Punish & Praise
A Dark Hockey Romance

ENDLEY TYLER

PUNISH & PRAISE:

A DARK HOCKEY ROMANCE

Second Edition

Standalone

Copyright © 2025 Endley Tyler

All rights reserved.

Blurb

The Praised

I binge, I break, and I hide behind my shame. But *he* sees me — the man on every sports channel. The hockey god with a wicked smirk and a promise: Submit, and he'll show mercy.

But he doesn't play fair — he destroys. My boundaries. My pride. My defenses. And worst of all... my heart. I should hate his games. But when he praises me, I burn for more. So, is this love... or a game I'll never escape?

The Punisher

I'm a savage on the ice. Violence is my life — then I met *her*. The fragile girl with a forced smile. I should let her go. But instead, I make her a deal: *Obey me, and I'll join your team.*

When she breaks my rules, I punish her. When she submits, I praise her. But she's sinking under my skin, and it's ruining everything. She was supposed to be my plaything, just a sacrificial lamb. So why do I crave her? I should have kept this a dark game. But now, I'm the one losing.

Content Warning

Dear Reader,

This story is a standalone dark romance that's not for the faint of heart. If you're new to the world of dark romance, let me warn you upfront — this genre is unapologetically raw, unconventional, and often ventures into themes that can challenge your comfort zone. It's not politically correct, and it's not meant to be. These stories thrive in the shadows, exploring the forbidden, the messy, and the morally gray.

This book is no exception. It's fast-paced, intense, and *dark*. If you're here for lighthearted romance or a clean-cut love story, you might want to sit this one out. But if you're ready for an emotional rollercoaster with flawed characters and boundary-pushing moments, then buckle up — you're in for a wild ride.

Triggers: This novel contains sensitive topics, including assault, non-glorified non-consensual (rape), child abuse, murder, violence, eating disorders, corporal punishment, and strong language. It delves into heavy, dark themes, so please proceed with caution. For a full list of triggers, visit my website: https://www.endleytyler.com/trigger-warni ngs

Spice Level: The heat level in this book is *very spicy*. Expect open-door intimacy, including scenes in public places, size difference, somnophilia, freeuse dynamics, a heavy breeding kink (yes, bodily fluids and reproduction-related themes), BDSM, DDLG, degradation, spanking, and plenty of praise. If we're rating on the chili scale, it's a 5/5 — the spiciest end of the spectrum in the dark romance world.

Tropes to Love (or Hate): This story blends classic and bold tropes, including 'touch her and die,' claiming, hockey, a troubled heroine, forced proximity, and power imbalance. I've tried to put my own spin on these themes, and I hope you enjoy the twists and turns I've woven into this darkly captivating tale.

Who This Book Is For: If you're a dark romance enthusiast who loves intense, morally complex stories with plenty of spice, this one's for you. If you're new to dark romance or unsure about the genre, I recommend starting with a softer introduction before diving in here. My characters are flawed, their actions aren't always admirable, and their choices might test your limits — but that's part of the thrill.

Dark romance is about exploring the extremes of emotion, desire, and morality in a safe, fictional space. It's not for everyone, and that's okay. But for those who are ready to embrace the shadows and the heat, I hope this story leaves you breathless and wanting more.

Don't say I didn't warn you.

Happy reading,

Endley Tyler
https://www.endleytyler.com/subscribe

Chapter 1

Emma

Love at first sight must exist.

There's no other explanation for the way my eyes are glued to this man — tall, tan, muscled, with that sinful smirk.

And *of course*, he's wearing a suit. A perfectly tailored one, at that.

My God, his blazer fits like it was sewn onto him. It hugs his waist even unbuttoned, just enough to tease of that rock hard body beneath it.

Someone help me.

It's been *too long* since I've been with a man. At this point, it's just embarrassing.

Not that I've had a lot of great sexual encounters... mostly disappointing. But I doubt he disappoints in bed.

With an air of confidence that matches that assumption, he lifts his chin in my direction, as if he knows my sinful desires for him.

I tear my gaze away, forcing a breath to steady my nerves.

Get a grip, Emma.

It's just hard to focus with how much this man oozes refinement and control, a stark contrast to the knuckle-dragging Neanderthals that usually roam this ice rink.

Besides, tonight is about figure skaters! We deserve this evening — an event unsullied by beer breath and sweaty jerseys.

Last year's disaster still stings: Igor sneaking vodka into a supposedly dry event, then vomiting all over the awards table. It's no surprise my father finally banned hockey players at this event.

A small act of mercy for his fallen daughter.

So I smile at how well things are going. My skaters are lined up on the ice, sequined costumes sparkling under the spotlight. Dreams waiting to take flight. My dreams for them, anyway. Because mine?

Failures.

"Pay attention, Emma," Mother hisses under her breath, jabbing her elbow into my side.

I flinch, blinking away my clouded memories. Her eyes are sharper than what's hidden in her hand.

I *hate* having a tiger mom.

"Sorry," I whisper.

She doesn't say anything more, just gestures impatiently to the medals. With a quick breath, I grab one and raise the microphone to my lips.

"Starting with our Junior Novice category, this year's award goes to Caylie Bing!"

The parents clap politely, a few cheers echoing through the rink. A sweet, Asian girl with pale skin and black hair breaks from her group, gliding forward with practiced grace. Her expression is pure, unfiltered joy.

For a moment, I see myself in her — young face, pink lips, that same hopeful spark in her eyes. Only, Caylie's eyes reflect something mine never did: double eyelids.

I know it's pathetic, but I'm absolutely envious of this child's plastic surgery.

Western beauty standards, even on the ice are paramount. Her parents surely made her get the surgery. I remember the pressure from my own mother to do the same. She insisted that success would only come to those who 'fixed their flaws.'

Dad fought for me back then, the only voice willing to say I was already enough.

Mother was right, though. My monolids scream, Foreign Girl, not America's Sweetheart.

"Coach Huang?" Caylie's soft voice pulls me back.

"Right, sorry," I say, forcing a smile. Mother's glare is a weight on my back, unforgiving. I slip the ribbon over Caylie's perfectly styled bun.

"Congratulations," I say gently, shaking her hand.

"Thank you, Coach Huang!"

She dashes back to her group, beaming. I focus on the ceremony, one award after the next, plastering on a smile that grows more automatic with each passing minute. Mother, ever vigilant, notices each time I drift and delivers a swift elbow jab like clockwork.

I *hate* it.

By the end of the evening, the clubhouse feels like a relief — warmth, laughter, cookies and soft drinks replacing the ice's biting chill. Parents mingle, students giggle, and for once, I let myself breathe. These are my wins.

My wins nowadays. Not as sweet, but nonetheless pleasurable.

I'm so lost in my small victory that I don't see him until his hand extends toward me, startling me from my thoughts.

"Good job, coach," says a smooth, deep voice.

It's him. *Suit guy.*

My heart stutters. For a split second, I take him in up close: towering, broad-shouldered, a jawline sharp enough to cut glass. Deep brown eyes. His short sandy blond hair is perfectly styled, but there's a ridge on his nose, a faint imperfection that somehow makes him look even more devastatingly masculine.

My ovaries are screaming.

And then he smiles.

So *sexy.*

"Did I scare you?" he asks, amused.

I let out a breath and shake my head. "No, just... lost in thought. I'm Emma Huang, and you are?"

"In awe of your beauty."

My cheeks burn, but I roll my eyes at the cheesy line. "Oh, geez."

He chuckles — a low, warm sound — and tilts his head. "We've met before. I'm Erik Sköll."

"Sköll?" The name pulls at something distant, nagging at me. My gaze drifts to the faint notch in his nose, then to his smile... and that one tooth. Slightly whiter than the rest.

Oh no.

"Your nose," I blurt out. "How'd you get that notch?"

His eyes brighten, like he's proud. "Puck to the face. Montreal game, two years ago."

My heart sinks as heavy as a lead weight. The muscles straining his suit, the fake tooth, the notch... The realization hits like a punch to the gut.

He's a hockey player.

Before I can spiral further, a woman's voice carries over the speakers, breathy and indecent.

"Oh, baby! Do me like that! Yeah! Eh, eh, eh!"

A deep, Russian man's voice follows. "Put a puck on each tit... Yah, like dat. Now I fuck you and see how long they stay on."

Laughter and gasps bubble through the rink.

The woman's voice giggles from above. "They didn't stay on for long!"

5

"I fuck like a stallion."

My jaw drops. Erik snorts, clearly trying to smother his laughter into his beer can — *beer*, I realize, not soda.

"Sounds like Igor took his date to the announcer's booth," he says, too entertained by this travesty.

I scan the horrified parents and their wide-eyed kids. My gaze locks with Dad's. Thankfully, his face mirrors my horror. He knows his precious hockey players are in the wrong this time. Mother stomps her foot, gesturing wildly for him to handle it.

The rest of the evening is a blur of apologies and silent self-loathing for not hiring security to keep those idiots out of the stadium.

By the time the rink is empty, I'm packing up the last of the snacks. Erik lingers, gathering stray napkins and wrappers. For a moment, I *almost* appreciate it... almost.

When I shoulder my oversized bag and make a beeline for the door, he intercepts me.

I pause, my heart stumbling again.

Hockey players. So irritatingly sexy *and* stupid.

"Want to grab a drink?" he asks, his voice smooth. Those dark eyes hold something magnetic, something I can't help but want despite my better judgement.

However, I couldn't let myself ever entertain the possibility. Hockey players are forbidden for so many reasons.

"Did you hear me, Emma?" he asks.

Chapter 2

Emma

Did Erik really just ask me out?

The audacity makes me cringe. Maybe I'm sexually frustrated by him, but I snap, "*Absolutely not!* Not even if we were in the middle of the desert and dying of thirst. Not even if my mouth was full of sand. I'd rather drink dust than date a hockey player."

His eyebrows lift, but he's clearly more curious than offended.

I draw in a deep breath, instantly feeling remorseful for being so curt.

"I'm sorry," I mumble.

He shrugs. "It's okay, but I promise I'm a good time," he says, those smoldering eyes practically melting my resistance.

I ball my fists, cursing my hormones.

Not today.

I can't let those eyes weaken my defenses, so without saying goodbye, I spin on my heel to make my escape... but walk straight into Dad's round belly.

"Ah, sweetheart!" Dad's voice booms, too chipper for someone who just helped me apologize to a string of disgruntled parents. His plump face shines under the fluorescent light.

I sigh. "I'm leaving. Thanks for your help tonight."

He smiles warmly. "My pleasure."

Erik steps forward and says with playfulness, "I was just asking Emma out for a drink. Seems even in a suit she denies me yet again."

"We've met?" I ask.

Dad chuckles. "Don't tell me you've forgotten Erik already."

My cheeks flush at my oversight. I shoot Dad an apologetic expression for not recognizing one of his prized oafs. "Well, I knew the name sounded familiar at least," I defend. "And isn't he the reason my academy's budget got cut? So you can bring in some overpriced hockey star?"

Dad holds back a laugh, and scrolls through his phone before handing it to me.

I reluctantly take it, the screen clammy from his sweaty fingers. A video plays, showing a man who looks like Erik but... *bigger*.

As I watch, the world around me blurs more. The man on the screen is... captivating.

His face is a masterpiece carved from ice and fire — strong cheekbones and a muscled jawline that looks capable of splitting stone.

His hair, dark underneath and golden blond on top is tied back carelessly, but the strands that escape frame his face in a way that's almost predatory, a faux softening of the warrior beneath.

And those eyes. Wow, those eyes. They're deep-set, their hue a ruthless blend of ice blue and stormy gray, like the sky before a winter storm. They don't just see — they consume, demanding attention without effort. Even through the tiny screen, I can feel their weight, as though he's stalking me.

His shoulders are massive, broad enough to carry the burden of any sin, and his arms — shaped with muscle, his veins raised in a testament of the power he holds — the kind of power that makes you wonder what it would feel like to be caught in them, trapped but never wanting to escape.

The video switches to an interview of him in a gym. His chest rises and falls with effortless strength, the fabric of his workout shirt clinging to every ridge and plane like it's ready to rip.

Once more the scene changes to him answering questions after a game, eager journalists facing the table he sits at. Even in a modern setting, there's something raw and ancient about him. A Nordic God, a Viking reborn and unrelenting, with a stoic expression and a body that could conquer any man who stands in his way.

My pulse pounds in my ears as I ogle him, transfixed.

If Erik was foreplay for the eyes, than this guy, he's the climax.

"How big is he?" I ask, still staring at the screen, barely recognizing my own voice.

"Well over six foot, 240 pounds of muscle," Dad says with admiration. "Joar Sköll. Power forward. Leading scorer. A rare find. He's strong enough to fight off defenders and get the puck into the net."

Erik sighs, clearly irritated. "Yeah, but with an ego too big to come to our team... despite being my cousin."

"The best players need big egos," Dad fires back dismissively, not even looking at him. Then to me: "Joar's a big draw, sweetheart. The Tampa Bay Lightning sells out every game. Best-selling jersey in the league, too. And, well, he's got his fans."

He skips the video to a shot of women in the stands holding signs: *Marry me, Joar!* Some are practically screaming, waving posters like it's a boy band concert.

"Oh, please," I scoff, suddenly remembering guys like him want puck bunnies. Not me. For a second there, I got too lost in those steely eyes.

Therefore, I fast-forward to another post-game interview, determined to find some reason I can accept for Dad to truly justify cutting my academy's budget.

Joar doesn't smile. Not once. No jokes. No softness. Just a cold, no nonsense presence.

He answers a couple of questions in clipped sentences before a reporter asks something that clearly hits a nerve. His expression shifts — not anger, exactly. More like irritation. Like he has no time for it.

And then he stands. Just... stands. Rising like a mythical God among men, looming over the journalist with a dismissive air that shuts everyone up. The team publicist tries to stop him, murmuring something, but he doesn't care. He brushes her off without a word and strides out of the room, unapologetic.

I freeze.

There's something so maddeningly sexy about it — that quiet defiance, the audacity to simply *leave*. Like he doesn't need anyone's approval. Doesn't care if he's liked.

The opposite of me, as I am the ultimate people pleaser.

"Not impressed?" Dad chuckles when I hand him back the phone.

"Nope. Just another overpaid hockey player," I quip, hiding my very real need to get home to my bob: battery operated boyfriend.

However, Dad is unsurprised by my perceived lack of interest. "I figured. Anyway, Erik's been here for five years, you know. Maybe you should learn the team roster. Then I can retire."

I fold my arms, smirking. "You'll *never* retire, Dad."

"Actually, dear, your mother insists it's time. I am looking into selling the team."

"What?" I choke.

Erik chimes in next with a sharp: "Tell me you're joking!"

"No joke. I'm speaking with investors." Dad shrugs, casual as ever. "Don't fret, either of you. I'm working to keep Emma's academy running as part of the deal. And the team will stay in Texas. However, Emma, your academy might be smaller. Less ice time."

My stomach twists. *Smaller? Less ice time?* My voice is shrill as I blurt, "You can't sell the team, Dad!"

"And who would run it? You?" His tone is teasing, but it stings. Hard.

"Uh... Yes! If it means saving my academy, I will." The words come out before I can stop them, conviction fueled by desperation. "I'll run this place. All of it. Give me a chance."

Dad stops laughing, his expression shifting to genuine surprise. For a moment, there's silence.

And then Mother steps in. Like always. Her presence, cold as winter.

"Emma? Run everything?" she says, her laugh as sharp as a 'Mr. Needle.' "Impossible."

Dad raises his hand to quiet her. He's still looking at me, assessing. Judging.

Finally, he says, "You want to prove yourself? Fine. Get the team to win the Stanley Cup this year. If you can manage that, I can trust you and won't sell."

I force a smile. The *Stanley Cup?* My heart stumbles. I want to laugh. Cry. Scream. But instead, I think of my precious academy. My sole purpose.

I lift my chin and say, "I won't let you down."

Mother frowns, her eyes burning holes into me. "Asinine! She can't. Too fragile to lead a team."

"I can try," I squeak.

Erik clears his throat, breaking the tension. "Emma, I can arrange a meeting with my cousin... if you'd like my help."

I blink at him, caught off guard. "You'd do that?"

"Of course." He gives me a sweet smile. "If you want me to, I'll go with you. Break the ice."

"That's great! When can we meet Hawl?"

Erik chokes on a laugh. "It's Joar. *Yoh-ar.* It's Norwegian."

"Oh. Ja-oar. Okay. Set it up, please!"

Mother steps closer. "I will attend the meeting as well."

I grimace and reply, "Um, I can probably handle this on my own."

"You can," she says smoothly, "with me by your side."

Her voice is calm, but I know her. The *storm* underneath. The message is clear: I can't be trusted to do anything on my own.

My pulse races, frustration and determination warring inside me. I have no idea how I'm going to pull this off.

But I can't lose everything.

And I sure as hell can't let *Joar Sköll* get the better of me. I have to convince him, even though my own dad, the best deal-maker I know, couldn't.

I just hope Joar likes Asian women. Maybe I should dress sexy?

Oh, no — I wouldn't have thought that if he wasn't hot. I definitely need to get on a dating app... or buy more batteries.

Chapter 3

Joar

I answer the front door and cock my head at my idiot cousin and the two Asian women standing stiffly behind him.

One is older — frail, moon-faced, with the kind of beady eyes that miss nothing.

The other is much younger, her figure hidden under an unforgiving blazer and pantsuit, yet somehow still keeping my attention.

Erik practically bounces in place, grinning like a fool.

"Hey, buddy!" he says, far too friendly. He's acting. He you usually greets me with a casual, "Hey, fucker."

"Dumbass," I mutter under my breath, already imagining how satisfying it would be to embarrass him. He's obviously trying to impress these women. For now, I settle for, "Hi, Erik."

I move my gaze to the women, holding out a hand. The younger one steps forward first, her small, soft hand slipping into mine. Her head bows ever so slightly as she greets me, and I have purse my lips to smother an unexpected smile.

Few things are as sexy as an obedient, respectful woman — even if her fingers are trembling faintly.

Also a turn-on.

"Mr. Sköll, I'm Emma Huang, and this is my mother, Mei Huang. We're from the Austin Rattlers."

My eyes narrow as I gaze at her. Something in the way she speaks makes me pause — her words are careful, rehearsed, like she's reciting from a script but doesn't feel worthy of the role. There's tension in her voice, but it doesn't match the calmness presented in those bright, upturned brown eyes.

"Yes, I know of your shitty team," I reply flatly.

Her lips part slightly, brow furrowing, as though she wasn't expecting my bluntness. Erik narrows his eyes, but Emma recovers quickly. She crosses her arms, almost defensively, and straightens her posture, squaring her shoulders.

"I would use more flattering adjectives for my team, like young and promising. But that's why I'm here — to make my roster better."

Her defiance almost makes me smile. Cute, not intimidating.

So I respond dismissively, "You'll need more than pretty words to get my attention."

Beside me, Bergen, my Lundehund, growls low and throaty, his attention locked on the guests. Mei doesn't flinch, her expression unshakable, but Emma visibly jumps. Her arms latch onto Erik as she shifts behind him, body tense.

"Bergen. Sit," I command.

My dog obeys instantly, his growl cutting off mid-vibration.

Emma peeks out from behind Erik, relief flooding her face. Her reaction is more telling than she realizes — she's on alert always, anything unexpected shakes her to her core. I find it... tempting.

"Come inside," I say, leading them to the front room.

Both women set down their purses, and as I glance at Emma, I find myself memorizing her figure: a mistake.

Never steal or fuck another man's girl, especially if that man is a part of your family. Erik wants her, so be it.

Ah hell, what's the harm in looking?

Hence, my gaze lingers longer than it should on the curve of her hips, the fullness of her thighs. She's not what society calls a perfect ten, but there's something undeniably lush about her. Her movements are precise, her shoulders straight, but there's a softness to her body that draws me in. I catch myself tilting my head, studying her ass from behind.

I can see why Erik is interested just by her curves.

I force my attention forward, though, motioning for them to sit. They do, both women prim and proper, their backs ramrod straight. They're practically twins, save for the years etched into Mei's face.

"You have fifteen minutes," I say, lowering myself into the opposite chair. I sit casually, bracing my elbows on my knees, deliberately letting my gaze settle on Emma. She shifts slightly under the weight of it.

I like that... seeing her nervous. Therefore, I add, "I've already spoken to your dad, so don't waste my time repeating his pitch."

Emma winces. She leans toward her mother and whispers too loudly, "I only practiced Dad's pitch."

I arch a brow, amused despite myself. Emma freezes under my scrutiny, then straightens her back so quickly it's almost painful to watch her display of insecurity. Her dark eyes dart to mine, full of barely restrained nerves.

For some reason, I don't look away.

Her face... Damn, her face is something else. Smooth skin, pale and clear as porcelain. The high sweep of her cheekbones, the delicate nose, and those innocent eyes — she's all softness, despite her sharp, defensive words.

"Well, Mr. Sköll," she begins, voice unsteady, "we offer you a unique leadership opportunity. Most of our starters have less than two years in the NHL—"

"I'm already the captain on my current team," I interrupt, keeping my tone even.

She falters, her confidence slipping for just a moment before she rallies. "On our team, you can solidify your legacy. Help bring a Stanley Cup to a franchise that's never won in our forty year history."

"I already won three cups for a team that had none."

Her lips part, and her gaze lowers to the floor, momentarily lost. The defeat in her posture is subtle, but it stirs something in me I can't place. Her mother nudges her — a swift jab of... something.

"We have warm weather!" she blurts suddenly.

I blink, stunned. Then I glance out the window, gesturing lazily to the ocean, the palm trees swaying under a cloudless sky.

"You are in Florida. Visiting me. Remember?" I say dryly. "Besides, I prefer cold weather. I already told your dad what I want — more money."

Emma glances at her mother again, her nervousness barely masked. Mei's eyes narrow ever so slightly, and Emma blurts once more, "We can find you sponsorships for the difference."

I tilt my head, more intrigued than I care to admit. *Why does she keep panicking and practically shout responses?*

Watching her closely, I reply, "I already have big sponsors."

Mei hisses something under her breath that I don't catch. The dynamic between them is growing harder to ignore. There's something off here — and based on Emma's crumbling exterior, I don't like it.

"Emma, talk," Mei says, low and venomous.

Emma swallows hard and blurts yet again, "You can play whichever position you want!"

I lean back slowly, a grin spreading across my face. How cute. I can't help myself and mock, "Oh, can I? I always wanted to be a goalie."

"Definitely!" she says, her voice laced with sweet hope.

Beside her, Erik grimaces, squeezing her shoulder gently. He says in a soft, consoling tone, "Emma. He's messing with you."

Her cheeks go red — a flush that spreads quickly. She looks ready to combust, but the look in her eyes is unmistakable.

She's embarrassed.

And desperate.

And... impossibly lovely.

"Do you know anything about hockey, Ms. Huang?" I ask, my voice calm, almost teasing. "Or are you just a spoiled, pretty girl your daddy sent in a last-ditch effort to sign me?"

Her lips part, and for a second, I think she'll snap back. Instead, she deflates, hugging herself.

"Honestly?" she says, her voice trembling. "I hate hockey and know very little about the sport."

Her honesty knocks me sideways. I should dismiss her entirely — a spoiled rich girl out of her depth. I should demand they leave for sending someone so unqualified. They're wasting my time.

Yet... my gaze lingers, my interest inching higher. She's defeated, but there's so much more there, too — such a desperate need to prove something. Or maybe survive something.

And she takes whatever it is quietly.

"May I use your restroom?" she asks suddenly, her voice barely audible.

"That hall. Two doors down on the left," I reply, watching her closely. She leaves the room like she can't escape fast enough.

I let Mei keep talking, her voice a drone in the background.

However, my thoughts are on Emma. The way she reacted to her mother... and what I saw. The effect she had on her daughter. That subtle, covert *something* that made her body as stiff as steel and poise implode.

Curiosity burns through me like a flame I can't put out. I excuse myself and head down the hallway.

From behind the bathroom door, I hear it: the quiet, unmistakable sound of retching. My jaw tightens. Then the faucet runs, followed by a pause, a sniffle, and the door cracks open.

She startles when she sees me. Her beautiful, dark eyes meet mine, and for the first time, the calm behind those eyes fades. The real woman she is looks back at me.

"Did you just throw up?" I ask bluntly.

"No," she yips.

"I heard it."

Her lips tremble. "You listen to people in the bathroom? That's... disgusting," she tries to scold, but her voice is shaky.

"Not as disgusting as lying." My gaze sharpens as I step closer. "What did your mom do to you out there? To make you fall apart like that?"

She freezes. But damn, those eyes. The fear and desperation they hold — so afraid yet eager to please.

Fuck.

I'd love to see her with that same look in her eyes, except while on her knees.

"Emma, I want to make a deal."

Chapter 4

Joar

"Really!" Emma says, her eyes beaming with pure joy. "You want to make a deal?"

"Yeah," I answer. "One with you on your knees."

Emma balks, her words catch in her throat as she struggles to process what I said.

Watching her squirm is... heavenly. I can't stop myself and reach out to calm those fragile nerves, soothe her with my touch as if I already own her.

I'm snapped from my trance as she shys from me, but I snatch her forearm.

"Are you touching me?" she says, disbelief etched across her face as she gawks at my hand wrapped around her arm.

I don't let go - I don't want to. What am I doing? I need to remember this is Erik's prize.

She stutters, her body tense, pointing at my hand, "I, uh, I won't be on my knees for you, you... pervert! So please let go."

For a moment, I imagine freeing her. Letting her run off to Erik. But damn, even upset, even talking back to me, she looks so innocent. So lost.

So... *tempting.*

Acting on my own selfish desires, I keep my hand cuffed on her forearm. "By on your knees, I meant symbolically. I simply want you to serve me — as my assistant." It's a weak recovery, but I feign innocence by adding, "I'm from Norway, my English is jumbled sometimes. Gets misinterpreted."

"Oh," she replies, though still looks skeptical. "Uh, sorry. Didn't mean to call you a pervert then."

"It's okay." Wanting to lower her guard, I switch the subject. "Why did you throw up?"

She veers her eyes. "I'd rather not say."

"I won't judge you. Please answer me," I say, but my voice is edged with impatience. I should work on that, but being overly polite instead of direct is an annoying American habit.

She scoffs at my prying, though, her smooth forehead creasing as she loses her composure. The skeptical mask slips just enough for me to catch the fragile, desperate woman beneath.

I jump on her weakness. "Tell me."

She panics and snaps, "I'm sorry, but that's none of your business." Then she adds in a disgruntled tone, "Besides, I'm not about to confide in a *dumb* hockey player."

I lift my brow. "Dumb?"

"Yeah." She lifts her chin, defiant and trembling all at once. "I hate dealing with *you people*. You're all vile, crud e... stupid men!"

Stupid. I've been called worse, but hearing it from her? I so badly wish I could discipline that mouth.

"Hm. You think I'm stupid?" I ask quietly, my grip tightening just slightly. It's enough to make her flinch.

Her eyes flicker to mine, and something deeper burns there. Her shoulders tense as though she's weighing her next words.

Finally, her voice flattens. "Can we cut to the chase, please? Is there any chance of you joining our team? Be honest."

"No way in hell," I lie, just to see how she'll react.

The despair in her face is instant, but she doesn't crumble. Instead, she presses on, her voice rising with a desperate edge. "Then we have nothing to lose. So yes — I think you're stupid. You all are. My parents were right, though. I probably can't run this team. I definitely cannot work with brutes like you. Even if it'll cost me..." Her voice cracks and tears pool in her eyes. "Even if I lose everything."

For a split second, she looks utterly broken. The sight hits me like a blow to the chest.

I want her. This broken, begging me to fix her.

She tries to yank her arm free, but I don't release her.

"Ms. Huang," I say dryly, "I'm not so stupid that I vomit because I can't handle pressure. Nor am I stupid to take a pay cut just to join your mediocre team. Only an imbecile would accept that deal."

Her tugging ceases. She looks up at me, blinking, her breaths coming unevenly. "But I don't know what else to offer you," she whispers. "We can't afford your asking price."

I stare at her - really stare - and my mind drifts back to the scene in the living room. Her mother's hidden cruelty, the something that made her stiffen in shock or pain, the way she took it without flinching.

Silent.

Enduring.

Obedient.

God, I want that for myself.

"What did your mom do to you? I saw you change."

She sighs, perhaps so defeated she doesn't care at this moment and confesses, "Mr. Needle... I mean, it's a needle. It helps me focus better. I have anxiety and get overwhelmed. But it's a very small needle. Not a big deal."

Something primal stirs deep in my gut. A dark need - one I haven't felt this strongly in years. A desire to possess *and* protect.

I imagine her kneeling before me, those pretty lips parted as she waits to either receive me or obey my next command. Not breaking eye contact. Not resisting.

Mine.

For ten years, I've fed that side of me with empty encounters - women who played along as a submissive, but never really kept my attention. It's never been the same as the first time I found a girl willing to give me everything. *Runa*. The memory flashes - brief and sharp.

But now... here she is. Not Runa. Not perfect. But something else entirely. Something just as interesting, though. Perhaps more.

"Joar?" Her voice cuts through the depths of my dark thoughts. "Are you sure there isn't anything else you'd like? I don't want to go back to that room and tell my mom I failed. Maybe we could talk about the assistant idea you mentioned?"

I smirk, restraining a bigger smile. Perfect. She's returned to the deal I most want. Now it's her idea.

"Yes, I suppose I may consider that arrangement," I say, my voice dismissive, pretending I don't really want it.

Her eyes brighten, a flicker of hope surfacing through the desperation.

"Oh? You need an assistant, right?"

"Yes," I say casually, but then move closer, crowding her until she tenses. "Do you think you could fulfill my needs?"

Her expression wavers. "Uh, if you mean being a personal assistant, then yes, I could do that."

I release her arm, letting the words settle. "I don't know. I am demanding. My last personal assistant couldn't keep up."

She jumps on my comment. "I'm a hard worker!"

"You think so? Because I want you to do what I want, when I want. No excuses."

"Um, I'm confused," she replies, stepping back as though I've scared her. "To be clear, you don't want me as your... sex slave. Correct?"

I laugh, a deep, taunting sound that rolls from my chest. "Who said anything about sex? I'm talking purely about being my personal assistant."

Her brows draw together, wisely suspicious. "Just a normal assistant?"

"That's right. No sex. No touching. Simple."

She folds her arms tightly across her chest, hugging herself as she bites on her bottom lip. The movement - innocent but unconsciously sensual - makes it impossible to look away.

She has no idea what she's doing to me. Hell, I hardly believe it myself. She's so... pure. So damn needy.

She asks cautiously, "And if I do this... you'll play for my team?"

"Yes."

"Why wouldn't you just hire an assistant?"

"Are you trying to talk me out of this deal?" I ask, amused. But then, I shrug apathetically and muse aloud, "Although, I suppose you're right. Maybe I should try another *local* personal assistant."

"No!" she replies quickly.

"Well, if you honestly think you can manage the workload." I extend my hand, but quickly stifle my smile, not wanting her to know how excited I am.

Eagerly, she shakes my hand. "Deal!"

"I hope I don't regret this, Ms. Huang. But if you simply do what I say, I'll play. Don't, and I walk. Easy as that."

She hesitates, her eyes flicking with that sweet sense of unease. Finally, she swallows and nods.

"I assure you. I can do this."

I don't end our handshake just yet. I step closer, towering over her, and slip my knuckle under her chin. Her breath hitches, her body tensing as it did for her mom earlier.

"Good. First order of business - I want you to promise never to throw up when you can't handle pressure or your mom jabs you with a needle."

Her brows shoot up. "Are you serious?"

"Dead serious. You simply come to me and I'll talk you down."

She hesitates again, but she relents. "Um, okay. I promise."

Hearing her say it so quietly — so quickly — sends a pleasurable shiver down my spine. Perfect. I can't resist, and trace my thumb along the underside of her chin for just a second longer before releasing her.

"See? Simple," I murmur, leaning down. I inhale deeply, catching the faint floral scent of her perfume. Subtle. Clean. I want more of it. More of her.

I give in, leaning even closer, my nose grazing her soft neck.

She steps back — but meets the wall and can't get far enough to escape me. Her dark eyes flick to mine, and for once, she doesn't look away.

"That's a lovely perfume," I say softly.

"Oh. Um. Thanks," she stammers.

"By the way, I look forward to working with you, Min Leketøy."

Her lips purse, her brow furrowing. "Meen la-tu?"

I bite back a laugh at her botched attempt. "It means 'my friend' in Norwegian. Now that we're friends, let's go tell your mom the good news."

Her face lights up briefly, only to falter. "Joar, can we not tell her about... the assistant part of our agreement? She doesn't need to know."

I smirk, enjoying her discomfort far too much. "Sure. I'll say you convinced me with your wit, charm, and beauty."

"Okay, but leave out the beauty part. That won't impress her," she mumbles, cheeks faintly pink.

I chuckle and nod. "Deal."

As I follow her back toward the living room, I let the satisfaction settle over me. She's not under my full control yet - far from it - but she's mine now even though she doesn't realize it.

And I can't wait to see just how far she'll bend before she falls to her knees and begs.

Chapter 5

Emma

The season opener against the Boston Bruins is packed to the rafters — the first game with Joar Sköll on the roster. Fans hurry to their seats, buzzing with excitement like they're witnessing the second coming.

It's strange. One hockey player shouldn't cause this much ruckus.

...Although, I get it. He's hard to ignore — that body, those broad shoulders, the raw, commanding presence.

I hate myself for the way my gaze lingered on him when we met. Especially when I, like a freaking puck bunny, *checked him out.*

For God sakes, I even stole a glance at his package like a starved animal! I hate when men do that to women by staring at our tits or ass.

My own hypocrisy doesn't taste good.

That's why after I left, I signed up for a dating app. Also, I put under preferences: must not like sports.

I need a man with intelligence, someone who challenges me. But, I must admit... if he looked like Joar? A bonus.

I look toward the rink, my heart filling with an unexpected swell of pride. Every game this season sold out in fifteen minutes the second Joar signed. Even Mother seemed impressed, which is saying something.

When I sit beside Dad in the owner's box, I can't help but smile — like I finally belong here. Like, for once, I measure up.

"This is wonderful, isn't it, Dad?" I say, wanting to hear the praise again, just to savor it.

He grins, his cheeks plump with satisfaction. "Oh, yes, sweetheart! You did good. Very good. And wait until you see Joar in action. I can't believe we have a chance to win the Cup this year."

I beam at his words, my chest swelling with triumph. That is, until a tap on my shoulder startles me.

I turn to find Mother leaning down, her voice sharp as she whispers, "Joar said he wants to speak to you before the game starts."

I blink. "He does?"

"Yes. And why would he?" Her tone carries a cold edge, like suspicion is already eating her alive.

"I don't know," I reply truthfully, though my pulse jumps.

Without waiting for further interrogation, I hurry out of the box, heels clicking against the stadium floor as I make my way to the locker room.

I pause at the door, drawing in a deep breath. Calm down, Emma. It's business. Straightening my blazer, I push the door open and step inside — into chaos.

Men everywhere.

"Oh my God," I mutter under my breath as Sergey, our wild Italian goalie, struts past me.

Fully naked.

His grin stretches across his impish face, cheeks flushed. "Ms. Huang!" he greets shamelessly, bright-eyed. "Here to hang out with the boys, eh?"

I jerk my gaze up to the ceiling, heat burning my cheeks.

"Hello, Sergey," I reply formally, but his laughter trails behind him.

"Sergey, get dressed!" Igor growls from across the room, his voice cold as steel. "Stop fuckin' around."

The energy in the locker room is manic, testosterone-fueled, and it burns against my skin. I don't belong here, and every fiber of me knows it.

Then, something brushes against my calf.

The sensation is slow, deliberate — a teasing drag of something foreign sliding up my leg. My body jolts, my skirt lifts slightly, and I spin around, fire in my veins. "What the—?"

A hockey stick.

My glare locks on its owner, and the world around me narrows.

Joar.

He stands there, completely at ease, his towering frame now leaning casually on the stick like he's baiting me to react. His piercing eyes gleam with something wolfish, predatory, as they rake over me unapologetically.

"Min Leketøy," he drawls smoothly, his lips curling into a smug smirk.

Heat explodes in my chest — a mix of rage and something worse. Something traitorous.

Ugh... those mesmerizing eyes.

I shake off his spell and snap, "Don't do that again!" I glare up at him as I take a step back, trying to put distance between us.

His gaze doesn't waver. If anything, it sharpens. He straightens, his full height amplified on skates. The closeness of him, the way he towers over me, makes me shrink. It's infuriating, and yet... it leaves me breathless.

"But you have such pretty legs," he says, his voice dipping, seductively. "I wanted to see more of them."

My jaw drops and my face burns.

Still using his stick as a prop, he leans on it while looking down at me. Strands of his hair fall forward as he says casually, "Do you skate, Emma?"

"Uh, yes. Actually, I was a seven-time figure skating National Champion. Took bronze at the Olympics in pairs skating too."

"Wow, an Olympic skater," he says, appearing genuinely impressed.

"Don't be too impressed. My mother gave me Kwan as my middle name, after Michelle Kwan, another Chinese-American figure skater. Probably the best figure skater in history. But Mother said naming me that was a mistake because 'bronze is for the second loser at the Olympics.'"

He must see this is a sore subject for me because he lifts his chin and taunts, "You're named after Michelle Kwan, huh?" then he flashes a wicked grin.

"It's not funny, and... yes," I reply, but have to look away to avoid seeing him wallow in my misery. Quickly, I summon my self-respect and deflect. "But now I teach the country's best to compete. Is this what you wanted to talk about?"

He's still smiling, like he's savoring that gem of truth, but eventually his grin warms. "So beautiful and talented. I'd like you to dress up like a geisha for me next."

I scrunch my brow. "A geisha?"

"Yeah, those fancy women that wear kimonos and serve men drinks... on their knees."

I roll my eyes and force a smile, if only to bear him testing me. "Oh, no, no, no. That's Japanese. I'm Chinese. That's a hard no for me. Listen. The game is starting soon, Joar. Just tell me what you wanted to discuss, please."

"Japanese, Chinese, same difference. Both beautiful women."

"No, there is a difference."

He shrugs, his lack of urgency is absolutely maddening. Especially as he says matter-of-factly, "I'm Norwegian."

"I *know*," I reply, my tone not hiding the confusion I'm feeling.

Yet, he continues, as if he decides what we talk about. "According to Old Norse mythology, Sköll is the wolf that catches the sun. Doesn't your flag have a red sun on it?"

"That's the *Japanese* flag," I correct sharply, making my impatience now loud and clear. "Is this really what you dragged me down here to talk about? Our names?"

He chuckles low, the sound challenging, even dangerous. "An Olympic medalist, a beautiful woman, and surprisingly mouthy. Interesting combination."

He stares at me, but suddenly, there is a dark intensity in his gaze that hints he's holding back, his thoughts unlikely to be as innocent as this conversation.

"Um, please... tell me what you want, Joar. My parents are waiting," I stammer, attempting to sound tough despite the growing anxiety squeezing my heart.

His smirk lingers, infuriatingly smug. "A kiss."

My mouth falls open. "What?"

"Before every game. And after." He says it so matter-of-factly, like it's already decided.

"This isn't part of the deal. We agreed: no sex!"

37

"A kiss isn't sex."

"It's... it's inappropriate."

"Not in Norway," he replies lazily, still watching me like a hawk.

A player brushes past me, making his way through the aisle toward the rink. Another follows, clipping me, forcing me to step forward toward Joar so they can get by.

Suddenly, I'm boxed in — my body pushed close to Joar, the locker room chaos swirling around. My palms press instinctively against his stomach, feeling the heat of his body even through his jersey. Players pass by, their burly frames taking up the aisle and keeping me wedged close to Joar.

I freeze.

His arm snakes around me, a heavy, unrelenting force pulling me even closer. My pulse spikes, panic and something worse fluttering in my chest. His head dips slightly, his lips hovering near my ear as he murmurs, "You feel good here, Emma. Soft. Warm. Small."

"Joar, let me go," I beg, though my voice doesn't carry the bite I want.

He ignores me. Instead, his large hand grips my jaw, forcing my face up to meet his gaze. His hold isn't rough, but it's firm. *Dominating.*

"One kiss," he says, his tone leaving no room for argument.

"Joar—"

He cuts me off. His hand slips into my hair, grasping it gently as he tilts my head back. Before I can protest, his lips crash against mine, firm and possessive, stealing the breath from my lungs. The kiss is everything I feared it would be — overwhelming, consuming, arousing.

In this moment, I'm paralyzed, torn between resistance and my very real need to feel another human's touch.

My fingertips dig into his sides, both hanging on, yet ready to push off.

Chapter 6

Emma

I remain frozen, shock coursing through me as Joar's mouth claims mine with relentless force.

"Get her, Joar!" cheers Igor.

Shoot! My sanity side-swipes me, snapping me back to reality.

My entire body tenses, panic sparking through me as his grip tightens at the roots of my hair. His fingers pull harder, holding me immobile as though he owns me. I try to turn my head, but his hold doesn't budge, and before I can think, his tongue pushes past my lips.

Humiliation flashes hot across my skin. Around us, more jeers and catcalls of his teammates, their laughter stings. Each sound makes the burn in my cheeks sear deeper.

I'm humiliated, furious.

And ashamed. Because the most terrifying thing is, this kiss has stolen all my fight — if only for this moment.

But my instincts kick in.

I bite down — *hard.*

My teeth sink into his tongue, and Joar jerks back, breaking the kiss as his grip loosens just enough for me to stumble free. My heart pounds wildly, my breaths ragged as I wipe the back of my hand across my mouth.

Joar runs his tongue along his teeth, testing for damage. Instead of anger, though, he smirks. The gleam in his eyes sends a jolt of unease straight through me.

"Tsk, tsk, Min Leketøy," he says, his voice carrying amusement. But then, it deepens to something darker. "That only turns me on more. I'll remember that." He licks his lips, savoring the moment.

"That was way out of line," I huff, though I can't meet his gaze. I hate the way his eyes hold me captive — the way they seem to unravel me apart, piece by piece, like he sees something in me I don't want to admit exists.

"You're... bratty," he says, leaning casually on his hockey stick once more.

"I'm not bratty," I shoot back. My fists clench at my sides, desperate to erase the thrill his kiss ignited deep in my chest — a kiss I can't stand to acknowledge happened.

His lips curve lazily, like I'm nothing more than a riddle he's already solved. So I hiss, "In fact, the only thing I am is angry!"

"And I'm ready," he replies, seemingly unintimidated by my tone as he adds, "for more."

"You're an animal."

Before I realize it, he reaches out, attempting to pull me back into his cage. My instincts explode in fury. I shove at his chest, my fists pounding as hard as I can manage, though his solid frame doesn't budge an inch. The bastard lets me struggle just long enough to send me into panic further, but I manage to twist free, stumbling backward.

"See you after the game, Min Leketøy," Joar calls, his deep voice dripping with satisfaction as I storm out of the locker room, humiliated and shaking.

I return to the owner's box, my chest still heaving. My lips still tingling.

I hate it — *hate him.*

How dare he. It wasn't a kiss; it was an assault. A complete violation of my boundaries, and I feel every inch of it, simmering like poison beneath my skin.

And the worst part? The worst part is that I didn't hate the feeling of his lips.

What's wrong with me?

I sink into my seat beside my parents, feeling out of place, like I no longer belong here. Dad doesn't notice. He's too busy cheering for Joar.

"That's our new boy!" he beams, pointing toward the ice where Joar glides effortlessly into play.

I barely look. Instead, I focus on trying to calm the sick twist in my stomach.

Mother, of course, notices immediately. "What did the hockey-man need to discuss?" she asks sharply, her suspicious gaze drilling into me.

"He asked if I skated," I reply quickly, which isn't technically a lie.

"Odd."

"Yes, he's very odd," I mutter, praying she'll drop it. To my relief, she does. I focus on the game instead, forcing myself to observe Joar on the ice.

I don't want to admit it... but he's mesmerizing.

He doesn't just play hockey. He owns the rink. Every stride, every move is calculated, effortless — a perfect balance of power and precision. He crashes into opposing players, checks them so hard they slam against the boards like rag dolls. He weaves through defenders like they're obstacles to be ignored, claiming the puck time and time again. It's almost beautiful, watching him dominate so completely.

I lose track of the score. I lose track of the minutes. He pulls me in, and I hate him even more for it.

So with determination, I fixate on my dating app and by the first intermission, I can't take it anymore.

I'm bored because my inbox is mostly dick-pics or short blurbs that don't seem like they read my profile. Besides, I'm rattled because of the kiss, and my stomach still feels off. Thus, I tell my parents I'm heading home.

"Hope your stomach doesn't calm down too fast," Mother remarks, her tone dripping with passive aggression.

I know what she really means: Skip dinner. You've gained weight.

I say nothing more and leave.

Once home, I pull on my softest pajamas and put on my guilty pleasure: Bling Empire.

Oh, and I snack on my other vice... chocolates. Which I'll purge, of course.

But as I cook dinner, I simmer my sauce with resentment in my bones. Joar has ruined everything. Hockey was bad enough before. Now it's worse because he's here — invading my thoughts, pushing boundaries, making me question things I don't want to question.

I'm halfway through making dinner — carb rich spaghetti to spite Mother — when the doorbell rings.

I pause, frowning. Who could that be?

Peering through the peephole, I groan.

Joar.

He's fresh from his post-game shower, dressed in a white tee-shirt that hugs his broad chest, and black athletic shorts that highlight his powerful legs. His hair is still damp, darkened, and slicked back from his face, exposing every sharp, perfect line of his features.

I open the door.

Damn.

His scent is like heaven, too, fresh with a soothing spice, a combination that coils around me immediately.

He gazes down at me, his presence unnervingly confident. "Naughty girl. Left my game early."

I force myself not to look at him too long and get lost in his eyes... and that body. Instead, I say, "How did you know I left?"

He grins. "You were in the owner's box. Then you weren't."

"I know I should stay, but I don't normally watch hockey," I admit stiffly. "Why are you here?"

"I told you — I want a kiss before and after every game."

I gawk at him. He's got to be joking.

"You can't be serious," I reply.

His grin fades. "Very serious."

"No. Absolutely not."

Joar steps into my house without warning, his massive, athletic frame forcing me back.

"Are you alone?" he asks, his tone far too casual.

"What...? Yes, but you can't just—"

He ignores me completely, stalking through my house as though it's his own. I follow him, spluttering. "Get out, Joar! You're trespassing!"

He checks every room before turning to me with a triumphant smile. "Good. No men. Only me."

"You are insane!"

He steps closer, crowding me. I back up until my spine hits the wall, his frame looming over me like a building. His hand shoots out, cupping my jaw, his grip firm, but careful, tilting my head to meet his gaze.

"A kiss, Emma," he orders, his voice a deep, seductive growl. "I told you. A kiss before and after every game. It's not a complicated request."

He's frustratingly calm, his composure intact.

"No, no," I insist, my voice smaller than I'd like. "You're taking this too far. I thought this arrangement was about personal assistant stuff — errands, schedules, *normal things*."

His expression doesn't change. If anything, his mesmerizing eyes grow more intense, more calculating. "I've just started."

"Started what?" I ask, my throat tight. "I'm not doing this with you."

"Why not?" he asks, though I get the feeling he's indifferent to however I answer.

"Because," I reply, grasping for control. "I'm... I'm not interested in you like that. I'm not attracted to you."

Joar stills, his eyes narrowing. The air between us thickens, charged with new tension. Then, without warning, he moves. His hand slips to the back of my neck, his fingers long and firm as they press into the sensitive area. I try to pull away, but his grip tightens just enough to remind me how much stronger he is.

His other hand takes my jaw, his thumb brushing over my cheek with a touch so deceptively tender, it sends a shiver down my spine. I freeze, my breath caught as he leans closer, his lips hovering near mine.

"You're lying," he says softly.

Before I can respond, his lips meet mine again, but this kiss is different. It's calm, sensual, like he's proving a point rather than taking what's his. The gentleness unnerves me more than his forcefulness — it's disarming, and I'm utterly powerless.

When he finally pulls back, his steely gray eyes hold mine, the mix of ice blue chilling me. "Even if it were true, attraction can develop over time," he says, his arrogance palpable. "I'll grow on you, but I think you already like what you see." His gaze lingers on me, slowly floating down my curves as he adds under his breath, "I know I like what I see."

I shove him, trying to appear tough, but barely hanging on. This guy is the human touch I crave. It's just so wrong for so many reasons. But despite my effort to thrust him away from me, he barely moves.

Clinging to my fragile sense of determination, "Get out!"

He chuckles, stepping back with infuriating ease. "What's for dinner?"

Chapter 7

Emma

Did Joar just imply he's staying for dinner?

"Oh, no... I made a deal with a psycho," I mutter, staring at him in disbelief.

He smirks, unbothered by my growing horror. "No. You made a deal with a man who understood the terms better than you. Guess I'm not so 'stupid,' hm?"

His smug assertion hits a nerve. I gawk at him, my mind racing through every twist and turn of this nightmare deal. Could this brute have actually outsmarted me? The thought is unbearable.

Abruptly, he turns toward the kitchen. "Now, back to the topic of dinner. What did you make us?"

"Us?" I echo, dumbfounded.

Ignoring me completely, he strides into the kitchen like he owns the place. "Spaghetti," he says, spotting the pot on the stove. Without hesitation, he finds a plate in the cupboard and begins helping himself.

"I made it for me," I clarify, incredulous.

"Yum," he says with maddening cheer, loading up his plate.

Before I can protest further, he's settled on my couch, flipping through channels until he lands on ESPN. My jaw nearly hits the floor as I watch him swirl spaghetti onto his fork, completely at ease in my space.

I linger in the doorway, horrified. The sight of red marinara sauce so close to my pristine white couch is enough to make me cry.

"I don't eat in the living room," I say, frantic, afraid any second of an impending spill. "Especially spaghetti."

Still focused on the screen, he replies, "I watch *SportsCenter* after a game. Come sit with me."

"Uh, nope," I state, unsure why he doesn't see how serious a tomato stain can be.

"Yes, sit, *Min Leketøy.*"

"Don't call me that! I am not your friend, Joar. I'm your boss."

His eyes meet mine, and a slow, sly grin spreads across his face.

"I lied. It doesn't mean 'my friend,'" he says casually. "It means 'my toy.'"

My upper lip arches in disgust. "Uh! I'm nobody's toy."

He sets down his plate, rising to his full height. My breath catches as he towers over me, closing the distance in two measured steps. Instinctively, I retreat, but his hand darts out, capturing my arm before I can escape.

"Joar, let go!" I demand, trying to yank free.

He doesn't waver, though. Instead, he drags me toward the couch with ease, his grip firm but not painful.

"Sit," he orders.

I stare for a moment, wondering if this is real. A darkness fills his eyes, the tension in the air like an electric wire snapping.

I pout, dropping onto the couch in an act of temporary surrender. But as I cross my arms and glance over at him, he shakes his head slowly.

"No. On the floor," he mutters.

"What?" I echo, appalled.

"On the floor. But close to me."

Before I can argue, he nudges me off the couch in a swift motion. My knees hit the carpet, and I find myself sitting at his feet like some obedient pet. Humiliation burns through me, but when I glance up, he's already focused back on the TV, as if my reaction isn't even worth his attention.

"Joar, I will not live like this," I say, my voice shaking.

"Then behave," he replies smoothly. "You left early and didn't give me a kiss after the game. That's your punishment."

"We never agreed to punishments," I balk.

Surely, he's joking.

"Would you prefer I fake an injury and not play the next game? We won tonight, by the way."

My mouth opens, but no words come out.

Ugh. This bastard... He's outsmarting me at every turn, leaving me spiraling with frustration and a gut-wrenching anxiety I can't shake.

"I need to use the bathroom," I blurt, rising quickly.

His hand clamps around my wrist. "Why?" he asks.

"Because I need to relieve myself, you..." I snap my mouth shut, afraid I'll say something to make him crazier.

After a moment, he releases me. "Be quick," he says, his voice heavy with suspicion.

Once I'm in the bathroom, I lock the door and kneel by the toilet, my hand trembling. I need this. I need to purge whatever is in my stomach — to rid myself of my anxiety.

I stab two fingers down my throat, and relief washes over me as a small flood leaves my body.

It's not much — mostly foamy bile. I haven't eaten except those chocolates I snacked on while making dinner, but it's something.

The panic within me ebbs, replaced by a faint sense of control. When I finish, I brush my teeth and stare at my reflection in the mirror.

How did my life come to this?

The door rattles, and my heart leaps into my throat. Before I can react, Joar's voice cuts through the door. "You threw up again."

Shoot.

"Uh, no I didn't," I lie, but the tremor in my voice betrays me.

I open the door, and he's there, stepping in and filling the frame, his eyes dark with disappointment. He grabs my wrist and leads me to the kitchen without a word.

"What are you doing?" I demand, but he doesn't answer. Instead, he lifts me onto the counter, his hands firm around my waist. My breath catches as his strength — his sheer physicality — leaves me momentarily stunned.

He twirls a forkful of spaghetti and holds it to my lips.

"Open," he orders.

"Oh, no. Nope."

His gaze hardens. "Open, or I'll make you."

Reluctantly, I comply, closing my mouth around the fork. It feels like I've taken a bite of poison. He watches intently as I chew and swallow, his expression unreadable.

"Good girl," he murmurs, spinning another forkful. "You'll eat, and you'll keep it down. No more throwing up."

"You definitely can't force me to do that," I reply with indifference. Not even years of Christian's therapy or self-help books have done the trick. But once my eyes meet his, his calm determination makes my resistance feel futile.

I shrug and add softly, "I can't stop. I've tried. So trust me, you can't stop me, either."

"I can," he replies simply. "And I will. I'm taking care of you now, Emma, because you're mine."

Squinting at him, my confusion lingering, I reply, "Uh... what did you say?"

Chapter 8

Emma

Joar calmly shrugs. "I said you're mine. I'm taking care of you moving forward."

"But I'm not yours," I say softly, afraid to entertain that notion. But the words feel hollow as Joar's thumb brushes against my bottom lip, wiping away a smudge of marinara sauce. Yet, the innocent touch sends an unwelcome shiver down my spine. I shake my head and repeat in a firmer tone, "Stop it, I'm *not* yours."

"You are, and you should be thankful. You need me," he says, his voice low and full of conviction.

I open my mouth to retort, but he silences me with another forkful of spaghetti. And though every bite feels like a battle, he's relentless. Each time I try to pull away or protest, he's there, ready, until I've eaten enough to satisfy him.

When it's over, he lifts me off the counter like I weigh nothing and sets me down gently, his hands lingering on my waist.

"No throwing up again. You can do this," he says softly, his tone surprisingly sincere. "I'll show you."

I squint but nod, just wanting him to get the heck out of my house.

He smirks and adds casually. "Also, no masturbating tonight."

"What?" I reply aghast, unsure I heard him correctly.

"Why are you upset? Did you plan to think about me after I leave?"

"No! It's just... we discussed no sex."

"You're exactly right, my pretty toy," Joar says. His gaze pins me in place as he leans in, so close I can feel the warmth of his breath against my skin. "You said 'no sex,' and that includes sex with yourself. Therefore, no mastur-bation."

His words send a jolt through me. My cheeks burn as I stammer, "W—What? You can't be serious."

"Dead serious," he replies smoothly, his lips curling into a faint, knowing smirk.

I gawk at him, struggling to comprehend how he's turned my own words against me so effortlessly. He couldn't have outsmarted me *again* — could he?

Nope... No way.

"Fine," I counter, but grasp at any scrap of leverage I can muster to win this battle. "Then that means you can't have sex with anyone either, or masturbate."

"I know," he answers without hesitation, as though this stipulation barely registers as a sacrifice.

I scoff, rolling my eyes in defiance, but before I can step back, Joar takes my wrist. His grip is firm, possessive, and unrelenting as he pulls me toward him, then slides my palm beneath his shirt! My fingers press against the scorching heat of his chest, and the sharp planes of his muscles flow under my touch.

The contact sends a rush through me, my breath hitching as he guides my hand downward with deliberate slowness, dragging my fingertips over the defined ridges of his abs.

Each movement feels purposeful, like he's carving the memory of his body into my mind, daring me to forget.

I try to jerk my hand away, but his hold tightens, his eyes locked on mine with a look so dark, it leaves me frozen in place. He stops just at his navel, his voice dropping to a low, velvety murmur.

"Should I go lower, you sad, deprived little thing? Give you something to dream about tonight? If it's about me," he pauses, his lips curving into a sinful smirk, "then I'll allow you to touch yourself."

I draw in a sharp inhale, the heat between us burning as his words settle over me. My mouth opens to protest, but nothing comes out — my mind is too busy processing the thrill of his closeness and the raw masculinity he exudes.

I tug at my hand again, desperate to break free, but he holds me fast, his thumb brushing over the sensitive skin of my wrist. The movement is infuriatingly gentle, a stark contrast to the power radiating from his body.

His lifted shirt exposes the sharp cut of his hips, the deep V that disappears tantalizingly into the waistband of his shorts.

My wandering eyes betray me further, sliding down those taut lines to the edge of his athletic underwear peeking above the band. My imagination runs wild, dark thoughts of pulling the fabric down, tracing the lines of his body with my fingertip, my lips—

Stop, Emma!

I veer my eyes away, my face burning with shame.

This isn't happening. It can't be happening.

With a surge of willpower, I pull back hard, finally breaking free of his grasp. I stumble away, my chest heaving, my hand tingling with the memory of his incredible body.

Joar doesn't chase me. Instead, he straightens, his smirk deepening into something darker, knowing.

"You're blushing, poor girl," he teases, his voice a rich hum that makes my skin prickle. "I'll take that as a yes."

"God, you're insufferable," I whine, crossing my arms in a futile attempt to shield myself from his penetrating gaze.

He chuckles low in his throat, his eyes raking over me like he's already won.

"You can lie to yourself all you want, but tonight, when you're alone, I'll be the only thing on your mind."

I glare at him, my heart racing as I fumble for a retort, but the truth in his words has me shaken.

With one last triumphant look, he turns and strides toward the door, leaving me standing there, reeling from the chaos he's unleashed.

After locking the deadbolt, I decide to take matters into my own hands — if only to spite him as I fantasize about someone else!

I'm absolutely not going to think about what he might look like beneath his underwear, peeling that tight fabric down. I refuse to imagine tracing my fingertips over those muscled curves, palming his annoyingly perfect butt. And I definitely won't visualize him stretched out naked on my bed, every inch of him hard as I... *oh God.*

I so need relief. A vibrator isn't cutting it anymore.

...Ah, hell with it. I'm totally masturbating to him.

Chapter 9

Emma

Christian and I skate side-by-side across the practice rink, his graceful, lean frame keeping pace with mine as we round the edge in perfect sync.

He's gorgeous.

I catch myself, my gaze lingering on him.

I focus my eyes ahead and we move as one, anticipating each step with the ease of partners who have known each other's rhythms for years.

A small group of elite pair skaters, just 16 and eager, watch us intently, observing every precise shift in our synchronized footwork.

As we come to a turn, Christian's powerful hands slide down to my waist, as if preparing to lift me like he did so many times in the past. But it's been two years since he's hoisted me into the air, and we both know that lift isn't coming. Still, the familiar touch makes my heart skip a beat, a reminder of all that's changed and everything that hasn't.

"Axel lift here, followed by the footwork we just showed you," he says loudly, his voice carrying across the rink.

Our students nod and the pairs begin the exercise.

I glance at Christian. His strong chin, shimmering skin, dark lips, long frame, and shoulder-length brown hair still has an irresistible allure.

There's no denying he's attractive — but not like Joar. Christian is refined, deliberate, thoughtful... more than a set of hard abs and nice biceps. And though Christian's body is far from muscled, his grace makes him captivating.

For years, I thought I'd marry him.

Foolish.

So foolish.

Out of the corner of my eye, I spot Joar slipping into the front row. Our eyes meet, and the brute has the nerve to wave and flash a grin. My stomach twists, letting me know a purge is already in the future.

"Darn it," I mutter under my breath.

"Who's that?" Christian asks, his gaze following mine.

"An animal that needs to go back to the locker room," I reply, my voice short.

I ask Christian to continue the lesson and skate toward Joar. While leaning over the barrier separating the ice from the seats, I glare down at him seated casually. He's reclining like he owns the rink.

"What are you doing here, Joar?" I whine, my fatigue clear.

"You'll watch my games, so I'll watch yours," he answers, lifting a white drink cup with a neon green straw. "Have you eaten today? Brought you a smoothie. Banana and strawberry."

I grimace. "I don't want that sugary mess. And this isn't a game. It's a lesson."

"It's your sport, so I care," he replies, his grin softening into something warmer, but no less calculated.

"Joar, we need to talk about last night."

"What's there to talk about? I had a great time. Didn't you?"

"No." My tone hardens.

"Did you think of me after I left?" he presses.

I balk, my mouth agape, stunned by his forwardness. Here. At work no less! He has no shame!

My cheeks burn hot, and I fumble to look innocent.

His handsome smile turns wicked. "Don't be bashful, needy girl. Tell me, did you touch yourself, thinking of me?"

"Joar!"

"I thought of you," he replies, his voice a seductive murmur, "while imagining you trembling for me."

My breath catches. I never had a guy masturbate while thinking about me! I hate to admit it, but it's flattering. But now I'm even more embarrassed.

I stammer, then finally manage to say, "I can't live like this. I'll run errands, cook... but all this other stuff? It's a deal breaker. If that's how you see a personal assistant, then this deal is off."

"No, you can't end the deal," he replies casually, his tone dismissive as he glances past me. "Who's that man?"

I follow his gaze to Christian, who watches a pair skate, his jaw resting on his hand.

"That's Christian, my old skating partner. But never mind him. Stay on topic, Joar. I *can* end the deal, so I'm ending it."

His eyes stay fixed ahead, watching Christian, his gaze darkening with fierce intensity. "This... Christian fellow, did you date him?"

"That's none of your business!" I huff, trying to show him I have limits and this is one of them.

"Are you dating him now?"

I roll my eyes, totally exasperated. "No, no. We dated in the past, but... he cheated."

"Oh?" The slightest smirk appears on his lips. "That's good."

"Good?"

Joar nods decisively, his smile infuriating. "Yeah. That means you're over him, right?"

"Again, none of your business. He occasionally teaches with me. That's all you need to know."

Joar shrugs, unimpressed. "I can skate with you instead."

I purse my lips, suppressing a laugh. "That's impossible. You can lift me onto a kitchen counter, but you can't lift me above your head while skating at full speed."

His brow raises, as if I just insulted him. "If that guy can do it, so can I."

"Even Christian can't lift me anymore. I've gained too much weight. But enough about him. It's time for you to go. Please?"

"No. I'm staying. Especially with your ex here. I don't trust him. I don't like the way he touched you, either." He smirks slyly and adds, "You're my girl now. Did you tell him we're dating?"

"You're not getting it," I reply firmly, stepping off the ice and stomping toward him. My skates squeak against the rubber mat as I close the distance. With conviction I didn't know I had, I point my finger at his face and say in my most commanding voice, "This is *not* a relationship. I'm not your girl, your toy, or anything else. Now, please, knock it off."

He leans back, his gaze dark and unflinching. Slowly, he licks his lips as he stares from under his brow. An artic wolf, ready to pounce. It's a look that causes me to cautiously retract my hand from him face, afraid he may snap if I don't.

I whisper, "Sorry."

After a painfully long silence that seems to amplify the tension between us, he says, "I thought you'd be more obedient. At least you're sexy when you stand up for yourself."

For some reason, I'm relieved that he isn't mad, but I'm still flustered. "Ugh, you're unbelievable," I say, but softer, as I'm uncomfortable being described as sexy, too. Guys never describe me as sexy.

Well, Christian called me sexy once. However, figure skaters strive to be graceful, elegant, refined. Not sexy.

But the compliment sure feels good, especially coming from Joar.

He tilts his head. "It's true. But you shouldn't stand up to me. Stand up to other people. Now go back on the ice and make your ex leave. I'll skate with you instead."

"No way," I say with anxiousness. "I told you. I'm too fat for Christian to lift, let alone someone untrained like you. It's a lot harder than it looks."

"You think you're fat?" he asks, genuine concern flashing across his handsome face.

"Well, yeah! Little tits, big hips." I turn to the side and swat my own ass. "Come on, Joar, I'm *obviously* fat."

"No. Your weight suits your body type."

"Thanks," I mutter sarcastically. "If by body type, you mean a frumpy pear."

He snatches my wrist, pulling me closer until I stumble onto his lap. His hand strokes my thigh, slow and comforting. "You're not fat. You're beautiful. You caught my attention the moment I met you."

"Don't lie," I whisper, hating when people tell me white lies to make me feel better.

He shakes his head, but gently, he takes hold of my chin. "I'm not lying. And I remember you hid behind my cousin that day because you were afraid of Bergen, my dog. But I'll protect you from now on."

I can't help but smile as I quip back, "Protect me from what? You?"

"No, not me. My cousin. My teammates. Your mother. Your ex."

It's been a long time since I got a compliment, or someone seemed to care about my body issues. So I relent. "Gosh. Alright. I guess you can stay, but *please* just behave. Stay here."

"Do you want a kiss first?" he asks, his voice soft and low, like a caress.

"You're joking," I reply softly, yet know he isn't. Worse still, my heart races wildly at the meer mention of kissing him again.

He sits back, his smirk widening. "You're blushing again."

I look away, desperate to hide the heat rising in my cheeks.

"You'll ask for one soon," he adds.

I refuse to respond, and for a moment, I hold my bottom lip between my teeth as I stare at this chest. The heat of his body radiates, drawing me in from the chill of the ice rink.

I really like it, being this close. I want to cuddle, be held, take his bait.

What a fool I am.

So, I force myself to leave the comfort of sitting on this man's lap. I rush back to the ice while I still have an iota of control.

When the lesson ends, he's still there, waiting.

He smiles warmly. "Good job. You're a great teacher. Your students admire you. I can tell," he says with sincerity.

His compliment is simple, yet stuns me more than his earlier *sexy* comment. Nobody ever told me that I'm a good coach. For a moment, I falter, unsure how to respond.

"Uh, um, thanks," I mumble.

"Do you want a kiss now?" he asks, his gaze burning into mine.

"No, Joar," I state firmly.

Well, if it wasn't *him*, a hockey player, a brute, a controlling insane person, I know the answer is yes. Especially as I find myself staring at his lips.

And as his lips curl into that maddeningly confident smile, my resolve wavers. His jawline, sharp with the perfect amount of scruff, draws my gaze, and my thoughts betray me. *God,* I do want to feel his roughness against my lips again.

His eyes flick to my parted lips, and his smirk deepens. "Emma?" His voice makes my pulse race. "See something you want?"

Chapter 10

Emma

Joar caught me. I stared at those luscious lips for a moment too long.

He freezes in place like a statue, and I can tell by his stillness that he's about to monopolize on my weakness. I edge further out of reaching distance in a casual manner.

But that slight, mischievous curl at the corner of his mouth is my warning before he's already in motion. I try to dodge, but his reflexes are just too fast; he catches my arm, pulling me back toward him. And then, before I can even protest, he leans in, capturing my mouth in a kiss — firm, deliberate, and... public.

I squirm as he presses forward, his pressure persistent, refusing to let me go, like he's proving a point.

Despite the irritation simmering in my chest, a part of me knows he isn't crossing a line; he's just disrupting my world in that maddening way only Joar seems to thrive on.

But with my students nearby, I can't risk a scene, so I reluctantly raise my white flag, muttering into his mouth, "Okay, okay. I give up!"

He pulls back, a devilish grin lighting up his face.

"Good. Give me a real kiss now," he orders, his voice a low, commanding rumble that's so hard to resist.

With an exaggerated sigh, I close my eyes and rise onto my skates, going through the motions as he cradles my jaw.

This time, he waits, so I push through this and lace my fingers behind his neck and stretch up, moving into the kiss first. But as my lips near, I find myself brushing his gently. My own motions have a tenderness that catches me off guard — and we kiss... a quiet, genuine kiss that lingers far longer than I expect.

When he finally pulls back, his expression has softened, the dominant energy fading into something deeper. I'd always dismissed hockey players as little more than overgrown boys, but perhaps that was my mistake — underestimating Joar. He's proven to be far more clever than I ever anticipated.

"Not so bad to kiss me, hm?" he says, his voice carrying that unwavering confidence.

"Oh, yes. I love your scheduled kisses," I reply with sarcasm, though a smirk tugs at my lips despite myself.

"You have a pretty smile," he says, causing me to blush. "Are you ready to go?"

"Where?" I ask, my voice cautious.

"Dinner. At my place."

"Uh. No."

"Too bad. Not debatable," he says, his friendliness suddenly gone, replaced by something colder. "My house is nicer, anyway. Much more appropriate for us."

I stare at him for a moment, frustration bubbling beneath my skin. I make another mental note to set plans with other people, like Christian, so I have an excuse when Joar pulls these stunts. But tonight, I'm cornered — no excuses, no solutions, no escape.

Joar waits patiently as I unlace my skates and slip on my shoes. Before I ask, he swings my duffle bag over his shoulder, adjusting it with a meticulous care that's somewhat off. As though he can't get the strap to sit right on his shoulder.

Then, without a word, he takes my hand and leads me out of the rink. When he hands me the smoothie he brought earlier, I immediately toss it into the first trashcan we pass.

Nope. He can't force me to eat that! Sugar is poison.

He stops mid-stride, his eyes rolling up to the ceiling as if searching for patience, as though I'm the unreasonable one.

After a moment, he gives me a dark, knowing look. "Defying me will only make this harder on you," then says nothing more. He tightens his grip on my hand and guides us to the parking lot, leaving me feeling both victorious yet uneasy.

Once in the car, he says, "I hope I don't have to be forceful to make you obey me every time. So naturally rebellious?

That explains why your mom had a needle in your thigh, doesn't it?"

"Obey you?" I repeat, astonished.

He leers at me but begins the drive to his place in silence. Time blurs before we arrive at his high-end, modern home — a unique blend of sleek sophistication and Texas charm. In his spacious dining room, I stab at a salad with my fork, pretending the crisp lettuce is his annoyingly handsome face. When *The Imperial March* from Star Wars sounds, I know Mother is calling.

With a heavy sigh, I retrieve my phone.

"Don't answer it," Joar says, setting down the main course: lasagna.

I swear this guy is trying to kill me.

"I don't eat Italian, or other carb-heavy dishes every day, Joar. And I have to answer. She'll keep calling if I don't."

I swipe accept, but he reaches over my shoulder and hits the speakerphone button.

Mom's thick Mandarin accent fills the room, asking me what I am doing. "Hāi, nǚ zài zuò shénme?"

Joar hits the mute button and orders, "Speak in English."

I glare at him but unmute the phone and reply to Mother, "I'm just sitting down for dinner." I then cover the phone and whisper to Joar, "Excuse me while I take this call privately." As I attempt to stand, his hands grip my shoulders, forcing me to stay seated. I sigh but say to Mother, "What are you calling about?"

"Where are you having dinner?" she asks.

"I'm home."

"No. I looked up your location and you are not home," she says in her usual, calm tenor.

I grit my teeth. "Sorry. I misspoke. I'm at Joar's place."

"You can't date players, Emma."

"I know, Mother. We're just friends."

Joar sneers in disgust beside me.

"Don't lie to your mother," she replies. "Christian said Joar was at your lesson."

"Oh, Gosh." I glance at Joar, who's now wearing a cocky smile.

She continues, "Christian also claimed Joar was... touching you inappropriately."

Although that isn't a lie, it's extreme. "He only kissed me. He didn't grope me."

"Kissing in public?" she says, her voice stifling outrage.

"Mom — obviously I didn't want him to kiss me in a public place, or kiss me at all. He just likes me, I guess."

Joar leans close, his voice low and dangerous. "No, tell her we're dating."

I stick out my tongue, mouthing "no," prompting him to narrow his eyes.

Mother's voice sharpens. "Ah. Joar coming to our team makes sense now. Why would he be interested in you, though?"

I glance at Joar, who gives me a warm smile, but I frown as I answer truthfully. "I don't know."

My words twist my gut as I feel my insecurity cause tears to well in my eyes. But honestly, why would any guy like me? I'm such a mess in so many ways. I'm lucky Christian dated me.

Joar, on the other hand, has a different reaction. His jaw tightens, nostrils flare, his patience clearly wearing thin.

Mother continues, "I assume you're having dinner to discuss boundaries and ending his advances?"

"Yes, Mother," I groan.

Joar scoffs and stands, balling his fists as he paces, his anger radiating.

"Besides, Emma. He's the most valuable asset on our team. We don't want his performance compromised because of you. Business only."

"Of course—"

"He needs to stay in peak physical condition, too. You're heavy like Buddha. We don't want your bad habits rubbing off on him."

He stops, his voice is cold, slicing through the tension. "Hang up."

Silently, I mouth "no" once more, causing him to thump the tabletop with his fist, making the silverware clatter.

I flinch, but tell Mother, "I agree. He made lasagna. He clearly chose such an unhealthy meal because I'm fat."

Joar rubs his face. For the first time, I see him undeniably frustrated. His clear lack of control in this conversation brings an unexpected smile to my face, though. I'm not powerless against this Nordic God at this moment.

Apparently, he cares what my mom thinks, so I add, "Don't worry, Mother. I'm not interested in hockey players, as you know. I'm simply being respectful and obliging him to a dinner, but I will let him down easy."

As hoped, the inkling of disappointment in her voice vanishes.

"Excellent. That is a relief. I suggest you are exceedingly polite and professional to spare his feelings and any embarrassment. After you leave, come over so your father and I can advise you on avoiding conflicts of interest in the future."

The familiar sense of dread sinks in as I imagine a three hour lecture with my parents about what I already know: don't date players.

Neither of them would believe me if I explained the deal, anyway. And even if they did, I bet they would blame me. Hopefully, Joar, hearing Mother's objections, will put an end to this situation once and for all.

So I close my eyes and sigh with a genuine sense of defeat. "Okay, I'll leave here after dinner and—"

The connection ends. My eyes snap open and I find my phone in Joar's hand.

"I didn't give you permission to leave," he says. "And you misbehaved." His voice is cold, commanding, as he sets his chair back from the table. Facing me, he extends his hand, his expression unreadable. "Stand up."

I stay seated, defiantly perched at the edge of my chair, even as I feel his gaze fixed on me, searing and intense. His displeasure radiates, coiling tension in my stomach, making my heart pound.

"Stand up," he repeats, "or I'll make you."

I hesitate, the broody storm in his eyes making it clear defiance won't end well. I sigh, slowly shifting to rise, but before I can fully move, his hand clamps around my forearm, his grip like steel.

With a swift, unyielding motion, he pulls me forward, my feet stumbling as his grip doesn't loosen. The force of his pull makes me wince, but he doesn't offer a single apology.

Instead, he maneuvers me over his lap. I start to push myself up, but his hand presses firmly into my lower back, keeping me pinned.

I barely have time to process what's happening before his hand descends, landing a sharp slap on my backside! The shock of it stings, sending a jolt through me.

Wait.

Did he just spank me?

"Stop, Joar! That hurts," I protest, my voice cracking, beyond confused.

Chapter 11

Emma

Joar's palm connects with my backside, sharp and hot, the *smack* cracking through the air as I cry out in pain. It's not just the sting — it's the overwhelming force behind it, the power in his strike, that makes my body jolt, and my cheeks burn with humiliation.

"Joar! Stop! You can't do this!" I shout, writhing against his iron grip, but he doesn't even flinch.

"You think you can break the rules? Disobey me?" His voice is deep and dark, yet disregards my protests entirely. He's irritatingly calm despite my panic, and in that obnoxiously dismissive tone, he adds, "You're weak because you let her control you. Because you've never had someone force you to face the truth: Your mom controls you."

Tears sting my eyes as his words cut deeper than his hand. "She does not, and I'm not weak!" I snap, even as my voice trembles.

His grip on my upper back tightens, pressing me down further. "You are weak. But I'll make you strong... after I break you."

Smack!

The pain blooms again, burning and unbearable, yet something inside me feels like it's unraveling. My walls — those carefully built defenses I've clung to for years — are shaking, and he knows it.

"Look at you," he says, his tone laced with mockery. "Letting a woman like your mother make you her little puppet. Do you know what I see? A scared little girl, too afraid to fight for herself."

Joar is twenty-nine. I'm younger — twenty five. But I'm not a little girl!

"You're wrong! She doesn't control me. She helps me," I cry out, the humiliation hitting harder than his strikes.

He leans down, his breath hot against my ear as he murmurs, "No. You need to hear this. You're pathetic because you let her win. Over and over again. That ends now."

I'm trembling, my pride shattering into pieces. His words make me want to scream and hide, but a deeper part of me — a part I don't want to acknowledge — feels drawn to him. To his strength. To the fact that he sees me, even at my lowest.

"Say it, Emma," he demands, his voice commanding and cruel. "Say she controls you. Admit it."

I press my lips together, my stubbornness clinging to the last shred of my pride. "No. I make my own decisions. She just... advises me."

Smack!

The sharp strike sends tears streaming down my face. "Try again," he orders, his tone unrelenting.

"Ugh," I pout, my voice cracking. "Okay, maybe she is a little too opinionated. Are you happy now?"

"No. Almost."

Smack!

"God! Fine! She is controlling. Now Stop!" I whine.

A smirk tugs at his lips as he straightens, his hand gently stroking the raw flesh of my round bottom, the tenderness jarring after the punishment. "Better. Not perfect. But you'll learn."

He pulls me upright, sitting me on his lap like a China doll. His arms encircle me in a possessive hold. My body feels small against his, but for the first time, the vulnerability doesn't scare me as much as it would before he swatted me like... a child!

"Emma," he says, his voice low but softer now. "You don't need her approval. You need mine. I'll teach you how to be strong, to stand on your own. You just have to trust me."

His words land with a weight that leaves me speechless. Something in his tone, in the steadiness of his gaze, makes me feel like he means it. Like he sees something in me worth taking care of.

I mean, he's a madman, but still... damn it, I am so confused.

My phone buzzes on the table, shattering the moment. He picks it up, holding it out to me. "Answer it. Tell her you're not going over there tonight. And tell her we're together."

My heart races as I stare at the screen, my mother's name glaring back at me like a warning. My fingers tremble as I take the phone, the pressure mounting with each passing second.

For reasons I don't understand, I bury my face in the nook of his neck. "I can't," I murmur, my voice barely audible.

"Yes, you can," he counters firmly, his grip on my waist firm. Gently, he strokes my hair, petting me! Yet the act doesn't feel belittling — like sitting on the floor — and I must admit, the effect is incredibly soothing. "You can do this, *Emmy*."

Oh gosh. That nickname. He's so good at calming me. But how?

His words and touch are intoxicating, yet make my chest ache, but the fear is too much. But the battle between his effect on me and that nagging ringtone collides in an overwhelming sense of chaos. I can't breathe. Suddenly, my pulse pounds in my ears and I push away from him, stumbling toward the bathroom.

"Emma—" he says, but I slam the door shut, locking it behind me.

My hands shake as I press them to my temples, my mind racing. Everything is too much. His dominance, his words, his unwavering presence — it's suffocating.

Bang. Bang. Bang.

"Open the door," Joar demands, his voice low and dangerous.

I ignore him, reverting to my failsafe. I fall to my knees as tears stream down my face. My fingers shove down my throat, the old habit promising its relief. But before I can act, the door bursts open with a splintering crack.

Joar steps inside, his towering form filling the small space. His eyes are fierce, yet there's something deeper there — a flicker of concern beneath the dark dominance.

Before I can react, his hands are on me, pulling me to my feet. "Why do you hurt yourself?" he demands, his grip firm but not cruel.

"Leave me alone!"

"Answer me. Now."

I pound my fists against his chest, the fight leaving me in broken sobs. "I can't do this! You don't understand!"

He catches my wrists in one hand, his strength overwhelming. His free hand brushes a tear from my cheek, his touch surprisingly gentle. "You can. And you will. Because you're mine, and I won't let you hurt yourself."

The doorbell rings, breaking the tension, but he doesn't move. His eyes stay locked on mine, his grip unwavering, as if daring me to run again.

Chapter 12

Emma

Thank goodness.

Mother is here. I'll be free soon. I know how to endure her. Joar encompasses a completely different set of problems I don't know how to solve.

I look up at Joar and say with apprehension, "Sorry, I have to leave."

He releases his hold and replies smoothly, "If you obeyed me, you would be happy."

I look away and step out of the bathroom, but Joar moves past me, heading toward the front door. His hand pauses on the doorknob as he casts a curious look my way. "Do you want to leave with her?"

The question catches me off guard, and I hesitate, glancing away as I try to make sense of the strange pull he has over me. A flicker of warmth — of wanting to be close to him — flashes through my mind, leaving me unsettled. I can't start feeling something for him... not after everything he's done to control me, especially refusing to let me purge and, yes, spanking me.

"No, I don't want to leave with her, but it's much better than sitting on the ground like a dog or being spanked like a child." I lower my voice. "I'm overwhelmed by you."

He tilts his head, a glimmer of something sinister in his smoldering, stormy eyes. He sighs and says, "Emmy, you realize you need me, don't you?"

I scoff, but lower my voice as I add, "Probably like I need a headache." I veer my gaze, now convinced this man is beyond reason.

"Look at me. You are not leaving my house. It's time for you to grow up and tell your mom 'no.' When I open this door, you better do that or I'll—"

Mother's voice sounds from behind the door. "Hello! Emma? Are you in there? Don't ignore your mother. Do you hear me? Are you in danger? Open this door or I'll call the police."

I dart my eyes to him and blurt, "Joar, I can't tell her off, but I don't want to leave you!" Just as quickly as the words escape my lips, I cover my mouth in shock.

A slow, deviant smirk spreads across his face. "Good decision. Ready?"

I look at the door. "No," I whisper, the sternness in my voice sounds weak even to my own ears.

"You are ready." Joar's smile doesn't waver as he opens the door.

Mother sweeps inside without a glance his way, her eyes focused on me with unmistakable disapproval. "Why didn't you answer your phone? Where's your purse? Grab it. Come along."

I glance at Joar, silently pleading for help. He tilts his head, urging me to speak up, but when I open my mouth, nothing comes out — I can only stammer under her harsh gaze.

He sighs, disappointment flickering across his face, but he steps beside me, draping his arm around my shoulder with a protective ease. "She is staying with me," he says calmly, his tone leaving no room for argument.

"Staying?" Mother purses her lips to hide her amusement, but her eyes shine bright. "Mr. Sköll, player relationships with owners are a serious conflict of interest and strongly discouraged by the league."

"But not prohibited," he replies. "I read the bylaws."

"Ah. Even so, I'm sorry to disappoint you, but my daughter understands your romantic interest in her is inappropriate and must not be indulged." She looks at me and adds, "It's time to leave, Emma."

Although I cannot speak, I summon the strength to move, and clutch onto Joar tightly. My eyes squeeze shut as I bury my face to his shirt. His powerful arm curls around me more, actualizing the fantasy I wanted since I sat on his lap in the rink. It's tranquil here, feeling completely impervious to Mother's commands.

"Goodbye, Mrs. Huang," Joar says to Mother.

A growl draws my attention to the floor as Bergen faces her. The light brown dog curls his lips, bearing his fangs.

"Oh my," she mutters, taking a cautious step backward.

The dog follows at the same pace, slowly herding her towards the door. Once she passes the threshold, Joar releases me and moves to lock the deadbolt. Once the steel lock slides into place, he pats Bergen on the head.

With the threat of Mother gone, the sense of needing Joar's help evaporates and before he looks my way, I rush to the bathroom again, my fingers down my throat before I've even knelt.

Just then, I'm jerked around, my fingers yanked from my mouth.

In what seems like a second, Joar pins me between the bathroom vanity and the front of his hard body. With both of us facing the mirror, his arms snake around my body, pulling me closer. My backside presses to him as his weight leans forward. My thighs dig into the marble countertop, causing me to wince.

He doesn't care, though, and asks, "Why is that your solution every time? Why do you hurt yourself?"

I cannot deny there's something incredibly comforting about being caught in his hold. However, I'm emotionally exhausted, and a second round of punishment is unthinkable.

Not wanting to upset him further, I answer without a fight, "Whenever I'm overwhelmed, it lessens my anxiety."

"Then open your mouth."

"Huh?"

He offers no explanation, and before I can react, two of his fingers press past my lips, sliding deep into my mouth until they reach his knuckles. My body tenses, spine rigid, as I watch the scene unfold in our reflection, my gaze locked on his intense, unyielding expression.

"Suck," he commands, his voice a low, steady murmur that sends a shiver through me.

"Er, um, I," I garble, unable to speak with my mouth full.

"Suck," he repeats.

Chapter 13

Emma

In the mirror, Joar's hypnotizing eyes hold mine, dark and unreadable, pulling me deeper into the moment.

Silently, I beg him to let me keep my last shred of dignity. But mercy doesn't seem like his nature. His cheek brushes against my temple, his warmth grounding and disarming all at once. My eyes flutter shut, fighting the human side of me that needs connection — a touch I've denied for so long.

"Suck, my poor, sad little toy," he commands.

I wince at his words, because deep down, he's right. I am sad. I'm starving for someone to help me who isn't my mother.

And since I can't escape his hold, I timidly apply suction, my lips closing around his fingers. His lips graze the edge of my earlobe, and he whispers, "That's my good girl. Only my fingers can be in your mouth when you're overwhelmed. Got it?"

My breath hitches, his bossy words both shocking and strangely soothing. His praise also warms something damaged inside me — a flicker of approval I didn't realize I need. My eyes close as I nod, savoring the moment of peace... an escape from my almost constant sense of anxiety.

His lips brush along the curve of my ear, his breath hot against my skin. The sensation is incredibly disarming, and I instinctively suck harder, desperate to hold on to the solace he's giving.

A low exhale sweeps down my neck as he bends his knees, lowering his hips to meet mine. The movement presses me harder against the marble countertop, the front of my thighs digging painfully into the edge. The friction between us intensifies, and I let out a sharp gasp as his jeans rub against my sore backside, the sting a cruel reminder of his earlier punishment.

My hand snakes between us, desperate to create a barrier. I press against his stomach, trying to ease the pressure, but he captures my wrist effortlessly, his grip firm yet unhurried. His smirk deepens.

I whine, "It hurts," but cringe instantly, as I don't want to sound weaker than I already do. I close my eyes, hoping for mercy.

His voice remains steady, though, holding only concern. "I hurt you that bad?"

I nod, my brow furrowing with the dual intensity of pain and longing. Surprisingly, his eyes gleam with compassion as he guides my hand away, removing the only barrier between us.

With one swift motion, he undoes his jeans. My breath catches as the rough denim falls away, leaving only the thin fabric of his underwear and my stretchy leggings between us.

The heat radiating from him is a soothing heat, and my body betrays me, leaning into the contact.

His voice drops, deep and primal. "Do you know how sexy you are? Do you have any idea how badly I want to fuck you? I want to give it to you so hard you squirm and beg me to stop. But I wouldn't... because damn, you need it."

I shudder, having never heard a man speak to me so brashly — making promises I never knew I wanted until they were said.

His fingers begin to withdraw from my mouth, but I bite down lightly, keeping them on my tongue. The anxiety that suffocated me minutes earlier is gone, replaced by an un-tamed need that surges through me. I suck harder, desperate to hold on to the fleeting peace his touch brings.

His hips grind against mine, and despite the soreness, I can't stop myself from arching back into him, now craving the friction. My hand slips between us again, but this time, it's not to push him away. My palm glides over the bulge in his underwear, tracing the length of him before giving a firm squeeze.

Damn. He's perfect. Maybe even too big.

As I rub him firmly, a low, husky breath escapes his lips.

"You little tease," he murmurs, his tone laced with desire.

"Mm-hm," I hum, shameless as I stroke him through the stretchy fabric.

Mother's words echo faintly in my mind, warning me not to indulge. And she's right.

Stop, Emma, I lecture myself. He's one of our players. This is so wrong!

Yet the thought of stopping only fuels my rebellion. I glance over my shoulder, then let my other hand slide behind Joar's neck, pulling him closer until his lips meet the sensitive skin just below my ear. His mouth is ravenous, tasting me with a hunger that sends waves of heat cascading through my body.

He wants me. This god of a man actually wants me, a frumpy pear.

Hell with it. I'm desirable... I think. Yes, okay. I'm *very* sexy.

I almost grimace at my inner pep-talk, but I cling to that notion, wanting to be confident for him.

And in a moment, I moan, arching into his touch, and guide his hand to my breast. His palm is warm and rough as he kneads the soft flesh, his thumb brushing over the peak with a tenderness that contrasts the ferocity of his earlier punishment.

"Joar," I whisper, my voice trembling. "I'm supposed to stop this."

"But you can't stop, can you?"

"No," I whimper and stroke his shaft firmly. The rock hard length is so incredibly tempting. "I... I think... I wanna know what you feel like."

He smirks, knowing I just confessed I want to feel him inside of me. His grip tightens slightly, and he grinds against me and I immediately imagine him thrusting into my aching warmth. His voice is seductively smooth as he says, "Oh? So my needy toy wants more? Do you think you deserve it?"

The question stings, but my desire is spilling over. I can't wait and slip my hand beneath the waistband of his under-wear, my fingers wrapping around his velvety smooth shaft as I stroke him with deliberate, eager motions.

"Yeah," I breathe, my voice full of angst I can't hide. "I deserve it."

His teeth nip at my earlobe, the sensation sending a shock of pleasure through me. "Say you'll obey me first. Then I'll give you every inch of me until you're shaking." His thick cock twitches in my hand, driving me mad.

And although the words seem so wrong, I'm tempted to say yes. But instead, a truth surfaces out of nowhere, slipping past my lips. "I think I have feelings for you, Joar."

His body stills, the energy between us shifting into some-thing more intense.

He's surprised, and his brow peaks.

Oh my gosh! What if... what if he doesn't have real feelings, too? What if this is just about sex and control over me? I shouldn't have said that. I'm so stupid!

Before he can respond, I panic and turn my head, capturing his lips in a desperate, passionate kiss — if only to silence his possible rejection brought from my careless words.

His stubble scrapes against my skin, the roughness igniting a fire in me that burns brighter with every second. My hands clutch at him, pulling him, needing more.

"Emmy," he murmurs into my mouth, his kiss as hungry as mine.

But then he reaches for my shirt, lifting it higher.

Oh, no! My stomach!

Panic floods me, and I yank the fabric back down, shielding myself from his gaze. My desire dims as I catch sight of our reflection in the mirror — his eyes burning with hunger, mine clouded with insecurity.

"Sex isn't part of our deal," I blurt, my voice high pitched.

"What! Fuck the deal," he bites back, his arms tightening around me as though he already knows I'm about to flee.

But I'm done. I shouldn't have let myself get so swept away. I'm not sexy. But I am stupid. Weak.

In a burst of energy, I duck under his arm and slip from his cage, keeping my eyes away from his glorious body and handsome face. I say as commanding as I can muster, "No. I don't want this deal, and I definitely don't want to change that rule."

He exhales sharply, his frustration palpable. It's something I haven't seen before: Joar impatient.

"Emma, I want to change the deal. Now. Don't fight this."

I meet his gaze, unflinching. The only thing I can say to end this is, "No. What are you going to do? Rape me?"

His eyes darken, a growl rumbling deep in his chest, and he steps backward. "I don't need to rape you. You'll be begging for me soon enough. But will it be too late?"

The words leave me speechless.

He walks out of the bathroom, leaving me with my reflection — and what always remains when I'm alone: anxiety. And although I deprived myself of sleeping with someone like him, it was the right thing to do.

After all, I don't deserve that kind of sex. That's for women who can please Joar. Who are perfect, unblemished, more experienced. Besides, I let my insecurities ruin that connection we could have had. My lack of self esteem won't change. Better than stopping mid-act.

It's for the best we don't cross that line, too. Sleeping together will only leave me broken when he moves on to the next girl. Mother always said Christian wasn't right for me and would find a better match, and he did.

Chapter 14

Emma

Unlike yesterday, tonight's dinner is my idea, not Joar's. This time, I insisted on a public place. My intentions are purely business-related: make amends and set boundaries.

He chose Bellagio, an upscale steakhouse, almost too dark to read the menu without holding my phone up for light. The fine linen tablecloths, waiters in sharp uniforms, and soft candlelight create an air of sophistication.

It feels out of place for us — well, for Joar.

"This is classy," I admit after the waiter takes our drink order.

"You sound surprised," he says, his lips curving into that sexy smirk.

Trying not to sound rude, I reply in a kind tone, but still answer truthfully. "I figured you'd pick a burger joint or a pizzeria."

"You really think that little of me, don't you?"

I shrug, trying not to smile. "Let's just say my experiences with hockey players haven't painted you guys in a flattering light."

"I'll change that," he says, his tone confident, bordering on seductive.

I'm about to reply with, "doubtful," but his unwavering gaze stops me. Instead, I sit straighter, lifting my chin.

"Mr. Sköll, I'd like to discuss our business relationship—"

He leans back, the corner of his mouth tugging up in amusement. "Let's not make this formal. You're killing the mood already."

"There's not supposed to be a mood," I retort.

"You look beautiful tonight," he says, effortlessly dismissing my protests.

Heat floods my cheeks, and I duck behind my menu, mumbling, "Thank you."

When I peek over the edge, my eyes are instantly drawn to his body. His crisp white button-up shirt clings to his broad chest, a couple of undone buttons hinting at the hard lines beneath. His sleeves strain slightly against his biceps, and I can't stop myself from wanting to see that shirt crumpled on the floor... while I lay on the bed and watch him undo his pants.

Abruptly, his dark, smoldering gaze meets mine, and I quickly redirect my attention to the menu.

"Say it," he orders.

I glance up. "Say what?"

"You were staring. You can say I look good, too."

"I... uh..." I stammer, but his smug grin makes it impossible to deny. "Um. You look... nice."

"That's better," he replies, his eyes gleaming with amusement. "Thank you, my beautiful toy."

"Geez," I bemoan, straightening in my seat. "That's one of the things I want to discuss. Your behavior — especially in the locker room and at my lesson — was completely inappropriate. So was... last night. We need to keep this professional."

His grin doesn't falter, but his eyes narrow just enough to make me tense.

He drums his fingers lazily on the table, leaning closer. "Man, you really need to relax. When's the last time a guy made your toes curl?"

The audacity of his comment makes me balk loudly, startling the waitress who just appeared to set down our wineglasses.

"I'm sorry," I say quickly, mortified by my outburst. They feign ignorance and pour the wine before leaving the table. I sip my Pinot Noir, hoping it will calm my nerves.

Joar chuckles, his deep voice infuriatingly smooth. "Why are you like this, you poor, poor thing?"

"Like what?" I squeak.

"So uptight."

I glare at him, wishing I could say something to hurt his ego. But, that's not how to manage employees. Therefore, I reply calmly, "I'm simply being professional."

"You call it professional. I call it sad," he counters, his gaze challenging.

I narrow my eyes this time. "Well, why are you so bossy and... unprofessional? You make everything so difficult."

"Emmy," he says, his voice softening.

"Don't call me that," I correct softly, the nickname stirring emotions I shouldn't be feeling.

"*Emmy*," he states more firmly, "last night, you said you had feelings for me. Are we pretending that didn't happen?"

"I, uh, I wasn't thinking clearly," I reply, crossing my arms. "I was caught up in the heat of the moment."

"You're lying."

"I'll get up and leave if we don't talk about something else," I warn, though I can't make eye contact. But to show him I mean business, I shift my body to the edge of the seat, ready to stand if he says the wrong thing.

He leans forward, resting his forearms on the table. "Okay. You want formalities? Will that make you relax? Then, let me get to know you as someone at my work."

I hesitate, his words disarming me. "What do you mean?"

"Let me ask you some regular questions," he says. "And answer honestly."

I purse my lips, debating whether to indulge him. Then I remember my father's advice about the importance of building trust with people at work. Little things, like knowing their birthday, interests, ambitions. That's normal. Harmless. So with a resigned sigh, I nod. "Very well. Go ahead."

His lips curve into a sly smile. "First question: What's your greatest fear?"

The question catches me off guard. "I have so many," I admit. "Losing my figure skating academy... disappointing my parents... never getting over Christian."

They rolled off the tongue, but I suppose I shouldn't be so candid, especially about my parents or dating life.

Joar nods, though, his expression stoic. "I thought you were over Christian?"

"I am!" I yip. "I just meant... I want to get over the damage he caused. I shouldn't have mentioned my dating life—"

"What if I told you I could help you with all of that?"

I blink at him, confused. "What?"

"I can help you run the team for one. I happen to know a lot about hockey. More than you."

The sincerity in his voice sends a wave of warmth through me, and I hate how much I want to believe him.

He continues, "I can help you with your parents and your baggage, too."

I quickly shake my head and say, "Next question."

"Okay. Then I'll just help you with your GM duties. Give you advice, suggestions, things like that. Is that alright, or is that unprofessional?"

It would be nice not relying on my parents or coaches for anything hockey related. I know they think I ask dumb questions. Thus, I give Joar a small nod.

"Good. Next question: Did you enjoy last night?"

"What!" I nearly choke on my wine.

"Be honest," he presses. "Didn't you feel better after I spanked you?"

I stare at him, flustered and ashamed. His deep-set, piercing eyes see right through me and I feel my composure chipping away. Desperate to set boundaries with our star player, I say firmly, "Joar. No. I didn't enjoy it. Business only, please."

"Emmy, the way you moaned for more—"

"Joar!" I practically yell, drawing the attention of nearby tables.

He looks disappointed as he leans back. "Okay, okay, calm down," he concedes, but soon, his grin returns. "Don't lie, you liked when I took control, didn't you?"

"I... no!" I stammer, but my voice wavers and I cover my face, the shame unbearable.

He doesn't care though, his gaze unrelenting. "You wanted it so bad, Emmy. You couldn't get your hand on my cock fast enough."

I'm speechless, my mouth opening and closing as I try to form words. I'm just about to storm out of here when our waitress suddenly reappears. With a glowing smile, she sets down our plates, then casually asks, "Is dinner tonight for business or pleasure?"

Her eyes dart between us, reading our expressions.

"Business!" I blurt, my pitch embarrassingly high.

The woman's brow lifts and her warm smile turns to something more amorous as she then fixes her gaze on Joar. In a suddenly seductive tone, she purrs, "I hope you don't work too late then. I get off in an hour."

Before he can respond, she has the audacity to wink at him and spin around, walking away with a wiggle in her hips. Clearly trying to tempt him!

I gawk for a moment, unsure if I just imagined that tacky exchange. I can't believe she just threw herself at him like that! I mean, this is a nice restaurant.

The gentle sound of a wineglass being set down draws my attention to Joar, who has just taken a swig. I meet his gaze, his eyes holding a sense of genuine confusion. Maybe I look stunned... because I am.

So I huff, "Well! That was incredibly rude of that woman. Wasn't it?"

Apparently, he's oblivious to what just happened because he replies, "What was rude?"

"How she propositioned you right in front of me."

He squints and leans forward as though he misheard me. "Emma, she asked if we were on a date. You made it clear we weren't."

"Oh now I am Emma!" I sit up, perhaps more astonished that he finds that woman's behavior perfectly normal. "Does that mean... you'll meet with that girl tonight?"

He cocks his head, and the corner of his mouth slowly arches. "My God, are you jealous?"

"No! It's just crazy that you would have sex with some random woman—"

"*Emmy*, you know I would be faithful to you?"

"Uh... I, I don't know what you're talking about." I grab my purse, but he reaches over the table and clutches my hand before I can leave.

"Is that what you are worried about if we date? Me cheating? I wouldn't. I'd be good to you."

His gaze is hypnotic and his eyes carry such sincerity that it doesn't seem like a line. Deep down, I want to believe him. I want to believe some men won't stray.

But that's how my heart shattered last time, and unlike Christian, Joar has far more opportunities to cheat. The temptations are endless, including a waitress who never gave me the impression she was interested in Joar until it was right in my face.

Like Ophelia.

I jerk my hand free from Joar's and say flatly, "Date or sleep with whomever you wish. I don't care. Our relationship is business only."

Before he can argue, I slide out of the booth and rush out of the restaurant.

Once I park in the garage, I turn off my car and rest my forehead on the steering wheel. Abruptly, tears well in my eyes. I sniffle them back, but I'm surprised I'm becoming so emotional. It's painful to admit, but I wish I didn't leave the restaurant. A vision of Joar meeting with that girl outside the restaurant causes more tears to cascade down my cheeks.

I know I'm being jealous for no reason. I just... Why can't I let myself be that girl? Not care about anything but what I want. That woman was so fearless.

And I am the opposite.

Tonight, she won. Only the brave win.

I *hate* that she is probably sleeping with him at this moment instead of me.

Chapter 15

Joar

"Fucking, Emma," I mumble, leaving me at a restaurant. Such a brat.

Focus.

The locker room's scent is thick with ice and musty equipment — a familiar mix that usually sharpens my focus before a game.

I sit on the bench, tightening my laces with practiced precision. My teammates' banter fills the air, their laughter a distraction from the tension thrumming in my chest.

The door swings open, and Emma strides in, her jaw tight and her fists clenched. Her eyes flick around the room, wary of the curious stares and teasing smirks from my teammates.

She navigates the mess of bags, sticks, and scattered gear with the determination of someone who refuses to back down, even when she wants to.

She stops in front of me, and the flowery scent of her perfume drifts through the cold, sharp air, cutting straight to me.

It should affect me — she's mine.

And it's that same lovely scent that clung to her when I kissed her neck, her helpless body trapped between me and the counter. The memory ignites something primal inside me. I smother the reaction before I get too turned on, forcing myself to meet her stormy gaze.

She leans down and presses her lips to mine — brief, emotionless, and painfully unsatisfying. But her beautiful scent of still lingers when she pulls away.

"Good girl," I say, keeping my voice low and taunting. "I see you got my text."

"You're such a horrible person," she hisses soft enough for only me to hear. "You threatened not to play. Don't think for a second I want to be here. I thought I made it clear last night. Business only."

I let an exasperated sigh, wishing she would let down her guard. "I meant what I said, Emma. I won't hurt you. I'm very loyal."

She mumbles, "Same thing Christian said."

That fucking name keeps popping up. I clench my fists.

Feeling impatient with her fixation on him, I lean closer. "I can get him out of your thoughts." I bite my tongue, but I'm unable to stop myself and add, "Sleep with me. One night in bed is all it'll take. You'll forget his name when you're screaming mine."

Her lips part in shock, but before she can retort, she spins on her heel and stomps toward the door.

I shouldn't have said that, but God, I love making her squirm.

"See you after the game," I call, loud enough for the entire locker room to hear. A chorus of whistles and hoots follows, and her cheeks flame. She glances back, her glare promising retribution, but I meet it with a devilish grin. She barrels out of the room.

I lean back, my grin fading as Erik leans in, his voice low but sharp.

"What the hell was that?"

I glance at him, making sure no one else is listening. "She accepted a deal."

"What? Like Runa?" His eyes widen.

"Yes," I reply, shrugging as though it's nothing.

His shock quickly morphs into disgust. "Blackmail? Really? That's low, even for you."

"It's not blackmail," I correct, my voice hardening. "It's a trade. She gets what she needs; I get what I want."

Erik shakes his head, running a hand through his hair. "She hates it. Anyone can see that. This won't end well — just like Runa."

I stiffen at the mention of her name, the familiar sting of guilt twisting in my chest. "I didn't force Runa into anything.

She agreed to the arrangement. Whatever happened after... that wasn't my fault."

Erik's expression is grim. "But it happened. And now you're dragging Emma into the same mess."

I glare at him, my voice dropping to a dangerous whisper. "This is different."

"How?" He scoffs. "Do you honestly think Emma wants you? Without this deal, she wouldn't even look at you."

I restrain the urge to slug this guy. "How would you know?"

"Come on, Joar. Get real. She's a billionaire's daughter, way out of your league. Christian's more her type — clean-cut, polished, her perfect little skating partner. Hell, they're probably still together."

The mention of Christian — *again* — sends a flare of irritation coursing through me. My mind flashes to the way Emma looked at him during her lesson, too. Not to forget, him touching her.

"Then I'll get rid of Christian," I reply, my voice cold and detached.

Erik's jaw tightens. "You're a piece of work, you know that?"

I turn to him, my eyes narrowing. "What's your problem, man? Why do you care so much about what I do with Emma?"

"I'm just being honest. She doesn't want you, Joar. And if you weren't holding this deal over her head, she'd walk away without a second thought. Clearly! Besides, talk about breaking the code."

It's obvious now. Erik still wants her for himself. I know it was wrong to pursue her since he was interested first. I just got so excited, I forgot.

"Sorry, Erik. But let's face it. You had five years to score a date with her. She wasn't interested. My turn."

His restraint snaps. He grabs me by the collar and slams me against the wall. However, I react fast, my fist connecting with his jaw before he has a chance. He swings back, but I block him, switching places as I pin him to the wall with sheer force.

"It is fair game at this point, you dumb fuck," I growl, my voice low and venomous. "And don't you dare even look at Emma again. Your chance is over."

Our teammates pull us apart, their shouts echoing. I shrug them off, my breathing heavy as I stare at Erik. His lip is split, blood trickling down his chin, but his glare is just as fierce.

"You're gonna regret this," he mutters, wiping the blood away.

I don't respond. Instead, I grab my stick and head for the tunnel, the roar of the crowd already vibrating through the walls. The game is minutes away, and I need to channel this fury into something productive.

But as I step onto the ice, Erik's words linger in the back of my mind.

Without the deal, she'd walk away.

I replay the way Emma clung to me the other night, the way her voice trembled when she admitted she had feelings for me. Was it really the heat of the moment, or does she want me as much as I want her?

Worse, it seems she prefers someone else. If she didn't want Erik, my cousin, a hockey player who looks somewhat like me, she may always resist — holding out for a guy like Christian.

The thought consumes me, and for the first time in years, I feel something more dangerous than rage: *Jealousy.*

Chapter 16

Joar

The roar of the crowd engulfs me as I step onto the ice.

It doesn't matter if it's home or away — when I skate out, the world watches. I'm a legend in my own right. People buy tickets to see me, the way they once did for Gretzky. This team should be groveling in gratitude for me dragging their sorry asses toward a championship. Without me, they'd be dead in the water.

No, actually, Emma should be grateful.

Too bad she doesn't seem to understand that truth. Getting her is proving far more difficult than I anticipated.

"Don't think about her," I scold myself as I skate a slow warm-up lap, the sharp chill of the ice biting at my face.

My gaze flicks upward toward the owner's box — a part of my ritual, imagining myself sitting there someday. Emma isn't in her seat yet, but she will be. She can't miss a game, and lately, I've found myself caring far too much about whether she's watching.

Focus.

I shake off the thought.

After the anthem plays, I settle into my stance at the face-off circle, my stick poised on the ice. The second the puck drops, I'm in the zone, every muscle coiled and ready. The cold, the sound of skates cutting through ice, and the adrenaline pumping through my veins — it's a symphony I've mastered.

But then, Erik's voice echoes in my head: "She wouldn't even look at you."

Forget Erik. Focus, damn it.

I push the distraction aside, driving toward the goal with a single-minded determination. The puck glides to me, and with precision, I fire it past the goalie into the net. The red light flashes, and the roar of the crowd fuels my hunger for more.

Midway through the second period, the puck is tangled in the chaos near the boards. I charge in, my eyes narrowing on the opposition. One player, a hulking asshole from the Sharks, throws his weight around, his elbows flying recklessly. When one connects with my shoulder, my patience snaps.

The next few seconds blur. My stick jabs into his gut, and I fling off my gloves, grabbing him by the jersey. My fists fly, each punch landing with the force of my rage. He hits back, but his punches are weak, fueled by fear rather than fire. I relish the feel of his body giving way under my blows.

The refs intervene, pulling us apart.

My chest heaves as I'm dragged to the penalty box, my knuckles throbbing, my adrenaline spiking. The crowd roars around me, some cheering, others jeering, but my focus shifts elsewhere — upward.

Emma is in the owner's box now, her lovely silhouette unmistakable.

My stomach twists as I notice her leaning toward the man beside her. His arm snakes behind her, pulling her closer.

Christian.

My jaw tightens. The sight of her laughing, her hand resting on his, sparks a fire in me hotter than any fight. She's too good for him. He's a fucking cheater, a coward, and yet, there she is, hanging on his every word like he's still her world.

I clench my fists, and try to pay attention to the game, but my mind betrays me, dragging me back to the other night yet again.

Fuck. The warmth of her body against mine, her soft whimpers, her hand gripping my cock, her needy look when I played with her nipple.

She wanted me.

That was real. That was mine.

But now, all I can picture is her doing the same to Christian, her pulling on his neck, her lips parting for him — her touching his dick.

The thought is infuriating.

The penalty ends, and I launch back onto the ice, channeling my rage into the game. The Sharks don't stand a chance. I'm faster, sharper, more ruthless.

But even as I dominate, my gaze keeps darting to the owner's box. Not once does she look my way. Not once does she acknowledge my existence.

By the time the final buzzer sounds, we've won. I skate off the ice, my chest heaving, but there's no satisfaction. The game was easy. Too easy.

And Emma? She didn't even notice.

I head to the locker room, ripping off my helmet and throwing it against the wall. Erik approaches, his expression smug.

"Nice game," he says, his tone laced with something that feels like judgment.

"Don't start," I warn, grabbing a towel to wipe the sweat from my face.

"You looked distracted out there," he says, crossing his arms. "Noticed Emma hanging onto that guy, huh? Welcome to my life. But don't worry, fucker. In five years, some asshole will take your last chance."

I glare at him, the fire in my chest reigniting. "Fuck off."

"I told you, Joar. You've got her tangled in this deal, but do you really think she'll ever look at you the way she looks at him? Just end the deal. It's fucked up."

Before I rip off his head, I go for the showers to cool down and reset. However, the icy spray does nothing to cool the fire coursing through my veins. Usually, it's my ritual after every game — washing away the sweat and adrenaline.

But tonight?

Tonight, I'm wound too tight. My thoughts are a storm of rage, frustration, and something I don't want to admit twice.

Emma better still be here. She owes me her post-game kiss.

I dress quickly, ignoring the usual banter in the locker room. My teammates don't matter right now, and thankfully, Erik's already gone, so I don't have to hear his nonsense again. I check my watch.

She should be here by now.

Irritated, I storm out of the locker room and head for the owner's box. I round the corner, eager to find her, but the scene that greets me stops me cold.

At the end of the corridor, Emma stands between Erik and Christian.

Erik's talking, his hands moving animatedly, his expression serious. Emma's eyes widen, her gaze locked on Erik as she listens intently. Then she gasps.

Christian moves closer, pulling her into his arms like he has any right. My fists clench at the sight of her resting against his scrawny chest, her head tilted up as if seeking comfort. Rage rises in my face, hot and consuming.

Erik doesn't like it either. His hands ball at his sides, the tension in his posture unmistakable.

Good. At least we agree on something.

I start walking toward them. Erik spots me first. His gaze sharpens, and he gestures in my direction. Emma and Christian turn, their eyes meeting mine.

"Why did you tell Erik about our deal?" Emma asks, her voice cutting through the air like a knife. "Who else did you tell?"

I mask my surprise, keeping my tone steady. "Nobody."

"And then you hit your own cousin?"

"He deserved it," I reply, my jaw tightening. I force myself to soften, knowing the rage I'm straining to suppress might frighten her. "He asked for it."

Erik smirks, the bastard relishing this moment. "What Joar really means is that he can't control his temper. Especially when I call him out for forcing women into situations they don't want to be in."

Emma's lips part, a whisper of disbelief escaping. "Oh my gosh."

"I can control my temper," I assure, but my voice is sharper than I intend. I take a breath, my composure chipping away.

Christian steps forward, positioning himself between us. My hands itch to swat him aside. Does he think I'm a threat? Or is he just staking his claim?

Either way, I'm this close to killing him.

Erik doesn't stop. "Joar apologized to me earlier. Isn't that right, cousin? You felt guilty about the deal and how you've been treating Emma."

"Really?" she asks, her voice soft.

"Yep," Erik answers for me, nodding like the snake he is. "Joar admitted it was all a twisted game. Making you kiss him before games, punishing you when you don't obey. That's why he hit me — because I told him it was wrong."

Emma's gaze flickers to me with confusion and hurt in her eyes.

"Has he punished you, right, Emma?" Erik presses.

"Punished?" Christian snaps, his voice rising.

Erik nods solemnly, keeping his eyes on Emma. "That's Joar's thing. Blackmail and punishment. He controls women, makes them follow his rules. But don't worry — I stood up for you."

"You did?" her voice trembles, her vulnerability slicing through me. I want to comfort her, draw her away from these idiots.

"Yes," Erik says, stepping closer to Emma. "I told Joar this isn't Norway. This is the United States — the birthplace of cancel culture and the *Me Too* movement. If the media got wind of this, his career would be over. That's why he attacked me. Because I threatened to expose him."

Emma's eyes widen, darting between Erik and me. "The deal is... over?" she whispers, more to herself.

Erik smiles, smug and victorious. "You're free, Emma. You don't owe him anything anymore. You can date whomever you want."

My hands ball into fists. The nerve of him, twisting the truth and using it to worm his way closer to her.

Erik leans in closer to Emma, his voice dropping to a hushed, conspiratorial tone. "I'm nothing like him, you know. I'd never treat you like that. I'd never blackmail or punish you."

I take a step forward, my presence swallowing the space between us. "Enough." My voice is low, lethal.

Emma flinches slightly, but it's Erik who tenses, his smirk faltering.

I turn to her, holding her gaze, forcing her to stay in this moment with me. "He's lying. Don't listen to him." My voice is controlled, but there's no mistaking the authority behind it.

She crosses her arms, her expression stoic, but the slight shake of her hands betrays her. "How is he lying?" she asks. "You told him about the deal, didn't you?"

I don't break eye contact. I refuse to show weakness in front of these men circling her like fucking vultures. But there's no easy way to undo this. I hate not having control.

"I didn't mean it like that," I say.

Her brows knit together, lips pressing into a thin line. She doesn't believe me. She's standing in front of me, but somehow, I feel her slipping through my fingers.

Erik smirks, Christian glares, and Emma... Emma steps back.

Like she's afraid. Like I'm suddenly a stranger.

The surrounding air is thick, the silence stretching, and for the first time in my life, I feel something foreign sink into my gut. Not regret. Not guilt. *Something darker.*

Because she is afraid. And part of me likes that.

But another part?

Another part of me wants to grab her, shake her, force her to see that I'm her only sanctuary. That I don't fucking share. That these men have no claim on her thoughts, her fears, her loyalty.

But she doesn't move forward.

And it *burns.*

This is my fault.

Erik leans closer to her, whispering something I can't hear. My vision tunnels, rage clouding my mind.

Game over — time to break skulls.

Chapter 17

Joar

When Emma's eyes meet mine, I have to draw in a sharp breath to control whatever fucking weird feelings I'm having.

My plan is imploding.

No *fucking* way is this over.

Her gaze flicks to Erik then me. And maybe she sees I'm a second away from killing my cousin, because she steps around him carefully, her movements cautious — like she's approaching a *beast* that could devour her whole.

Without a word, she reaches for my wrist, her fingers barely brushing my skin as she guides me down the hallway. I let her, though every instinct screams to go back and obliterate those two bastards.

When we're far enough from the others, she stops, and tilts her face up to me. There's hurt in her eyes — real, deep, *gutting* hurt.

"How could you tell anyone about our deal?" Her voice is barely above a whisper, strained with held-back emotion. "I'm *mortified*, Joar."

I hold her gaze, unmoved. "Who cares what they think? Listen, I—"

"Does Erik know everything about... what you did to me?" She whispers, "The spanking?"

"It doesn't matter."

"It does to me! And what about other women? How many others do you make deals with and punish?"

I exhale slowly, fighting the urge to grab her chin and *force* her to look at me properly. To make her *see* that nothing matters except *us*.

"Erik doesn't know specifics," I reply evenly. "Just that we have an arrangement: you obey, and I play."

Her shoulders tense. She looks down, her fingers twisting together like she's bracing for something worse. Then, in a voice so soft it barely reaches me, she asks, "*Please...* answer the other question... How many other women do you punish?"

I blink. *Fuck.* The jealousy in her voice is staggering. Hm. Maybe she wants to be the only one. "Since we met, just you. Before that, there were ten or so."

"*Ten?*" she breathes, her voice laced with distress.

Oh, yeah. She doesn't share.

Now there is no doubt in my mind: She wants me.

And she's standing here, trying to convince herself she *doesn't*.

I watch the way she wrestles with her own mind, the way her lips press together, the way her small hands fidget — like she's holding herself back from clinging to me.

Her body knows what she *needs*. It's her mind that fights it.

I take a slow step forward, savoring the way she tenses.

"You don't want this deal to end," I murmur.

Her head snaps up, panic flashing through her expression.

"I do want it over! Things are getting out of hand anyway," she says, but it sounds like she's trying to convince *herself* more than me. "I just pray Mother doesn't find out. At least... this insanity is over."

The moment those words leave her lips, something inside me *snaps*.

A slow, consuming rage unfurls in my chest, wrapping around my ribs like barbed wire.

Over?

That means I can't touch her again. Can't control her. Can't *protect* her.

She thinks she can just walk away? She's wrong.

My voice is final. "*Nothing* is over."

She blinks. "What?"

I step closer, trapping her between me and the wall, letting my presence engulf her. "This deal isn't over. I don't care who knows about it."

Before she can argue, I grab her wrist and *drag* her down the hall to where Erik and Christian are waiting. She stumbles slightly, but I don't stop.

When I reach them, I lift my chin, pinning Erik with a sharp, merciless stare.

"If you go to the media or breathe a word about my deal with Emma," I say in a calm tone, "you'll upset her."

I glance down at Emma, my grip on her wrist tightening. "Isn't that right?"

Her head bobs quickly, her voice tight with anxiety. "Yes. I would be horrified if my parents found out. It would be humiliating for them, too. And I don't want that kind of attention. Fans will blame me if Joar is suspended."

I smirk at Erik. "And if I'm banned, the team is far less likely to win the cup. You may go your whole career without a single championship."

The flicker of hesitation in his eyes tells me everything.

His ego. His legacy. That's what matters to him. Not Emma.

Satisfied, I turn my attention to Christian, the fucking weakling who dares put his hands on my girl.

I take a slow step toward him. "If you say anything, I'll break your fucking legs."

He swallows hard, taking a step back, the color draining from his face.

I smirk. "And don't put your greasy hands on her again."

Christian's jaw clenches, but he doesn't say a word.

Good. Because Emma is untouchable.

I don't share, either.

Both men side-glance at each other but nod in defeat. Like wounded animals, they limp away.

Emma folds her arms and looks at the floor again, apparently afraid to make eye contact. The tension between us is so thick that it feels electric. I just want to hold her, but I wait to see her reaction.

After a moment of her silence, she finally says, "I guess I should have known you would keep me trapped. You even figured out how to get me to beg others to keep the deal going. Gosh, you're impossible."

Hearing the sadness in her voice irritates the fuck out of me. "Emma. You don't want the deal to end anymore than I do."

"No! That's not true! I, um, I—"

I step closer, my presence crowding her against the wall. The hall feels smaller, the air between us charged, heavy with something I know she feels too.

"Are you still in love with Christian?" I ask.

Her body stiffens. "What?"

"You heard me," I press, my gaze boring into hers. "Are you?"

Her arms curl around herself, her fingers nervously rubbing her upper arm. "No."

The way she avoids my eyes, the way her voice lacks conviction — it might as well be a yes. A lesser man might dwell on that, might let it fester. Not me. I'll deal with him later.

For now, I say sternly, "I want to be clear. You are mine, not his. Don't see him outside of work."

Her lips press together in that stubborn little pout that always tempts me to fuck the attitude right out of her.

She squeaks, "I swear, we're just friends."

I point near her face like I'm scolding a child. "And only I can end the deal, anyway. Not you, and not them."

Her lips part slightly, but she doesn't argue. That surprises me. Instead, she drops her arms and sighs. "Actually, we didn't talk about this over dinner last night, but I'm kind of surprised you still want the deal. Seems like you could be with better women. Why waste your time on me?"

I lean in, gripping her jaw between my fingers, forcing her to look up. "You don't think very highly of yourself, do you?"

Her cheeks flush deep red, but she quickly averts her gaze and tries to step around me. I don't let her. I press in, pinning her with my body until she has nowhere to go. She should know by now — I won't let her run.

Suddenly, she blurts, "Joar, did you go home with that waitress?"

I hide my smirk.

My grip slides down, my hands claiming her waist as I lower my forehead to hers. The tension between us is electric.

"No, I didn't go home with her," I answer. "Emmy, why would I? I can't stop thinking about you. It was impossible to concentrate during the game." My thumbs stroke slow, possessive circles along her hips. "Have you been thinking about me, too?"

She squirms under my touch, her pulse fluttering wildly against my chest. "Well!" she huffs. "I've been trying not to think about you, but it hasn't been easy."

A dark chuckle rumbles from my chest. She's always fighting me. Always resisting what she so clearly wants.

"Where's my post-game kiss?" I challenge, my voice dipping lower. "Or are you still too scared to take what you want?"

She hesitates, battling herself, and I wait. The moment she takes that breath, the one that gives her away, I know I've won. Without another word, she reaches for the back of my neck, her fingers threading into my hair, tugging me to her mouth.

I smirk against her lips. *Finally*.

She pulls me harder, and I oblige, slipping my tongue past her lips as she parts for me. The kiss is deep, slow, dragging her under with me, stripping away all her defenses. Gone is the careful, hesitant girl from before. This time, she gives in.

And fuck, I love it.

The weight of her body against mine, the way she grapples at me, like she needs this as much as I do — it does something to me.

The kiss deepens, my control fraying at the edges. I nip her bottom lip between my teeth, biting down just enough to make her whimper. Her hips shift, her body asking for more.

This. This is what I wanted.

Her surrender.

Against her mouth, I murmur, "Next time, don't make me wait."

Once again, she whimpers, kissing me harder before breathing out, "Okay, I promise, I won't make you wait."

Oh, such beautiful submission.

My grip tightens. *Fuck*, my dick is begging me to take her right here. I glance side-to-side.

Coast clear.

I reach down to undo my pants.

Abruptly, the sound of a throat clearing causes us to startle.

Emma slinks away quickly, her face flushing as she visibly cowers under her mom's gaze.

Mei's disapproval radiates, her presence demanding respect and fear. But she won't get either from me.

I reach for Emma, but she's already just out of my grasp. Forcing her back to me in front of Mei isn't an option, though the urge simmers beneath the surface.

"Inappropriate visits to his home and now this? Kissing a player in the stadium?" Mei's voice is flat and sharp.

Emma's shoulders slump, and she bows her head. "I'm sorry, Mother," she mumbles.

Mei steps closer, clasping her hands together. "As interim GM, what happens if the other players find out about your affair? What if a reporter makes it a scandal?"

My jaw tightens as anger churns inside me, but Emma doesn't argue. She just lowers her gaze. The sight makes me sick. If she's going to submit, it damn well better be to me — not her mother.

"Come with me," Mei commands. "We'll discuss this further at my house."

Emma glances at me, her eyes filled with remorse and longing. But she doesn't resist. She turns and follows Mei.

Disbelief courses through me. I stalk forward and clutch her arm, making her face me. Lowering my voice, I speak so only she can hear. "Emma. Stand up to her. Tell her we're dating."

She cringes, her voice strained. "I told you — I can't. Why don't you get this?"

"Do it," I demand, my tone harsh as my grip tightens. "I know you want to leave with me. I felt it in your kiss."

"Yes, okay? I'd rather leave with you," she admits, her voice rising with desperation. "But I can't. I'm not that kind of person. I can't just say no to my parents."

"Then I'll tell her about the deal," I threaten, hoping she doesn't call my bluff. I need her mom to like me for my plan to work.

Emma's eyes dart to Mei, who stands waiting with an icy expression. She sighs. "Joar. Just let me go with her, and we'll talk tomorrow. Please."

Her words are a punch to the gut. Not the babbling, but the fact she's defying me. If Mei wasn't here, I'd bend her over and spank some sense into her.

Swiftly, she lets go of my hands and turns away. I sigh in contempt as she walks off, the side door closing softly behind her.

Chapter 18

Emma

How did I end up in a hotel room with a hockey player? Yet here I am, perched on the edge of the bed, watching Joar rummage through his bag.

"I need to head to the rink in fifteen minutes," he says without looking up.

I swallow, trying to regain some control over this situation. "Joar, I should probably go back to my hotel room. I'll see you after the game."

He turns, his voice gruff. "Yes, you will. Because you are staying in my room tonight."

"I think it's... well, it's just more professional if we set some boundaries," I start, reciting Mother's words. They're now burned into my brain after spending three days with her. "Besides, where am I supposed to sleep? There's only one bed."

Folding his arms, he gives me a once-over. "Obviously my bed, although lately, I'd say you belong on the floor."

"I'm here, aren't I? I came to your room to give you a pre-game kiss, as you asked for over text," I point out.

He glares with disdain in his eyes. "You said if I let you go with your mom, we would talk after. Then I didn't hear from you for days. I give you an inch, and you take a mile."

"No, I didn't—" I start, but he cuts me off.

"And you didn't stand up to your mom, tell her we're dating, or respond to my texts. You were never home, either. Where were you?"

I sigh, doing my best to remain calm under his intense stare. "I've been staying at my parents. I'm here to watch your away game, though. And I haven't purged."

That's a lie, and the guilt tugs at me, but living with Mother has been harder than dealing with Joar's overbearing demands.

He watches me, his expression just as cold. "I'm adding rules," he says firmly.

"We have enough rules, and—"

"When we get back to Texas, you're moving into my place. You'll stay with me tonight and every night moving forward. Remember, you're mine. Do as I say."

I roll my eyes and mumble, "I'm not yours, Joar."

His voice deepens. "Choose your words again." He cocks his head. Apparently not letting this go, he waits for me to say something.

Having forgotten this guy administers corporal punish-ment, I begrudgingly soften my tone and clarify, "I meant, I'm not a piece of property you can own."

A dark smile tugs at his lips, and he leans in. "It's like you're asking to be spanked with that mouth."

Oh, no. I'm desperate to prevent this arrangement with Joar from spiraling out of control again. Being apart from him has allowed me to approach this situation with a rational mindset.

Distance from Joar is healthy. I was losing my sanity.

In fact, maybe after the game, I won't give him my room number. I'll ignore his texts. Yes — that's exactly what I'll do. Give him just enough, then add space. He may get mad, but he'll still play if I don't completely cut him off.

Feeling reassured by my plan, I lean back as he resumes searching through his bag. Still, I can't stop myself from watching him. The way his biceps stretch the sleeves of his shirt stirs up thoughts of those arms wrapped tightly around me. I ache to rest my cheek against his chest, remembering the quiet peace of that night, the intensity of his hold. And that last kiss at the stadium before Mother interrupted — I was so caught up, the energy between us undeniable. The truth is, I haven't stopped thinking about him.

And every day apart has only made me miss him more.

The realization hits me so abruptly, I almost gasp aloud. Horrified by the notion that I actually missed him, this con-trolling hockey player, I drop my gaze to the carpet, struggling to keep my reaction in check. Joar is saying something, but his words blur as I scold myself silently.

Suddenly, he steps forward, lifting my chin so I'm forced to meet his gaze. "Pay attention. I expect you in this room after the game tonight, understand?"

I nod, hesitant, wrapping my arms around myself and shutting my eyes, trying to block out everything. But immediately, a vision flashes — Joar, shirtless, moving over me on the bed, his sculpted body close, the heat of his hips between my legs.

My eyes snap open, pulse racing.

Holy... Is there no escape from these sinister thoughts?

Frustrated beyond reason, I blurt out, "Look. I know this whole deal is about sex. I didn't agree to that, and I told you from the beginning I won't waver on that rule. So, let's end this now."

He arches an eyebrow, his tone shifting to something unreadable. "You've had sex before, right?"

I balk, feeling my cheeks flush. "Oh, so you don't deny this deal is just to sleep with me?"

"I deny it. Now answer my question. Are you a virgin?"

"No... I've had sex..." I pause, swallowing as I glance away. "Of course, the lights were always off to hide my disgusting body, but I'm definitely not a virgin."

His expression hardens, his voice low and firm. "*Never* call yourself disgusting."

I return an inauthentic half smile.

Calmly, he shakes his head and leans against the wall, arms crossed, muscles bulging, sexy as hell.

"Seriously, Emma. Please tell me you do not think you're disgusting. You know you're beautiful, don't you?"

My cheeks rush with heat and I look at my lap, my heart fluttering fast. I catch myself, though, realizing I need to ignore these feelings around this man. They aren't real. They're obviously hormone driven.

Everyone has hormones.

To avoid losing my self-control or getting swept away by empty compliments, I reply with conviction, "Quit trying to fill my head with lies. I'm not beautiful. I'm overweight like my dad. That's why I failed to win gold at the Olympics. That's why my skating career was cut short. Too heavy for Christian to lift. Nothing you say can change that fact."

"Emma, that guy is weak—"

I stand up abruptly, frustration bubbling over as I throw my hands in the air. It's exhausting to have him brush off these truths as if they are imagined, as if ignoring them makes them any less true. My voice trembles slightly as I say, "*Please*, stop. It's not just my weight. I'm not the coach I should be. My students deserve the best, and yet only a quarter of them have made it to Nationals. They should all be champions."

"Many of your students won. Others went to the Olympics too. I looked it up," he counters, appearing confused by my logic.

"Those skaters did well because they are wildly talented. Not because of me."

Joar opens his mouth to respond, but I cut him off yet again. "And my mother is probably right. I'll fail as interim General Manager. I'm not fit to run a hockey team. I'll mess it up. I already have! Just look at this situation. I'm somehow at the mercy of one of my players. I'm breaking every conflict of interest rule, too. I'm your superior, yet you're bossing me around. I've failed."

"Emma. Calm down. I've already started intercepting questions that aren't worth your time." He then shakes his head and walks to my side. With a gentle touch, he glides his hands from my shoulders to my elbows, cupping them. He leans in, but I step back. However, he tightens his hold, keeping me in his trap.

"You sad little toy," he says.

"Don't call me that!"

He holds back a smirk, his intense eyes softening with an unexpected warmth. "Don't you see? You so clearly need me. I'm not your problem, I'm your solution."

I sigh loudly.

He moves even closer and in a split second, his body heat warms my skin as his lips brush near my ear. His mouth opens, causing my breath to hitch. His thick tongue tastes the delicate skin below my ear, awakening my body against my will. But instinctively, I lean away from his touch, desperate to suppress my desire. If I'm being completely honest with myself, it's more than my body that wants Joar.

No! Don't think like that, Emma. Be professional. Save your academy. Make Mother proud.

Yet, despite my resistance, I'm anchored by the closeness and warmth of his towering frame, feeling secure in this moment. He soon pulls away, though, and says, "Sit down."

That's a request I don't mind, more than willing to add space between us and calm my body. I return to my seat at the end of his bed. But he follows and stands facing me. He lifts my chin with his knuckle, bringing my eyes to his. As I gaze up at this intimidating man, I feel physically tiny.

"Don't you want to please me?" he asks.

My shoulders give a slight shrug and I answer, "I guess. Then I won't get spanked or sleep on the floor."

"Let me rephrase. If I tell you I'm pleased you came to my hotel tonight, does that make you happy?"

I think for a moment, then reply, "Not happy. More like relieved. I did what I was supposed to, and the pressure is off."

He sighs. "Isn't that how you feel when you obey your parents?"

"Um... Actually, yeah."

"Yet, you throw up because you can't stomach doing what they want instead of what you want."

"Not uh! Not true," I balk.

"It is. Pleasing me should make you happy, not relieved. If it doesn't, then—"

I can't help but roll my eyes and interrupt. "Oh yeah? When should I have been happy since you've taken over my life?"

"Emma, I know I make you happy. Did you know, you make me happy, too?"

I consider his question, but I'm a bit jarred. I didn't think I ever pleased him, let alone made him happy. I guess he must like something about me. Nevertheless, I'm simply unable to justify Joar as a positive in my life. No rational woman could.

Hence, I put on my professional persona and reply, "No, I didn't know I made you happy, but that's unimportant. We are business associates."

"Emma, I want you. I have feel—"

Oh no! I can't have him speak those words. I'll never recover.

I'm possessed, and shout, "Stop! Stop! Don't you dare! I'm not happy. And I, uh, I hate you!"

I gasp, in shock of my outburst, yet desperate for control.

A flicker of darkness fills his wolf eyes, his jaw flexing as he watches me. I shrink back a little, uncertain, his reaction pulling me into silence.

"You hate me?" His voice drops to a chilling whisper. "I don't buy it. I think you want me, too, but you hate yourself so damn much, you don't think you deserve it, or let yourself admit it."

I tense, instinctively pulling my chin to my chest as he drops to his knees, leveling our eyes. My fingers grip the edge of the bed, a wave of panic rising as his hands slide over my knees, inching my skirt up my thighs. I squirm, grabbing for the hem and yanking it down, but he smacks my hands away with an infuriating calm, like disciplining a child for touching something they shouldn't.

"No, Joar!" I plead, clasping my hands into a tight ball next to my chest and rubbing the hot skin he swatted.

He returns a death stare that is so intense I'm frozen in fear. His hands take hold of my skirt once more, pushing it up in a sharp thrust. I try to keep my knees squeezed together, but he unhinges them in a powerful motion. He moves between my legs, the heat of his body radiating through the fabric of his shirt. The sensitive, thin skin just outside my underwear presses to the shirt's soft cotton.

I shoot my hands over my crotch to create a barrier between us.

"Joar," I squeak, the panic in my voice unmistakable.

Chapter 19

Emma

Joar always carries a taunting quality around me, constantly pushing, sparring in that infuriating way of his.

But right now, the man kneeling between my legs as I sit on the edge of the bed is a stranger. There's no hint of warmth, no trace of his teasing smirk.

Trying to reach that softer, less intimidating side of him, I raise my brow and murmur, "Hey, I'm sorry, okay? I don't hate you."

His response is flat, unwavering. "Take off your shirt."

"No, no, no, no," I ramble reflexively, my hands rushing to guard the front of my button-up shirt.

"Yes. Take it off." His finger slips beneath the neckline, tugging lightly on the fabric near the first button, his gaze steady and unrelenting.

I curl my fingers tighter, creating a steel grip on my blouse's row of buttons. "Joar, I'm not ready for this," I whine, my throat tight as nervousness engulfs me.

He leans closer, voice low and certain. "You're ready. You're overdue."

His words are firm, yet reassuring, but I just need to escape. I can't keep losing control just because I find this man... incredibly handsome. Plus, it's obviously getting more difficult to resist him, so I must prevent this from advancing. Even kissing is too much!

As I move to rise, he grabs my hips and jerks me back down. With lightning speed, he easily pries through my grip and tears open my blouse, causing buttons to scatter through the air and land in every direction. My breath catches and I pull my top closed and cover my stomach.

Like it's so damn easy to overpower me, he removes my hold by grappling my wrists and restraining them with one hand. Using his other, he yanks up my bra, exposing my chest. The underwire digs into my flesh, pressing into the slope of my breasts. I grimace and hunch forward, trying to curl into a ball and hide my nakedness.

With a gentle touch, Joar takes hold of my chin and forces my gaze up from my lap. "Relax, Emma. Tell me you don't fucking want this."

He's so sexy as he licks his lips, causing me to swallow as my body screams to give in. I can practically taste the pheromones drawing us together.

I bite my bottom lip as I fight this crippling indecision. And even though having Joar this close is so damn wrong, it feels so right.

He must take my silence as a 'have your way with me,' because his mouth moves toward my chest.

I stay hunched and nervous, and despite my posture, Joar still forces his way to my chest. His jaw opens and before I know it, his tongue swirls over my nipple. As he snakes his other hand behind my shoulders and brings me to him, I take in a sharp breath and remind myself to relax. I tremble as he holds me in place, though, my eyes still snapped shut. As his teeth apply pressure to my sensitive nipple, every muscle in my body flexes.

Then his jaw opens wider, trying greedily to devour every inch of my flesh. With his hand on my back, he brings my body forward more, pushing my breast against his mouth with greater force.

I swallow hard and remain stiff and uncomfortable. But then, my eyes dart to his hand still clutching my wrists. To my surprise, his fingers unravel and move to my lower back. His pace slows, and he sucks my breast in long, sensual pulls. His mouth roams to the other side, taking his time.

Yet, the sudden shift of his touch from forced to tender leaves me more torn as it resurfaces feelings I keep trying to stuff down. And although far less rough, the strength of his pulls hold an insatiable hunger, and with it, I feel desirable — faults and all.

I love feeling his touch.

Surprising me even more, my body tension eases and I exhale a shaky breath. It's a small, but noticeable moan, and a glaring moment of the weakness within me. Such a betrayal of my body. I know I must fight my own rising desire before it's too late.

Just then, in a deep, soothing voice, he breathes against my nipple, "Stay calm, baby."

He knows I'm struggling. It's so grounding to have someone understand there is chaos consuming me — killing me slowly.

His encouragement of such simple words are so powerful. They somehow charm me just in time. In fact, I find my hands magically floating to his shoulders, and his body heat radiates through his shirt to my palms. The muscles underneath are so defined, and I'd love to feel them without the fabric between us.

But can I give myself to this man?

...Oh yeah.

I can do this.

I might get over Christian, too!

Slowly, I lift my hands and slide my fingers behind his neck, feeling the warmth of his skin under my thumbs. With my head lowered, I let my cheek rest against his soft hair, closing my eyes as I confess, "Joar... I want to... you know."

My words cause him to pause, but only for a moment, then he resumes feeding on my body. But soon, he draws in a deep breath through his nostrils and says against my flesh, "You want more?"

I swallow, my heart pounding, and whisper, "Yeah. I fantasize about you, you know, on top of me."

"You do?" he asks, causing me to blush.

His mouth continues to tease and suck my nipples, his lips shockingly affectionate in their pressure. Soon, he gives a gentle kiss on my nipple before leaning back and looking into my gaze. There's a warmth in his eyes that wasn't there before. Nevertheless, a wicked glint soon appears.

"Emmy. Beg for it. Be a good toy and earn it."

My eyes widen, torn once more. He always pushes me. He has to know it makes me uncomfortable.

Stranger still, I want to submit. I want to lose myself under his power. Yet, it feels so... degrading. However, at this moment, my desire outweighs my inner conflict.

"Um, please?" I whisper, heart fluttering as I give him what he wants.

He chuckles darkly. "Is that the best you can do? Because it's not enough."

Nervousness twists in my stomach, but as my fingers thread through his soft hair, I find the courage to reply in a shaky voice, "I don't know what you want. But I swear I want to sleep with you. Please?"

Joar smirks, as if my surrender is laughable. But then, his hand moves across my body. As his hand reaches my underwear, my breath hitches. With gentleness, his thumb strokes over the thin fabric, moving up and down my slit at a sensual pace. When he nears my entrance, he pushes against the delicate material of my panties, teasing me. I can't help it and clench, tilting my hips forward.

He licks his lips, then speaks, his deep voice curling around me like smoke. "I can feel the heat radiating from between your thighs, my desperate little toy. Your panties are drenched. Pathetic how your needy pussy aches to be filled with my cock, even when you know you don't deserve it."

Chapter 20

Emma

I'm ashamed — hating that Joar knows my attraction to him is this strong. Hating that he's denying me. But I don't understand what he wants. I am begging. I said please!

His eyes narrow slightly, and he must notice the flicker of self-loathing in mine, because he kisses the inside of my thigh gently — soothingly. "It's okay, my anxious girl. Just do as I say. Give me your pride, and I'll give you pleasure better than any man has or ever will. Really beg."

I panic and explain with angst in my voice, "Joar! I don't know how."

He chuckles softly, more to himself than me. I bite my bottom lip, feeling so inadequate.

When my chin quivers, his taunting nature leaves, shifting to what looks like sympathy.

"It's okay, Emmy," he says. "I'll help you." Slowly, he pulls down my underwear. I draw in a sharp breath as his mouth returns to the inside of my thigh. His lips caress me softly, trailing closer. "Start by saying you are my toy and want me to pleasure you."

I hold my breath as he then gently drags his knuckle along my bare slit. I can't help but moan, despite that part of me that's uncomfortable begging. Maybe he is right. Maybe it is my pride.

So I try.

My voice is unsteady and small as I say, "I, um... I am your toy and I want you to pleasure me, please?"

His fingertip then parts my slit. My thighs flex in anticipation as he travels down, swirling the pad of his finger along my entrance. When he doesn't enter, I'm quick to plead, "Don't stop!"

Joar nods slowly, approvingly. His finger pushes forward and the sensation makes me clench down hard. Now with his finger in deep, he chuckles once more. "God, Emmy. You're so wet."

"It's not funny," I whisper.

"It is. You need to be fucked so bad." He leans forward, replacing his finger with his tongue. He swirls and massages, lapping up my arousal. My legs trouble, the feeling so euphoric. When he pulls away, his chin glistens and he has to wipe it away. "Fuck, baby, you're a mess for me. I can't get enough."

I exhale a breath I didn't know I was holding, relieved he wants more, too. He returns his fingers, sliding in a second —

and it's heavenly. When he curls his fingers and massages my g-spot, I shudder. "Mmm, please Joar. Please give me more." I reach forward, desperately pulling on his shirt, wanting to undress him.

"Very good," he praises. "That's what I want. Now say I can play with you whenever and however I want, and I'll give you more." To tempt me further, he exhales a hot breath on my throbbing clit.

My legs tremble as the warm air sweeps over the sensitive skin. I can't restrain myself and blurt, "I'm your toy! Joar! You can play with me whenever and however you want. Please, please!"

His tongue dips out and wets my bundle of electrified nerves. I gasp, my legs shaking around his head. I claw at his back, wanting to yank him on top of me and give me every inch.

But he ignores my attempts.

His huge hands palm my hips. "And are you going to make me cum like a good girl?"

Those words crash over me like a tidal wave, leaving me breathless and hollow. A relentless reel of images floods my mind—beautiful, flawless puck bunnies, their perfect bodies writhing beneath him, their honeyed words and practiced touches drawing out his deepest pleasure. They give him everything he wants, sending him to heights I'll never reach.

How can I ever compete with them?

He stops, drawing his perfect mouth from my pussy. His brow lifts, waiting for my answer.

When I still don't answer, I grimace, hating myself. The disappointment clouding his face is punishment enough.

"Emma—"

I hang my head. "I'm sorry. I don't deserve this and I don't deserve you," I explain, something I never imagined I'd say to a hockey player. Yet, every self-loathing thought comes crashing down. Every insecurity. Every failure. I even imagine us sleeping together — and after — seeing the same intense disappointment in his eyes.

I'm out of my league in so many ways. I'd rather deprive myself of any pleasure than have another failure.

He stares, his expression incredulous.

"You should get to the rink," I insist, the tension so thick I can barely breathe.

"Don't do this, Emmy," he warns, but the petname jars me more. It deepens my self-loathing because it sounds like he actually cares about me — as if this is about more than sex.

I just need this to end, stop the chaos, so I do the one thing that will break the spell.

With the last ounce of willpower I can muster, I let the name fall from my lips like poison. "I'm still in love with Christian."

Joar glares, striking into my very soul like a whip. For a split second, his expression is dark — stunned, maybe even angry. The moment stretches, heavy and suffocating.

"I'm sorry," I murmur.

But the shift in his expression changes fast. His eyes narrow, dimming with something primal and dangerous. His jaw clenches, a muscle twitching as he processes my words.

"Even if you are, so what?" he challenges.

"I just want to be with him," I lie, panic swelling in my chest as he rises to his full height. For a fleeting second, I think he's retreating, stepping back in defeat. I make my move toward the door, desperate to escape the storm I've unleashed.

But I don't make it far.

His hand shoots out, gripping my jaw in an iron hold, yanking me back with such force that I stumble. My body freezes under his grasp, my breath catching as his fingers press into my skin, sharp and unforgiving.

"Don't ever run from me," he orders, his tone sharp enough to slice through the air. His face is inches from mine now, his gaze burning into me with a fire so fierce it burns.

"I'm sorry," I recite, the words tumbling out as my chest tightens. "I can't help how I feel."

His other hand tangles in my hair, jerking my head back so my neck arches, exposing my throat to him. The sudden, violent movement sends a shock of fear coursing through me. My pulse pounds in my ears as his grip tightens, his thumb brushing against my vulnerable throat, reminding me of just how much power he holds over me.

"Do you think this is a game for me?" he asks, his tone razor sharp.

My lips tremble as I force myself to meet his gaze. The weight of my guilt crashes over me, suffocating and undeniable. I hate myself for pushing him this far, for crossing a line I can't uncross. But most of all, I hate that I couldn't do it. That I chickened out.

I wish I wasn't cursed with so much anxiety and fear. My negative thoughts are like a soundtrack I can never turn off, pushing me endlessly into a dark world I can't escape.

"Joar, I'm not right in the head," I whisper, my voice shaking, but the words feel hollow against the storm brewing in his eyes.

His grip loosens slightly, just enough to let me breathe, but the intensity in his gaze doesn't fade. His lips curl into something dark and unforgiving as he leans closer.

He suddenly releases me, searching for words before saying, "Emma, I know what I want, and it's you. Figure out what you want."

Without another word, he leaves.

Chapter 21

Emma

"Emma!" The sound of a woman's voice cuts through the chaos in my mind as I walk through the hotel lobby. I turn slowly, dreading what I know I'll see: *her* — Ophelia.

The woman who ruined everything.

"Oh, hey," I reply, forcing a tight smile. "I didn't know you'd be here tonight."

Ophelia beams, her pretty brown eyes sparkling with confidence. Everything about her is a slap in the face — her long, flowing hair, her flawless skin, her radiant energy. Even the way she moves seems effortless, a sharp contrast to the awkwardness I feel in my own skin.

She's the better version of me. Perfectly polished. A Singles skater who shined three years longer than I ever did. Now a Marketing Director who somehow convinced Mother to give her a role at the top. And of course, she's thriving in it.

She always does.

And Christian chose her, at least in bed.

My stomach twists at the memory, but I shove it down, keeping my mask in place.

"Are you heading to the stadium now? Let's go together!" she chirps, holding up a homemade sign with bold black letters: JOAR! BET YOU CAN'T SCORE 3 GOALS.

I stare at the sign, my heart stuttering.

"What is this?"

She giggles. "I've been trying to get him to meet with me forever. He's ignored every attempt, so I figured I'd shake things up. Maybe if I piss him off, he'll want to meet me after the game, if only to tell me off."

Her laugh bubbles up, light and carefree. But her words? They land like daggers in my chest.

"You're meeting Joar tonight?" My voice wavers despite my best efforts to keep it steady.

"That's the plan. Front-row seat, so he can't miss me. I'm stopping at the locker room after to ambush him. He won't expect me at an away game. He seriously needs to get on board with the Marketing department. Do more interviews, help sell merchandise."

I'm losing air. My chest tightens as the panic sets in.

"I should sit with you instead of the visitor's box," I blurt, the words tumbling out before I can stop them.

Ophelia tilts her head, her expression curious. "Oh, bummer. I only got one ticket."

"I'll see if the person next to you will sell their seat," I insist.

She blinks, a flicker of surprise crossing her face. Then she smiles sweetly, tilting her head in that innocent, calculated way of hers. "I'd love that, Emma. It's nice to see you wanting to spend time with me again."

I smile back, but my teeth ache from clenching so hard. I'd rather be around Mother.

But deep down, I know it's not her I want to be near. It's Joar.

I can't stand the thought of Ophelia anywhere near him. Even though I'm too screwed up to be with Joar, my feelings for him are real. It would be so painful to see him date Ophelia.

Oh, God. I bite my bottom lip, my worry compiling. She is just the type to seduce him, too. Ophelia is like the waitress. Beautiful. Brave.

�֍ ⅲ————— ••• —————ⅲ ❧

At the game, I pay a sizable amount to get the seat next to Ophelia.

I don't know what I am doing other than staying close to this temptress — as if I have any control over what happens between her and Joar.

When I catch sight of Joar glide onto the ice, his gaze flicks up to the visitor's box, surely looking for me. He sighs, clearly mad. As he does a warm-up lap, Ophelia leaps from her seat as he approaches and taps the glass.

His attention snaps to her. She puts the sign against up and he reads it as he nears. His expression is unreadable. But then, he does a double-take, noticing me as I sneak up beside her and give a small wave.

The slightest smile curves the corners of his mouth. I can't deny his subtle approval gives me a sense of relief — and happiness.

But the moment quickly ends as the game starts.

We sit down and Ophelia is fast to tease, "How adorable! Are you blushing? Is Emma crushing on our star player!"

I shrug. Maybe if I tell her yes, she won't hit on him. So I reply, "I guess I like him... a little."

"Oh my God, Emma! That's so cute. I'm telling your mama!" she teases, knowing Mother would never approve. We grew up together. She knows my mom all too well.

And although I know she is joking about telling Mother, I am quick to say, "Please don't."

She laughs, smacking her leg.

I sit back in my seat, fidgeting. The reality is, she knew I loved Christian, and that didn't stop her. I guess I don't feel any better having told her the truth. Actually, I feel more vulnerable because now, if she does something, it would hurt more.

I draw in a deep breath and focus on the game.

Our team is immediately put through the wringer. Hard checks, high sticks, and a slew of other penalties seem constant. The first period is a brutal struggle.

Then, it happens.

Joar, with a burst of speed and precision, scores. It seems almost effortless. The crowd erupts with a mix of boos and cheers.

"Alright, Joar!" I clap wildly.

Ophelia and I high-five.

To my side, I notice an opposing fan giving me a smirk. I shrug my shoulders and explain, "We are big fans of the Rattlers."

He chuckles. "Uh huh, I bet. Probably cuz you guys got Joar Sköll on your team this year."

I return a smile and nod.

Just then, Joar taps the glass with his stick to get my attention. He points at the net as if I didn't realize he just scored. I can't help but chuckle. For a fleeting moment, his gaze darts to the guy next to me, then back. I roll my eyes, but deflect from his apparent jealousy and applaud dramatically to acknowledge his accomplishment.

If only he knew the woman sitting next to me has sparked a jealousy in my heart that burns ten times hotter than whatever he feels.

"Good God," says Ophelia. "Look at him trying to impress the boss." She playfully elbows me. "Must be nice to have all these men try to be on your good side instead of canceling meetings."

"Oh. Uh, yeah."

"I know why you're crushing on him. The guy is like Thor level hot." She fans herself. "Hockey players are so sexy."

I have to look away. "They're okay, I guess. I mean, he's cute and all but, I wouldn't say sexy." I silently pray she doesn't think he is as attractive as I find him.

She giggles. "Oh, come on, Emma. He is beyond sexy. They all are. I love hockey players. Hell, I love this sport. It's such an aggressive game. Look at how much protection they have to wear and they still get hurt. Hitting the ice is like slamming onto concrete. They take pucks and sticks to the face. Get hit against boards, elbowed in the ribs. Fists fights break out. It's so different from figure skating."

I never really thought of it like that. I just assumed most sports have men overflowing with testosterone and fighting to win. I guess it is kind of dangerous.

"Yeah, I see what you mean," I reply.

"Did Joar say he is dating anyone?" she adds... *out of freaking nowhere!*

I freeze, trying to choose my response carefully. "Um—"

"You probably don't know, huh? Have you even talked to him yet or does your mom talk to the players still?"

"Yeah! I have talked to him," I say, aghast. "I was the one who convinced him to join our team."

"For real?" she says, genuinely appearing shocked. "Wait, you aren't seeing him, are you?"

I cover my face with my palms and like the coward I am, I mutter, "No." I feel my world caving in. Despite not being with Joar, a part of me loved being the object of his affection. A big part.

Damn it.

My heart races and I stammer, "He's probably dating someone." No, *be more definitive.* "I think he is serious with a woman. I mean, I know he is."

She side-glances at me, perhaps confused. But soon, she shrugs. "I guess I'll find out tonight. By the way, Emma. You should give hockey players a chance one day. They are more than eye candy. They're good in bed, too. Never found one that wasn't."

I force a smile, but inside, I'm barely hanging on.

Chapter 22

Emma

I settle in my seat, determined to stay calm and not start crying in public.

Ophelia jumps from her seat again as Joar skates by, holding up two fingers, taunting him for two more goals. He removes his glove and holds up two fingers, then points to me. I sit up straighter, unsure what that meant.

Ophelia looks my way. "Oh! I think he is saying he'll get two more for the boss! Lucky!"

I'm sure I'm blushing.

She plops back down beside me. "I'll be shocked if he does, though. It only happens in about 5% of games. Very rare."

"I'm sure he'll try. He is persistent."

By the end of the first period, Ophelia seems to be correct about it being difficult for one player to score three goals. Joar hasn't score a second.

Once the next period starts, it's just as rocky. In fact, the intensity only ramps up. Bodies colliding, sticks smacking the ice, and the sound of glass rattling is fairly constant.

However, Joar remains relentless, often working to get the puck rather than waiting to be set up to take a shot by his teammates. I don't think they mind though, as everyone looks tired.

The home fans roar as the Panther's score.

But not long after, another loud buzzer sounds. At the end of the rink, Joar holds up his stick in celebration.

Against the odds, he somehow scored a second goal.

My heart races. Cool. Two down.

Once again, he skates to me and stops. He taps the glass twice with his stick. I clap for him and he grins — which make me feel all fuzzy. God, I'm so into him.

"Wow, I am impressed!" says Ophelia. "This is exciting!"

Now I'm really focused on the game as I watch Joar, hoping he can make a third goal. As if somehow, that effort is just for me. That he isn't trying to prove Ophelia wrong, nor care what she thinks.

Unfortunately, it's obvious Joar is just as tired as everyone else. To catch his breath, he coasts to the middle of the rink to face-off rather than skating swiftly. He slowly takes his position, both players looking exhausted.

When the puck drops, the battle continues with the same intensity. It's a great game and everyone is on edge. By the third period, everyone, including myself, is anxious as hell.

A player from the opposing team hooks Joar with his stick and then trips him, causing Joar to fall face first onto the ice. I gasp and shoot to my feet, wanting to see if he's hurt. When Igor helps him up, blood drips from Joar's chin. He skates toward the bench and is quickly replaced by another player. A team athletic trainer takes him to the locker room to assess the damage.

I sit back down as the game continues, watching the clock go down. I cross my arms, worried about Joar. However, I just want to know if our star player is badly injured. That's what GM's should do.

Suddenly, Joar returns to the game with a bandage on his chin.

I close my eyes, relieved that he's okay. But the pressure remains immense, and I wince as he is cross-checked into the glass. The opponent's stick thrusts into his side. Joar snarls, but doesn't lose his temper and risk a penalty - despite the attacker getting away with the unfair play.

Red numbers on the display edge lower.

Thirty seconds.

I clasp my hands together in a nervous ball and rise from my seat, squinting to see the puck slide back and forth as players work frantically to win in the last seconds.

Ten seconds.

I draw in a sharp breath as Joar skates at full speed to the net, the anticipation building with each stride. In a final attempt, the blade of his hockey stick swiftly sweeps under the puck, launching it into the air. The goalie lifts his glove, and in slow motion, the puck glides effortlessly through the small gap between the glove and the net's vibrant red frame.

The buzzer sounds, announcing the end of the game.

I stand there, still holding my breath and in awe at the sheer intensity of the moment. The stadium echoes with an overwhelming chorus of boos and cheers.

Instead of celebrating with the team, Joar breaks free from the players and skates directly to me. He stops in front of the glass with a proud, cocky grin. Beads of sweat roll down his temples, and he breathes in ragged breaths.

Removing his glove, he raises three fingers, then points at me — as if saying they were a gift. I smile sweetly and mouth, thank you, clapping once more.

But suddenly, his brow lifts and he gives me the same look I last saw in the hotel when he told me to figure out what I want.

I stammer, unsure how to respond. He shakes his head, his expression holding such disappointment that it feels like a knife to the heart. Before I can respond, he skates away.

I turn around and Ophelia is gone. Damn it! I have to stop her!

Just then, *The Imperial March* plays, and I begrudgingly answer my phone.

"Emma. Come to the third floor. Box E. I need to introduce you to some important people as part of your GM duties."

⚜ ⚜

Standing in the hotel's hallway, I knock on Joar's door... four hours later. Mother dragged me to a dinner with some NHL hotshot. It was boring, and the whole time, I kept picturing Joar fucking Ophelia.

I don't know why I am here other than to confirm my fear. To stay in my dark place.

That's why I'm determined to stop overthinking this and squash these feelings. So when he opens the door, I don't bother smiling.

"Hey. Good game."

He holds up his chin, now adorned with only a steri-strip over the cut. His posture is relaxed as he replies, "Thanks."

Those steely eyes are so cold. He's mad.

It pains me and I murmur, "Joar, I know you're upset, but I told you... I'm not right in the head. I don't know what you expected."

"To be happy that I got that hat trick for you. To show up after the game, give me fucking kiss. Not come to my hotel room hours later without an explanation. I don't know — just give a fuck about someone who care about you."

My chin trembles as I fight back tears.

"Joar," says a woman's voice.

Every vertebrae in my spine stacks flush with the other, straightening my back in a perfect line. My eyes dart from him, then search for a gap in the doorway to see around his body and find the mystery woman in his room.

But I already know who it is.

166

Joar opens the door wider, giving me full view of Ophelia seated seductively on the edge of the bed, a wineglass in her hand.

When our eyes lock, the tears I've choked back unleash. "Why!" I cry out to her.

She rushes to her feet, setting the wineglass on the TV stand. "Emma, I didn't—"

"I just told you at the game I liked him!" My voice cracks. I wipe my face, the tears running like a river.

"I... I thought you had a silly crush. You wouldn't date a hockey player. But Emma, if I knew it would bother you—"

"You are such a bitch," I interrupt, but the words are weak as struggle for breath.

My world shatters and I start to hyperventilate.

Swiftly, Joar hooks my waist and drags me out the room, closing the door so we are both standing in the hallway. I crumble in his arms, crying against his broad chest. I both want to push him away, and get the comfort I know only he can give.

"Emma, why are you this upset?"

Between sobs, I say, "Did you fuck her?"

"Hell no."

"No?"

"She met me after the game, we got some drinks at the hotel bar, it closed, so we hung out here. I waited for you, Emma. I texted and called. You obviously don't care who I fuck. That's what you said, remember?"

I want to believe him, but who invites a girl up to his hotel room just to hang out. "I think you're lying."

He sighs, his exasperation thick. "I'm not. I want you to be my girl. What do you want?"

I nervously bite down on my bottom lip.

I want him.

But how do you take what you want will you have no self esteem? How do you believe someone when you're incapable of trusting anyone?

My voice is small as I reply, "Have fun with Ophelia. Christian did."

"Emmy, stop," Joar soothes. "I've been talking about you all night. That's all. Ask her."

Since he can't force me to do anything while Ophelia is just inside his room, I back away. He calls after me, but I'm numb, determined to feel nothing for him.

Chapter 23

Emma

The next game, I head to the locker room with a single purpose: to apologize.

I've replayed our last encounter a hundred times in my head. The way Joar looked at me, the way he left without a fight—it's haunted me. I need to fix this. To tell him I'm sorry for overreacting and to wish him the best... with her.

The idea makes my stomach twist, but I push the feeling down. I need to show him I'm mature, professional, and not the weak, emotional mess he probably thinks I am.

As I step into the locker room, the air feels heavy, charged with the energy of pregame routines. Joar stands near the entrance to the tunnel, his broad back to me, the number **91** bold across his jersey.

He turns, his gaze catching mine immediately. His jaw tightens, his expression unreadable.

Before I can speak, he strides toward me, his towering frame commanding attention. His hand wraps firmly around my upper arm, not painfully, but with a grip that brooks no argument.

"Come with me," he says, his voice low and clipped.

He leads me away from the other players, and my heart pounds in my chest. His presence is overwhelming, and even though he's not saying much, his silence speaks volumes.

Once we're alone, he stops and turns to face me. His eyes pierce into mine, and I struggle to hold his gaze.

"Why are you here?" His tone is sharp, almost accusatory.

I stammer, the words tumbling out in a rush. "I... I just wanted to apologize for how things ended. I shouldn't have left like that. I wasn't thinking clearly, and I—"

"You weren't thinking clearly?" he cuts me off, his brow arching.

"No," I admit, my voice small. "I... I wanted to tell you I'm sorry. And... I hope things go well for you and Ophelia. I mean, professionally, of course. I'm sure you two will work well together."

His eyes narrow, and he takes a step closer, the cool fabric of his jersey brushing against my arm. "That's what you think this is about? Ophelia?"

I swallow hard, unable to answer.

"Tell me," he says, his voice dropping an octave. "When you left my room, did you want me to go to her?"

"What? No!" I gasp, my heart lurching at the accusation.

"Be honest," he presses, his gaze unrelenting. "Did you want me to fuck her that night? Is that what you're here to say? That you're fine with me burying my cock inside her?"

The vulgarity of his words makes my cheeks burn, but the jealousy twisting in my gut is worse.

"Of course not," I whisper, my voice trembling.

"Then why did you leave?" he growls, his hand tightening slightly on my arm. "Why did you run away instead of staying and fighting for what you want?"

"I didn't run away!" I snap, though the words lack conviction.

"Didn't you?" His tone is mocking now, his smirk cutting me to the bone.

Tears sting my eyes, but I refuse to let them fall. "I... I thought it was better this way. For both of us."

"Better for both of us?" He steps closer, his voice low and dangerous. "Or better for you? Because you're too scared to admit what you really want?"

"I don't—"

"Stop lying, Emma," he snaps, his patience wearing thin. "You want me, but you're too much of a coward to face it. You're too afraid to let go of the control you think you have."

The tears spill over, and I bite my lip to keep from sobbing.

"Look at you," he murmurs, his voice softer now, almost pitying. "You're a mess, Emma. You push everyone away because you're terrified they'll see the real you. But I already see you. And I'm not going anywhere."

"I don't need you to save me," I choke out, my voice barely audible.

"Good," he says, his tone firm. "Because that's not what this is about. This is about you learning to trust me. To let me in."

I shake my head, the weight of his words too much to bear. "I can't."

"You can," he insists, his grip on my arm loosening slightly. "But you won't. And that's the difference between you and someone like Ophelia. She wouldn't run. She'd stay and take what she wants."

The mention of her name feels like a slap in the face, and I flinch.

"Maybe you should be with her, then," I say bitterly, the words tasting like poison.

He smirks, but there's no humor in it. "Is that what you want? For me to find someone else? Someone who isn't afraid of me?"

I can't answer, the lump in my throat making it impossible to speak.

"Fine," he says, stepping back. "I'll find someone who isn't such a coward."

And with that, he walks away, leaving me standing there, shattered.

The game begins, but it's clear Joar isn't playing at his best. His movements are sluggish, his shots lack precision, and he seems completely disinterested.

From the owner's box, I watch in agony as the crowd grows restless, murmuring their disappointment.

Beside me, my father's jaw tightens. When the final buzzer sounds, he turns to me, his expression grim. "You need to fix this, Emma. Whatever's going on with him, it's your job to sort it out."

I nod, the weight of his words pressing down on me like a ton of bricks.

Later that night, I lie in bed, staring at the ceiling. My mind is a storm of emotions, my thoughts circling back to Joar and the things he said.

I can't stop imagining him with someone else—Ophelia, puck bunnies, faceless women who would give him everything he wants without hesitation.

The thought is unbearable.

Before I know it, I'm in my car, driving to his house.

When I park in his driveway, doubt washes over me, but it's too late. My legs carry me to his front door as if on autopilot.

I knock once, then twice, my heart pounding in my chest.

Bergen's barking grows louder as he nears the door, and I hold my breath, praying Joar will answer.

And dreading what I'll find if he does.

Chapter 24

Emma

When Joar opens the door, the sight of him steals the breath from my lungs.

He's wearing nothing but red athletic shorts, his chiseled chest and abs are a masterpiece of raw strength and power.

Finally shirtless, just as I've imagined a thousand times. A trail of hair starts at his navel, leading down to the waistband of his shorts, drawing my gaze lower, straight to that tantalizing line of his groin. Every inch of him is carved, unapologetically seductive, and I don't want to look away.

However, I'm here for business. So I pry my wandering gaze up, avoiding the outline I shouldn't be looking at in the first place.

But now focusing on his sculpted face, I'm paralyzed by those cold, stormy eyes glaring down at me.

Subtly, he shakes his head in a disapproving manner. "What do you want now, Emma?"

I try to appear casual, but honestly, I find myself struggling to steady my voice while also sneaking glances beyond him. I want to see if anyone else is here.

Just... curious.

"Um, sorry if I woke you, but I'm concerned. It looked like you weren't playing your best tonight. Is that because of me?"

His eyes narrow, and he crosses his arms over his chest — where I wish I could rest my head.

Be professional, Emma!

He says dismissively, "I was distracted. I'll try harder next time."

"Okay, good. Because I know you want a fourth championship."

"Is that really why you think I joined your team?"

His words and unfriendly demeanor leave me somewhat lost, suddenly unsure what I'm doing here. I scan the ground as I search for more ideas, but I give up pretty quickly as I find myself stealing another glance past Joar.

...Fine. I admit it. I'm desperate to know if a woman is here.

He waves his hand in front of my face, snapping my attention back to him. "Something you are looking for?" he says, his expression taunting, yet impatient.

"No! Uh. Joar, please don't make the team suffer because you're mad at me. They need you. You'll be a legend with four championships," I reason, my voice breaking despite my best efforts to remain composed. But this time, I don't bother being subtle as I stoop down to look around him and see into the house.

He sighs loudly, then steps back, moving to slam the door in my face.

Panic surges through me, and without thinking, I stick my foot in the doorway to stop him. The door thumps against my ankle, sending pain rocketing through my toes and up my calf. Although it definitely hurts, I know right away it's not bad. However, this is just what I needed to keep talking to him, so I cry out, taking hold of my ankle like I'm in agony. Joar reopens the door swiftly, having realized my foot intercepted it.

"Emma!" he says, the coldness in his voice replaced with genuine concern.

I scrunch my face, pretending I'm near tears as I inhale through clenched teeth. Suddenly, my body lifts into the air as Joar carries me inside. Gently, he sets me on the couch and takes hold of my injured foot, slipping off my shoe.

"Let me see," he says softly, his touch surprisingly tender. The dismissiveness he showed earlier is gone. After examining my faux injury, he grumbles, "Stay here," then jogs down the hall, returning shortly after with a small bag of ice. He rests it on my ankle, which I hope he doesn't notice isn't swelling.

I look at him and say meekly, "Is somebody here?" But he remains silent, his expression returning to cold as his deep gray eyes certainly see right through me. Despite his lack of warmth, just having him within touching distance is so... *comforting*. I don't know what overcomes me, but suddenly, I blurt without shame, "If you want me to try the deal again, I will. Uh, I mean, if that's what it will take to get the cup, I'll do it."

Where did that come from? I've lost my mind.

He stares at me, his icy expression unchanged. Since he isn't softening, I cringe and try harder. "Joar, what do you want? We could add it to the rules, okay?"

"You know what I wanted in that deal, Emma: You."

My heart skips a beat. "I feel like I tried. I definitely did as you asked... most of the time."

"I wanted all of you. I wanted you to obey *me*," he clarifies. "Which meant no making excuses, and no bending the knee to your parents or anyone other than me. No wanting other women to sleep with me so you can hate me and run away."

"Honestly, I don't know if I can," I admit.

"You can, but you don't want to."

"I do!" I exclaim so loud it surprises both of us. I lower my voice and rephrase. "Could we try the deal again? Please? I'll... behave."

He grimaces, looking disgusted at my proposition. "Why don't you get this? I don't care about the deal anymore. I want you."

My cheeks burn, but I remind myself to avoid getting swept away without facing my most pressing fear. "Tell me the truth. Did you sleep with Ophelia?"

He smirks but answers in a serious tone, "I haven't slept with anyone since I met you. She came to my hotel room. I made her leave after you ran off."

Now my cheeks might as well be on fire, and putting my better judgement aside, I reply, "Well, I have to admit that is a relief. I have some issues about cheating."

"To cheat, we would have to be together, anyway."

"So you did cheat!" I say haughtily, sitting up in a tizzy.

He chuckles. "And you think I'm the problem?" he replies, which prompts me to slump back on the cushion and pout. But he takes my hand and strokes it gently with his thumb. "I'm not your ex. If we're together, I wouldn't cheat on you, but that's the only kind of deal I want."

"So, you still want to date me then?" I say, but I'm unable to hide my excitement.

"Not date. That implies you can date other people. We'd be a couple. You have to be mine. Agree?"

A thrill runs through me at the seriousness of his tone, and I nod, managing a hesitant, "Uh, yeah, if that means no cheating."

"Okay," he replies, his gaze darkening. "But know this: I expect you to stop fighting me moving forward. Give yourself to me completely. Agreed?"

There's something unsettling in his tone, yet I can't deny the giddiness rising inside me at the thought of being with a man again — being with *him*.

He's the only guy who I've felt these kinds of feelings, the safety and thrill that only Joar seems to give me.

Therefore, I nod, my pulse quickening in anticipation.

He doesn't rejoice, though. His expression is shrouded with skepticism.

"Okay. The let's see if you're really committed." An almost sinister smile graces his lips. "We'll start with your punishment."

He tilts his head, gesturing pointedly to his knee, silently instructing me to get into position. My eyes widen, disbelief tightening in my chest. "Uh, you... still want to spank me? But there isn't a deal I have to follow."

"Same rules, though. You disobeyed me and haven't been punished. If we're together, I have even higher expectations for you," he replies casually. "Take it or leave it."

It's hard to imagine being in a relationship with someone who has rules. Although, I guess it isn't much different from a 'no cheating' rule. His rules are simply less conventional. I should at least try. In fact, I want to try.

I take a deep breath and reluctantly settle myself over his lap, lying on my stomach.

Chapter 25

Emma

In one swift motion, Joar lifts my skirt, exposing the black thong tight between my round cheeks. My eyes snap shut as his dominance weighs heavy on me, my teeth sinking into my bottom lip as I brace for what's coming.

The first crack of his palm against my bare flesh echoes through the room, sharp and punishing. The searing heat spreads across my skin, and I can't hold back the small, muffled cry that escapes my lips.

"That's for pushing me away," he says, his voice low and edged with menace. "For talking back, and for letting your mother control you like a puppet."

Another slap lands, harder this time, the sting making me flinch. I try to hold still, but my body betrays me, squirming under the force of his hand.

"And this," he growls, "is for saying you love another man. Do you know what that does to me?"

"I'm sorry!" I yip.

The next smack sends my head snapping up, a gasp tearing from my throat.

"And this is for making me wait in the hotel. For hours. You don't keep me waiting, Emmy. Ever."

The next strike is punishing, the force stealing my breath. "Joar! I get it!" I cry out, twisting my head to glance back, my voice trembling with both pain and desperation.

His dark gaze meets mine, but there's no softness there, only calculated control. His hand lingers on my burning skin, roaming his palm as he savors the feel of my soft flesh. The heat of his touch soothes me despite the sting. And then, his hips lift slightly, pressing his hard length to my body.

"Are you ready to beg, Emmy?"

I hesitate, unsure how to answer, but the delay earns me another sharp slap that sends me burying my face into the pillow.

Yet again, Joar's hand comes down sharply on my ass, the sting pulling a cry from my throat.

"Answer me, Emmy," he snaps. "Is my needy, pathetic toy ready to beg?"

I tremble under his gaze, my breath hitching as I realize I can't fight it anymore. A part of me — a deep, primal part — yearns to be what he wants. To make him happy. To see that look of dark satisfaction on his face.

"Yes," I whisper, then louder, with more conviction, "Yes, I'm ready! I'll beg."

I think...

Oh, no. I hope I can do it right this time! I don't want to let him down.

A wicked smirk curves his lips, his eyes gleaming with triumph. "That's my girl," he murmurs, his tone softening just slightly. His hand grips my ass cheek. "You'll beg *and* take every punishment I give you until you learn to obey. But I doubt you can handle it."

Despite the shame and the lingering sting of his dominance, I feel a pull within me that craves his control and his approval.

"I can!" I assure, my throat tight but tone certain.

"Good start," he says. His fingers hook under the waistband of my thong, dragging it down slowly. The cold air meets my exposed skin, and I tense.

"Joar," I whine, my voice small.

"Relax," he commands. "You're mine now. That means I can do whatever I wish with you."

One long finger sinks into me, and I gasp at the intrusive sensation.

I attempt to lift my belly from his lap, but his powerful arm pins me down, holding me firmly in place. "Stay still," he orders.

My insecurities rush to the surface: my naked body, my limited experience, my relentless anxiety. I stammer, "Joar, I'm getting overwhelmed. I just—"

His other hand moves to my mouth, two fingers pressing against my lips.

"Open," he orders.

I hesitate, but his fingers press harder until I comply, taking them into my mouth.

"Suck," he says.

My body tenses more, but I obey, the act still humiliating but just as calming. My anxiety slowly dissipates as I focus on his fingers in my mouth and the rhythm of his hand between my legs.

"That's better," he praises, his voice a mix of mockery and satisfaction. "You're so much prettier when you behave and take what I give you. Such a good little plaything, aren't you?"

I wince at his words, the degradation cutting deep, but I can't deny the way my body responds to him because I arch my back and suck harder.

"Good girl," he murmurs, slipping another finger into my warmth, the stretch making me moan despite myself. He adds, "You like this, don't you?"

"Yes," I whimper, my voice muffled by his fingers.

He chuckles darkly. "Of course you do. Did you know, you were made for this? To be used by me."

His words are jarring, but as his fingers continue their steady, sensual rhythm, my shame melts away, replaced by pure, unfiltered need.

Suddenly, he flips me over and lowers his mouth to my clit, and the world fades away. His tongue and fingers work

ENDLEY TYLER

in perfect harmony, pushing me to the brink of euphoria. "Mmm. Oh, Joar," I moan, my body shaking.

His skill is flawless, and it is clear he's enjoying it. Somebody is enjoying *me*. And soon, my orgasm crashes down. It's heavenly. In a state of bliss, words spill from my lips before I can stop them. "Joar!" I gasp, then breathe out, "I love you."

What a perfect moment.

As the pleasure ebbs, though, I freeze, the weight of my confession settling over me like a rain cloud.

Why, Emma! I'm so stupid! Why did I have to say that?

I *hate* myself — I let the 'L-word' escape. I didn't even know I loved him... but now that I admitted it, I know it's true. And sure, a climax suspends logic, but still, it shouldn't have been enough to completely abandon all caution. I glance at Joar, finding his mesmerizing eyes looking back at me from between my legs.

He gives a tender kiss on my tingling bundle of nerves before saying, "See how good I treat you when you behave?"

"I uh," I stammer, then try to rise as insecurity envelops me.

He didn't say it back.

Of course he didn't.

Before panic takes root, his body shifts. He looms over me, his broad shoulders and chiseled chest casting me in shadow, cocooning me in his massive form. The intensity of his presence steals my breath, his bare skin radiating warmth onto mine. His sculpted body is unmatched, every inch of him muscled with power.

186

My heart stutters as his tip presses against my entrance, and the intensity of what's happening sends a jolt through me.

"No... don't, don't, don't!" The words tumble out, but his reaction isn't what I expect.

He stills, his sharp gaze narrowing as he studies my face. Then, slowly, a knowing smirk tugs at the corner of his lips. "Try again."

"But... I'm just not ready," I explain, my voice wavering.

He tilts his head, his smirk deepening. "Not ready?"

"Yeah... everything is moving so fast," I manage, my voice trembling. "Can we... slow down?"

His chuckle is low and rough, sending a chill down my spine. He lowers his head until his lips brush against my ear, his voice a dark whisper that coils through me. "You're ready, you poor little thing."

His words ignite a flood of desire that I can't deny, no matter how much I want to.

His cheek grazes mine, the faint stubble scraping my skin in a way that's both grounding and electrifying. "You want to feel me claim you. I see it in your eyes, hear it in your voice. Stop lying to yourself."

My breath catches, and before I can form a reply, his hips press forward, the pressure at my entrance increasing.

I'm rigid as steel.

"Relax," he commands, his tone firm but soothing. "Don't fight me."

My knees press against the sides of his powerful body, torn between trying to stop his advance and doing what he wishes. But it's no use either way — he's in control, and I know it. I remain still, holding my breath as his shaft inches forward.

"That's it," he murmurs, his voice smooth. "Good girl. Let me in."

Chapter 26

Emma

Slowly, Joar fills me, stretching me with deliberate care but leaving no doubt that he's taking what he wants.

Reflexively, my hands clutch his muscled yet soft, velvety sides, and my nails pinch in as I brace myself to take all of him. My knees squeeze his wide body harder. The pressure edges me to my breaking point, but finally, his formidable length is fully inside.

"Oh yes, little Emmy. You're mine now," he murmurs, his voice dark and possessive. "Say it."

My heart races as I grasp for my sanity, caught between defiance and surrender.

"Say it," he presses, his tone softening slightly but losing none of its dominance. His hand cups my jaw, tilting my face up to meet his eyes. "Say it, you trembling, needy girl, or this will hurt."

The threat is a promise, and the power in his voice leaves me shook. Besides... apparently, I love this difficult man, so I nod and whisper, "Okay... yes, I'm yours."

His expression doesn't shift, as if he knew I'd comply.

"Good girl." Then slowly, his hips begin to move, each stroke still deliberate but sensual, igniting every nerve in my body. The friction makes my muscles tense from a mix of pleasure and very real pain.

After a minute or two, he stops.

"Are you okay?" he murmurs near my ear.

I nod eagerly, though deep down, I'm unsure. He's so much bigger than anyone I've been with, and it feels as though he might tear me apart if he's not careful.

"Does it hurt?" he asks, his dark gaze boring into mine.

I try to mask it, but he sees right through me. I wince, feeling exposed. "Um... how can you tell?"

His lips curl into a knowing smile. "Because your nails are digging into my sides like you're clinging for dear life," he answers, his tone filled with dark amusement. "And your tight little body is fighting me. You're strangling my cock."

My cheeks burn, and I quickly release my nails from his flesh, feeling foolish. I want to impress him in bed, not disappoint him. "I'm fine. Don't stop," I assure, but my meek voice betrays me.

"God, you are pathetic," he jabs, his voice thick with mockery as he watches me adjust beneath him. "You're so needy — so desperate to please me. You'll let me ruin you, won't you?"

I frown, his words cutting deep, but then, his hand brushes over my cheek with such tenderness. "That makes you precious. You may be a mess, but you're my mess, and if you keep taking me so pitifully, I won't let you go."

My mouth parts, shocked he wants to keep me despite my floundering performance thus far.

Before I can respond, his hips begin to move again, even slower this time, but deeper. His thick length fills me with care each time. I try to shift, unsure how to angle myself, but he catches my movements and chuckles low in his throat.

"Squirming only makes my cock harder," he warns.

Abruptly, he rises onto his knees, his strong hands gripping me. With one fluid motion, he lifts my hips, my back arching as he holds them suspended off the couch, my back still rested on the cushion.

"Lay back and relax," he orders, his voice cutting through the haze of arousal and apprehension. "I'll decide what your body can handle."

"Um, okay," I whisper, the words slipping from me like a reflex, my resistance dissolving under his control.

The back of my legs press to his body, my ankles on either shoulder. His hands tighten on my thighs, the grip possessive, firm, as though daring me to defy him. He moves with calculated focus, his eyes fixed on my expression. Each thrust is a test, his pace slow, his control absolute. I can feel him gauging my every reaction, pushing me just enough, stretching me, owning me.

"Look at you," he growls, his tone dripping with disdain and hunger. "So uptight, so anxious. Just trust me."

I nod, accepting that he sees my anxiety. In fact, it lets me relax more knowing I can't pretend around him.

It doesn't take him long to find an angle my body doesn't resist so much. He steadily increases his pace, still measured and not too fast. In time, my breath begins to grow shallow, and I moan ever so softly.

He grins. "That's it. Make those pretty noises for daddy."

The word "daddy" slams into me, leaving me breathless and off-balance. It's both unexpected and arousing, making me feel vulnerable in a way I've never experienced. Another moan escapes my lips, louder than I intend, and I turn my face away, confused that a word could stimulate me so much.

"Don't hide from me," he says, his voice sharp. "Always show me your pleasure or shame. It's your gift to me." His pace quickens, the intensity pushing me closer to the edge of discomfort.

Faster and faster.

Soon, it's too much, and despite wanting to impress him, I cry out, "Joar! That hurts. Please, um, slow down."

His response is immediate. "No. Say, 'Please slow down, *daddy.'"*

I squirm in his hold, my body instinctively trying to escape, but it's useless. His dominance wraps around me like a vice.

"Joar, I can't—" I begin, but his voice cuts through me.

"Stop fighting me, Emmy." He presses his lips to the inside of my ankle, the touch surprisingly gentle. "Behave."

His words and touch are like a tether, pulling me back to him, grounding me. Despite my turmoil, I find myself nodding.

"Um, please slow down, *daddy*," my voice trembling but obedient.

"Such a good girl," he praises, his grip loosening. His pace slows, his thrusts becoming more controlled, more careful. He finds the perfect rhythm, coaxing my body to respond, to yield to him entirely.

And it does.

"That's it," he breathes, his voice smooth with approval. "See what happens when you stop fighting me? I can be gentle... but I have to tell you: I'd love nothing more than to fuck you as hard as I can right now."

His words send butterflies through me, a thrill and desire curling low in my stomach. He wants me.

I glance up at him, his bottom lip caught between his teeth as he reins himself in, his mesmerizing eyes burning with restrained hunger.

Part of me yearns to tell him to let go, to take me completely, but I can't find the words. I also can't bear how badly that would hurt. So instead, I let myself sink into the electric pulse of his steady rhythm, my body shaking as it strains to accommodate him, yet wanting more of this powerful man.

His lips brush against the inside of my ankle once more. Then, his tone completely changes to stern and serious. "After this, are you going to run from me, Emmy?"

The answers flows from me without delay. "No. I won't."

He nods, though skepticism clouds his eyes. "You sure like pleasing me, don't you? Saying whatever I want."

He doesn't believe me.

I want to prove it to him. So I close my eyes and scrape for all the courage I can muster.

"I won't run away." I swallow hard, then purr softly, "I'm yours. See? Watch me, daddy."

My hand drifts to my clit, circling the sensitive nub as waves of pleasure ripple through me. His hands clamp down on my thighs, his breath ragged as his eyes lock onto my fingers. Indeed, he watches my every move as I put on a show for him.

"Fuck," he groans, his voice holding angst and surprise. "You *are* desperate to please me. Keep going, you sweet girl. Let daddy see how much you supposedly *love* him."

Oh my God!

That rattles me, and my breath catches. He's acknowledging everything I'm feeling — my vulnerability, my longing, the fact I *fucking* love him — but still, he doesn't say it back.

My chest tightens, a lump forming in my throat as my self loathing claws at me. The silence between us feels suffocating, and before I can stop myself, the words slip out in a broken whisper.

"I wish you loved me, too, Joar."

He stills for a moment, his sharp gaze slicing through me as his lips curl into a wicked smirk. "You wish?" he taunts.

Heat rises to my face, shame crushing me as I realize how immature I must sound, but before I can backtrack, he leans down, letting my legs curl around him as he moves over me. His hand grips my jaw, forcing me to look at him. His gray eyes gleam with cruelty that sends my heart racing.

"Listen to yourself," he says. "You're begging for something you haven't earned. Do you think whining like a little girl will make me love you?"

Tears prick my eyes, and I shake my head. "No, I just—"

"No?" he cuts me off, his grip tightening slightly. "You just what, Emmy? Thought I'd say it to you because you're desperate enough to admit it?" He chuckles darkly, the sound sending a fresh wave of humiliation through me.

Tears spill over now, unbidden and unstoppable, and my voice cracks. "Please, Joar. Please just say it! I *need* to hear that you love me."

"You need to hear it? You're so spoiled, just a crying little rich girl, so used to getting what you want."

A sob escapes my throat, and I'm lost now, my hands clutching at him as though he's my lifeline. "I do deserve it. I love you, Joar! I love you so much, and I... I just need to know you love me back. *Please*."

The words feel like my final surrender, and in that moment, I realize I just put my fragile heart out there to be crushed. I just love him so completely, so desperately, that the thought of him not loving me in return is... unbearable.

A flood of tears unleash and I sob more. Really sob. Ugly cry sob.

Joar's smirk falters, his expression shifting as my tears wet my face, each gasp for air wracking my body. His hand loosens on my jaw, and his thumb brushes over my wet cheek, wiping away tears. For a moment, he just stares at me, his stormy eyes softening, something raw and possessive flickering in their depths.

"Emma," he murmurs, his voice lower now, almost reverent. "You really love me that much?"

"Yes," I whisper through the tears, my voice trembling. "I love you more than I've loved any guy. I just couldn't admit it because if I said it and—" I choke back tears and can barely breathe.

His lips part, then he exhales a long breath, and I know his cruel game is over.

"Emmy... I need time," he says, his tone shifting entirely, full of pity!

His words crush me, and fresh tears spill over.

"Why can't you say it?" I cry, but I immediately stop myself. I know the answer.

Because he doesn't love me.

One thing is for sure, though: I don't want to lose him. I can't scare him off by moving too fast. That's what I did. I moved too fast. I let my guard down. That was a mistake, but I won't do it twice.

Thus, with every ounce of strength I have, I choke back tears. I take a deep breath, then speak with conviction. "I thought that's what you wanted me to say and do — say things like that, cry and beg. I didn't really mean it."

His brow lifts, the skepticism behind those striking eyes is so obvious. However, I persist. Despite my weaknesses, I've always hidden my emotions from my parents. Crying in front of them was never an option. I can do the same with him.

"I mean it, Joar. I was just playing the part you wanted me to. Right? This is all a game."

His forehead presses to mine. "Emmy, you don't have to lie—"

"I'm not lying," I interrupt. "I don't really love you. I can beg like you want."

At this moment, I know he's not happy, but I'm unsure why. He looks away from me, seemingly contemplating.

When he finally nods, I breathe a sigh of relief, desperate to move on and pretend that never happened.

Then... he moves closer, giving me a passionate kiss. When our lips break, he presses his cheek to mine as he rolls his hips. He nuzzles in my hair and murmurs my name near my ear. He says things I don't expect: *You're perfect, Emmy. Precious. So beautiful. My girl. I'll take care of you. I promise.*

He's soothing me.

And not long after, I give in and, steadily, he raptures me. And despite my moment of distress, I block it out, determined to be present. To be sexy and desirable. I do everything I think I should, and he seems to enjoy it. Many times, he even tries to restrain his force, and although he mostly succeeds, eventually, I am sore, weary, and fully under his cruel spell.

When he sees me spent underneath him, broken and completely unraveled, his hips hold in for a moment as he releases inside me. I relish the moment, exhaling as his body lowers onto mine.

He catches his breath, then places a gentle, lingering kiss on my lips. It's sensual, even affectionate. It's a kiss that leaves no doubt: he likes having sex with me... I didn't disappoint.

Unfortunately though, this closeness, those eyes, that body, his masterful skill, those soothing words, his achingly gentle touch... it's too much, and now, I love him even more.

He was right. I wanted to please him so badly that I let him ruin me for other men, and without those three words, I *hate* him for it.

Chapter 27

Emma

Joar left a note on the bed, saying he had errands to run before the gym and didn't want to disturb me. No 'good morning,' 'had fun last night,' or anything.

It's unsettling.

I hate to admit it, but I suddenly regret having slept with him. I kind of feel... used. As my anxiousness ticks up, I remind myself not to spiral. But I can't stop from texting him, yet he doesn't respond.

Damn it, Emma. Don't freak out.

At work, I suffer through meetings, but of course, I can't stop worrying. Right now, Joar should be in the gym, working out like he usually does at this time. Therefore, I head towards the weight room. The clang of steel plates and light chatter bounces off the walls.

I scan the area, noting a few players pushing themselves on various machines, but Joar is nowhere to be found. My heart sinks slightly, but I refuse to let my insecurities take over — even though they probably already have. But I still pretend to be determined and make my way to the physical therapy rooms.

As I enter the doorway, I stop in my tracks.

Joar is lying face down on a massage table, only his tight blue athletic underwear covering his hips, leaving his muscled legs and sculpted back in full view.

A cute brunette with a petite nose and big cheeks wears khakis and a blue polo. Standing over him, her hands work expertly along his shoulder blades and lats. She digs her elbow into a particularly tight spot, causing Joar to grunt a short, husky breath. It's a sound that brims with pleasure.

"That the spot?" she asks.

"Yep, that's perfect. You are amazing, Bri."

A surge of jealousy shoots through me, and my fists clench at my sides. I hate myself at this moment. I don't need to be the jealous girl anymore.

But the sight of another woman touching him, making him react with pleasure, feeds my regret of sleeping with him.

Maybe I too cold when I lied to him, claiming I was role playing and didn't really love him. Yes. Maybe I pushed him into the hands of this woman!

Perhaps more gut wrenching is to hear him praising her instead of me.

Gosh, I wish I didn't love him. I don't want to lose him when I finally have the courage to act on my feelings. Nevertheless, I mustn't forget to resist looking desperate.

But then, she leans over his back, her slim belly touching him. I'm torn between the urge to watch how far this goes versus my desire to storm forward and claim my territory.

'My territory?' *Whoa.* Damn it again. This isn't who I am. I refuse to stoop so low!

So I step further into the room, clicking my heels loudly against the hard floor. The sound catches Joar's attention, and his eyes turn in my direction, locking onto mine. For a moment, there's a flash of happiness in his gaze, quickly replaced by something more guarded.

"Emma," he says, his voice holding genuine curiosity. "What are you doing here?"

I force a smile, trying to mask the insecurity boiling beneath the surface. "I was looking for you. We need to talk about... something."

Bri steps back, apparently sensing the tension. "I'll give you two privacy," she says, her voice smooth and professional. She gathers her things and exits the room, leaving us alone.

Joar sits up, swinging his long legs over the side of the table. His gaze is unwavering, challenging even, as if daring me to say something about what I just saw.

He starts, "What's on your mind?"

I take a deep breath, struggling to focus on the real reason I came here. Trying to keep my emotions in check, I slip into professional-mode. "The coaches want to make sure you'll perform better than yesterday. We need you at your best, especially now."

He raises an eyebrow, a small smirk playing at the corners of his lips. "That wasn't clear last night? Remember? When I made you cum so hard that you said you loved me?"

The words hit me so hard I flinch. My face burns hot with embarrassment. But I force myself to stay composed, refusing to succumb to the insecurity that is gnawing at me.

I manage to look at him, but surprisingly, he veers his eyes. His jaw tight, expression calm, yet I know immediately: he's remorseful.

This is so unlike Joar. I've never seen him say something he regretted.

Oh my God. I hope he isn't pulling away already.

Quickly, I say, "I thought I made myself clear. I was just role playing. Anyway, your gameplay is all I needed to discuss." My words are perfectly gathered, yet I can't help but wonder if he can see the turmoil within me.

He sighs heavy, but seems to gather himself, too.

"Are you jealous, Emma?" he asks brusquely, taking me aback.

"What? No!" I assure.

He has to bite his bottom lip to hold back a smile, but it doesn't work. However, he quickly resets his expression from amused to calm. "Why are you jealous? What are you worried about?"

It's nearly impossible not to scoff and yell, '*because I freaked you out by professing my love too early and I think you're about to leave me for someone else,*' but I restrain myself. "I'm fine, Joar."

"No, you're not."

Like he just ripped off my tough-girl mask, my chin immediately quivers as I struggle to keep my eyes from watering.

How does he disarm me so easily? I stare at him for a moment before saying, "I don't want to feel like this, Joar. I don't want to worry about other women."

He extends his hand, and I walk to him. He doesn't delay, drawing me in his warm chest in a tight, comforting embrace. "You realize I only have eyes for you, right?"

"Yeah?" I reply, not believing that for a second.

He nuzzles his face to my neck and soothes, "We're exclusive. Like I told you, I have been since we met."

"Really?"

"You can watch all my massages. I don't give a fuck. Whatever makes you feel better."

I don't want to do that, but I nod, letting him know I appreciate the offer. "Are you nervous about this, too? About us?"

He does a double-take, and after a moment he shakes his head. "No. Not at all."

Joar gives a reassuring smile as he stands up from the table. "Everything's fine, Emma. Just remember, I'm not your ex. Don't worry about my loyalty to you." He reaches into his gym bag on the counter and pulls out a key, pressing it into my hand. "Here. This is for you. I had it made this morning. You can move all your belongings into my house whenever you're ready."

I stare at the key, the weight of it solid and real in my palm. It's almost like a form of praise, a step forward that I didn't expect just 24 hours ago.

Wow! I guess I didn't scare him off.

Joar kisses my forehead and I smile. "For now, go pack some of your things for staying over tonight."

I grin, feeling a wave of relief wash over me. "Okay. I'll do that."

"One more thing." He pulls out a silver necklace. "Lift up your hair."

I do as he says, and he loops it around my neck and latches it in place. It's tight, like a choker. I feel the metal between my fingers. It's elegant, but still thicker than a regular necklace. "Wear this for me. Never take it off, okay?"

"*Never?*" I ask with a smirk.

"Never. Oh, and Emma."

"Yeah?"

"Don't role play anymore."

Slowly, I nod, but focus on the gift. It's proof Joar isn't as freaked out as I thought. He gave his girlfriend a gift. And the key in my pocket is a sign that he isn't playing a twisted game with me, like Erik claimed.

With a nervous smile, I head home, pack a few essentials, and return to Joar's house, wearing my new necklace proudly.

Joar is *not* my ex. Christian never invited me to move in with him or bought me gifts. In fact, I should tell Christian about Joar! Now that it's official, he should know. We're still close.

Yeah... That's it. We're close. Christian *needs* to know I've moved on.

Chapter 28

Emma

Christian sighs and takes a sip of his drink, his eyes fixed on mine with a mix of disbelief and sharp curiosity.

The tension is thick, cutting through the noisy bustle of the restaurant. His fingers rake through his long, brown hair, his jaw tightening as he leans forward. His gaze makes my stomach twist, but not just with unease. It's something darker, something sinful I can't fully acknowledge. Not now.

"I can't believe you're seeing this guy," he says, his tone flat but dripping with judgment. "Joar. Really, Emma?"

I shrug, feigning indifference even as heat rises in my cheeks. "It's not what you think."

"Oh, it's exactly what I think. Erik told me what he's like. Emma, the guy punishes you."

The word drops between us like a bomb, and I immediately look away, embarrassed that Christian knows. The urge to defend Joar, to defend myself, wrestles with my growing frustration.

"Not really," I mutter, but my voice is unconvincing.

Christian raises an eyebrow, his lips curling into a skeptical smirk. "Really? Because from what Erik told me, it sounds like he gets off on spanking you."

I wince, my stomach churning. "Erik told you that! Well... It's not about getting off, okay? It's just... complicated."

"Complicated? Emma, you're letting some guy hit you because you think it's normal? Since when did you start letting anyone treat you like that?" His voice is louder now, drawing glances from nearby tables.

"Keep your voice down," I hiss, glancing around nervously.

He leans back, his eyes narrowing as he studies me. "Unbelievable. The Emma I knew would never let a man dominate her like that."

His words sting, though I can't tell if it's from shame or the growing awareness of how true they are. The Emma he knew wouldn't. But that Emma didn't have Joar.

Christian's intense gaze pins me to my seat, and despite myself, I notice the curve of his lips, the way his shirt clings to his chest. It's infuriating that, even after everything, I can still find him attractive.

I scold myself, gripping my glass tighter. Stop it. You're with Joar now. Thinking about Christian this way is wrong.

Then Christian speaks again.

"Does he degrade you, too? Call you names? Insult you?" he asks, his voice quiet but cutting.

I bristle, refusing to meet his gaze. "No!"

"Come on, Emma. You're sitting here telling me this guy spanks you for breaking his so-called rules, and you expect me to believe he doesn't humiliate you?"

I cross my arms, my voice defensive. "It's not like that. I mean, sometimes he calls me 'my toy,' but it's innocent. Um, like playful."

"Playful?" He scoffs, his jaw tightening.

Toy is nothing compared to the other adjectives he uses to describe me.

The memory of Joar's deep, commanding voice whispering the words *pathetic, sad, desperate* makes my cheeks burn hotter. I glance down at my plate, unwilling to elaborate.

Christian leans forward again, his expression softening but still full of pity. "Emma, I know you. You're not built for this. You're too guarded. Too independent. You can't handle a guy like Joar."

His words cut deeper than I expect, and I blurt without thinking, "What makes you such an expert?"

He hesitates, his gaze wandering as if he's deciding how much to reveal. Then, to my shock, he says, "Because I'm into BDSM too. I'm a dom."

My heart skips a beat, disbelief washing over me. "What?"

He shrugs, his cheeks tinging pink. "I didn't tell you because we weren't compatible. You couldn't handle that side of me, Emma. You were too... closed off."

The words hit like a slap, and I stare at him, unable to hide the sting of jealousy that flares in my chest. "You never gave me a chance."

Christian sighs, running a hand through his hair. "I did, Emma. But you were too uptight. You didn't trust me enough to let me lead, and I couldn't be what you needed, either. That's why I..."

He stops, and my stomach drops. "Why you what?"

He hesitates, then looks me in the eye. "That's why I cheated with Ophelia. She was everything I needed — a perfect submissive. She trusted me. She let me lead."

Finally, the truth is spoken.

The air leaves my lungs, and for a moment, I can't speak. The humiliation, the betrayal, the sheer audacity of his confession leaves me reeling.

"I wasn't enough for you," I whisper, my voice trembling.

He shakes his head. "It's not about being enough, Emma. We just weren't compatible. You're not a submissive. You're too guarded, too controlling. And a dom needs a sub who trusts them completely."

His words dig into me like daggers, each one twisting the insecurity I've tried to bury. "I trusted you," I say, though even to my ears, it sounds hollow.

Christian's expression hardens. "No, you didn't. You barely let me touch you. You panicked every time you weren't in control. Emma, you're not cut out for this lifestyle. If anything, you're a dom, not a submissive."

His words echo in my mind, and for a moment, I feel like I'm free-falling. The doubts he's planted about Joar, about myself, grow louder, drowning out any defense I could muster.

"What if you're wrong?" I ask, my voice small.

He shakes his head, his expression pitying. "I'm not. Joar's dangerous, Emma. And when he realizes you can't be what he needs, he'll move on. Just like I did."

Tears prick at my eyes, but I refuse to let them fall. "You don't know him."

"I know guys like him," he counters. "And I know you."

But the truth is, I'm not sure I know myself anymore. Sitting across from Christian, I realize why I wanted this lunch in the first place. It wasn't just to tell him about Joar. I wanted him to want me. I wanted him to regret losing me.

And Joar... Joar terrifies me because I know Christian might be right. I'm not enough for him. I'm not kinky enough, not submissive enough. Joar deserves someone like Ophelia, someone who can give him what he needs.

Joar seemed to like last night, but what do I know? I can't read men. Apparently, Christian, the guy I dated and knew since we were kids, is into BDSM and I had no idea!

The thought makes my chest ache, and I stare at my plate, my appetite gone. By the end of lunch, Christian has planted seeds of doubt that I can't ignore.

When I leave the restaurant, I feel more lost than ever. Joar's world is dark and full of desires I don't understand. And now, I'm not sure if I can measure up.

Chapter 29

Emma

As soon as I'm home, I flip open my laptop and start researching BDSM. Hours pass, the words on the screen warping together in a sick blur of leather, collars, restraints, punishments, and humiliation. I feel like I'm spiraling.

Joar cannot possibly expect me to do these things. He's just a little aggressive. He can't actually be into all of this... twisted stuff.

I press my fingers to my temples, exhaling shakily. My stomach churns at more thoughts of what I've read — choking, CNC, impact play, ownership, and of course, degradation. And the worst part: Christian was right.

The things Joar has done to me already — the spanking, the name-calling, the rules — they fit right into this world.

A wave of nausea rolls through me.

I flinch as the front door opens. Joar's heavy steps enter the room, and I quickly slam my laptop shut. His gaze lands on me instantly, taking in my stiff posture. His handsome face is unreadable, but I swear there's a flicker of amusement in his shadowed blue-gray eyes.

I force a smile as he leans in and tenderly kisses my temple.

God, why does he have to be so sweet... so good-looking? I try to focus on something, anything else, but my eyes betray me, drinking in his powerful form that shook my world last night. Oh, and the way his broad shoulders stretch his dark shirt.

Gorgeous.

But like Christian, we're not compatible.

"Emma." His deep voice snaps me back to reality.

I straighten. "Uh, what?"

He tilts his head, studying me. "Are you listening to me? Did you eat dinner?"

I blink, thrown off by his concern. "Oh! No. I had a salad for lunch."

His smirk deepens as he heads to the fridge, pulling out fruit and yogurt. He sits down beside me, his presence intimidating even in something as mundane as getting food.

"Pre-dinner snack. Take a bite," he orders, holding a spoonful of yogurt to my mouth.

Normally, I'd scoff and swat him away, but the air between us is thick — charged. My throat tightens as I realize what he's doing. Feeding me is dominance. A silent form of control.

But the strangest thing?

I obey.

I open my mouth, my lips brushing the spoon as he slides it in. The tangy bitterness makes me wince. "Gross," I mutter.

His smile is slow, knowing. "Don't like Greek yogurt? I thought you wanted me to feed you healthier foods."

Before I can argue, he holds a piece of cantaloupe to my lips, his other hand grazing my thigh. I hesitate, but he quirks an eyebrow. The look alone makes my stomach flip.

I take it.

As I chew, he watches me too closely. It's like he's measuring something. Analyzing.

I swallow hard, my skin buzzing under his scrutiny.

"Joar," I say carefully, shifting my weight. "Why do you make me eat?"

His muscled shoulders lift in a slow shrug. "You have food issues we need to work on."

We.

I inhale sharply. There's that goddamn word again.

I shouldn't feel so vulnerable, but it's as if he's stripping me down mentally, emotionally, layer by layer — until there's nowhere left to hide.

I straighten my spine. I need answers.

"Joar... um, are you a dominant?"

His expression stills. For the first time, a real flicker of surprise flashes across his face. "What?"

"A dom." My voice is firmer than I feel. "In BDSM, a dominant is the person who has control over their submissive, who—"

"I know what it means," he interrupts smoothly. His brows furrow as he regards me, his gaze dark. "What brought this on?"

I cross my arms. "Please, just answer the question."

Silence stretches between us, thick as molasses. His stormy eyes roam over my body, cataloging everything — my guarded stance, the way I bite my bottom lip, my clenched fists. He's too perceptive, too calculating.

Finally, he leans in, his voice as smooth as silk.

"Yes, Emma. I am a dominant."

I exhale shakily. *Of course he is.* Damn it.

My next words make me wince as I speak them. "And you want me to be your sub?"

"Not a sub." He tilts his head, his voice dropping lower. "*My* sub."

I swallow hard, hanging my head. My worst fears confirmed.

Joar strokes my thigh again, but this time, it's deliberate. Slow. Hypnotic. His palm is warm through my leggings.

"Relax, Emmy," he comforts.

I jerk away. "I can't! I thought things would get more normal. Or that spanking and a couple of rules were all I had to worry about. But now, I find out that's just the start. And if I stay with you, it will just get crazier and... more dangerous. I don't think we are a good match."

He exhales sharply, his patience ebbing. "Never talk about us breaking up."

I laugh, but it's humorless. "You cannot control what I say, Joar."

His eyes flash with something menacing. Something possessive. "You need to understand something, Emmy."

I cross my arms, trying to keep a strong exterior. "Oh? I think I understand this clearly."

His thumb brushes over my jaw, firm enough to silence me.

"You think this is just about sex?" he asks, his voice dangerously soft. "It's not. This is about you needing structure, care, and rules. I know what you need, even if you don't."

My breath catches, his words hitting too deep. "You don't know me. Not fully."

His smirk is infuriating. "I know you better than you know yourself. I know your nature. I know you need me."

I glare at him, but deep down, a big part of me wonders if he's right.

His fingers trace a slow path down my arm, his touch calm, controlled, consuming. "Have you heard of DDLG?"

I blink, thrown off. "What?"

"DDLG. Daddy Dom, Little Girl."

Heat rushes to my face. Oh, gosh. I read about that.

My mouth opens, but no words come out.

He leans in, his voice a velvet rasp. "It's not what you think. It's about trust. A woman like you... thrives on it. Structure. Protection. You need someone to take care of you, don't you, my helpless little one?"

My heart slams into my ribs.

Little one.

His eyes glint as though he can see the battle waging inside me. I hate the way my body reacts, my heart racing.

No. No, no, no.

I lean back. "I know what you're doing. You are trying to manipulate me into your twisted world."

Joar sighs, but his lips twitch in amusement. "Fine. I won't push... for now."

For now.

I sigh heavy. "Joar, we need to talk about—"

His expression darkens. "I know you had lunch with Christian."

My stomach drops. How did he...

His grip tightens slightly. "Let me guess. He fed you his bullshit about how I'm a predator?"

I swallow. "Joar—"

His voice is eerily calm. "Did you want him to be jealous? Make him regret cheating on you?"

I jerk back. "That's ridiculous!"

"Is it?"

Tears sting my eyes, frustration clawing at my throat. I hate how well he sees me.

"It was just to tell him about us, but it exposed who you really are." My voice drops. "I didn't mean to hurt you."

Joar's gaze is unreadable. "I'm not hurt. Just surprised after last night. Do you love him more than me?"

My jaw drops and I stammer, "I, uh. I told you that was role playing!"

"Emmy." His expression shifts to compassionate. "The way you begged... those tears. That was real."

I gawk, my insecurity urging me to run. I squeeze my eyes shut. "Joar... this isn't going to work. I think... we're over."

Silence.

He stands and pulls me close.

Then — his lips brush my ear, his voice like a promise. "That's not how this works, you sad little thing. I'm not done with you. Now answer my question. Do you love him more than me?"

Chapter 30

Emma

I know Joar is mad. His whole presence is a storm looming, but I can't hold back anymore. I'm too anxious, too hopeless.

...And the fact he knows I love him, it makes me feel worse. So, I deflect his question of whom I love more to keep my last ounce of dignity. "I didn't want us to break up, but BDSM? It's just... not for me. It's wrong and twisted."

His expression darkens, a shadow flickering across his features.

I blink at him, suddenly remembering *who* I'm dealing with. He's staring at me like he's deciding whether to punish me for that remark or let it slide. A chill runs down my spine, and I try to soften my words, my voice barely above a whisper.

"I meant, you are too *advanced* for me... I can't do BDSM. I'm... I'm sorry."

His smirk is slow, almost cruel. "We already do it, Emmy. And you're enjoying it."

"I am not!" I try to sound firm, but my voice wavers.

Joar chuckles, shaking his head. "Yes, you are. We don't need to label what we have. Besides, what exactly are you so worried about?"

"Everything!" My heart thrums. "I read all about it. Whips, torture, cages—"

His hand moves so fast I don't see it coming. A sharp tug at my waist, and suddenly, I'm flush against his body, my breath stolen. His fingers dig into my lower back, holding me in place with little effort.

"Those things are not my style," he murmurs, his lips brushing my cheek.

The heat of his body against mine makes me tingle, but I swallow, now trembling. "They're not your style?"

"No."

Relief washes over me, but it's short-lived as I force myself to ask, "Then what is? What about insulting me? Calling me names? You already call me your toy."

Joar trails his knuckle along my jaw, his voice dropping smooth. "I call you my toy because that's what you are. *Mine.* To use, to play with, to take apart piece by piece until you can't imagine belonging to anyone else."

I already do. I just rather be single than wait for Joar to cheat on me with a better sub.

I instinctively grab onto his wrists to pry them off and escape, but my fingers barely wrap around them. His strength is suffocating, paralyzing.

"Emma, do you think that's an insult? It's not. It's reality."

I shouldn't feel better at all, but a small bit of me does. And I hate myself for it.

Still, I linger in his gaze, my body betraying me, tilting toward his touch. When he cups my cheek, my breath catches, the heat of his palm sending a pulse of longing through me.

I ask, "Do you expect me to be your 'little?' And you be my 'daddy?'" My voice wobbles. "That's why you want me to call you that, isn't it? I would never like that, Joar."

His lips twitch, eyes glinting with wickedness. "You can't stop me, Emmy. I'll call you whatever I wish. You don't want me to stop, anyway."

I shove his chest, but he doesn't move an inch. He only laughs, the sound low and indulgent, like I just confirmed something for him.

"Relax." His lips skate along my neck. "The DDLG kink is perfect for you, though, and you need it."

I shake my head furiously.

"You're addicted to control, and it's killing you," he murmurs, his hand trailing up my waist, his fingers pressing into my ribs. "That's why I need to take it from you. It's balance. Moderation. It's what's missing in your mind. You can't be trusted with control over yourself."

"That's not true!"

"Isn't it?" His hold tightens. "I see how fucking lost you are. How much you need someone to take care of you. And it makes me hard as hell knowing that person is me."

I inhale sharply, my whole body burning, hating the way his words send my pulse racing.

"But I don't like all of it," he muses. "In fact, I hate the brat element... that is, until I met you. My subs always pretended to be brats. I don't play games, though. I want my sub submissive. But you?" His lips curl. "You can't help yourself, can you, you sad, desperate toy. So hungry for my discipline."

I sniffle, my chin trembling. His hand grips behind my neck, steady and possessive. "Calm down. Stop fighting what you already know is true. Being with me has helped you, and it will continue to help you. If there's something you need — a punishment, a lesson — I'll give it to you. And you'll thank me for it."

"Something I need?" I shake my head. "I don't *need* to be punished."

"I'll decide what you need."

I'm trying so hard to make excuses for Joar. There's so much I like about him, including being in his relentless hold. But honestly, it seems wrong.

"No. I don't agree with you, Joar. I don't need punishments."

His eyes brew with something I can't name, and before I can move, he grips my chin, forcing me to meet his gaze. "There's the brat in you. Defiant, running, fighting what you want," he scolds. "I hate that... and I love it. I can't wait to truly wreck you."

Then his lips are on my neck, hot and searing, his tongue indulging in the sensitive skin just below my ear.

I freeze, my fingers clutching his shirt.

"Joar—"

"Shhh." His hand remains on the back of my neck, keeping me still. "You were fine before your lunch with your worthless ex. You're letting someone weaker than you put nonsense in your head. He's trying to pull you away from me and I won't have it."

"But I can't trust you."

Which is true. I can't trust anyone.

However, his patience vanishes, his grip too tight, making me blurt, "You aren't even a good dominant. The articles say you should have gotten my consent before anything like spanking—"

"Fuck your articles." His voice drops, low and stern. "You want a contract, Emma? Want me to write it out in pretty little words for you?"

"That's what you were supposed to do! Not disciplining me or gifting a collar without explaining what it was."

I don't respond fast enough. Joar loops his finger under the chain around my neck and tugs just enough to steal my breath.

"Collar or necklace, what's the difference? You've been wearing it like one. Don't act like you didn't already know I claim you every chance I get. You love it."

I open my mouth, but no words come.

"I've been patient with you," he continues, dragging his lips over mine. "I've been so *fucking* patient. But don't mistake my patience for weakness. You're mine. I own you, Emmy. There's no way I'm letting you go, and I know you don't want me to."

I'm dizzy. I can't think, can't breathe.

He exhales. "But if you want to run, the door is open. You can leave." His fingers trail along my jaw, his thumb now pressing lightly against my parted lips, his arm still locked around me in an unrelenting grip. "However, I wouldn't wander off if I were you." His smirk is dark, knowing, like he's already won. "Because if you do, you'll miss me too much. You'll have to crawl back on your hands and knees, all broken and needy, begging for what only I can give you."

His finger dips into my mouth and holds down my tongue. "Because that's what you are, aren't you? A helpless, desperate girl who needs me more than she can admit."

Just then, his hand moves from my mouth and slips lower, jutting into my panties, his fingertips teasing, invading, stealing my breath. He thrusts his long finger into my warmth and a sharp gasp leaves my lips as he begins to take exactly what he wants: my will.

My body twists, instinctively resisting — but his grip tightens, keeping me caged against him.

"Stop... don't fight me," he murmurs, his voice thick with satisfaction. His pace is tortuously slow, yet powerful, coaxing pleasure from me with every deliberate movement. "You're driving your daddy crazy when you squirm like that."

My legs weaken, my body betraying me as I sink against his chest, my whimpers muffled against the soft fabric of his shirt.

"*That's right*," he breathes. "Such a sweet little thing." His voice drops as he adds in a surprisingly almost pained tone. "You're fucking up everything I thought I wanted. All my plans. I can't let something as precious as you be taken from me by a lesser man. No more lunches with your ex — *ever.*"

I don't move. I don't run. Because I know he's right. At this moment, all my anxiety dissipates. I'm his. Not Christian's.

He murmurs, "Now, who do you love more?"

Damn. He knows. He sees me.

Again, I whimper, my cheek pressed to his chest. With regret in my voice, I utter the truth: "I love you more."

With incredible tenderness, he kisses the top of my head, rewarding me.

I add in a whisper, "I wish you loved me, too. And please, don't tease me for saying it."

He doesn't speak. A rare moment where Joar neither punishes nor praises. I just don't understand why he won't say it since he supposedly wants me so much.

Chapter 31

Joar

This is a good day for Christian to die.

That fucking parasite wiggling his way into Emma's already overloaded mind is infuriating. She's weak when it comes to him — her resolve crumbling at the hands of the man who should disgust her. Yet she lets his words eat at her. That ends tonight.

I watch from the shadows as Christian tosses his car keys into a decorative bowl near the garage door, completely unaware he's already signed his death warrant. His lazy movements are those of a man who thinks he's untouchable.

He heads down the hall, flicking on the living room light as he passes through. Before he even turns around, I'm already in motion, my hockey stick raised, my grip tight.

The first swing lands across his ribs with a satisfying *crack*.

Christian stumbles forward, his body buckling from the force. He gasps, clutching his side as he staggers to keep his balance. His hand presses against the injured area, his wide-eyed gaze darting back to me.

"You?" His voice is strained, barely a whisper.

I nod, the grin on my face stretching slow and cruel. "Take a seat," I order, nodding to the chair I've positioned in front of his massive TV. He hesitates, eyes flicking toward the door, but one look at my stance — stick in hand, ready to swing again — tells him this isn't an option.

He lowers himself into the chair with a slow, careful movement, his breath coming in sharp, pained inhales. "For a guy who figure skates, this is a nice place you've got," I remark, glancing at the expensive furniture and the grand piano collecting dust in the corner.

"A good career and social media," he mutters. He's trying to keep his voice even, but I hear the waver.

Perfect.

With his coffee table already shoved aside, I step to the center of the room. Next to my shoes is a neat little stack of hockey pucks. One by one, they'll all serve their purpose.

Christian shifts uncomfortably. "What the fuck are you doing?"

I don't answer. I send the first puck flying straight at his expensive TV. The impact is deafening, the glass spiderwebbing on impact. He flinches hard.

I grin. "Why did you have lunch with my girlfriend?"

"She's my friend!" he spits out, wincing as his ribs still protest.

"Not anymore." I send another puck flying, this one skimming the top of his shoulder before shattering the liquor cabinet behind him. The glass explodes, raining down in shards.

"She invited me, man! Besides, she'd think it's weird if I suddenly quit talking to her after all these years. We work together. Be realistic."

"I *am* being realistic. You dated her. There's no reason for you to still be around." I cock my head. "Resign and get a new job."

Christian sighs, exasperated. "Jesus Christ, trust me. Emma and I will never get back together."

I grip my hockey stick tighter. "Best not," I sneer.

He scoffs but takes a sharp inhale. "Date her long enough and you'll see for yourself. She has some *issues*."

I raise a brow. "How so?"

Christian hesitates.

I flip my stick around, pressing the end firmly against his groin.

His breath hitches.

"How so?" I repeat, my voice dangerously low.

He squirms but doesn't answer, his lips pressed into a tight line.

I push harder.

"*Okay!*" he yelps. "She's... too fucked up, alright? She's a prude. And it makes her boring in bed. I'm into the scene, like you — BDSM. I need a sub. She's a dom."

I freeze, the words sinking in.

Emma? A dom?

That's the biggest load of bullshit I've ever heard.

I exhale a slow breath, shaking my head. "Wrong."

"No, I'm serious, man. She might be submissive to her tiger mom, but she's not in the sack. Her mom *fucked* with her head bad." He leans forward slightly, ignoring his pain, as if this is his chance to *warn* me.

"Do you know anything about that type of Chinese parenting? It's fucking brutal. I never saw Mei give her a hug. Not once. No praise. No *'good jobs.'* No 'I *love yous.'*" Not to her or me, even when we won competitions. It made Emma *uptight as hell.* Do you know about Mr. Needle? How her mom jabs her with pins to secretly correct her behavior in public. Ask who taught her how to throw up to lose weight. She was eleven! Ask her about the lighter! Mei is bonkers."

I stare at him, knowing little about tiger moms other than they are strict. Poor girl. I know Emma's got issues. Her insecurities, her fear of failure, the way she shies from attention yet begs for it — *it all makes sense now.*

Christian keeps talking. "Hell, in all the years I've known her, she cried once: When she found me in bed with another woman."

I hide my smile, loving that my Emmy has already bared her soul to me several times. I love her tears. They're raw, and now, they're apparently reserved just for me.

I shrug. "I know about you and Ophelia. Pathetic move."

"Phh! Sleep with her! You'll see. She thinks everything is degrading. Doggy style? Nope. Blowjobs? No chance. If I so much as grabbed her wrist, she'd tense up like I was about to murder her. She has no trust, and I wasn't willing to waste my time fixing it."

I blink, trying to rid my mind of visions of this guy fucking my girl.

Fuck it.

My stick swings full-force, colliding with his forearm.

A *snap* echoes through the room.

Christian screams, clutching his now *very* broken arm as he hunches over, his body wracked with pain.

But I'm not finished.

I drop the hockey stick and grab him by the collar, dragging him out of the chair and onto his knees. His face is already pale, his forehead beading with sweat.

With a single punch, I break his nose.

He chokes on a scream, blood gushing down his lips and dripping onto the pristine hardwood floor.

I don't stop there.

I punch him again. And again.

His face swells, both eyes turning dark, his lip splitting open. His body sags under the weight of my blows, but I hold him up, making sure he takes every hit.

By the time I'm done, he's a fucking mess.

I crouch in front of him, gripping his shattered forearm in my hand and squeezing hard enough to make him nearly pass out from the pain.

"If you call the cops," I murmur, my voice eerily calm, "I'll get out on bail and finish the job."

Christian nods weakly, tears mixing with the blood on his face. "I — I won't," he croaks. "You fucking psycho..."

I release him, standing to my full height. I should kill him. I *want* to kill him. But I already got what I came for.

As I turn for the door, my mind is racing.

Is Emma going to be this difficult *forever*? Or will I have to break her little by little until she finally lets go? I don't mind a fight, but I refuse to battle her every damn day.

And now, after what I've just learned...

She *is* my submissive. I can't let her go.

And I know why.

Chapter 32

Emma

I can't wait to get home to Joar — to feel his strong arms hold me, to talk about our day, to lose myself in the quiet comfort of being his. It's a rare feeling, knowing someone will be happy to see me.

To show him my appreciation, I got him a gold watch. He doesn't wear one, but I don't know what else to give a man like him — a hockey player, a force of nature. Christian was so different.

Just then, the elevator doors slide open, but I don't move. My breath catches in my throat.

Joar stands in the middle of the busy lobby, his oversized hockey bag slung over his broad shoulder. He's smiling wide, laughing.

With *her*.

That evil, evil... *bitch*: Ophelia.

The doors start to close, and I lunge forward, stepping out. My pulse pounds as I approach, each step slower than the last as I take in the scene. Her hand reaches out — *touching him* — playfully pushing against his chest.

My vision tunnels and I hurry my pace.

"Hi," I say curtly, my eyes darting between them.

Ophelia's lips part slightly before she forces a smile, her tone airy but losing its excitement. "Oh, hey, Emma... Just catching up with our star player here." She flicks her gaze toward Joar, teasing under her breath, "I always have to ambush you, don't I?"

My fingers twist together as I bite my bottom lip, my pulse inching higher.

She doesn't know we're together. No one does. I assume Joar understands that my mother would kill me if she found out. Kill *us*. But that doesn't explain why Ophelia is so damn comfortable touching him.

Plus, she saw my breakdown at the hotel!

She knows finding them together upset me. She wouldn't — *she couldn't* — be pushing it further.

Not after I found her in bed with Christian, him fucking her bent over, her perfect body wrapped in red lingerie.

I shake off the horrific memory.

Joar's eyes are already on me. Without thinking, I step between them and face him as though I'm a barrier. I'm desperate to break their connection as I stumble for an excuse. "I need to... speak with Ophelia... about stuff."

I nudge his arm, urging him to leave. But he doesn't budge. Instead, his expression sharpens, his head tilting slightly as he assesses me. His stare says everything: *Don't tell me what to do.*

But I'm not intimidated. Not with her so close. So I push him harder, both hands against his chest as I plead with my eyes.

His glare darkens, and he drops his bag onto the floor with a thud — *a punishment.* Like he's planting his stay, daring me to try that again.

My stomach clenches. *Fine.* I spin to Ophelia, taking a single step closer.

I'll just block her out myself.

The tension between us tightens to the point of snapping, though. Ophelia shifts, glancing between Joar and me with curiosity. "So, uh... are you two seeing each other or something?"

My breath stalls. She's *too* perceptive. Always has been. The ultimate social butterfly.

Across the lobby, I spot Mother leaving for the day, her sharp, no-nonsense expression scanning the room, but not spotting us in the bustling area. Still, the pressure mounts in my chest, my throat closing in panic.

I blurt out, too loud, too fast, "God no! We're not together. I'd never date players."

Ophelia blinks. "Oh. Yeah, I get that. Being GM and all. It's good to be... so professional."

My ears ring. My heartbeat is deafening against my eardrums. I want to turn, to cling to Joar, to beg him to make this moment disappear.

But instead, I nod like a *fucking* coward.

She says cooly, "Good, because after the hotel, I was worried your little crush on our star player was something we should talk about."

"Oh, no! I was emotional that night. Too much to drink!" I yip, my face hot with shame.

I glance at Joar, who holds such disgust in his gaze that I have to look away.

And just when I think it can't get worse, Dana — the overly friendly blonde from marketing — breezes in. "Hey, hey, hey," she practically sings, her hand outstretched to Joar. "Here's our reclusive player!"

I step back as she snatches his hand, my stomach twisting further.

"You sure hate giving interviews, don't you?" Dana laughs. "Ophelia has to work overtime to wrangle you."

Joar merely nods, unimpressed. "They aren't my favorite."

Dana gushes, "Gee, you are *so* handsome." Then, *out of fucking nowhere*, she reaches over and lifts his shirt to his chest, revealing his washboard abs. In what feels like slow motion, her slender fingertips float down their ridges.

I might die as I recall his naked body over me, that rippled stomach radiating heat on my skin. His powerful hips between my legs.

He was mine. But with one flirty touch, now he isn't.

Dana doesn't know my heart is stuttering hard. She grins. "Look at his abs! We should do a calendar with you and some of the other starters. Sergey, Ivan. Our female fans would *love* that."

"And some men, too," Ophelia adds with an impish smile.

Dana nods enthusiastically. "Yep, yep, yep! Why don't we get drinks now? Go over the details?"

I try to gasp, but my chest is frozen. A reel of the three of them together plays, drinking, laughing, late into the night. Ophelia's hand sliding up Joar's thigh. Her breath against his ear. Joar's arm slung around her, a lazy smirk on his lips as he pulls her closer. She slips onto his lap. They kiss.

Hearing gone.

Breathing gone.

Darkness.

A voice, distant and muffled crisps. "Emma! Emma!"

Everything is blurry — faces merging, voices echoing in disjointed panic.

"Emmy," says a deeper, familiar whisper. The heat of an arm securing me against something solid.

Joar.

Dana's hand squeezes mine. "Jesus, Emma! Are you okay? Should we call an ambulance?"

My head spins. My body sways as I slip from Joar's hold.

No, *no*. My coworkers are staring. Gawking. Their concern only fueling my humiliation.

PUNISH & PRAISE

"I'm fine," I force out. My voice is wrong, weak, pathetic. "I didn't eat today. Low blood sugar is all."

Tears sting my eyes. I will them away as I always do in public. I sling my purse over my shoulder, trying to stand taller, trying to salvage what little dignity I have left. "I'm fine. I swear."

I can't even look at Joar.

And then I see her. Ophelia. Her gaze pins me in place. She knows. She knows this wasn't low blood sugar. It was a panic attack. And worse? She knows exactly *why*.

She saw me break over Christian. And now, she's seeing me break over Joar. Maybe that's her thing. Maybe she enjoys taking what other women love.

More tears threaten. I can't be here. I *have* to escape.

"I have a snack in my desk," I mutter. "I'll eat before I leave."

I don't wait for a response. I slip away and rush toward the elevators, my heels clicking against the tile as I all but flee. The moment I step inside, I stab the button, my breath ragged, my chest aching.

The doors start to close, but Joar steps in.

I stiffen.

The second the doors shut, his tone is sharp. "What the *fuck* was that?"

I cover my mouth, shaking my head, trying to erase the last five minutes from existence. "Nothing," I whisper. "I do that sometimes when I haven't eaten."

241

His stare pierces through me. He sees the lie, the shame, the way my shoulders hunch. He sees everything... And I break.

My chin quivers, my breath shattering into a sob — one I can't hold back, one I don't even try to.

Joar immediately pulls me in, locking me against his chest, his arms forming an impenetrable cage around me.

I cling to him, shaking. "I *hate* that woman." My voice is muffled against his shirt. "Please, Joar... don't fuck her. It will kill me. You have no idea!"

"Shh," he soothes, stroking my head, petting me. "You're my girl. Only you."

I squeeze him tighter, desperate to believe it. Desperate to drown in the security of his touch. He holds me like he means it, like he's anchoring me down before I disappear entirely.

I sniffle, my voice small. "Please don't bring this up. I don't want to talk about it. Can we just go to your place?"

He nods. But for the second time, *he* seems lost. Just like when I confessed that I loved him. My panic attack rattled him. It's as if he doesn't know what to do with this version of me. And that, more than anything, makes me feel *defective*.

Maybe I've scared him again — or repulsed him — enough that he will leave me this time.

God! Why can't I be normal? I hate being such a nervous, high-strung person.

He whispers once more. "Emmy, I want everyone to know you're mine. We should tell people."

I squeeze my eyes shut. "I... it's too soon."

An irritated sigh follows, prompting me to snap, "Well! You let other women touch you! You'll probably cheat and then I'll look like a fool at work."

"Women touch athletes. They think we like it. A lot of us do. But I pushed her hand off, or did you not see that?"

"Uh."

"And that was after you told Ophelia you would never date me. Come on, Emma. Do you want me or not?"

I search for words, but I falter. I suddenly realize I am the bad guy. I didn't consider how I would make him feel. He always seems so unaffected by everything.

"Sorry," I squeak.

"Figure it out, Emma. Because right now, I don't feel like you want to be with me."

I squeeze him so tight, showing him how much that is untrue. He has to feel my distress as my body trembles in his arms.

Yet, he says nothing more.

It must be true. He's rattled.

Chapter 33

Emma

Later that night, I sit up in bed while Joar sleeps beside me. I glance over, wondering if he considered leaving me today in the elevator. The doubts fester despite my best efforts to believe him, making the desire to binge and purge overwhelming.

I'll just slip out of the bedroom, raid the fridge, and purge in the kitchen sink so he won't hear. That will make me feel better.

Just as I move to rise from the bed, I glance at him again. My stomach clenches like I've already failed him. I replay my last punishment — how his powerful hand stung across my backside, how sharp the pain was, how relieving it was afterward when he pressed his fingers between my lips, letting me suck on them.

An escape.

If I suck on his fingers again, maybe it will help.

My pulse quickens as I weigh my options: Purge... or try something else.

I crawl back onto the bed, careful not to wake him. Without moving his arm, I slowly take two of his fingers into my mouth, stopping at the second knuckle.

The effect is immediate. A wave of calm blankets me, warmth spreading through my limbs. I curl up against him, clutching his wrist like a lifeline, my tongue gliding softly as I nurse on his fingers. This is comfort. This is connection. This is safety.

If he woke up — *God*, he would think I'm so weird. But with this much anxiety, I feel like I'm dying anyway. I choose comfort.

And for a moment, it works. The desperation to purge dissipates.

But my anxiety is a relentless beast, whispering insidiously in my ear, twisting, growing louder as the minutes pass. My thoughts spin out of control, flooding my mind with every terrible possibility.

I keep replaying all my conversations with Joar. There is one thing that keeps bothering me, though: The door is open and I can leave.

Now that he witnessed me publicly fall apart, I fear he'll push me out the door. Or maybe my value to him is contingent on whether I make our relationship public... or become a less uptight person.

But, I'm can't and I'm not. I'm a disappointment. I always have been.

I imagine living with him for a year. A perfect year. Then one night, I open the bedroom door and find him in bed with Ophelia. She has a black mask, tied up, latex lingerie, begging him to give it to her harder — the perfect submissive he actually wants.

And like Christian, Joar defends himself, saying he cheated because I wasn't enough. I didn't satisfy him.

I failed. *Again.*

My eyes snap open. My pulse hammers in my ears.

Joar is still asleep, but I feel worse than before. I tighten my lips around his fingers, sucking harder, seeking that same numbing relief.

But it's not enough.

My anxiety snowballs — memories flashing, thoughts slamming into me, heart pounding against my ribs.

Ophelia talking to him. Dana touching him. A lobby full of people judging me.

My skin flashes hot. Sweat beads along my spine. My breath shortens, chest clenching, panic mounting. I have to do something.

Desperate to stop the spiral, I turn off every reservation, every hesitation, and seek the one thing that has always grounded me.

Sucking on Joar.

But this time, I want more than just his fingers.

I want him.

Gently, I kneel beside him and peel down the front of his underwear. His cock is warm and heavy in my hand, already half-hard.

I hesitate. Just for a second. Is this wrong?

No. He's my boyfriend.

With the lightest touch, I lower my mouth. The tip brushes against my lips, and I freeze.

Is this rape?

No. He wants this. Guys love this.

When he doesn't stir, I part my lips and take him inside my mouth, letting his length slide along my tongue.

The relief is instant — better than his fingers. The panic, the noise, the storm inside me — everything slows.

I exhale through my nose, sinking deeper, taking him to the back of my throat, fitting as much as I can without hitting my gag reflex. My lashes flutter shut, and I apply gentle suction, savoring the closeness to him, the way my lips mold around his girth.

Then it happens: His cock twitches. His thighs tense.

I freeze. He's waking up. My breath catches in my throat as I feel his body rouse beneath me.

A slow inhale.

A subtle flex of his muscles.

And then, a shift.

His heavy gaze drifts downward, locking onto me.

I lift my head, my face burning as I release him from my lips. I don't know what to do. What to say. So I stammer, "Uh... I um... was anxious, and I want to please you."

Joar doesn't move. His chest rises and falls steadily, his stare piercing into me.

Finally, he speaks. His voice is low, cautious. "Okay. Good."

But something's off. Something changed since the lobby.

His gaze stays on me, sharp and calculating. He looks at me like I'm unpredictable. Like I'm something he can't quite trust.

Still, he licks his lips, and slowly, he threads his fingers into my hair.

With the lightest pressure, he pushes my head back down.

My lips part as I take him into my mouth again. But the security I felt moments ago is gone.

Now, there's only insecurity.

I start overthinking: Is a sub supposed to do this differently? Am I doing it wrong?

I force myself to focus, to push away the doubt. But then — a terrible thought... Ophelia sucking Joar better than me.

The image guts me.

Determined, I hollow my cheeks, working him with more effort. I need to be better than her. Or any woman. I need to prove I can please him fully. But the anxiety creeps back in.

I hesitate. Glancing up, I search his expression. "Am I doing this how you like it?"

Joar's eyes are still fixed on me, dark with approval. His hand tightens in my hair, his voice deep as he murmurs, "You're doing everything perfectly. Such a good girl. Keep going."

The words ripple through me like a drug. A rush of relief. A pulse of arousal.

Being called *good girl* has my clit throbbing so hard, I can't stop myself. I start grinding against his leg, dragging my soaked panties along the hard muscle.

Joar groans, his fingers curling tighter in my hair.

"That's my needy girl," he breathes, voice strained. "Just like that."

But then it happens. An abrupt, violent realization. If I like this, then who am I? I wouldn't have been this comfortable with Christian. Damn, I love Joar. I love him so much. And I'm going to lose him.

Because of *this*. Because I can't shut off my brain.

I falter, slowing.

Joar notices immediately. His voice shifts — commanding and firm. "Don't stop."

I stop entirely, lifting my head, whispering, "I can't do this, Joar. I'm not what you want."

His hand ghosts along my jawline before gripping it fully. His tone drops lower, sharper. "Oh yes, this *is* what I want. Now put those pretty lips back around my cock."

I shake my head, eyes stinging. "But I can't do it right..."

His fingers tangle in my hair. He tightens his hold. "Listen carefully. You will make me cum in that tight little throat of yours. And after I cum, you will swallow every drop to show Daddy how much you love him."

A sharp, breathless gasp escapes me.

He's not asking. And God help me — I obey.

I wrap my lips around him again, hollowing my cheeks once more, taking him deep.

"That's it," he growls, his muscles firm beneath me. "But now, take off your panties and ride my leg again. I want to feel your little, wet cunt beg for more."

I do as he orders and slip off my underwear. Then I grind against him and suck at the same time. And to my surprise, I'm ravenous. I love it. Not long after grinding my clit against him, I come undone.

As I return to my senses, I'm trembling against him. My mind had turned off and my body took over.

"Wow, little one," he breathes, his voice low and husky as he takes in the sight of my shaking body. "You look so pathetic like this, and it drives me fucking insane."

With force, he feeds his cock back into my mouth, and this time, his pull on my hair is almost painful. Yet, I want more, and suck him with greater vigor, bobbing my head faster.

"Oh, fuck, Emmy," he moans, his eyes closed. "You're ruining me."

He might just be caught in the moment, but hearing that deep voice speak those words, and that glorious moan coming from his sexy lips... it's utterly euphoric.

I release my mouth from his shaft, gasping for air, then purr, "Good, because I want to ruin you the way you ruined me."

The second the words leave my lips, I regret it. What did I just say? Those are not my words. That's not me. I'd never say something like that. Never mean it so completely.

Yet, it's true.

It's because I love him so much. Because I do want to please him, taste him, fall prey to him. And yes, I want to ruin him. I need him in a way that terrifies me, but still, he needs to be mine. Only mine.

Oh no. Panic crashes down. He can't leave me. He can't. Because if he does, I don't know if I'll survive it.

I push up on my elbows, my breath ragged. I meet his gaze, searching wildly for reassurance, for something to grasp onto before I fall apart completely.

"Joar," I nearly shout, fear slicing through my voice. "Tell me you're not leaving me after what happened today in the lobby. *Right now!* Please! Tell me this isn't just about sex. Tell me you don't think I'm unlovable because I'm so messed up. God, Joar! Why don't you love me?"

Chapter 34

Emma

Joar glares down at me, the same intimidating expression he wore in the lobby. A flicker of something sharp and assessing glints in his gaze, like he's weighing me, dissecting me, deciding something I'm not privy to.

I *hate it.*

I want him to look at me the way he did before — like I was his, like I was something precious. Now, his stare feels different. Detached. Calculating.

It's killing me.

"Calm down, Emma. Maybe you need sleep," he says, his voice flat, apparently dodging my questions.

I swallow the lump rising in my throat. "No, Joar. I *need* answers. Are you leaving me? Am I unlovable after you saw me freak out in public? You're looking at me differently."

Slowly, he sits up, his expression guarded. Emmy..." His gaze flicks down to his rock hard cock, and I know, he's confused by my abrupt outburst in the middle of such an intimate act.

But I can't pretend we are fine when my heart tells me otherwise. "Did I ruin everything in the lobby today? Answer me, please!" I beg.

"This is about the lobby?"

"Yes! Do you think I'm defective?" My voice trembles, but I don't care. "I scared you, didn't I?"

His lips twitch into a sly smile, and for a split second, I see the Joar I recognize — the arrogant, unshakable man who doesn't flinch at anything.

I pout, desperate now. "*Please.*"

He rolls his eyes, but there's something almost indulgent in the action. Like I'm a child throwing a fit over something he already has the solution for. As if my emotions are a game he's already won.

With indifference lacing his voice, he says, "Come on. Get dressed. I want to take you somewhere." He gets out of bed, pulling on his shirt and pants before grabbing his keys.

After a quick drive, we pull up to the stadium.

"Joar, what are we doing here?" I ask as we walk inside.

"Get your skates and meet me on the ice," he replies and heads for the locker room. I rub my eyes, still wondering why the hell he brought me here, but do as he ordered.

Once on the ice, I look around the bright, giant space. The whole stadium is empty this late. No Zamboni driver, skaters, custodians, or fans. Just me and Joar.

He glides to my side and hands me a hockey stick before heading to the empty net, holding a goalie's stick. He gestures to a cluster of pucks in the middle of the rink. "Go ahead and take a shot."

I scoff and fold my arms. "First of all, I will not hit a puck at our seven-million-dollar player who has no pads or helmet. Secondly — why?"

"What? Do you think you can actually hurt me?" he asks.

It's clear he's taunting me, but my competitive side can't resist the challenge. Once I skate to the pucks, I pick up a few, stuffing them into the pockets of my jacket.

Casually, I skate toward Joar, stopping about five yards in front of him.

He shakes his head. "What are you doing? You have to hit from the middle of the rink."

"Why? Are you scared I'll hurt you?" I tease and drop a puck. Just as quick, I swing the stick as hard as I can, making good contact with the side. The black disc speeds across the slick ice, heading straight for a gap into the net. Yet, he casually blocks it with his skate.

"Maybe you should come even closer," he jeers.

I sigh and tilt my head. "Joar. Why are we here?"

His expression remains calm. "I want to make a bet. If you score, I'll answer your questions. But if you don't—" He pauses, his lips curling at the edges. "You drop to your knees and finish what you started earlier."

My stomach plummets.

"In the middle of this rink?" I gape.

He nods. "Your knees on this cold, hard ice."

I clutch my stick tighter, pulse spiking. "But if I win, you'll answer all my questions? Truthfully?"

He nods again, but there's something else in his gaze — something dark.

Disappointment?

"Okay... deal," I say.

With my answers so close, I quickly strategize. I don't know how to get a puck airborne high enough to slip past him. And I doubt I'm fast enough to sneak one through.

Joar squares himself by the net, waiting.

Just then, an idea sparks in my head.

I smile. "Ready?"

He nods, and I start skating forward, guiding the puck carefully with my stick's blade. His brow lifts, clearly surprised I'm moving with it instead of shooting from a standstill.

As I close in on him, I scoop the puck as best I can, launching it toward the net. Joar extends his arm, blocking it easily.

But I was ready for that. Quickly, I pull a second puck from my pocket and flick it into a gap. It lands in the net before he even realizes what happened.

Got him.

"I win!" I cheer, throwing my arms up. "No freezing knees for me tonight!"

Grinning smugly, I start a victory lap around the rink, reveling in my own genius. I glance back, expecting to see his usual smirk.

But instead, his gaze is locked on his palm. It's smeared with blood.

"Oh my God! What happened?" I gasp and hurry to him, my skates cutting through the hard ice.

Chapter 35

Emma

Joar's front incisor is missing, and blood outlines his teeth.

My eyes widen in shock, but the moment I register the gaping hole in his perfect, cocky grin, a laugh bubbles up uncontrollably. I shake my head furiously, pressing a hand over my mouth to contain it.

"Oh my God, your tooth! I'm so sorry!" But I still can't hold back my laughter, the absurdity of the situation making it impossible.

Joar smirks, running his tongue over the empty space. "You high-sticked me, you dirty little player."

My laughter only increases. "I *told* you I didn't want to hurt our most valuable player!"

His eyes darken with a mischievous glint, and I instinctively tense. That look never means anything good for me.

"It's okay," he says, closing the space between us, his lips twisted into something wicked. "Come here. Give daddy a kiss to make it better."

My heart jumps into my throat as I skate backward, my laughter turning into nervous shrieks. "No way! Stay away from me!"

"Just one kiss," he coaxes, his pace quickening with little effort.

I squeal, still giggling, but I know I'm doomed. In one powerful stride, Joar closes the distance, his arms wrapping around my waist like a steel trap. I press my hands against his chest, trying to push him off, but it's useless. He leans in, his mouth *too close*, teasingly hovering against mine before pulling back a smidge.

"Behave," he taunts. "I want my kiss."

I can't stop laughing and trying to pry myself free.

Finally, he releases me, allowing me to skate away. He watches with that smug, knowing grin, the one that always makes me feel like I'm losing some silent battle.

"See how happy I make you?" he says.

I shake my head, but chuckle as warmth blooms in my chest. "You make me *something*," I reply, heading toward the players' bench.

Joar follows, stepping off the ice as I rummage for a towel. I find one and turn to face him. "Here," I say, gesturing for him to sit.

He straddles the bench. I wet the rag and start dabbing at the blood on his jaw. As I wipe beneath his chin, his light stubble grazes my fingertips. My touch lingers, my eyes studying the sharp angles of his face, the softness of his lips. The tension shifts — no longer playful.

"Do I look better?" he asks, voice low, eyes locked onto mine.

I swallow. "No more blood," I say softly. "But smile for me."

He flashes a big, toothy grin, and I burst into laughter again. "Oh gosh, I'm definitely with a hockey player now. I'm so sorry I hit you."

Joar smirks, unbothered, and takes the water bottle from me. He rinses and leans over the boards, spitting red onto the ice. I make a disgusted sound. "Ugh, Joar! You're such a brute."

"Yes," he agrees casually, grinning wider.

Now that I know he's okay, my confidence surges. "Well, I won."

He leans in, his lips grazing my cheek before he murmurs, "That was a clever goal. Yes, you won the bet, my sly girl."

My stomach flips. He must see the heat in my cheeks because his smirk grows bigger. "What? Why are you blushing?"

I nod, biting my lip. "I guess you surprise me sometimes. You're unpredictable, rough, stubborn... but sometimes you can be so sweet."

Joar chuckles darkly. "Then you'll probably think it's extra sweet that I let you keep your victory, even though that goal didn't count."

I narrow my eyes. "What do you mean?"

"You high-sticked me. Goaltender interference. That goal would be disallowed."

"What! So I didn't actually win?"

He shrugs. "Emma, I planned to step aside and let you score at the end. The point of this wasn't to make do anything. It was to prove that I could force you to your knees in the middle of this rink... but I didn't."

My breath catches.

Joar watches me intently, his voice soft but firm. "See? This isn't about sex for me. But you should know that by now." His fingers trace the edge of my sleeve, grounding me, tethering me to him. "To answer your other questions — what happened in the lobby didn't scare me. And no, I don't think you're defective. You're *wounded*, Emmy. But I want to heal you."

The words hit like a freight train.

"You okay?" he asks.

I look around, feeling unsteady, like the weight of his words is too much to absorb. Buy I also know he's avoiding my biggest question, but I can't bear the answer. Therefore, I ask the lesser of the two remaining. "So... so, you're *not* leaving me?"

His gaze sharpens, his teasing gone. "Leave you?" He exhales slowly, shaking his head. "That's cute." His fingers slip beneath my chin, tilting my face up to his. "But I wouldn't ask that question again unless you want to be bent over my knee."

A helpless smile tugs at my lips despite my best efforts to suppress it. I look down, trying to hide how much that answer soothes me. But as my eyes drop to the bench, an intrusive thought surfaces — giving Joar a BJ right here, in the middle of the empty stadium.

It's completely outside my comfort zone. But I *want* to do this for him.

"Joar, um..." I wet my lips, summoning courage. "I want to finish what I started."

His eyes darken instantly, his entire body going still. Then, slow and deliberate, he smirks. "*Is that so?* You want to please me?"

I nod. "Yes. But... not here. Please?"

His smirk doesn't fade, but his voice drops an octave, thick with amusement. "Okay."

Joar moves.

Fast.

His fingers lock around my wrist, yanking me forward so suddenly I stumble. My heart slams against my ribs as he spins me around, bending me over the boards before I can protest. My hands splay against the cold surface, my breath coming in sharp gasps as my chest presses flush against the board's hard edge.

The sound of his zipper fills the air.

"Joar! Not here!" I gasp, squirming. "And I meant a BJ! What are you doing?"

He exhales, the sound low and wicked, sending a shiver down my spine. "Finishing what you started," he says.

I try to push up, but his hand is already on my back, holding me down. His grip is firm, immovable. "You're not going anywhere," he growls. "Not until my cum is dripping from your cunt."

The dominance in his voice seeps into my bloodstream, a powerful mix of fear and anticipation twisting in my stomach. There's no stopping him now.

And God help me — I don't want to.

Chapter 36

Emma

I am about to have sex here. At work. In an ice rink!

I can't. What if someone walks in? A BJ is one thing, but I'm so powerless to hide being bent over and in Joar's grip.

Determined to end this madness, I push up on the boards once more, but Joar holds me down and scolds, "Tsk, tsk. Don't make me punish you first."

"It's just... what if we get caught?" But my words fall on deaf ears as I hear him spit and lather his cock. Then, the sensation of his blunt tip meets my entrance, followed by a powerful thrust forward. His shaft tears through my hips and strains my sides. Despite his abrupt entry, I'm still worried about being caught. The reel of possible scenarios plays. "Joar! What if a player sees us? I'm half naked!"

In a disinterested tone, he replies, "No talking. Your only job right now is to take me — and this is gonna hurt, my pretty fucktoy."

His words are jarring, and I balk. However, he doesn't acknowledge my concern. And like he's been dying to do this, Joar grips my hips and pummels me, penetrating with powerful, deep thrusts!

But despite his force, I've been sexually frustrated since we left the bedroom. The friction of his cock alone easily intensifies the lingering ache in my hips. Soon, my arousal slicks his long shaft, and as he pumps and warm streams roll down my thighs. I cringe, overwhelmed by my need to keep everything clean, and my fear Joar will be repulsed.

I guess this is a good thing, though... I don't know what every guy wants to see in bed, but I assume a very wet pussy is desirable.

A stab shakes me to my core, and quickly, I realize he hasn't been putting in his full length until now.

Oh no... His cock hits so deep, so hard, that I have to brace myself and clutch the board's edge with all my might. Although it's great to have a guy with the length and width of Joar's, it can definitely hurt.

"Not so deep, please!" I beg.

"Breathe through it. You're made to take me, Emmy."

However, he does slow down a little, making it more bearable. I squeeze my eyes shut, knowing I can't escape him — nor want to.

I override my mind and put in an earnest effort to focus on how good it feels to be ravaged by this man. Yes — I'm giving up my control. Having control just causes stress, anyway, so him taking it is actually a huge relief.

Thus, I savor the burden being lifted. I also repeat the many times Joar has said I'm beautiful, reminding myself to be more confident in my body.

In time, my crumbling inhibitions allow pleasure to build and override the pain. The friction on my g-spot, the steady give of my pussy to fit his shaft, and the closeness of his incredible body pushes me higher. I enter a state of increasing euphoria and can't help but let my doubts and self-loathing fade as I moan his name in a loud, ethereal cry. My outburst causes him to pump even faster, and I practically yell again and again, "Ohhh, Joar. Joar! Mmm!"

"Is my mouthy brat enjoying herself? I told you I'd get you to scream my name," he says, triggering me to clench down hard.

"Mm-hm." I nod as I look back at him.

He returns a devilish grin.

That sexy smile and his touch send me into a hazy, erotic state where the only thing that matters is him. The tension in my muscles eases, and the sharp edges of discomfort blur.

"Such a good girl," he praises, his voice rough with approval.

He snakes his hand under my hips and finds the nub of my clit. He massages the concentration of nerves and slows his pace, giving me deep sensual thrusts to intensify my pleasure. His fingertips and steady rhythm cause my body and mind to give in more than ever before. My sides clamp down and my body tremors as I near my apex of bliss.

In a husky voice, he breathes out, "Fuck, I'm addicted to making your body shake like this."

Hearing his words is pleasurable on its own, let alone him fucking me at the same time. It's perfect, and I come undone. His arm hooks under me as euphoria weakens my body, my knees buckling to the rush of endorphins. I claw the board, trying to keep upright as I practically pass out. As he holds my hips up, I savor the blissful sensation of his hard, throbbing cock deep inside me. My orgasm is so intense that my fingertips slip from the edge. But I don't fall, secured in his powerful hold.

His voice cuts through, "That's right, cum on daddy's cock with your pretty pussy."

I shiver.

That sexy tone in his voice is earthshaking, and as I catch my breath, I murmur breathlessly, "You're my everything, Joar. If you only knew."

Just as quick as the words leave my mouth, his body tenses, breath cuts short, and his eyes snap shut. Right away, I know he's cumming. I tilt and swirl my hips, giving him extra friction as he reaches the height of his pleasure.

He takes heavy breaths and comes down from his high, his cock still buried inside. When his eyes flutter open, I'm looking over my shoulder, feeling like a schoolgirl with a crush. He doesn't return a smirk like I expect, though.

What's wrong?

I'm a little nervous by his coldness. The only thing I can think to say is, "That felt good, huh?"

He nods as he does up his pants.

I dress too, then squeeze his hand, feeling anxious.

Oh, I know! Maybe he is mad about earlier. "Uh, Joar, is it okay that I gave you a blowjob when you were sleeping... and that I woke you?"

"Yes. You're supposed to wake me when you're anxious."

I blink, his words catching me off guard. "I am?"

Before I can process it, he yanks me close — *hard*. His arms coil around me like steel, his hold unrelenting, forcing the air from my lungs. My hands press against his chest, but there's no escaping. His body is tense, his breath heavy near my ear as he speaks — low, raw, almost desperate.

"To answer your question, no, you are not unlovable. Don't ever fucking ask that again."

The sheer force of his words roots me in place, my pulse hammering.

"I haven't felt this way about anyone before. That's why you have it reversed. You're everything to *me*, and I've been losing my goddamn mind trying to get you to trust me. You're fragile, flighty, always pulling away. But I keep trying. I keep fighting. Because I want to keep you. Because — fuck — I'm so in love with you."

His confession shatters me. The stadium tilts. My vision blurs.

"You... you do?" I whisper, barely managing the words.

His lips hover near mine, his voice thick with frustration. "You really don't see it, do you? How fucking obsessed you've made me? Emmy, you're my world, and—"

My breath stutters, my legs wobbling. The weight of his words crushes me, consumes me, drowns out every other thought.

"Uh," I squeak, feeling dangerously close to blacking out.

In fact, the world goes black.

Completely, utterly black.

The light returns as I come to. Joar is holding me, his gazed fixed on my eyes. His deep voice cuts through the haze as he says, "Emmy, you okay?"

"*Damn it*," I curse myself, and veer my eyes, feeling so mad I interrupted the words I've been dying to hear. "I'm sorry I'm weak! Keep talking, *please*."

Gently, he kisses my forehead. "Be as weak as you want. I got you. I'll be your strength. And, I was just saying I love you too. I've loved you for some time."

"You are gonna make me pass out again," I whisper, my face surely pale.

He smiles warmly. "Then pass out. I got you."

I've never had someone who didn't treat my anxiety as something shameful I should hide. He seems to think of my weaknesses as the opposite: something that needs attention and shouldn't be a secret to endure alone.

"Let's go home." His fingers thread through mine, his grip firm.

As we turn to leave, something catches my eye — the glint of gold on his wrist. My breath hitches. *The watch.* The one I gave him. The one I assumed was tossed in a drawer, forgotten because I'm terrible at picking out gifts.

"You're wearing it?" My voice comes out softer than I expect.

Joar smirks, glancing down as if only now remembering. "Since the moment you gave it to me. Haven't you noticed? It wasn't a line. I am obsessed with you."

I blink, thrown completely off balance. No. I hadn't noticed. Not because he hasn't shown me — but I guess because I never believed I was worth being loved like this.

The realization crashes over me. I've spent so much time tearing myself down, assuming he only wanted to sleep with me, to own me in a twisted way. But this... this is something else entirely.

He really *loves* me. And I never even let myself see it. *Whoa. I'm lovable.*

Swallowing hard, he leads me forward. Wherever he wants me to go, I'll follow.

Chapter 37

Joar

The hot water from the shower does little to ease the tension in my shoulder. The workout had been brutal, every movement reminding me of the cramping and strain in my rotator cuff. The fucking deterioration has been creeping up for years, nagging at me like a slow, inevitable death.

One more season. That's all I have to get through.

I close my eyes, my mind looping back to telling Emma the truth. She is stronger than she thinks, because she was able to say it far earlier than I did. Hell, she's turned my world upside down. Nothing makes sense anymore. Everything was so easy before.

I towel off roughly, irritation simmering beneath my skin as I throw on my clothes and head out of the locker room. The crisp air does little to cool my temper. The weight of exhaustion sits heavy on my body as I make my way to the physical therapy area, craving relief.

When I step inside, I expect the familiar sounds of Bri or Helga moving around, prepping for another session. But the room is eerily still.

Too still.

I push myself up onto my elbows, scanning the space, when the sound of someone clearing their throat draws my attention.

Mei stands in the doorway, her presence as sharp as a blade.

I stay propped up, unmoving, my gaze locking onto hers.

"Joar," she says, stepping further inside, her tone clipped and formal. "How is our top scorer?"

"Fine." My response is flat, indifferent, though my pulse ticks up a notch. Mei doesn't come here. Ever. The fact that she's standing in my space, looking at me like I'm some unruly dog that needs to be put down, doesn't sit right.

She moves closer, calculated as always, her beady eyes studying me. "I wanted to talk to you about my daughter," she says, her voice carrying an edge that puts me on alert. "It seems I cannot get either of you to respect professional boundaries."

I exhale through my nose, irritation spiking. "Us being together wouldn't affect the outcome of a game."

Her lips purse, unimpressed. "And Emma's role in all this? Are you pressuring her to cross these lines? Because this kind of conduct is beneath her, though her meek disposition makes her susceptible to... persuasion."

Something in my chest tightens.

I sit up fully now, swinging my legs over the side of the table, my feet hitting the floor with a dull thud as I stand. "Emma wants me."

Mei's expression remains cold, her scrutiny unwavering. "So you had nothing to do with her abandoning her ethics?" she challenges. "Because security showed me footage of a late-night tryst — in *my* stadium. Who I saw on that tape was not my daughter. That woman was a disgrace."

I hold her gaze, my face an unreadable mask, but inside, my blood simmers with controlled rage. "Sorry you saw me rail your daughter," I say, my voice deliberately casual. "I'll have to ask security for a copy, though."

Mei doesn't react the way I expect. No flash of anger, no sharp retort. Instead, she tilts her head slightly.

"How's your tooth?" she asks coolly. "Looked bloody."

I smirk. "Already fixed. I fix problems quickly."

She lifts her chin, her expression unfazed. "Do not press an enemy at bay."

A chill slips down my spine, but I don't let it show. I straighten, my stare hardening. "Did you just refer to me as your enemy?"

There it is again — that flicker of satisfaction, subtle but unmistakable.

"Do you ever miss your ex, Mr. Sköll?" she muses. "The one who died in Norway?"

The words hit like a gunshot to the ribs.

My entire body locks up. "Who told you that?" My voice is firm now, no longer playing along.

Mei smiles, just the barest hint of one. Then she turns on her heel, striding toward the door. Just before stepping through, she tosses over her shoulder. "Brianne and Helga are busy, but we hired another physical therapist just for massages. Enjoy your... therapy."

And then she's gone.

For a long moment, I stand in absolute silence, my jaw clenched so tightly it feels like my teeth might crack.

That wasn't a conversation.

That was a goddamn warning.

I rake a hand through my damp hair, inhaling deeply through my nose. The tension in my shoulder is long forgotten. My mind is somewhere else entirely.

Mei *hates* that I have Emma. And I don't just mean she disapproves. This is deeper than that. She wants me *gone*.

She is mine.

I didn't know I wanted a brat for a girlfriend, but fuck, I *love* it. The way she fights me. The way she submits. She's not like my other subs — those women were placeholders, distractions. Emma, though... she fucking needs me. She's the perfect sub because she doesn't even realize she's mine in every way. And she *will* stay mine, no matter what her mother does to stop it.

The soft sound of approaching footsteps pulls me from my thoughts.

I don't bother looking that way. "Good," I mutter, lying back down, assuming the new massage therapist has arrived.

Then a woman's voice greets me.

"Hello, you must be Joar? I'm Aina."

The Norwegian accent snags my attention instantly. My head lifts, my gaze settling on the woman standing before me.

Tall. Slender. Blonde. She's... very young. The kind you want to check her ID so you don't end up in jail. Too young. But it's not her youth that has my stomach twisting.

It's that she looks like *her*.

Like Runa.

Aina lathers lotion into her hands, her movements smooth.

"Anywhere you want me to focus?" she asks, her flowy accent like a ghost from my past. "Helga's notes say it's mostly your shoulder?"

I swallow hard. "Yeah. My shoulder."

She nods and gets to work. Her touch is different. Slower.

The scent of her lotion mixes with something sweet — her perfume, probably. My jaw ticks as I force myself to relax under her hands. The room is silent except for the soft slide of her palms over my skin.

Then she leans in. Her tits brush against my arm, her breath warm as she whispers, "Is that enough pressure?"

The way she says it — the breathiness, the suggestiveness — sends a sharp, unwelcome shiver down my spine.

I force another swallow. "Yeah."

She shifts slightly, her ponytail slipping forward. Blonde strands dangle near my face, triggering an image that hits me like a truck.

Runa. Her hair falling near me as she straddled my lap.

I squeeze my eyes shut, gripping the edge of the table.

Focus. Stay present. Zero sexual thoughts.

"You know," Aina murmurs, dragging her hands down my back, fingertips skimming under my underwear's waistband, "you have an incredible physique. Do you work out every day?"

I flex my jaw. "Almost."

She hums. "I can tell."

Her hands are still on my lower back, her fingers dangerously close to where they shouldn't be. I inhale sharply, willing my body to stay unaffected.

It doesn't.

My cock twitches, heat stirring low in my stomach as it grows rock hard. I shift suddenly, sitting up and swinging my legs off the table, making it clear that I'm *done*.

Aina pauses, confusion flashing across her face. "Everything okay?"

"Uh huh." I stand, my back to her, grabbing my black shorts to cover up the unfortunate reaction.

And that's when the door opens.

"Hey, Joar!" Emma's voice is bright, cheerful.

Too fucking late.

I barely manage to get my shorts on before she bounces toward me, wrapping her arms around my neck.

And then she feels it.

Her entire body goes rigid. She pulls back just enough to glance down.

Her eyes widen.

Fuck.

Chapter 38

Joar

Emma's eyes snap down, locking onto the evidence of my betrayal — at least, that's what she's convinced she sees.

Her entire body stiffens, arms dropping limply from around my neck as she steps back. For a second, she just stares, her gaze flicking between me and the blonde, her expression morphing from shock to hurt. I'm sure she didn't even realize the woman was in the room.

"*Emmy*," I say sternly, anticipating a meltdown.

She backs away.

Not *happening*.

I seize her arm in a firm grip, holding her in place. Her shock evaporates into fury, her nostrils flaring, her chest rising with a sharp inhale.

"Let me go," she snaps.

I don't. Instead, I glance at the blonde, catching the way her eyes flick to my hips, lingering on the part that's still betraying me. She scurries out, the door clicking shut behind her. Good.

Once she's gone, I release Emma's arm — but I don't give her space.

"Nothing happened," I state, my voice steady.

"Yeah huh!" She jabs a finger toward my dick, her face shrouded in panic.

I drag a hand down my face, forcing a slow exhale. "She—"

"Gave you a hard-on!"

I hold her gaze. "I didn't want to have any reaction. I was leaving."

Her eyes flash. "Oh? So if you hadn't left, something would have happened?"

I grit my teeth. "Emma—" I keep my voice calm. "She was touching me. Whispering in my ear. Leaning her tits on me. My body reacted."

"That's all it takes?" Her eyes glisten, and her voice drops to something small, something fragile. "She doesn't even look like me, Joar. How am I supposed to compete with that?"

Oh, that *fucking* insecurity.

I squint. "I wouldn't have slept with that woman."

"But you don't deny she's attractive. You don't deny that if you'd stayed, you would've—"

"No, Emma," I say, my voice clipped. "I'm with *you*."

It doesn't soothe her. It should, but it doesn't. She flinches at my tone, glancing away, and I can see her shutting down, spiraling, preparing to run. She turns and heads for the door.

Balling my fists, I warn in a dark, threatening tone, "If you walk out that door... I'm *not* gentle when I'm mad."

She freezes, then, with a defeated sigh, she moves back to me, her steps slow. She doesn't look up.

Unacceptable.

I seize her chin, forcing her gaze up to mine. Her neck bends back, exposing the vulnerable column of her throat. "I won't explain myself again," I say, my grip firm. "So listen carefully."

She swallows, lips trembling.

"My body reacted, but not me. I left because that was the right thing to do. And that's the difference between me and the weak men you've dated before. I control myself. Do you understand?"

Just then, the door flings open. Dana saunters in, her face lit up. Following closely: Ophelia.

Could this get any worse?

Without a second thought, I snatch Emma's arm, knowing she'll flee the first chance she gets.

"I had to hunt you down again!" gushes Ophelia. She holds up a calendar. "Look at this! The National Ice Skating Association created a calendar with all the best looking guys. This is what we need to do with you and the other starters — but hotter." Ophelia flips to a page and hands it to Emma. "Christian is February! Isn't he so handsome?"

I glance over Emma's shoulder at the image. Christian's face is okay — for a guy — his arm is firm with muscles as he supports a woman above his head with one hand. The veins on his forearm stand out, giving him a shred of masculinity. But the sequined shirt? Laughable. No way a real woman finds that attractive.

"He's hot," says Dana coyly.

Emma's eyes gloss over the picture and, slowly, she nods. "Yep. Look at him," she murmurs, almost dreamily.

I grimace. "Emma — you think that picture is hot? His shirt is girly."

"I know but, he's..." She looks at me. Suddenly, her expression shifts from defensive to smug. "Christian is very... sexy. It's a good picture of his face, too. And his arm and shoulders are... all flexed."

A deliberate jab.

I know that's a challenge and I don't back down. "Oh? It's almost like you can be attracted to multiple men. Tell me, Emma. If you were in a relationship, would you cheat, or could you control your body's desires?"

Her hands clutch her hips as she balks. She tries to speak, but no words come out.

Ophelia cuts in, her voice playful. "See, Joar. Even robots like Emma love man-candy. Women like Christian because he's so strong and doesn't have to worry about looking tough." Her gaze swoops up my body, her eyes lingering as they trace along my bare chest — *thank God* I'm not turned on still. She continues, "That's what makes men truly sexy. Confidence. Quiet strength. Like you — our top player. Confident and quiet. A mystery every girl wants to pin on her wall and stare at all month."

Emma shakes her head, her black hair swaying. "Yeah, but nobody buys calendars anymore."

"They are promotional, Em-ma," hisses Dana. She rolls her eyes. "Don't discourage him. We will give out calendars in the pro-shop. Hopefully drive ticket sales. The other starters are on board. Just wanted to know if Joar is still on board. The photoshoot is Monday."

I smirk and gaze down at Emma. "Well, boss. Should I do it? Since women like you—"

"Joar and I are dating," Emma blurts. "I don't want him to do the calendar." She then heads for the door, and just before leaving, she turns around. "And to clarify, we're together. Not just dating." She then taps the door frame and leaves.

"Is she serious, or was that joke?" Ophelia asks.

I'm smiling widely, loving that my girl finally claimed me. "Yep," I answer. "I'm hers."

⚜ ⊱─────••─────⊰ ⚜

I sit on the patio, a drink in hand as I gaze at the stars above. The warm air swarms around me in a gentle breeze. It's a calm, pleasant Austin night.

Emma worked late, but I hear the garage door close in the distance. I lean toward the open sliding glass door and call to her.

When she finds me, I give her a lazy smile — I'm gloating, having smiled most of the day.

Her cheeks flush red and she says, "That rumor spread like wildfire. Everyone knows we're together now. I even had an uncomfortable phone call with my dad. Of course, a long lecture with my mom too. I hope you're happy."

"Yep. Come. Give daddy a kiss." I clutch her wrist and pull her onto my lap. Her lips meet mine and I kiss her gently, soft and sensual. A reward.

After our lips part, I retrieve the sissy-skater calendar I hid beside me and hand it to her. "Want to hang this up on Christian's picture?"

She grapples for it and tosses it onto the patio bar. "Very funny," she pouts. "I get your point. I guess it's normal to be attracted to other people as long as we don't act on those physical... feelings."

"Good girl."

She hesitates, her gaze flicking downward. Her voice is small. "It's just that... I always feel like I'm not enough for you. Like you haven't realized it yet. You're so desirable to women and—"

I laugh, a cruel, deep sound that has her blinking up at me, startled.

"Not enough for me?" I taunt, dragging my knuckles down the delicate skin of her throat, enjoying the way she shivers. "Poor little thing. Look at you, sitting here, all fucking timid, thinking you don't satisfy me. You don't even know what you do to me, do you?"

Her lips part, but she has no words. Only the rustle of the cedar leaves fills the air, sending a light scent of the pool's chlorine in our direction.

I stare at her lovely face, enamored by her beauty and sense of angst. "Oh, Emmy. So pathetic," I add, shaking my head.

Before she can process my insult, I rise and strip her. Fast. Harsh. Her breath hitches, her pupils dilating as I manhandle her onto an outdoor lounge sofa.

She tries to sit up, but I glare. "Don't test me, little one."

She goes still.

I move on top of her, caging her in, owning every inch of space between us. She wiggles, weakly resisting, but she's fighting something inevitable. I shove two fingers deep into her pretty mouth, then move them to her entrance. I feed them in with care, and as I suck on her humble, supple breasts, I finger her, prepping her for what's coming. She gazes at me, surely wondering how kind I'll treat her helpless little body.

I smirk, then gently, I drag the head of my cock along her slit. "You nervous? Nervous I'll take you like last time?"

She nods.

I chuckle, but offer no reassurance. Instead, slowly, I slide some of my cock into her... her tight sides so heavenly. She braces herself, her bottom lip held between her teeth. I take my time, though, warming her up in slow, partial thrusts.

After all, she finally told others about us. She deserves to be pleasured — not hurt. And soon, the tension eases in her body. Her fingers gently trace over my back, her hips rising as she anticipates my next move. She's not fighting anymore. She's slowly drowning in me.

"So sweet, aren't you?" I praise.

She whimpers.

I kiss her neck, wetting her skin as I breathe. "You like my attention, don't you?"

She practically melts.

That's all it takes. Her nails pinch into me, her lips parting as she breathes in tiny gasps, all her focus on me. I feel it — the shift as she steadily surrenders.

I own her. And fuck, it's intoxicating. Her submission has me straining to hold back, but I manage, working her open more and more, feeling the pulsing, hot squeeze of her wrapped around my cock.

And then... she tenses for a second and says barely above a whisper, "Am I being a good submissive right now? Is this how you want me to be?"

That insecurity again. That damn doubt.

I clutch her jaw with one hand, forcing her to look at me. "I want you as you are. I'm yours, Emmy. Say and believe it."

"Um, you're mine?" she murmurs.

A dark smile curves my lips. "See? Good girl."

Her eyes flutter, her body trembling under me, sinking into obedience. I keep her there, fucking her slow, careful, until her small gasps turn into breathy moans, until her muscles shake, until she gives herself over completely.

She needs this. Needs me to remind her she's my only choice.

With tenderness, my thumb swirls around her swollen clit as I finally give her my full length. Her face contorts for a moment, her body tightening. I leave my shaft in deep, wanting to stretch to her — so I can fuck her without causing as much pain — so she can enjoy it tonight like she deserves. "Shh, relax."

She swallows, and her body calms some. I retract my hips, and this time, I pump just as deep as before. She takes it, her hands gripping my hips, clearly trying to control my pace — and depth. But I'm patient, and I go slow, but deep each time. Soon, her hands push against my hips less.

Which is great, because eventually, she's just too damn fuckable, and I can't help but give it to her faster and harder. But this time, she loves every inch of my shaft, her body having surrendered as much as that rebellious little mind of hers. She clings to me more, panting, her voice broken as she reminds herself, "you're mine."

"Yes, I am," I praise. And when she ultimately falls apart beneath me, she shatters and cries my name, I press my lips to her ear and soothe, "You are enough for me. More than enough."

Gratitude, but also a powerful sense of possessiveness, of love, overcomes me as I look down at her trembling body.

My climax hits hard, accompanied by a thought that strikes so sudden, it fucking paralyzes me: I *must* keep her.

I need this. This fragile woman who consumes my mind, body, and soul.

I look into her eyes, and without a second of hesitation, I say, "Fuck. Be my wife. I'm so in love with you. As your husband, I'll take care of you for the rest of your life. I'll prove to you every day that you're enough."

Her eyes go wide. I didn't plan to say it. But that's what she does: fuck up all my plans. And there's no doubt, I meant it. This woman is my future wife, so she better say yes.

Chapter 39

Emma

The crowded bar is a roaring sea of voices, laughter, and clinking glasses. Joar and I sit at a long table, surrounded by his teammates, coaches, and staff, all basking in tonight's win. My fingers drum against my thigh, my mind elsewhere — on the *blond*.

Aina.

The woman who got my boyfriend hard. I don't even try to suppress my hatred for her.

It doesn't matter that Joar reassured me. It doesn't matter that he fucked me that night, that he left me shaking in his arms, whispering that I was enough. It doesn't even matter that he proposed, his voice raw and urgent, demanding I belong to him forever.

Because she's still here.

And the way her eyes linger on Joar — *I see it*. She wants what she saw, and if I showed up a minute later, would I have walked into something much worse?

I glance at Joar, my heart racing. I lean into him possessively, staking my claim, daring her to keep looking at him like that. She meets my glare, her lips twitching like she enjoys this little game.

Joar doesn't notice our silent war, but his arm tightens around my shoulders. He presses a kiss to my temple, soft but instinctual, like he's soothing something inside me before it even has the chance to spiral.

My phone vibrates, and I check it.

Ugh. It's Mother texting me to come over for dinner. I roll my eyes and reply to her that I can't. Joar squeezes my thigh affectionately and whispers, "*Very* good girl."

I look up to find his eyes on my phone screen. I blush instantly and respond with a sense of pride, "Thank you."

He retrieves his phone from his pocket and taps the screen a couple of times. My phone lights up with an incoming call from 'Mine.'

I bite my bottom lip and glance over at him, feeling embarrassed for having changed his name. It just felt right.

To my surprise, though, he doesn't tease me. He moves his mouth closer to my ear. "That's probably the sexiest thing you've done. I can't wait to get you home and make you fucking scream for being such a sweet girl."

I nearly whimper.

291

My gaze shoots to my lap, unable to hide my flushing cheeks from the happiness and pride caused by his words.

God, I *love* him.

From that moment on, I'm desperate to get the hell out of here and back home to receive my reward. But I stay and play the role of the responsible General Manager I'm supposed to be. I won't be the first to leave.

And as the night carries on, it's no surprise that the players are becoming increasingly rowdy and intoxicated. Sergey is particularly drunk, his eyes glassy and unfocused. Pinching the pronounced bridge of his nose, he tries to steady himself before looking up at us. He stumbles over his words, but his voice cuts through the noise.

"Hey, Joar, you and Emma together for real, eh?" he slurs, a smirk on his face.

Joar lifts his chin as his arm tenses behind my shoulder. "Yes, we are."

Feels good. We still aren't making it official with the NHL and press, but it is nice to be honest with the people we see every day.

"Cool. I always wanted to be with an Asian," he continues. I brace myself, knowing nothing good can come from this. "Heard they're kinky. Ever watch tentacle porn together? That kink started with the Chinks."

I roll my eyes and reply, "No more kinky than hockey players."

Sergey laughs and smacks the table. With an impish grin, he leans forward and says to Joar, "In the bedroom, do you blindfold her with dental floss?" He bursts into riotous laughter at his joke, and explains to others at the table, "Ya know? Because their eyes are tiny slits!"

I veer my eyes to the floor, the curse of my monolids rushing back from my competition days as a skater. Even Sergey, foreign born, makes me feel less American than him.

Just then, Joar's chair scrapes back. Before I can blink, *before I can even grab his arm,* he snatches up a beer bottle and *smashes* it against the side of Sergey's head.

Glass shatters.

Blood spills.

The table *gasps.*

Sergey clutches his head, blood and beer dripping down his dark hair and pale face. All eyes on are us. My heart races, adrenaline flooding through me as I cover my mouth.

Joar is towering, his presence sucking the air from the room. "Get the fuck up," he growls at Sergey, his voice calm — too calm.

"Babe, no—" I grab his arm, but he doesn't even feel it, his muscles locked with violent intent.

Sergey stumbles, still dazed, Igor and Aina trying to help him.

Joar doesn't hesitate. He moves around the table, his fists clenched, his eyes black with rage.

Erik throws himself between them. "We need to leave now," he warns.

Joar shoves him aside, grabs a fork, and rams the prongs into Sergey's *fucking* eye!

The bar erupts into chaos. Some women scream, men shout, and chairs clatter to the floor as a wave of people surges forward. I'm pushed back, lost in the crush of bodies as everyone floods toward the scene. My view is blocked, as pandemonium takes over.

Panic grips me as my vision blurs, my throat seizes. I can't *breathe.*

I stumble toward the exit, shoving through the bodies, my fingers clawing at my collarbone, desperate to breathe. The cold night air crashes into me as I stagger outside, gasping, trembling, seconds from passing out.

Then — *hands.*

A *vise* around my wrist and I'm yanked sideways.

Joar.

He doesn't speak — just scoops me up, Erik leading the way, heading to the car.

"What the *hell* were you thinking?" I cry as Joar shoves me into the backseat, slamming the door behind us.

His jaw is tight, his knuckles white as he fists stay balled. "He asked for it."

"You *stabbed* him in the eye!"

Joar exhales slowly, still buzzing with violence. "I gave him a couple of broken ribs, too. Still not enough."

Erik barks a laugh from the front seat. "Told you he has an anger problem."

I ignore him, turning to Joar. "Why?" My voice is softer now. "Why do you over-react?"

Joar stares out the window, silent. Then, finally, he speaks, his tone flat. "Sergey wanted to get fucked up, so I beat his ass. He deserved it."

I inhale sharply. "Joar, I don't need a bodyguard to protect me from racist jokes."

His head pivots toward me, his gaze burning. "You don't fucking get it."

I freeze.

He sighs. "I'm supposed to protect you from everything." His voice drops, quiet but seething. "You think I care about some stupid fucking joke? I care about what it does to you. What it makes you feel. I care about the way you looked at the floor instead of ripping that fucker's throat out. I care about the way you shut down — like some pathetic, helpless little thing that needs to be saved."

I flinch.

"But I'm the one who saves you, Emma. Always. I don't tolerate disrespect. Not from some useless piece of shit like Sergey." His grip tightens. "So don't ever fucking expect me to stand by and do nothing."

My stomach flips. He's both terrifying... yet comforting. I swallow, my breath shallow. "I just... don't want you to go to jail."

He smirks. "Relax, you needy thing," he murmurs, his thumb stroking my lip. "I'll take care of it."

His certainty soothes something deep inside me. I sigh, my body sinking into his.

He chuckles, low and dark. "See? There's my good girl. You don't need to *think* — just trust me to handle everything."

I bite my lip, my breath hitching. Once I exhale, all the panic, worry, and stress leaves my body.

He leans in, kissing me slow, *filthy*, like he owns my freaking soul.

And maybe he does. He definitely owns my heart.

Our lips part, and his voice, low and seething, cuts through my haze.

"I am your future husband. I'm losing my patience, Emma. It's driving me fucking insane, and I'll keep cracking skulls until you realize what I already know."

A tremor courses through me. Is this my fault? Is my hesitation to marry him what unleashed this violence tonight?

But any reasonable woman would feel these doubts.

Can he stay loyal, or will he leave when the excitement fades? He's a star — adored, wanted. My father's warning rings in my ears: *Athletes make the worst husbands.*

Then there's Mother. She'd rather bury me in shame than see me with Joar. She reminds every time I see her.

The academy — my passion — would I lose it in a scandal for being *the GM who sleeps with her players*?

And what if he goes to prison for assaulting Sergey? What if he *kills* someone the next time he loses control?

Loving him is unstoppable — But marrying him? On paper, Joar is the last man I would choose, but in my heart... he is the first. And thus, logic has endlessly battled my emotions since he proposed, making it impossible to give Joar an answer.

So, I murmur timidly, "I'll decide... soon," hoping to quell his impatience for now.

Chapter 40

Emma

Someone at the bar took a video of Joar stabbing Sergey, sold it to TMZ, and within hours, he became a household name.

The thirty second clip catapulted him into instant stardom far beyond hockey.

Upon seeing the footage, I cried in his arms, knowing his arrest was inevitable.

He didn't seem worried though and instead began a live stream, which was short and to the point: "Sergey was being a racist piece of shit. I took action to stop Asian hate."

But just as I feared, the police were soon knocking on his door. Of course, I cried more watching him being hand-cuffed.

The video he posted went viral, though, and in less than twenty-four hours, Joar was released from jail on bond. His mugshot looks the same as his roster photo, but because of that clip, women began sharing it by the millions.

Now more than just puck bunnies want to fuck my boyfriend. And instead of #stopAsianHate trending like Joar probably intended, his mugshot is viral, and regularly captioned with #puckMeHard #stabMeInstead, and my least favorite, #would.

When I first saw the latter, it took everything in me not to rush to Ophelia's IG and see if she posted the same. But even if she didn't, millions of other women apparently 'would.' He's become an Asian hero who isn't even Asian. It's just like Joar to get people to think he's a saint instead of the unpredictable, dangerous man I know.

It's infuriating.

But I still love him.

I just hate his new fans. Thus, over the last couple of weeks, I've become one of 'those women.' The kind who are so insecure that they do crazy things. When Joar leaves a room without his phone, I check it and delete new DMs as fast as I can. After practice, I go to the physical therapy area and make excuses to talk to him. I've also insisted that Aina never touch him, but he seems to avoid her, anyway. I keep tabs on his schedule too, and ask in casual ways where he was during time slots I couldn't track him.

It's pathetic. I'm ashamed. But I don't care.

I tell myself all the time, '*Emma, he wants to marry you! Stop being jealous,*' but it does little to calm my nerves. Actually, married people still cheat. If I can't trust him now, what hope do I have if we say 'I do'?

Yet one day, the paranoia boils over. My voice comes out too sharp, too desperate. "Can you share your location with me on your phone?"

"A tracker?" he says with his eyebrow raised.

"Yeah, is that okay?" I ask, my voice small and hesitant.

His knowing gaze pierces me, and I feel the weight of his judgment. Finally, he shakes his head and says, "If you marry me, you won't feel the need to ask. Or better yet, disclose to the media and the NHL that we're together. Problem solved."

"I think the NHL's already mad enough, trying to figure out whether to suspend you after Sergey lost his eye," I reply, my voice tinged with bitterness. "Besides, they'd look like they don't support Asians if they do. And they've made a fortune off you. Your jersey sales are through the roof. Fans are wearing capes with your number, like you're some kind of hockey superhero."

It's the truth, but it only makes me more anxious. Joar's handling the fallout effortlessly, manipulating public opinion like it's a game. Meanwhile, I'm falling apart, in awe of the way he manages to twist every mistake into an advantage.

When he doesn't respond, I hold his gaze, my eyes begging for reassurance.

Finally, he nods, his smirk softening into something warmer. "Sure," he says. "You can track me. I already have a tracker on your phone, anyway."

"You *what?*" I huff, my voice climbing in disbelief. "Like my mother?"

He chuckles, reaching out to ruffle my hair like I'm a kid. "Except I'm responsible for you. She hasn't been since you turned eighteen. I need to know where you are to keep you safe."

The protectiveness in his voice hits somewhere deep in my chest.

I hate it.

I love it.

I need it.

Still, no matter how much he reassures me, I can't stop replaying the moment I caught him with an erection for someone who looks nothing like me.

He's done everything to assure me otherwise. Last night, he whispered how beautiful I am, how much I turn him on. But I'm convinced it's only because of all the female attention he's getting. It's damage control. Not genuine desire.

At least I haven't been binging.

Though I *have* started adding a couple of cosmos to my nightly routine. The sweet burn helps. Like tonight.

I sit on the couch, sipping my drink, my foot bouncing as I wait for him to get home.

He'll be out late for the bachelor party.

He offered to stay home — Joar always knows when I'm close to breaking — but like an idiot, I insisted, No, *go have fun!*

God, why do I push him away? Why did I *let* him go?

A knock at the door startles me from my self-loathing.

I set down my drink and answer it.

"Hey, Emma," Erik says, looking polished as ever in slacks and a blazer. He's effortlessly handsome, just like at the awards ceremony.

"Hi. What are you doing here?"

"I left my watch by the pool last time I visited," he explains, stepping inside before I can stop him.

"Oh," I reply, trailing after him. We step outside onto the dimly lit patio. The evening air is thick with humidity, the scent of chlorine clinging to the night. Erik scans the area, then spots his watch sitting on the bar.

As he clasps it on his wrist, I ask, "Are you going to the bachelor party when you leave here?"

"Yeah. About to head that way. Just running a touch late. Are you okay?"

I press my lips together and shrug.

"Emma." He smirks. "You look like you're about to implode."

I huff. "I'm just nervous about tonight. Strippers and Joar don't exactly mix well in my head."

"Why would you worry about that?" Erik replies, feigning innocence. "My cousin is with *you*."

I let out a dry laugh. "There are a million Instagram models in his DMs. And before that? I caught him hard after a massage."

"With the new blonde?"

"Yeah, Aina."

Erik's smirk grows. "Ah. I see. She does look like Runa."

My stomach clenches. "Runa?"

"His ex." Erik swipes through his phone, then hands it to me.

And there she is. A gorgeous blonde, curled against Joar, his arm *tight* around her. She looks *exactly* like Aina. And even if I lost fifty pounds, I'd *never* look like that woman. I can't grow taller. I can't make my eyes bigger. I can't change my frame.

My chin trembles.

"Yikes. What's wrong?" Erik asks.

I swallow hard. "I guess I'm jealous. And Joar kind of... lied to me."

Erik chuckles. "Runa was always his type. Total babe. Dating an Asian woman is the unusual part."

"A fat Asian," I mutter.

"You're not fat, but yeah, Joar mentioned he'd like you to lose some weight."

I gasp, my hand flying to my mouth. "He did?"

Erik nods, then pours me a shot. "You need this."

I grab the glass with trembling fingers and down it without a second thought.

"What else did he say?"

Erik sighs, hesitating before locking eyes with me. "He said if you were thinner, he'd enjoy sex with you more."

My breath stutters.

Erik slides me another shot. "Bottoms up, sweetheart."

I down it. Then a third.

And then, before I can even react, Erik's mouth is on mine!

Chapter 41

Emma

Erik's lips crash against mine, the reek of whiskey on his breath making my stomach churn. I twist my face away, my hands shoving against his chest, but he's solid, immovable.

He smirks, dark and arrogant. "Forget Joar. He doesn't appreciate you. I've always wanted that fat ass of yours. You're so sexy and I bet you don't even know it."

Disgust coils inside me like a living thing, and I shove harder, trying to slip past him. But he anticipates my move, boxing me in, his body a wall of muscle against mine. Before I can open my mouth to scream, his hand rushes to my breast, squeezing hard!

My palm flies across his face. The crack of the slap echoes through the kitchen. Pain jolts up my arm, but Erik doesn't even flinch. He just grins. A devilish grin. "You know you want this, too."

The words make me scoff. My stomach clenches, bile rising.

I couldn't want this if I tried. I shake my head. "Ew, Erik! Get off of me. I love your cousin!"

But he just snickers, his fingers brushing the stinging heat of his cheek. "Ew?" he mimics mockingly. "Why? Joar's been lying to you. That whole fucking deal? It's all bullshit. He's using you. Like he used Runa."

My breath hitches at the name.

"Runa died because of him," Erik continues, his tone shifting, becoming even darker. "You know why? Because he took his kink too far. Choking. Non-con. Knotting. Orgies. He forced her to do things she hated. Things he's probably making you do, too."

I go rigid. My head spins, but I latch onto one thing — Joar isn't the sharing type.

So, I shake my head weakly. "No. Joar wouldn't do orgies. You're lying."

Erik strokes my cheek, but I jerk away from his touch. His expression hardens. "Quit believing his lies. He's a fucking psycho, Emma. He treats women like toys. That's why Runa's dead. And it'll happen to you, too. He's dangerous."

The word echoes through me. Dangerous. Just like Christian warned.

I'm so caught in my thoughts, so drunk on alcohol and confusion, that when Erik's mouth finds mine again, I freeze.

My body stiffens, my mind locking down in a haze. His lips are soft, his warmth pressing to me, coaxing—

Like Joar.

Ah!

A wave of nausea punches through my stomach, snapping me out of my paralysis. I twist my face away, my breath hitching.

"Damn it! Don't fight," Erik growls.

"Erik! Joar loves me. What are you doing?"

"Joar loves you? For Christ's sakes, Emma. That's lust. Can't you tell how much I love you? Have you really never seen how I look at you, or how many times I've tried to ask you out? How I hang around in the lobby just to talk to you after work? Why can't you look at me the same way?"

I gawk, shocked he had feelings for me.

He continues, "Hell, I introduced you to Joar to help you with your parents, not to hook up with him!"

"I... I'm sorry. I didn't realize you felt that strongly."

He blinks, waiting, as if I'd say anything in his favor. "Well?"

"Well, it's too late. I'm in love with Joar."

Suddenly, I'm airborne. My back slams onto the hard wall. The impact knocks the air from my lungs, leaving me gasping.

"He's using you!" Erik snarls. He jerks me by the arm like a ragdoll, forcing me onto a table.

My shirt flies over my head. My skirt is shoved up. "I'll show you what it's like to be with a real man who isn't using you. Who actually loves you."

A new kind of fear seizes me — a primal, suffocating terror I've never known.

I can't move.

I can't breathe.

My panties are yanked aside.

Oh, God.

Erik's face lowers between my legs.

No.

No, no, no!

A scream rips from my throat as I slam both hands against his forehead, pushing with everything I have. "Erik! Stop! Don't—"

He laughs against my skin. "Come on, don't be frigid. Just like Joar said — you're an ice queen. But I'll get you to give in."

"Stop saying awful things he told you! And stop doing this!" I scream. Panic surges through me, giving me strength. I thrash wildly, kicking, clawing at his hair.

Abruptly, he rears up, yanks down his zipper, and pulls out his dick!

"Fine." His voice is absent of warmth, his smile gone. "I'll just fuck some sense into you."

Adrenaline explodes inside me. I roll off the table at just the right second, then run to the kitchen. I lunge for the dirty butcher knife in the sink, wrapping my fingers around the handle. My grip is iron-clad as I whip it toward him.

I lunge forward, but somehow, he's faster and grabs my wrist, wrestling for the blade in my grasp. The struggle is vicious, the metal glinting under the overhead light. He yanks it down hard, and I feel it — a hot, stinging slice along my stomach.

I choke on my breath as warmth seeps over my skin.

Blood.

Erik curses, dropping the knife onto the floor with a clatter.

Erik roars, "Goddamn it, Emma! Why did you make me do that?"

Before I can even process the pain, he forces me to the cold tile.

I try to rise, but he knocks me down. Pain detonates through my hip and shoulder. My head hits the ground so hard my teeth *clack*. Everything spins.

"Ouch, Erik! Fucking stop!"

I barely register his hands on me again. He flips me onto my stomach and yanks my panties down to my knees.

I crawl fast. Clawing, dragging myself forward with my elbows.

He persists. "Come on, baby. I swear I love you. You'll see. I'll show you."

A careless, drunken hand slams between my shoulder blades, driving my chest into the tile. My forehead smacks the ground. Stars burst behind my eyes.

Spit.

A sickening *schlik* sound.

Then... utter *fucking* agony.

A force unlike anything I've ever known rips into me. A tearing, brutal intrusion that shatters my mind. I scream, and the sound bounces off the high walls. He grunts, his breath ragged. His weight crushes me, each thrust searing through my body like fire. I claw uselessly at the ground, my fingernails breaking against the tile. The pain is blinding.

Soon, I know I'm not escaping. My cheek smooshes against the cold tile as I sob, my tears pooling near my temple.

"Oh, Emma," Erik moans in a shaky breath. "I knew your ass would feel this good."

I nearly vomit, but for once, my panic attack is welcome. Finally, darkness falls, swallowing me whole.

❧ ⊶————•••————⊷ ☙

When I wake up, I'm still on the kitchen floor.

My stomach throbs, my shoulder pulses, my head aches. My throat is raw from screaming. My hands shake. But it's the deeper ache — the unbearable, searing violation — that makes it almost impossible to move. Every shift, every breath, sends fresh agony through me, a cruel reminder of what was done. My body feels foreign, ruined. The damage is done.

I pull my panties up with numb fingers. I am alone.

I should call the cops.

But my mind races with all the reasons I can't.

Compared to Sergey, Joar would probably *kill* Erik for this. He'd go to prison. He already has an open case. The media would eat this up. An epic scandal. The GM of the team at the center of a rape and murder case!

Okay, then Mother.

No. That's not gonna happen. I already hear her: "I told you so. Don't date your players. Don't put yourself in those situations."

I guess... No one can know.

I repeat that mantra as I move like a robot, wiping the floor, washing away the blood, throwing my ruined shirt in the trash. I shower and scrub my skin raw, but I can't get clean. I just can't erase Erik. I slip into an oversized shirt to hide the bruises setting in.

Not long after, the sound of the garage door closing sends a jolt through me. My heart pounds as I lie in bed, the hours of waiting for Joar's return amplify my anxiety. I've rehearsed a hundred ways this could go, but none of them feel right.

When Joar steps into the bedroom, the tension in my chest tightens. I keep my eyes closed, feigning sleep, but I can hear him undressing — the soft rustle of fabric, the faint *clink* of his belt buckle. The air shifts as he moves closer, and I feel the bed dip under his weight. Then, unexpectedly, his fingers brush a lock of hair from my face. I fight the urge to flinch, the memory of Erik doing the same so fresh.

Joar's fingers slide down my jaw. His touch is gentle, tender in a way that nearly undoes me into sobs.

I pretend to stir, rubbing my eyes as I mumble, "Hey."

"I'm home," he says, his voice holding warmth. "I missed you, my sweet girl."

His words trigger such shame inside me. I feel dirty. Not worthy of his affection. I want to melt into his arms, but doubt lingers like a shadow I can't shake. "Yeah?" I murmur, my tone guarded.

I reach for the bedside lamp, flipping it on, and the soft glow illuminates his face. He looks calm, almost serene, but my mind slips to my default: suspicion. Yes — jealousy is a much better feeling than accepting what happened tonight. That I was violated in such an embarrassing, painful, and horrifying way.

Thus, I let my gaze roam over him, searching for signs of betrayal — almost hoping for it as a distraction I desperately need to hide the truth.

Find it! Find something, I plead to myself. Stripper glitter, the faint trace of perfume, make-up on his shirt, or anything else that shouldn't be there.

He catches me mid-scan, his lips twitching into an amused smile. "Looking for something?"

Heat rises to my cheeks, and I cross my arms defensively, feeling small under his steady gaze. It's all too much — the weight of what Erik did, the lies, the mistrust. Finally, a sob bubbles up, the first since the assault. Tears spill over, and my shoulders shake as the emotions I've been suppressing break free.

Joar sighs deeply and pulls me into his arms, holding me close against his chest.

"Emmy," he says, his voice calm and tired. "You're such a lost girl, aren't you?" His hand rubs soothing circles on my back, his warmth enveloping me. "I won't give up, though."

If only he knew I am too broken now to be worth his effort.

Perhaps worse is the irony that the one man who can make Erik suffer is also who I can never tell. The last thing I want is another reason for Joar to end up in prison forever.

He pulls back slightly, his hands framing my face as he studies me. His brow furrows, the concern in his eyes cutting through the haze of my doubt. "Just so you know, I didn't touch any of the strippers. I wished coach well, had a couple beers with the boys, and left. That's it."

His voice is steady, firm, as though he's trying to anchor me. And for a moment, it works. I force a small, trembling smile, trying to match his resolve.

But Joar isn't easily fooled. "What aren't you telling me?" he asks.

I quickly look away, switching off the lamp. The darkness feels safer, like a shield between us. "Nothing," I say softly, squeezing his hand as if the simple gesture can push away the storm inside me. "I love you."

"I love you, too." His tone is distant, the weight of unspoken truths hanging between us like a wall. He knows something is wrong — of course he does. Joar is too sharp not to notice the cracks in my facade.

And underneath, I'm just as broken, my entire being shattered.

Chapter 42

Emma

Is the old Emma dead? I feel so different. Like I've aged years just from one traumatic moment.

Making it worse, the day crawls by, each minute stretching unbearably, my body stuck between exhaustion and raw nerves. Every noise startles me. Every shadow in the hallway makes my stomach clench. I can't focus. I can't breathe.

I feel Erik's hands on me even when he's not there — I see him, smell him, hear him.

I sit in my office, gripping the edge of my desk, trying to will my hands to stop shaking. The air is too thick, pressing against my ribs, making each breath a struggle. Then — three soft knocks. My heart stops.

I force myself to glance up, but the second our eyes meet, my stomach lurches.

He's standing in the doorway.

Erik.

The man who—

I lean back stiffly, pressing into the chair, trying to ground myself. The phantom pain is still there. The memory slams into me so hard I nearly gag. My fingers curl into my palms, nails digging into flesh, anything to keep from breaking down in front of him.

His face is serious, but his eyes—God, his eyes aren't the same as last night. They aren't filled with sex and alcohol. There's no arrogance, no threat. Just an unsettling softness that makes my skin crawl.

"Emma, can we talk?" His voice is low, almost gentle.

I flinch at the sound of my name on his lips. It's wrong. It's vile. It makes me want to run, to scream, to disappear.

I reach for my phone slowly and unlock it, punching in 911. "Stay right there. If you move, I'll press this button," I warn.

He glances down the hallway outside my office, double checking if anyone can hear. After, he returns his gaze to me, his posture awkward and uncertain.

"I need to apologize for last night," he begins, his words spilling out in a rush. "God, Emma. I was drunk and I fucked up. I have a problem with alcohol, and it makes me do stupid things. I'm *really* sorry."

His apology is ridiculous. People don't just get drunk and turn into rapists! That's an easy excuse. An easy out. So I squint at him, searching for any hint of a lie, but all I see is remorse.

"Uh, Erik, what do you want me to say? It's fine? We all have too much to drink sometimes?" I reply sarcastically, not wanting to give him an ounce of forgiveness.

He nods, his expression seeming sincere. "I get it. You're mad. And I promise I'll never drink again. I'm trying to get better, to handle my issues... did you tell Joar? About what happened?"

I hesitate, his question leaving me surprised. I tilt my head and glare. "Don't you think you would know if I did? You would have worse than a fork in your eye. Besides, I didn't want him to kill you if he found out. It was hard enough to calm him down after Sergey's joke, if you recall."

Erik exhales a heavy sigh of relief. "Thanks for thinking about me. I don't want to die, either."

I lift my chin. "You are unbelievable! I didn't do it for *you*. I don't want Joar to go to prison. You should be the one behind bars! I hope you haven't assaulted other women?"

"Of course not!" he says.

"I guess I am just the lucky one, huh?" I snarl, but my whole body trembles.

"Emma, I meant what I said. I do... love you. You're not some random—"

I hold up my hands to stop him from speaking. "You know what, Erik? Just stop making this worse. Okay? Moving forward, you have to understand, I don't want to be in the same room as you. So leave any room I enter. Don't come around.

Don't visit Joar. I don't want to see you again. And expect to be traded to another team as soon as possible."

He looks relieved, but before he steps away, I hold up my hand and with a hint of apprehension, I add, "Wait. I need to know something."

He cocks his head, his brow furrowing. "What is it?"

I lower my voice. "Last night, you claimed Joar said I don't satisfy him, my chest is too small, and I'm overweight. Is that true? Did Joar really say those things about me?"

Erik's eyes widen, and he shakes his head vigorously. "No, Emma. That wasn't true. I was drunk, and I said things I shouldn't have. Joar never shared anything bad about you."

Some relief fills me, but it's tinged with lingering doubt. Joar told Erik about our deal. Why wouldn't he confide in him about other personal stuff. Therefore, I press on. "Are you sure? You're not just saying this to keep me quiet? And Joar doesn't have a type, like Runa?"

He bites his bottom lip and shrugs.

I frown. "Just tell me. You owe me that much!"

"Okay... Joar did say those things... I'm sorry. And yes, he definitely has a type, and it's Runa. As well as her lookalikes he dated over the years."

My heart cracks. "And what was the arrangement he had with Runa?"

He stares for a moment, then rubs the back of his neck. "She was his submissive, but he took it too far. I know I shouldn't judge after last night, but Joar is dangerous, and that's why Runa is dead. But come on, Emma. You already know he's unhinged when you saw him flip out over Sergey's joke."

I swallow hard, knowing I need to be certain. "So he *really* killed her? I mean, that's basically what you are saying."

Erik sighs and answers as though he's in pain. "Yeah... but I won't say anymore. Ask him about it."

"Why! Just tell me!" I snap.

"It's not my place."

I scoff. Like this asshole has some kind of moral code! Give me a break!

If I could flip a switch to drop Erik to a shark tank below, I would at this moment. Instead, I nod slowly, not wanting to let his words poison anymore of my brain. All I can muster without losing my cool is, "Okay. Now, *leave*."

Erik gives a weak smile before stepping away. None of which gives me peace of mind. I hunch in my chair and glare down at my keyboard.

God, Mother was right. How did I end up in this mess?

Maybe I should trade both of them. Both liars. Both dangerous, *violent* liars.

Chapter 43

Joar

Emma is a riddle I can't solve.

As I head up the stairs to her office, the frustration simmering in my chest grows hotter. Her behavior last night and this morning was strange — jealousy sharpening into something jagged and cold.

Ever since she saw me with Aina, she's been pulling away. I did nothing wrong, but I can't seem to break down the walls she's built. It's as if she doesn't want me to get close anymore.

But why?

When I reach the top step, I freeze. Erik strides from her office, his swagger too casual, his smirk too satisfied. My jaw clenches, and a growl builds low in my throat.

"What the fuck?" I mutter under my breath. What the hell is he doing here?

A flicker of unease settles in my stomach, but I push it aside.

Once Erik is out of view, I head into her office. She's sitting at her desk, fingers in her hair, looking down at the keyboard. Her posture is so tense, I feel her anxiety from the doorway.

"Hey pretty little thing," I say, trying to keep my tone light. "How's your day been?"

Her head snaps up. The forced smile on her lips is pathetic.

"It's been fine," she says, much too quick, too fake.

"Don't lie to me, Emma," I reply, stepping closer. "You're anxious. What's going on?"

She waves her hand, brushing me off like I'm a fly buzzing around her head. "I said I'm fine, Joar. Just tired."

Dismissing *me*?

I lean over her desk, my hands braced on the surface. "I saw Erik leaving your office. Tell me what he wanted."

Her eyes widen for a split second before she molds her expression into something more neutral. "He was asking about next season. Contract stuff. He wants to be traded."

My knuckles tighten on the edge of the desk. "I *hate* being lied to, Emma. Try again."

"What! I'm not lying!" she protests, her voice climbing in pitch.

Unacceptable.

I move around the desk in two long strides, grabbing her arm and pulling her to her feet. "You're lying," I growl, my grip firm but not painful. I hold her chin, forcing her to look at me. Her wild brown eyes meet mine, and for a moment, I see the flicker of something I didn't expect: genuine fear.

No, *terror*.

I unlatch her arm in an act of mercy. Something is deeply wrong.

"You've been pulling away," I say, my voice dropping to a less aggressive pitch. "I won't allow it, though. I don't care what you think Erik knows or what bullshit he's feeding you. You *trust me*. Above all."

Her voice is shaky, but her words are defiant. "What if I... don't trust you? What if I wanted to leave? Would you force me to stay in this relationship?"

"*Leave?*" I say, indignant. My entire world shifts. "Emma. What the fuck?"

"I, uh... I didn't mean to say that," she stammers, but the fear in her posture tells me otherwise.

I coach myself, trying to be so delicate when I rather let my inner demons take over. But when I reach out to embrace her in my arms, she flinches like I'm about to hit her!

This isn't just fear of being spanked. I see it in her eyes. She thinks I'm a *lethal* threat. "Talk, Emma. Why are you so afraid of me?" The disbelief in my voice is genuine. The thought twists in my gut.

Her response is too fast, too loud. "I'm not afraid of you!" She leans back, her eyes darting around the room like she's calculating an escape.

Before she can make her move, I catch her arm again, holding her steady. But she yanks free in a burst of energy and makes a run for the door.

Wrong move.

I lunge, blocking her path, forcing her back until her ass hits the edge of the desk. There's nowhere to go. I crowd her, trapping her to sit on the desk.

"You think you can just run from me?" I say, my disgust evident.

"Joar! Someone could walk in!" she whines, struggling against me.

"I don't give a damn," I bite back. "Stop deflecting, Emma. Answer me."

Her bottom lip quivers, signalling a meltdown. Where is this coming from? I need to calm her down.

Wanting to regain the progress I've made with this woman, I slip my hand under her skirt, push her panties aside, and sink my finger deep into her pussy. Yes, I want to control her, make her remember I'm her answer in every regard, not someone to fear. However, this time my touch only causes her to be more panicked.

"Joar," she says in a frantic but hushed tone. "Stop. I mean it!"

"Behave," I order, placing my mouth on the velvety skin of her neck. She squirms and resists, not softening at all. She clamps onto my wrist, trying to remove my finger from her heavenly warmth. But I don't retract my hand, nor does she stop resisting.

Something is so different in her fight. Sure, I scared her before, but this... there is no desire behind it. She doesn't want my attention. Instead, her body stiffens further, and her fingers dig into my wrist. "Damn it Joar. I said no!"

"I wasn't asking," I reply, my tone losing its patience. I'm confused. Maybe she needs it rougher. I slide in a second finger, and can't help but wish my cock was inside her instead.

Great idea. A good fuck always makes her defenses crumble as she melts for me.

Now determined to make that happen, I hurry to unzip my pants. But her tense body and frantic expression only intensify. She takes hold of my shaft, digging in her fingernails as hard as she can.

Did that just happen? I look down at my dick, studying the red marks she left.

She's especially confident now, her expression icy, defiant in a way that sets my teeth on edge as she says, "If I had a knife, I'd put it in your chest for doing that. I told you — *not in my office.* Now get out."

She just bossed *me*. Who is this woman?

I stuff my cock back in my pants and stare, my head titled. She cowers, knowing I'm not going to fucking leave.

Her lips purse together tightly, the truth just behind those pretty, lying lips.

Where did my submissive toy go? It can't just be Aina or the attention of women online that's making her hate me. It can't be Erik, either. She would never trust him over me. What else? I search around, trying to find an answer to explain the meaning of this sudden shift. Yet, her pristine office shows no obvious clues.

But then, I spot her purse is open beside her, and something catches my eye. An unlabeled pill bottle, half-hidden but unmistakable.

I reach over and take the bottle out, unscrewing it and shaking a few pills into my hand. They're white, small, and have a simple cross etched on one side.

"What are these?" I ask, my tone hardening.

She looks up at me, her angry expression replaced with a cautiousness. "They're vitamins," she says, her voice unsteady.

I can see the lie in her eyes, her nervous behavior, and the way she can't quite meet my gaze for long. Having reached my last ounce of patience, I say one last time, "Emma. *Please* stop lying before you send me over the edge. Now what are they really?"

"Vitamins!"

I'm going to fucking lose it.

Then, Mei walks into the office, her composure as reserved as ever. She inhales, her hands held together and chin lifted high. There's a sense of arrogance in the way she surveys the scene, Emma perched on the desk, me angry as I glare down at her, the tension between her daughter and me thick enough to cut with a knife.

Mei revels in it, of course, loving the sight of us arguing.

I sigh, her presence adding to my already heightened level of frustration.

Of all times for her to walk in, it had to be now. I glance at Emma, whose face is a mix of relief and anxiety, then back to Mei, who stands there, a smug smile tugging at the corners of her mouth.

"Joar, Emma," Mei greets us, her voice dripping with insincere politeness. "Am I interrupting something?"

I grit my teeth, trying to keep my anger in check. "What do you want, Mei?"

She steps further into the room, her eyes gleaming with satisfaction. "I came to discuss some business with Emma, but it seems I've walked into something far more... interesting."

Emma shifts uncomfortably on the desk, her eyes flickering to me, then back to Mei.

"Joar was just leaving," Emma says, sliding off the desk, her body language now in the same formal posture as her mother.

I fucking hate that.

My anger possesses me. I throw the open bottle against the window, the sound of pills scattering as they land in every direction. Emma flinches, her body rigid with shock and fear.

I turn back to her, my voice seething. "I don't know what's gotten into you, but this isn't over, Emma."

Without waiting for a response, I head towards the doorway, my stride swift and purposeful. Mei's stoic expression persists. Only her eyes move as she watches me approach.

Just as I pass, she says calmly, "When the common soldiers are too strong and their officers too weak, the result is insubordination."

I snarl at her and step through the doorway. However, her smug tone continues, "Emma, have you been weak?"

Shit. This problem keeps compounding, and now includes Erik, mysterious pills, and this conniving pint-sized woman. I need to fix this and fast, or all my plans will be ruined. Most of all, I *can't* lose Emma.

Plus, after she tried to maul my dick, I've never wanted to punish a woman more.

Chapter 44

Emma

I'm not looking forward to speaking with Joar about his outburst at my office.

When I hear him enter the room, my body tenses. I bury my focus in my laptop.

He leans in, pressing a kiss to the top of my head. But I can't get swept away.

"Emma," he says, his voice smooth, but the tension coils beneath. "We need to talk."

"I'm kind of busy," I deflect, clicking on an email at random. It's the *National Ice Skating Association's* newsletter. I scan the first line and gasp.

He swivels the laptop toward him and reads aloud, "Congratulations to Ophelia Lee, selected for the Lifetime Achievement Award to be presented at our annual awards ceremony..."

I balk. "I cannot believe it! Now I have to see that woman be loved by everyone all night. Ugh! Why does she have to be better than me at *everything*?" I fumble for my phone. I need to call Mother.

Joar watches me as I rummage through my purse, but his words cut through my despair: "I'll get a tux."

I freeze, then slowly, I lift my gaze to him. "What?"

"For the awards ceremony," he says, his tone calm but pointed. "I'll get a tux."

My stomach twists. *Oh God.* He wants to go with me. "Joar, uh, this really isn't a hockey player thing. It's a night of refinement. Very formal. You would hate it."

He crosses his arms. "Emma," he says, his voice on edge. "Start over."

Panic flutters in my chest. "Well... it's just... Christian was my skating partner for years. It makes sense for him to be there."

His eyes darken, the sharp line of his jaw flexing. "You want to bring your *ex-boyfriend* instead of me?"

I hesitate, floundering. "Yeah... Christian probably has his own invitation. Oh! My mother," I blurt. "She'll want to be there." But then, I add in a bitter tone, "To support Ophelia, the daughter she never had."

"I'm sure they'll let your parents attend, too." His tone is clipped. "But I'm talking about *your date*. You and me, Emma. Or does the idea of being seen with me embarrass you?" He steps closer, his towering frame casting a shadow over me. "Or are you worried about your mom again?"

He reaches for my hand, but I flinch and cower.

His voice drops to a rough growl. "Goddamn it. Why are you so afraid of me?" Again, his hand reaches for mine, but I recoil, blurting out the first thing that comes to mind:

"Because you're scary!"

He snatches my arm. I stumble as he pulls me toward the front door. When he swings it open, hot night air blows inside. The first drops of rain scatter across the pathway. The storm brewing outside swirls, the thick scent of rain permeating everything. He gestures sharply toward the dark world outside.

"I don't know what's going on with you," he says. "But if you're afraid of me, the door's open. Go. Leave. Run away if you think I'm a threat."

The words hit me like a punch.

He means it.

I look past him toward the front yard, to the swaying trees and gathering storm. I open my mouth to speak, but just then, his lips crash against mine, silencing me. He kisses me with a sense of passion, yet anger. When he pulls back, his forehead rests against mine, his voice gentle but firm. "Something is wrong, Emmy. Fucking tell me. Tell me why you want to walk through that door."

The tenderness in his tone kills me. I glance toward the open door again, the rain growing heavier.

The truth claws at me, desperate to escape: *I think you're a liar. I fear you'll betray me — hurt me — make a fool of me. Your cousin raped me, and I can't tell you because you'd destroy him and yourself. I suspect you killed your ex... and I could be next. I'm terrified of you. And worst of all... I'm waiting for you to leave — Because I love you — But I'll never trust you.*

Instead, I murmur, "I just need time."

"Time? I'm trying to be patient, Emmy, but it's not my nature. Go with whomever you want to your awards ceremony, but, if you don't accept my proposal by the end of the week, I'll push you out that fucking door. That's all the time I'll give you."

I stare at him, stunned. And as he turns and walks away, a cold emptiness creeps in.

<hr />

It's been almost a week, but I'm still lost in doubt.

Focus on the present. This is what a good coach does. Support your students.

That's what I tell myself as I walk into the banquet hall. It's drenched in warm golden light. The scent of gourmet cuisine mixes with fresh floral arrangements, and laughter hums across the room.

Christian stands beside me near the piano, his bow tie perfectly matching my dress, a coordinated relic of our years skating in sync. We were a perfect team once. Safe. Predictable. A stark contrast to the storm that is Joar.

Christian's voice is weary as he asks me, "Emma, are you sure Joar said it was okay to be your plus one tonight?"

"Yes! Why do you keep asking me that?"

"No reason," he mumbles.

Just then, Mother joins us. She gives a small bow and scans me from head to toe.

"Lovely, Emma."

"Thanks, Mother," I reply, feeling relieved she approves of my gown.

"I'm quite pleased to be here. Ophelia deserves this award. I'm sure her mother is proud."

I swallow a knot down, forcing myself to nod. Ophelia deserves it. She worked hard. But so did I. I don't need an award, but I wish *just once* Mother would be proud of me.

Christian takes my hand in his, an act of support that he's done countless times before. The gesture always comforts me.

"You look beautiful, Mei," Christian says.

She smiles, but doesn't return the compliment.

Then something shifts.

A presence.

I don't need to see *him* to know he's here. The air changes, growing electric. It's not the soft kind of heat Christian provides — it's darker, rawer. Undeniable.

I spot Joar across the room, his tall, powerful frame standing out even in the dim lighting. Dressed in a tuxedo that molds to his body like sin, he looks completely at ease, as if he belongs in this world of refined elegance. Except, he doesn't. Not really.

I mutter a quick excuse to Christian and push through the crowd, dodging tables, barely breathing until I'm right in front of him.

"What are you doing here?" I say.

His stormy eyes flicker with amusement. But before he can answer, a stunning woman in a black dress steps closer, hooking her hand on his bicep.

"I think it will start soon," she says.

I stare at her, then at him, my stomach twisting.

His expression is indifferent to the horror I'm feeling. He replies smoothly, "Oh, this is Li. My plus one."

My throat tightens. *Plus one?*

"How did you even get an invitation?" I ask.

Joar gestures toward Li.

She smiles at me, warm and polished. "You must be Ms. Huang," she says pleasantly. "It's nice to meet you. I'm a big fan."

"Thanks," I murmur.

Joar grins. "Li's from Japan. Can you believe she was a geisha before coming to the United States?"

She swats his arm playfully. "I wasn't a geisha! My goodness! He's been making me laugh all night."

All night?

I glare at him, my heart thrumming in my chest. I can't help it and blurt, "This isn't funny."

Joar leans in, his voice more taunting. "What part? That you're here with your ex-boyfriend instead of me?"

I scoff. "Christian is *not* my date!"

He studies me for a long moment, then turns to Li. "Can you give us a minute?"

She nods with a knowing smile and steps away.

Joar watches her leave. "Fuck, that woman is so obedient. You can learn from her."

A sharp pain twists in my gut, jealousy so ugly and raw it burns through my veins like poison.

"If this is a punishment, *please stop*," I whisper, my voice breaking. "You know how jealous I am."

The teasing vanishes from his face. For a split second, I think I see remorse. But I wipe a tear before I can be sure.

"God, Joar! Why do I have to love you so much?" The words spill out before I can stop them. "I know you're mad at me. And I know I'm a mess. But *this*... This is another reason why I can't marry you. You already have too much power to hurt me. So there's your answer! No, I can't marry you... you *bastard!*"

Before he can say anything, the speakers crackle overhead, announcing for guests to take their seats.

I spin on my heel.

"Emma—"

I don't stop. But once back at Christian's side, I glance over my shoulder.

Li returns, and Joar pulls out her chair like a fucking gentleman. Women around the room steal glances at him, their eyes filled with desire, envy. He plays the role of charming suitor effortlessly, like he was built for seduction.

And I hate him for it.

Soon after taking our seats, the event starts. I silence my inner turmoil to support my students as the night progresses. And then, an unexpected name echoes through the speakers.

"Please welcome Joar Sköll, three-time Stanley Cup champion and all-time high scorer in the NHL, to present the *Excellence in Coaching*, an award to those who mold the next generation of elite skaters."

The whole room claps with enthusiasm. Thanks to Joar's overnight fame as an apparent ally to Asians, everybody knows him here, too.

And I'm shocked, my jaw dropping as Joar walks onto the stage.

What. The. Hell?

Joar steps up to the podium with that effortless confidence of his, adjusting the mic like he owns the stage. His tux fits him like sin, his presence commanding, the room hanging on his every word before he even speaks.

"Didn't think I'd end up at a figure skating banquet," he starts, his deep voice smooth, laced with amusement. "Hockey's more my thing, obviously. But Emma Huang is someone worth showing up for."

A murmur ripples through the room, and I feel my pulse hammer against my ribs.

"When I met her at the start of the season, she convinced me to leave a franchise I had zero intention of leaving. Didn't matter that I was comfortable. Didn't matter that I had nothing to gain. Emma looked me in the eye and we made a deal I couldn't refuse."

Joar's gaze sweeps over the crowd before landing on me.

"She has that effect on people, though. You all know it. You've seen it. For years, she dominated the ice, one of the greatest in her sport. A two-time National Champion. A goddamn Olympic medalist. Christian Poole might've been her partner, but she was the one we couldn't take our eyes off. The one who made you hold your breath every time she stepped onto the ice."

He leans forward slightly, voice dropping to something deeper. More personal.

"But that's not what impresses me most about Emma. It's what came after. The way she poured her soul into coaching, into building something greater than herself. She doesn't just teach kids to skate — she gives them something to believe in. I see it every time I watch her at the rink. And yeah, I watch. More than she realizes."

A knowing smirk curves his lips, and I hear scattered laughter. My face *burns*.

"Her students work to impress her. Because she makes them want to be better. That's the kind of coach she is. But she never sees her worth, even when it's written all over the people she's changed. So tonight, I'll spell it out for her." He pauses, his next words holding intensity. "You are enough, Emma. More than enough. And tonight, you're getting the recognition you deserve."

As I step up the stairs and walk across the stage, I approach this man who completely blindsided me. Just as I reach his side, he says into the microphone, "Ladies and Gentleman, Li Chen."

Suddenly, Li walks out from behind the curtain and announces to the crowd. "Ms. Huang, as Executive Director of the association, we are proud to present you with this award."

Oh. That's why Joar was with her!

I take my plaque and stare at Joar, wide-eyed, breathless. He doesn't offer a handshake. He pulls me in, arms wrapping around me in a way that makes my heart stutter.

His voice is a whisper against my ear. "Congratulations, Emmy. I am a bastard, but I still love you."

Tears sting my eyes. Without thinking, I lean into the mic. "Just so everyone knows — Joar is not stalking me when I give lessons. He's my fiancé."

Joar grins — wicked, sexy, devastating.

The room erupts in applause. I don't even look at Mother. She may never love me, but this man does, even if he scares the hell out of me.

Chapter 45

Emma

Last night was the *best* night of my life!

I walk to my office with a pep in my step — I can't believe I was recognized *and* got engaged. I've been smiling so much, my cheeks hurt.

Someone in my peripheral catches my eye and I look in their direction. Mother stands in the doorway. The expression on her lined face is cold and intense.

"Emma," she says without warmth in her voice.

"Good morning."

"I *wish*. Unfortunately, I've spent much of my morning dealing with phone calls."

"Oh?"

She steps inside the office and closes the door. "Have a seat," she says, directing me where to sit. Before I move, she's already heading to the chair behind my own desk!

As soon as she takes my chair, she makes small adjustments, repositioning the angle of my picture frames and keyboard. Although I consider protesting, I don't want to get worked up after such a lovely night. I want to stay in the afterglow. Thus, I swiftly take a seat and gesture for her to speak.

"The league was surprised as me to learn you are engaged to our star player. As well as the media, who has been hounding our PR department all morning."

I can't help but cringe as I give a weak shrug. "I didn't intend to make the announcement last night. He proposed weeks ago, and I was unable to give an answer."

"Ah. And in all your wisdom, you determined last night was the appropriate time to do so?"

"Yes, it was a bit impulsive, but—"

"Immature, foolish, and yes, impulsive."

I draw in a deep breath and grip the armrests. However, I can't allow Mother to shame me for something that isn't against the rules. I'm doing my job, too.

"Mother, I will formally disclose the engagement to the league today."

"Indeed, you will." Mother rises and walks to the door. With her hand on the doorknob, she adds, "Your father and I wish to discuss the matter further over dinner — *without* your future husband present. Be at our house at five."

I nod, not as intimidated. I know what I want: Joar. I'm ready for my parents' lecture, but it won't change my mind.

Father gladly welcomes me with a warm hug and pat on my back. I bow to Mother and we head to the dinner table.

As normal, Father takes heaping servings, while Mother prepares a plate of salad and side of soup for me. Soon, Father sets down his fork and begins the conversation.

"Sweetie. I first want to say I'm happy you have found someone you wish to marry.

"Thank you," I reply, my cheeks flushing.

He returns a weak smile. "*However*, we want to safeguard you — limit your exposure."

"What?" I interrupt.

"Joar is a wealthy man, but he will gain an empire upon marrying you. In the event of a divorce, he will walk away with far more than he has now. Not to forget his recent legal issues. Sergey is suing him for the loss of his eye — probably after he loses at trial and goes to prison."

The direction of this conversation is now clear, but I can't let their concerns discourage me from being with him. "I understand, Dad, but I love Joar and he loves me. I think if I trust him, we'll last."

"A good business woman should always plan and protect herself from unnecessary risks. That's why I must insist you have Joar sign a prenuptial agreement."

Instantly, I frown. "Again, I understand your concerns, but I am confident—"

Mother pipes up. "Unfortunately, your father and I are not confident. "If you don't protect yourself from the fallout of a divorce, how can we trust you with the family business?"

I sit up straighter, pleading with my eyes as I look at my dad. "We all agreed if I led the team to the Stanley Cup, I would be given the organization when you retire?"

"Yes, sweetie, but that agreement did not include you marrying a player. That decision is not only a tremendous conflict of interest that compromises your business ethics, it also presents an incredible liability to our franchise."

"So, what are you saying? If I don't get Joar to sign, you're breaking our agreement?"

"Yes, you would force our hand in the matter."

I jolt to my feet so fast, my chair falls backward. "That's unfair! At least Joar never backed out of our deal."

"What deal with Joar?" asks Mother, setting down her silverware.

Shit.

I didn't mean to say that, but their ultimatum shook me. Knowing I am in the right, though, I have nothing to hide. So I lift my chin and say without reservation, "Joar and I made a deal that if he traded to our team, I would do simple things for him."

Father's eyes blink several times as he processes this information. I don't bother looking at Mother.

He presses, "And what is entailed in these 'simple things.'"

"Running errands."

Mother interjects, "Ah. And sex?"

"No!" I balk, but my parents know I'm telling half-truths. I was never a good liar under their heavy scrutiny.

"*My God*, Emma. Are you telling us you only secured our star player because you offered him sex?" says Dad.

"No! The only thing I had to do outside of a typical business deal was give him a kiss before and after games. That is far less unethical than changing our deal just as we approach playoffs. I'm succeeding in meeting the original requirements we agreed upon, and now you're retracting your side of the bargain!"

"And what if you refused to meet Joar's demands?" Mother asks.

I shrug. "Then he will not play."

"Blackmail," Father says bluntly, prompting Mother to nod in agreement.

"It wasn't blackmail!" I defend, but for the first time tonight, I lack conviction in my voice.

Mother rises from her seat. "It seems our concerns are justified and more pressing than originally thought. You will get Joar to sign the prenup, otherwise, our agreement is over and we will sell the team at the end of the season."

"I agree with your Mother. This is outrageous. I am shocked how far you have fallen from what we taught you."

"This is so wrong! I'm doing a good job."

"Oh? That reminds me," says Dad, "I heard you are trying to trade Erik. That will *not* happen. It's insane to trade a top starter before playoffs."

The blood drains from my face. I desperately want Joar beside me. The intensity of my need for him cements that I made the right decision to accept his proposal.

I move to speak, but Mother holds up her hand. "Enough, Emma. Erik stays, and Joar must sign the prenup. Now, go to your room. You need time away from that man to think clearly. In fact, you will move in with us."

"Excuse me?" I say, unsure I heard correctly.

"And give us your phone." She extends her hand, waiting patiently.

"I'm *not* a child," I reply, still uncertain if this is real or a dream.

"Do you want your academy, the franchise, *our* legacy? Or do you wish to lose it all for a man? A man that forged a relationship with you using blackmail." She steps closer and repeats, "Phone."

I glance at Dad and swallow, but he looks away, evading my plea. I protest anyway. "This is crazy, right, Dad? I'm a grown woman."

Silence.

Suddenly, Mother snatches my phone, leaving me breathless and gawking at my open palm. "Upstairs. Now."

I don't know what to do. Leave and go home to Joar, but lose everything I wanted before I fell in love with him? Lose myself entirely to a man. But I don't have a quick solution, so I trudge to my room. Mother follows closely, joining me inside the haunting space I've suppressed since childhood. I glance around the four walls a moment too long, and Mother's hard palm smacks my face. I grimace and clutch my cheek.

"Purge before bed. You are chubby in the waist," she says, her voice colder than ever.

After shutting the door, she locks me inside like she's done so many times. I tread to the adjoining bathroom and purge. After I rinse my mouth, I gaze into the mirror, recalling Joar pinning me to the sink as we looked at our reflections.

Both Mother and Joar are controlling. The difference is, Joar's touch can be tender. Mother never hugged me or said I love you. She only punished — never praised.

I guess my parents are not completely wrong. Prenups are common. And It's foolish to trade Erik before playoffs just because... I cringe.

I *need* Joar. People say I can't trust him, but as I sit here, trapped in my childhood bedroom, it's me I can't trust. I'm the one who walked in here!

Chapter 46

Joar

The moment evening arrives, I can't sit still. I pace back and forth by the door, checking my phone every few seconds, hoping Emma will finally respond.

Dinner at her parents' should be over by now, but my texts remain unanswered. I tell myself to believe her, to stay out of trouble. I remind myself that I asked her to trust me, so I need to do the same.

But by nine o'clock, my patience has run dry.

That's it.

I grab my keys and speed toward her parents' gated community. When I arrive, I demand the security guard let me in. He makes a call and then hands me the phone.

"Emma doesn't want to see you," Mei answers smoothly.

I blink. Once. Twice. Trying to process the audacity of this woman.

"Put her on the phone," I say, my tone calm, lethal.

"Emma is unavailable," she replies, her tone condescending. "It would be wise to keep your aggressive nature on the ice. And even wiser to keep business and personal relationships separate. In war, the way is to avoid what is strong is to strike what is weak. Emma has always been weak."

"War? What the *fuck* are you talking about?"

"Behave, Mr. Sköll. You're already on a tight leash with the police."

The call ends.

I grip the phone so tightly I nearly crush it. The security guard, sensing my rage, clears his throat. "Sir, Mrs. Huang has requested the authorities escort you off the property."

Fuck that.

"Open this goddamn gate before I rip off your head!"

Instead, he scurries into the guard shack, locking the door behind him. I slam my shoulder against the door. It cracks, splintering open. I grab that fucker and fling him onto the pavement. My fists rain down, my knuckles cracking the bones in his weasel face. "I told you to open the fucking gate, you piece of—"

Sirens.

Screeching tires.

Patrol cars surround me like they were waiting for this moment.

That *bitch.*

In the morning, I walk out of jail after posting bail. I told the cops Emma was in danger, but apparently, they did a wellness check and she's "fine."

Now, I dodge reporters asking about my arrest as I head through the airport. I hurry to the team plane headed for our next game, hoping Emma will be onboard.

She's not.

Just before the plane door shuts, a guy steps on board. "Joar Sköll?"

I nod. "You have been served." He hands me an envelope before leaving. Inside? A restraining order from my *fucking* fiancée.

Give me a goddamn break. Like I'll stop. I immediately call her.

Voicemail.

Then text:

> Emma if you don't show up before the game, I won't play.

By the time I arrive at the stadium, I'm dying to kill someone. I lace up my skates with sharp, jerky movements, ignoring the chatter around me. Every few minutes, my gaze snaps toward the entrance, heart hammering whenever someone walks in.

I rest my head against the locker room wall, trying to keep my fury in check.

I feel a light tug on my jersey.

My eyes snap open, and I look down.

Emma.

She stands before me, eyes glossy with unshed tears, her bottom lip trembling as she looks up.

I grip her wrist and drag her ass away from the team, leading her into an isolated corner of the locker room.

"Emma," I say, my voice dangerously on edge. "Explain."

Her fingers twist together as she stares at the floor, refusing to meet my eyes. She talks fast, frantic."Joar. I missed you so much. I'm sorry! I'll do better—"

I scoff. "I went to jail because you wouldn't talk to me."

"I know, but please! Don't punish me." She throws her arms around my waist, burying her face against my jersey.

I don't hug her back, just snarl, "And you filed a fucking *restraining order?*"

She squeezes me tighter. "Please don't be mad at me, Joar. I had to!"

I grit my teeth. This woman. *This fucking woman.*

"Had to?" I repeat sharply.

Before she can answer, the locker room door swings open. Emma stiffens as Mei strides in, her gaze scanning the room before landing on us. She lifts her chin, composed as ever.

"Did you give the boy his pre-game blackmail?" she asks smoothly.

Blackmail?

Emma leans against me more. "Not yet," she answers quietly.

"Hurry. Then come along," Mei commands.

Emma shifts like she's about to move, but I lock my arm around her finally. "She's not going anywhere," I state.

Mei's expression remains unreadable. "You haven't told him, Emma?"

Emma swallows hard. "Not yet."

My eyes narrow. "Tell me what?"

She speaks like a robot, but softly. "I want to postpone the engagement."

My pulse thunders, a deafening roar in my ears. "You don't want to marry me now?" I manage, my voice flat, but the rage underneath is bubbling up.

"I do! I just..." She composes herself and looks at Mei. As Emma speaks, Mei mouths along word-for-word. "I think you should go to counseling first. Your anger issues..."

My vision blurs. She was mine. She fucking belonged to me. And now? Now, she's slipping through my grasp.

I glance at Mei, that scheming, manipulative bitch. I tilt my head, envisioning my hockey stick cracking across Mei's smug face.

"Joar," Emma whispers.

I look down, but her eyes suddenly hold panic... fear. Her gaze is so intense, she radiates anxiety. Her fingers dig into my sides like she's trying to hold on for dear life. I can barely hear her as she says, "*Help me.* Please don't let me leave with her."

Oh.

Everything shifts. This isn't what I thought it was. This isn't my girl obeying her mom. It's my girl trying to *escape* her mom.

Mei clears her throat, flicking a glance toward the door. "Hurry up."

Emma presses her cheek to my chest, her whole body trembling.

Gently, I kiss the top of her head, petting her hair in comforting strokes. I soothe, "You're okay, Emmy. I got you now." Her arms squeeze me harder, as if she doesn't believe me.

I glance over at Mei. "Shoulder is killing me tonight. Can't play. I'm taking Emma back to the hotel."

Mei shakes her head. "Then I'll call the cops for breaking the restraining order."

I smirk, dark and wicked. "Go ahead. Kiss your fucking championship goodbye."

Mei's jaw clenches and I know this is a battle I've won.

For now.

<hr />

Something is terribly wrong with Emma.

She doesn't say a word during the drive from the stadium. I haven't seen her this detached. Pale as a ghost, lost in her mind. I don't pry yet, giving her time to calm down.

Once we are in my hotel room, I gaze at her. She stands small, her shoulders curled inward, her eyes welling with tears. A scared little rabbit. She does look beautiful, though. My little doll. My toy. My pet.

Thank God she's back in my possession. What a fucking relief.

She keeps her eyes on the carpet, her fingers twisting together.

I take a slow step forward, closing the space between us. "What's wrong, Emmy? Tell me what happened and—"

She blurts out, "Are you going to punish me, too?"

Her words stop me cold. Too?

My hand lifts her chin up, forcing her to look at me. Her eyes glisten with tears, and the way she trembles beneath my grasp fuels the fire burning through my veins.

"Too?" I echo, my voice low, dangerous. "Did Mei punish you?"

She shrugs.

I snarl, my grip tightening just enough to keep her from turning away. "Stop protecting her. Tell me what she did."

Emma shakes her head and mumbles, "Nothing."

I exhale sharply. She's brainwashed. Too broken to even recognize how much damage Mei has done to her.

I sit on the edge of the bed and bring her to my lap. Slowly, she lets herself sink into my hold, her body small against mine.

I rub slow, firm strokes along her back. It's only when she finally exhales that I murmur, "That's my girl. I'm here. You're safe."

Her tiny fingers curl into my shirt, gripping me like she's afraid I'll disappear. "Joar..." she whispers, her voice cracking. "I don't want to be seperated from you again."

I slide a hand up, cupping the back of her head, tangling my fingers in her hair. I chuckle softly. "Like you have a choice."

She sniffles, nuzzling her face against my neck. The tension in her body starts to give way.

Good.

We sit like this for a while, but I don't miss the way she keeps shifting and winces, trying to get comfortable when my palm roams over certain parts of her back.

I don't ask, I simply turn her and yank up her shirt. She squirms, but she isn't going anywhere.

The second I see the burns, I inhale deeply through my nose.

"What the *fuck* is this, Emma?" My voice is sharp, but I already know the answer: The 'lighter' Christian mentioned. The shape of the burn marks is unique. Mei must have heated the metal top, then scolded her daughter at least twenty times.

Emma pulls her shirt down, looking ashamed. She sighs heavily. "My mom was mad at how I've been messing up... how I let them down."

"So she *burns* you," I state, not a question.

353

Emma just stares at the floor, refusing to answer.

I shake my head in disbelief. "And you think this is normal?"

With a subtle shrug, she answers, "It's not deep enough to scar me. She's trying to help me do better. I shouldn't have gotten into a relationship with one of our players."

I release her and comb both hands through my hair, trying not to put my fist through the wall. She is so fucked up. So goddamn brainwashed she can't even see that her own mother is a monster.

I grab her by the waist, tossing her onto the bed.

Emma gasps. "Joar—"

"No talking," I order, yanking off her pants. "You don't know it yet, but you need this."

I settle between her thighs, nuzzling my face against the soft skin of her thigh. She's trembling, but I can feel the way her body is warming, softening.

"My poor, *stupid* little doll," I murmur against her leg, pressing a kiss there. "You really think you deserved that?"

She squirms, shaking her head. "I don't know..."

I bite down on her thigh, just enough to make her squirm. I add brusquely, "Wrong answer."

"Joar!" she yips, flinching.

I soothe the bite with a lingering kiss, then trail slow, wet caresses up. "You'll never be punished like that again," I soothe, nipping at her skin. "Not by anyone, not even me. That's beyond cruel, Emma. You don't deserve that kind of pain."

She swallows thickly. "You... you don't think I deserved it?"

That right there. That *fucking* question.

I slide a finger under the waistband of her panties, snapping it against her skin.

"Look at me."

She does, her lips parting, eyes glassy.

"I own you," I remind her. "Your body. Your pleasure. Your pain. You are mine, and nobody touches what belongs to me. Not even your bitch of a mother. Understand?"

She nods weakly.

"Say it."

"I... I understand," she whispers, her tone holding such a desire to be loved.

I hum my approval, sliding off her panties. Her breathing is uneven as I drag my fingers through her wet heat. I slip a finger inside, causing her to exhale, my touch close yet comforting. "That's my good girl." I kiss the inside of her thigh once more, watching the way her body melts.

And as I devour her, touch her, worship her the way only I can, I vow that no one will ever hurt this broken, sweet woman again. Not Mei. Not herself.

Nobody.

I failed to protect her once. I won't twice.

Chapter 47

Emma

My fingers glide through Bergen's thick fur as he pads toward the back door, his powerful frame moving with quiet authority. He's always patrolling the backyard, circling the perimeter like a watchful sentinel.

Ever since I returned to Joar, he's been the same way. I don't think he even sleeps anymore. If he does, it's only after I've passed out in his arms, exhausted from his touch, from his claim. But protective doesn't even begin to describe him.

Possessive. Obsessive. Watchful.

He never lets me out of his sight unless it's unavoidable. And when he does, he demands to know every detail — where I am, who I'm with, how long I'll be gone. I should feel suffocated.

But I don't.

Because with him, I'm safe.

I stretch out on the couch, my feet resting in Joar's lap as he massages them. His eyes are glued to some sports segment, but I don't care. I don't need his words to feel wanted. His touch alone is enough.

My gaze lingers on him, memorizing the sharp cut of his jaw, the way his brow furrows slightly as he listens to the TV. My strong, violent, terrifying man.

Mine.

He catches me staring and smirks. Lifting my foot, he presses a slow, deliberate kiss to the top.

"What's on your mind, my anxious girl?"

I blush, biting my lip. "Nothing. I'm just happy."

"Good." But there's a flicker of something in his eyes — something unreadable.

Before I can ask, my phone rings, slicing through the warm silence like a blade.

My stomach knots. I know who it is. I changed the ringtone.

Joar tenses beneath me, his grip tightening slightly around my ankle.

I sit up calmly. "Probably work. I'll take this real quick. I need a drink anyway."

His eyes narrow slightly, his fingers brushing along my calf. A warning. A silent: *'Don't test me.'*

I flash him a reassuring smile and retreat into the kitchen before answering.

"Emma," Mother's sharp, clipped tone greets me, devoid of warmth. "Have you spoken to Joar yet?"

I swallow hard. "Not yet, but I will soon." I change the subject to what I really want to discuss. "I know you and Dad don't agree with me, but I feel *strongly* that we need to trade Erik."

Silence.

Then, "No. The priority here is the pre-nup, Emma."

I grip the fridge handle, bracing myself. Mother's voice softens — too soft, like a snake preparing to strike. "If you are afraid to ask him to sign one, is it wise to marry him?"

Her words sink their claws into my chest. A part of me knows she's manipulating me. But another part — the part she's shaped and controlled my entire life — whispers, 'What if she's right?'

My breath shortens and pulse spikes. But I can't lose Joar. I can't.

I rip open the fridge, searching for something to calm me.

Chocolate. Yogurt. Pretzels. Cheese. Anything to make it stop.

I tear into the chocolate, shoving a bar into my mouth, barely tasting it before reaching for something else. A *carrot. Some turkey. Crackers.* One bite after another, anything to drown her voice out. The sound of my own chewing fills the silence until—

"Emma?"

I freeze, my stomach flipping.

"Are you eating?" she asks. I quickly cover the speaker, chewing faster, swallowing hard. She continues, "Those pills won't work if you eat garbage."

My grip on the fridge tightens.

"Don't you see?" she adds, her voice almost pitying. "This man is ruining you. If you keep this up, you'll look like Buddha, yet lack the wisdom."

Each word feels like a fresh cut, each syllable another slice to my fragile self-worth. I grip the edge of the counter, blinking back tears. I mumble, "Mom, I'll call you back," then hang up and turn on the faucet, letting the sound of rushing water drown out my impending wretching as I lean over the sink.

With shaking fingers, I reach to the back of my throat. The moment my knuckles graze my tongue, the faucet shuts off.

The room is dead silent. My stomach drops. I already know.

Slowly, I lift my gaze from the sink's drain. My eyes follow the line of sight until they meet his.

Joar stands, his eyes black with fury. I try to speak, but my voice cracks. "Joar, I was just rinsing my mouth. I think the milk is spoiled—"

He snatches my wrist, leading me to bedroom. I stagger behind him, barely able to keep up. Before I know it, he bends me over the bed, rips down my shorts, and smacks my ass so fast, I'm speechless!

"I'm sorry! I'm sorry!" I plead.

"For what?" he scolds.

"Uh, I just... trying to throw up." My voice chokes off, tears spilling over. "I know I shouldn't eat so much. I know I'm fat and disgusting, and I'm sick of it."

Joar moves. In an instant, he yanks me to a stand, spins me around, and clutches my jaw hard. "Don't you *ever* say that again," he warns. I tremble, my lip caught between my teeth. He narrows his eyes. "Who was that on the phone, Emma?"

"Coach."

"Why do you lie?" He cocks his head. Before I can protest, he strips me of my clothes. I tense, my body going rigid.

I bite my lip, shame crashing over me. *I hate this.* I hate seeing myself. But Joar's hand is firm on my waist, his voice velvet and steel.

"You will learn to love what belongs to me." He whispers against my ear, "Now, it's time for you to tell me the truth, Emmy. No more lies. And I can see them all, so doesn't bother trying."

I stay as still as possible, trying to look innocent. "This is unfair, Joar. I shouldn't be punished that much. I didn't actually purge..." When he doesn't soften, I sigh loudly. "Okay, fine! It was my mom that called, alright?"

Joar doesn't get mad. If anything, his amusement grows. Then he forces me down on my knees! I scoff, but I know better than to fight. So I wait, completely still, looking up at this powerful man.

His fingers wrap around my jaw. His thumb presses against my bottom lip, pushing it into my mouth like he owns me. "Some bad girls have to learn lessons the hard way."

Then, he undoes his pants, his movements sharp and pace steady. My stomach tightens as my gaze betrays me, flicking down. He's hard.

I purse my mouth shut, bracing myself. He strokes himself slowly. "Open wide," he instructs. "You're lying little throat is about to hurt."

I freeze, my pulse hammering. I should have seen this coming. I should have known he wouldn't let my defiance slide — he never does.

"Joar! I told you the truth. It was my mom that called!" I reason. When he doesn't waver, I yelp out in a panic: "If you try that, I'll bite down!"

His eyes narrow for a moment, perhaps surprised I threatened him. *Hell*, I'm surprised. But he doesn't retreat, his stormy eyes cloud more. "That's cute, little one. However, if you do that, I'll fuck your throat so deep you'll pass out. When you wake up, you won't know what happened."

An icy chill races down my spine. I don't know if he's bluffing. And I don't want to find out. His hand weaves in my hair, yanking me forward. The blunt tip of his cock grazes my mouth. His pre-cum seeps out as he traces my lips, coating them. To my surprise, he's turning me on despite this degrading act of dominance!

He's just so maddeningly sexy — his touch, his control over me. And he knows I'm so weak for him. I burn for him, my ally, my protector, my safe place.

I focus, though, coaching myself to stay strong because I told the truth. I don't want my throat to hurt, either! So, with his cock pressing forward, I'm ready to snap my jaws on his shaft as it pushes past my teeth.

His voice drops. "Guess what, my toy? I'm *angry*."

I glance up, startled by the shift in his tone. Where did the amusement, the taunting, the dark playfulness go?

He pauses. He's waiting. His fingers stroke my cheek with his cock rested in my mouth — mocking me.

"I've been patient because you needed me to be after your mom's abuse," he says. "But that's over."

My stomach tightens, and I furrow my brow.

He continues, "I'm mad about Erik hanging around your office for no apparent reason. I'm mad about the unmarked pills in your purse. I'm mad that you nearly broke our engagement because of your bitch of a mother. I'm mad that you tried to purge again."

I go rigid and strain to reply, "They were vitamins. And Erik wasn't—"

His fingers pull on the roots of my hair. "Lies." He powers his shaft in deep enough to hit my gag reflex. He smirks something wicked before retracting, letting me speak.

"I swear! I'm not lying!" I reply, but my voice lacks conviction.

Joar sighs. He's disappointed. Like I'm letting him down. "Such a *frustrating* girl," he mutters to himself. The tip of his cock pushes against my lips again. I open my mouth to defend myself, but he drives forward, silencing me as I gasp just before he fills my mouth.

His deep voice murmurs, "Did you know I have a camera in the driveway?"

I never noticed, so when he withdraws just enough to answer, I garble, "Erm... no."

He strokes my cheek once more, his touch so soft. "Want to know what I am most mad about? I checked the footage before I came in here. The day before Erik was in your office, he came over. The strange thing was, he didn't leave for twenty minutes."

My heart stops.

Lungs freeze.

Joar smiles, but it's dark and sinister. He pushes his shaft deeper. Not all the way, but enough that I gag more. He clutches my head firmly, holding me there as tears roll down my cheeks. I beg with my eyes, whining with a full mouth for mercy. He withdraws. "Enough? Then tell me, little liar, why did he visit you that night?"

I cough softly, but I can't tell him the full truth. *I can't!* So I answer, "Um. He... he forgot his watch. We talked about work for a little bit. That's it."

Joar's jaw flexes. Slowly, he shakes his head. "I can tell by that slight quiver of your chin that's another lie," he exhales. "Why do you do this to yourself?"

I shake my head frantically. "It's not—"

"I can't keep being easy on you," he cuts in. His fingertips graze my throat, and his voice drops to a dark murmur. "I hope for your sake, this little throat can take all of me."

I go still.

He grips my jaw, forcing me to look up. "I'll ask you *one more time.*" His cock pushes into my mouth again. "Are you hiding something from me?"

I force myself to breathe through my nose and shake my head no.

Finally, Joar's composed expression falters as he groans heavily, but his steely eyes darken. Without another word, he rams his cock deep into my throat. I gag violently this time, his thick length stretching me. I've never deep-throated a guy before, *and it hurts!*

I scramble, pushing at his hips, but he clutches my head to hold me in place. More tears stream down. He moves his hips, giving me deep digs that make it impossible to breathe. He savors it, watching me struggle with each forward thrust.

"Tell me," he orders as he pulls back.

I gasp for air, my throat on fire. I race for answers. Every lie I come up with feels less convincing than the last. My chest heaves as I glance up into his unforgiving eyes. To my surprise, I know that look he's giving me. He's pleading with me to end my own suffering. To trust him.

That look makes it so hard to defy him... and I break. I confess, "He made a move on me that night."

Joar freezes.

His hand clamps around my upper arm, jerking me to a stand so fast my shoulder feels like it snapped out of the socket. "Erik made a move? How?"

I flinch as I try to soften the truth. "He... he tried to kiss me."

Joar's rage is instant. His voice is sharp, slicing through me like a blade. "And you didn't think that was important enough to tell me? Why? Did you do kiss him back?"

"I told him no!"

"Oh? Because I have cameras in the house too, Emma. Why don't we watch it together and see what happened? I waited just for you — to see if you're lying — *again*."

In that instant, I know my world is about to shatter.

Chapter 48

Emma

Joar presses play.

The video displays its horrifying reality — the kiss, the struggle, my muffled protests, my attempt to crawl away, and then... the rape. I veer my eyes on Erik's first thrust, hearing it is torturous enough. It's just too unbearable.

The recording pauses, but the silence left behind is worse. My stomach lurches. Hesitantly, I glance up at Joar's face, dreading what I'll see.

He doesn't blink. Doesn't breathe. He just stares at the screen. His fingers are tight around his phone, his knuckles white.

"Joar," I whisper, my voice trembling. "I'm so sorry I lied. I just — I saw how you reacted at the bar with Sergey, and that was over a joke. I didn't want you to *kill* Erik. I don't want you to do something stupid and go to prison forever. So I—"

My voice catches.

He slowly looks up at me, those blue-gray eyes shifting darker than I've ever seen before. His chest rises and falls, but no air seems to pass through his nostrils.

Ten seconds.

Ten unbearable seconds before he moves.

Joar yanks on clothes and snatches his keys.

Oh, God.

My heartbeat a violent drumming in my ears. "Wait! Don't go after Erik!"

He doesn't stop.

He snatches my wrist, and drags me to the bed. It happens so fast, but suddenly, I'm handcuffed to the bedpost, cowering on the floor, my arms hooked above my head!

"What is this?" I panic.

He crouches down next to me, and in a soothing manner, he strokes my head, as if I am the one who needs to be calmed. "Emmy, you can't stop me because I love you. I don't think you know what that means. Maybe you were too abused, too deprived of love to ever feel it. But this is what it means to be loved."

I whimper at his accusation, sniffling back tears. "You're wrong. I know I love you, Joar," I say softly, my fingers twisting together. "I lied for you."

He rubs the top of my head, tousling my hair like I'm his pet. Then — suddenly — he leaves!

I call for him until my voice is raw. I pull on the hand-cuffs, my skin grows red and swollen. My arms ache. And I weep until I have no more tears.

He's gone, surely doing the devil's work.

※ ———••——— ※

Hours.

Joar left me cuffed to this bedpost for hours.

My arms are numb, the unforgiving metal biting into my wrists. My body aches, my ass burning from the rough carpet, my pulse erratic from the agony of waiting.

I shift, desperate to find relief, but it's useless. There's no comfort. Not when I don't know what he's done.

Then I hear it — *footsteps.*

My breath stops, my heart pounds so violently it hurts. Please, let it be Joar.

The door creaks open, and there he is.

He doesn't speak. He barely looks at me. His presence fills the room like a storm, tension crackling in the air. His shirt is stained red. My breath stutters. *Blood.*

"Joar!" I pull against the bedpost, frantic. "What hap-pened?"

No answer.

His face is unreadable, locked behind an impenetrable mask. Without a word, he strides past me and disappears into the bathroom. The sound of the shower running makes my head spin. I should be relieved — he's back, he's with me — but all I can think is: Are police coming next?

I kneel, naked, frozen in place, waiting for something — anything. But time drags, stretching unbearably. The water stops, steam curling into the air as he finally emerges.

His hair is wet, dripping down the hard lines of his chest, tracing the ridges of muscle that are usually a source of temptation.

Joar walks to me, his shadow stretching across the room. His warm fingers unlock the cuffs, freeing my wrists. I barely have time to move before he scoops me up effortlessly, carrying me into the bathroom.

The giant tub is filling fast, water swirling with foam. He lowers me inside, the heat soothing my body. I curl into myself as the bubbles rise around me, but before I can process anything, he climbs in, pulling me onto his lap. His strong arms cage me in.

I break.

A sob rips from my throat as I collapse against his chest, shaking with exhaustion, fear, and relief.

His large hand cradles my head, his other smoothing down my back. "Shhh, don't cry, you tiny, poor thing."

But I can't stop. "What did you do?" I whine, my voice trembling.

His fingers stroke through my damp hair, slow and possessive. "What you feared."

My breath hitches. *God, no.* My sobs muffle against his skin as I cry out, "You ruined everything! They'll take you from me! Forever!"

His arms tighten almost painfully, his voice dropping low and dark. "*Nobody* will take me from you. But Emmy, I'm the one person you should have told and you suffered alone. You must feel so... *sad.*"

There is something in the way he said that, something that tells me he's uncertain. The unease in his voice lances through me. My strong, invincible Joar doesn't know how to help me beyond his violent nature.

And when he growls, "I let it happen too. In *my* house. My own fucking cousin! I brought that hell into your life. I'm so sorry, Emma."

My lips part, but I hesitate. He's not just mad. Not just lost for answers — there's guilt.

I shift, straddling him, our bodies close, but he doesn't react — not like he usually does. His hands rest on my hips, but there's no hunger in his touch, only a need to hold on to me.

"Joar," I plead. "I love you. Don't be sorry."

His knuckle traces down my chest as he studies me, following the slope of my breast. But his expression grips my heart.

He's not present, not truly, as he says in a dull voice, "You're not capable of love, Emmy. A woman should rely on her man in her darkest hour. But you don't trust me to take care of you. But I will, anyway. So don't you worry, little one."

I pout. I can't stand it. I can't bear him treating me like something broken. Like now, I'm too fragile, too pathetic, too *sad*. Like I'm not the same girl he can have his way with. That I'm so damaged, I'm incapable of love.

He's dead wrong. One thing I know above all, is I love this man.

So I kiss him — *hard.*

It's a collision of lips and breath, my nails scraping against his scalp as I devour him, desperate to pull him back from the abyss. I roll my body, beckoning him to return from his dark thoughts. Soon, his arms pull me against his chest, his fingers digging into me as if he's terrified to let go.

I drag my pussy, pressing against his growing length, trying to wake him, trying to remind him I'm still here — not too abused to love.

He groans, hesitant, his mouth pulling from mine. "Emmy," he breathes against my lips. "Look at you: perfect. Always trying to please me—"

I shake my head violently. "Joar! I want you!" I frown and lower my voice. "I'm not too traumatized. Not with you."

His eyes study me, and slowly, he nods. "Okay, just know, I'm a storm of rage inside. But I'll give you whatever you want, you precious thing. Tell me if I get too rough." Then, his hands lock around my hips, lifting me with ease. I gasp as he fills me, stretching me deep. His lips brush my ear. "Relax for me."

I nod, my body melting into him, my walls giving around his length.

"That's it," he praises, voice dark. "Take me like that, you perfect girl."

And he moves, his strong hands guiding my hips. Slow. Deliberate. But I feel the anger simmering beneath.

A whimper escapes me, and Joar exhales sharply. "Don't look at me like that," he warns, his jaw flexing. "You'll make me lose control. Then... it'll hurt."

I tilt my head, teasing. "Like this?"

His muscles tense, his lips curling into a dark smirk. "Oh, you bad girl."

He repositions my back against the tub wall, and takes me harder, his touch punishing, but full of worship. The water splashes with each, deep, powerful thrust. He fists my wet hair, he bites my skin, he dominates. Droplets roll down the ridges of his sculpted body. Every muscle is pronounced, the adrenaline mixed with anger making his entire being flexed and ready to kill.

And right now, I'm his next victim.

His assault on my g-spot is relentless, along with his fingers massaging my clit under the water. By the time my third orgasm crashes through me, I don't feel anything but his love.

As I tremble helplessly, utterly his, Joar buries his face in my neck as he nears his apex.

I adore his affection and smile as I moan, "Mmm, I love you."

But he freezes, his smile disappearing as he sits and pulls me with authority to straddle his lap once more. I'm uncertain why, until... His hand drifts down my spine to the curve of my ass. His fingertip glides between, and slowly, he circles my tight opening.

I draw in a sharp breath as he teases my puckered ass.

"How much do you love me, Emmy? A lot?"

I nod, knowing instantly, he wants what Erik had.

The pressure *there* builds as his finger advances. I tense, but he waits for me to relax before pushing further.

I kiss his mouth as he pumps his finger, then breathe, "You can have all of me, Joar. I want you to." And without hesitation, I turn around, positioning myself on all fours. With my wet bottom in the air and the suds sliding down, I wiggle my hips a little, baiting him.

The water displaces as he rises and kneels behind me. His thumb plays with my tight, twisted hole, opening, preparing me before slowly wedging the head of his cock in place. I close my eyes as his hips lean forward, my teeth clenched as I take every inch of Joar the best I can.

It's uncomfortable, painful, and at moments, triggering. But I don't protest. I want Joar to have all of me. To claim me. To know I love him so much, that my fragile mind can seperate his touch from Erik's.

And he does. He claims me *slowly*.

The water lightly splashes as his body moves, his hands branding my skin with such a powerful hold on my hips. He doesn't prolong my gift to him, surely an act of mercy. With one final thrust, he hunches and groans my name, spilling deep inside me.

His breathing is shakey, his grip unyielding. When he finally speaks, his voice is hoarse, raw with something terrifyingly real: "I love you, and I swear on my life, I'll die before another person hurts you."

A shudder rolls through me. I believe him.

Yet, a quiet, aching voice whispers in the back of my mind: This is the beginning of the end. People can't murder someone and get away with it.

Chapter 49

Joar

The low hum of the sushi bar fills the space between us, the sound of clinking glasses, hushed conversations, and the rhythmic chopping of knives behind the counter.

Emma sits across from me, dainty fingers plucking an edamame pod from the bowl, slipping it between her lips as she savors the salty taste.

She looks relaxed... content, even. Not me.

In her eyes, it's probably been good for us for the last several months. She's safe, untouched by her mother's poison, by Erik's filth. She's finally mine in every way that matters. Soon, she'll be my wife. Soon, no one will have a say over her but me.

I love it — nobody can fucking hurt her again.

But *there*, hidden in my mind's eye, flashes the visual of my girl and Erik. As I've done thousands of times since I first saw the travesty, I suppress my grimace.

Poor Emma. I can't seem to get over having failed to protect this woman. This fragile little doll. She cries about everything... except what happened.

To pull myself from my despair, I rest my hand on her thigh, squeezing gently, grounding myself in the warmth of her body being in my control. She's here. She's mine. She's *safe*.

"Do you like this place?" I ask, wanting to make sure she's comfortable. "I picked it for you."

She glances around, taking in the ambiance before smiling. "Yeah, it's nice. Why for me?"

"They speak your language."

She snickers, playfully nudging me. "Joar, this is a *Japanese* restaurant. The chefs are speaking Japanese. I can't understand what they're saying, but thank you."

"Oh? Then I wonder if they have geishas here to serve me?"

She swats my arm, giggling. "Hopefully *not*. I'd like to get that idea out of your head."

"Maybe for our honeymoon."

Her lips part into a wide smile, eyes glowing with something soft, adoring. She looks at me like I hung the fucking moon, and I swear, I just wish—

Her phone rings.

Emma sighs and answers, her expression immediately shifting to rigid, more businesslike.

"Hi," she says, her voice formal. A pause. "Uh-huh, yep, I know... I'm with him now." Then she mutters something in Mandarin before hanging up.

I narrow my eyes, my good mood rotting by the second. "What was that about?"

She inhales a deep breath, as if bracing herself, and reaches into her bag. Her fingers wrap around a stack of papers. "I was planning to wait until after we ate dinner, but I guess now is as good a time as any." Her voice is too steady... that professional bullshit. "Joar, I need you to sign these documents. Please read them and let me know if you have any questions."

She hands me the papers, my nerves already on edge before my eyes even land on the words: *Prenuptial Agreement.*

Instantly, my blood boils. My jaw locks as I force my eyes back to hers. She looks... nervous. Not ashamed. Not apologetic. Just nervous.

"I hope for your sake this is a fucking joke," I say, my voice dropping to a dark lull.

She tenses but keeps her posture straight. "It's to protect both of us."

"No, it's not," I refute. "I have less money than you, Miss Billionaire's Daughter."

"Okay, but you're still a millionaire. It shouldn't matter if you sign."

I shake my head. "It matters because it means you think we'll *divorce.*"

She winces.

Good.

"I'm not worried we'll divorce, Joar," she says softly. "It's just... the wise thing to do."

My blood pressure spikes. She really fucking believes this.

I lean in, my voice sharp. "Did your mother put this nonsense in your head?"

Her expression hardens. "No. Please don't make this about her."

I scoff. "It's *always* about her."

She reaches for me. Her delicate hand rubs my thigh, as if she can soothe me into this insane idea — *a goddamn prenup!* It makes me angrier by the second.

"I'm not signing these fucking papers, Emma." I hand them back to her.

She hesitates, then lowers her voice like she's afraid someone might overhear. "Then... you don't want to get married?"

I gawk at her. Is she serious?

She tenses, uncomfortable under my stare, but she doesn't take it back. She doesn't *fucking* take it back.

"Joar," she continues, "I just mean, if you love me like you say you do, then you'll sign it to be with me."

My jaw drops and I blink a few times. She's lost her damn mind. "Are you giving me a fucking ultimatum?"

"No," she breathes. "I'm just — giving you a choice."

379

A laugh punches out of me, humorless and sharp. A choice. A fucking choice. I shake my head slowly. One step forward, ten steps back.

"Let me ask you this one more time — did your conniving bitch of a mother put this in your head?"

Her throat wavers, but she keeps her gaze level. "She may have suggested it, but I agree with her. You have a lot to gain if we divorce."

My vision blurs red, but I maintain my composure.

"Emma," I say, staying as calm as possible. "Listen to me, and listen carefully. Mei is *poisoning* you. She is pulling us apart. And you, my clueless, naive woman, are letting her."

She shrugs.

A *fucking shrug.*

And then, like she hasn't just stabbed me in the gut, she has the audacity to say, "Well, I'm becoming concerned that you're fighting this so much."

I snap. I grab the papers back, slowly rip them in half, and thump them onto the bar.

"This is disrespectful," I add, my voice venomous. "Apologize *now*."

Her lips part, but she says nothing. She just shakes her head — barely, but I catch it.

Oh... *That attitude.*

I lean back. For a moment, I don't even recognize her. *This is Emma?* The woman who clings to me in her sleep, who begs me to not leave her, who promised to be mine. And

380

yet, it only takes one whisper from her mommy to turn her against me.

I glare down at her. "You're a 25 year old woman still sucking on her mom's tit. You'll never be free of her."

"I am not!" she whines, her face flaming in humiliation. "But you are a 29 year old man who will retire sooner than later and have no job prospects. All athletes burn through their money and have nothing left. I'm your free ride."

That's her mother talking, but every second that passes, I believe it less and less. There was too much conviction in her voice.

I'm speechless.

With one last look, I lay some bills and walk out.

An hour later, Igor and I are six beers down and just served another. The light buzz tempers my rage, but it doesn't fix the festering wound in my chest.

Prenup.

Emma should be beside me. Not in her mother's pocket. Not making me beg to marry her. Not making me question if she's ever truly been mine.

"Are you Igor Patlov and Joar Sköll?" a flirty voice asks.

I look over. Two women — one redhead, one blonde. My gaze sweeps over them. Full tits, nice ass, both sexy as hell. They smile, their bright eyes dripping with the kind of thirst I usually ignore.

"I'm Cheyanne," the redhead says, "and this is Rhea. We're really big fans."

What a time for puck bunnies to appear.

Chapter 50

Joar

The scent of Cheyanne's perfume is suffocating — sweet and overwhelming, luring me like honey, but I know it's rancid. Her body presses against mine, soft curves molding into my side as she casually drapes her arm over my shoulder. She fits against me well, too well.

I barely acknowledge her. *I don't want her.* Not her flirty smiles, not the way she bats her lashes, not even the way her body moves like it's made to be fucked.

Because even now, I can't stop thinking about that *frustrating*, fucking woman!

My Emmy, with her lovely, stupid lost eyes, handing me a goddamn prenup like I was some replaceable man instead of the one who owns her. Who keeps her from ruining her own life. Who protects her.

But... I didn't protect her.

My gut twists.

I failed my girl.

Fuck.

Maybe she's having second thoughts, and rightly so. I've let her mother abuse her, my cousin rape her.

The version of Emma I left back at the sushi restaurant — cold, calculated, formal — maybe that is her. The result of my failure to care for her the way she needed. Now, she's Mei's puppet again. And though it kills me, I can see why she went back.

I swallow the burn of my whiskey and tap my fingers against the side of my glass, tension knotting in my shoulders as I fight the urge to leave this place and find her. But why? It's hard to imagine that the woman I love might be better off with someone else.

Hence, I don't.

Instead, I let Cheyanne hang off me, let her play her little game. Let her push her tits against my arm and whisper about how she's "not like other girls."

And I almost let her keep going — until my phone vibrates.

Emma's name flashes across the screen.

The pull is instant. Despite my anger, I want to answer. I want to hear her voice. But my jaw tightens as I glance at the redhead wrapped around me like a fucking boa constrictor.

I push off my seat, untangling her from me as I step away, ignoring her little pout as I find a quieter corner of the bar. It's still too loud, the low bass of the music pulsing through my head, but it'll do.

"Joar? I see you on the tracker. Why the *hell* are you at a bar?" Emma's voice bites through.

That tone.

My grip on the phone tightens. First, she gives me an ultimatum, now she's speaking to me like I answer to *her*? I close my eyes, inhale through my nose, and force myself to stay calm.

"Start again," I command.

A heavy sigh follows before she tries once more, this time softer. "Joar... *please* leave the bar. Please, come home."

Come home?

I see red. This fucking woman.

She tests me. Doubts me. Asks for a prenup. Now, she suddenly wants me home. Before I can respond, Cheyanne appears at my side, sliding her hand behind my back. Her lips part into a slow, knowing smile as she says, "There you are! Come back to the table. We're doing shots."

I sigh in exhaustion, knowing Emma hears Cheyanne's voice.

"Who was that?" she demands.

I grind my teeth. I may have failed her, but I don't want to deal with her jealousy. Not after the stunt she pulled today. Not when she's the one who tried to act like I was some fucking temporary thing.

"That voice? That was a redhead," I say flatly, watching Cheyanne through narrowed eyes. She wants me. And maybe, right now, I want to be tempted. So I add into the phone, "A redheaded puck bunny, and she wants me to fuck her."

Cheyanne doesn't deny it. Instead, she bites the tip of her pinky, her eyes flicking between me and my phone.

Of course, Emma gasps. I hear the panic in it. The desperation.

"Don't! Joar! Come home, *please*."

My jaw ticks. I should cave. The rape flashes before my eyes, making my desire to keep her wage war with the reality: I keep failing to protect her. Such a poor fucking girl.

I should have prevented it.

I have to be honest with myself. The prenup isn't pissing me off. It's just the spark that ignited a mountain of guilt dynamite. Murdering Erik didn't extinguish this feeling, not even close.

Therefore, I deflect from the truth once more, scraping for anything to distance myself, to distract, to escape reality. "Still want a prenup?" I challenge, my voice razor-sharp.

"Joar, if you cheat with that girl, I won't *ever* talk to you again!"

Her threat, her avoidance of my question, is the answer I wanted, the excuse I need to hang up.

She doesn't call back. *Good.*

Without a second thought, I return to the table and let the drinks pour.

I don't know what time it is... but I'm not wasted.

I refuse to be.

But I feel it. The heavy warmth in my limbs, the slight disconnect between thought and movement. It slows me down just enough to make me dangerous.

Cheyanne is on my lap. *Again.* I don't know how she keeps reappearing here, but she's warm. Soft. Her ass molds against my cock, pressing, rubbing. Begging to be spanked.

It feels so wrong. I know it's wrong.

But I'm so goddamn angry, and I wonder — would *this* be easier? Fucking her, cheating to swiftly end the relationship.

Then, Cheyanne leans in, lips ghosting over my neck, whispering about a stripper pole in her apartment. My grip tightens around my glass, picturing her naked as she twirls around it.

I don't want to, but I can do this. Emma can be done with me for good, and God willing, find someone better...

Fuck, that thought kills me.

But as Cheyanne's teeth nip at my ear, I just can't enjoy it. This isn't right. No matter how drunk I get, my mind, my body, my fucking soul are hers. Also, I can't hurt Emmy — can't scar the poor girl more.

"Get the fuck off me," I growl at Cheyanne.

She pouts, but before I push her off, a firm tap lands on my shoulder.

I turn my head, and there she is.

Emma.

Her eyes are hard, her jaw set, shoulders square. She looks like she's about to kill me.

"Joar," she says, voice firm.

"Emma," I mock with a slight slur. I move to face her, but my hand knocks over my beer. The glass tumbles, shattering on the floor, shards skidding in all directions.

She scoffs. "Joar," she says, her voice louder. More *dominant*. That's new.

I don't like it.

Then, the last words I ever expect flow from her lips: "I *fucking* hate you right now." Her hand flies through the air, her small palm connecting with my face.

I hardly feel it, but a ripple of silence washes over the table.

Cheyanne gawks, then snaps, "*She's* your fiancée?"

Emma doesn't look at her. Doesn't acknowledge her. All her focus is on me. Then, she grabs my jaw, making me wonder: *who is this woman?*

"Look at me," she demands. "Get her off your lap and stand up."

Something about the way she says it — steady, unshaken, certain — stirs something dark inside me. I grab Cheyanne's waist and shove her off. Then, I rise, using the table for balance. I stay calm, towering over her. Honestly, I can't be mad at her. She has a right to be mad.

I sigh. "Go back to *your house*, Emma. Take your prenup with you," I bite out. But for the first time since meeting her,

I can't look at that sweet face and veer my eyes. I simply can't face her.

She exhales, clearly tired. But she doesn't falter. Shockingly, she takes my hand, fingers lacing with mine. "Joar, you're drunk. Just please. Come home."

I draw my gaze to her, genuinely surprised. "Why?"

Then, she does something that undoes me completely.

She lifts my hand to her lips and kisses my knuckles — soft, lingering. "Joar, you know me," she whispers. "I'm barely holding it together... seeing a woman hanging on you in a bar. It's a nightmare. But I'm here, fighting for you." Her voice loses its toughness with each word. The slight tremble of her chin is disarming. I want to give in. I want to take her in my arms and comfort this sad little creature I love so dearly. She's fucking precious and doesn't even know it.

"Did you hear me?" she says with angst, stepping close and snuggling her cheek to my chest. "I need you... and I love you. I'm so sorry. So, so, sorry. You have no idea how sorry. No prenup, okay? Just come home. I just want to marry you." She gasps for air, her throat tight as she chokes back tears. "Please. Joar."

I can't help it. I pet her and kiss the top of her head. "Emmy, you know this isn't about the prenup, don't you?"

Her forehead creases deep in confusion, but after a moment, a look of recognition blankets her expression as she says, "*Ohhh.*"

She knows.

I exhale heavy. "Twice, Emma. Fuck, I don't want to lose you, but you deserve someone—"

"*Don't,*" she interrupts. "You know the rules, Joar. You set them. We can't talk about breaking up. Remember?"

"But Emma—"

"I know what you're feeling. I see you struggle every day with what happened — more than I do. I see the stress in your eyes, in the way you carry yourself, the way you disappear in your thoughts, how you ball your fists and grind your teeth. I know you're angry and worried about me all the time." She lightly glides her fingers along my jawline. "But you need to realize: it was *not* your fault."

And fuck — that hits hard. I shake my head. "It was."

"No, Joar. It wasn't. *None* of this is your fault. I pushed you to go out that night. Then I let a man into the house late. I had been drinking and didn't notice the signs fast enough."

"Emmy, it's not your fault—"

She holds up her finger with authority, pointing it in my face. "It's Erik's fault... and guess what? I haven't cried since you took care of that problem."

"I know, but you can cry about it. To me." I wrap my arms around her trembling body, and it's like I'm whole again. The world around us is a blur of neon and noise, but everything about Emmy is clear and peaceful.

She squeezes me tight, as if I may float away. She says, "I don't need to cry, Joar. Not about that. Not when I have you. Bad things happen to me when *you're gone.* I'm safer with you. I need you, so let's go home." She takes my hand and jerks on my arm, pulling me toward the exit. I follow, smirking at this little thing leading me with such determination. She doesn't look back. Probably afraid I'll stop. It's cute.

I let her lead.

Just this once.

Chapter 51

Joar

This.

The worst part about being an athlete is losing, but *this* is a close second: interviews, dinners with strangers, dumb events. And when your girl is the GM, there's no skipping out.

Which is why I'm here tonight, in this ballroom hellscape, stuffed into a suit, acting civilized. At least it's for a charity saving cats and dogs.

Emma stands beside me, stunning in her pink dress — classy, yet sinful the way it clings to every curve. My eyes can't help but drift lower. Fuck, I'd like to punish her for wearing it — parading that perfect ass where every man can see it.

Across the room, Mei lurks, throwing her usual daggers of disapproval. She won't even meet my eyes — just glares at Emma like she wants her skates melted. Gremlin.

Before I can blink, Mei's in front of us — fucking witchcraft.

"Come, Emma. I want to introduce you to the Commissioner's wife."

Emma offers a polite smile and follows, leaving me to watch her hips sway through the crowd. But I trail close — where she goes, I go.

A soft, cool touch brushes my wrist, stopping me.

"Joar."

My jaw tenses as I look down. Eh. Ophelia.

Her catlike eyes flicker under layers of smoky shadow, her lips painted a predatory red. The high cut of her gown flashes her smooth thigh as the fabric shifts with every subtle movement. She's a sexual weapon, always dressed for one purpose.

"Do you have a minute?" she purrs, her voice thick with lust.

I flick my gaze toward Emma's shrinking figure. "Not now."

"It's about *that night*," she says, and the air snaps cold. "You know, about the guy I was sleeping with?"

My spine stiffens, and in a flash, the memories crash — blood on floor, Erik's body bound to a chair, the knife in my hand, the door creaking open... and her. Ophelia's stricken eyes, the only witness.

He was seeing her, and I had no fucking idea.

"Talk *here*?" I growl.

"No. Somewhere private." She tilts her head, a dare.

My teeth grind, but I begrudgingly nod.

She saunters ahead, hips swaying with practiced grace, different than Emma's innocent walk. Ophelia knows what's she's doing with every step, guiding me upstairs to a dim office. The soft *click* of the door echoes like a trap snapping shut.

"How are you?" she begins, voice dripping with mock sweetness.

I cut through her act. "What do you want, Ophelia?"

She smirks — such a sinister smile — as she perches on the desk, legs crossed, champagne stem dangling from her fingers. "What are you doing with Emma?" she muses. "Surely you know you're a terrible match with her."

"Explain," I say with disinterest, wanting to speed this up.

Her eyes gleam. "You and I both know what you need. Emma? She's sweet, but you'll break her. She'll never understand your... cravings."

"This conversation is over."

Her voice carries softly. "Walk out, and you'll regret it."

I freeze, my pulse inching higher. "I wouldn't threaten me," I warn.

"Very well. I'll cut to the chase. I want what Emma has — and that's you."

I furrow my brow, finding that statement ridiculous. "What the *fuck* is your fixation with Emma? It's cruel to pursue the men she loves."

"You mean, the men I love." She slides off the desk, moving to me. "Emma always had it all. The money, the perfect parents, the gorgeous skate partner — Christian. The same guy she knew I loved first. She stole him from me!"

"I'm sure Emma didn't date Christian to hurt you—"

"Yes! Yes, she did! But that is beside the point. That's the past. This is beyond first loves. We both know you and I have a connection that you can't have with her. She doesn't know the real you. Not like I do. She'll never understand the man beneath the mask. She wouldn't survive your darkness."

"She knows me." I glare down at her, not warming, hoping to intimidate this treacherous woman.

Ophelia shakes her head and stands firm. "Emma may know what you did, but it's one thing to *know* someone's sins, and another to *see* them."

I consider for a split second what Emma would have done if she were in Ophelia's shoes that night, but quickly disregard the thought.

Her eyes burn into mine. "But I saw. I didn't run, did I? I fell to my knees, ready to be next. Either your submissive or your victim. But you left me knelt. You let me watch. And you—" Her lips curl. "You liked that I did. Admit it. It turned you on. We saw each other that night. Let's finish what we started. I want you to fuck me. Right here. Right now."

I step back, disgust curling my lips. "No."

A flash of teeth. "Then I tell Emma. And her parents. And the press. I'll describe it all — how I walked in and caught you torturing the guy I was dating — your cousin. I'll describe all that blood, and that evil look in your eyes. I'll tell her how Erik begged for his life. That you killed him because you *liked it.* That you threated to kill me if I went to the police."

I inhale sharply, my heart a live wire. But just then, she closes in, her fingertips slide just under my waistband, causing me to step back. However, she follows, her thumbs hooked on my belt as she stays close.

"Ophelia, this isn't going to happen," I assure, unlatching her hands from me. "Emma won't believe you. Nobody will. Erik is missing. There isn't a body."

"Everyone will believe me. Especially Emma," Ophelia presses, now circling like a panther. "Especially when I tell her about your ex. *Runa*, is it? Erik gave me the full story."

I freeze. My voice pure ice. "Tread carefully."

"It is just facts," she slithers. "How you *snapped* — and she never walked away. Runa couldn't handle you as her dominant. I can. What do you think Emma will do when she wonders if she's next? She'll *never* trust you."

I step forward, the urge to end this with my hands surging through every muscle. "You're playing a dangerous game."

"And I'm winning," she taunts, her gaze pinned on mine. "Face it. You want me so bad. I bet you're hard just having me this close. Oh, Joar... if I don't make your toes curl, if I don't make you cum harder than you ever have in your life, then go be with Emma. I'll leave you two alone. But I know who you are, baby. You're a killer. You're a dominant. And me? I am your prey you want to toy with. The girl you're dying to punish just for forcing this choice on you. Because I'm your perfect submissive. The only one who sees you — the real you."

She tilts her head, lashes lowering. "And I know what you need, Joar. I saw it the night you killed him. You wanted me then — you wanted the girl who *stayed*. You wanted to wreck me. So wreck me." Her hands trail up my chest, and she sinks, slow and deliberate, to her knees.

I try to speak, but nothing comes out. I just stare down at this woman.

In a raspy voice, she whispers, "What will it be? One harmless night with me? Just one. Or shall I return to the party and destroy your life? Make Emma run from you for good?"

My pulse thunders, adrenaline and rage bleeding into something primal. I could kill her. But this is different from Runa. This is a whole different situation.

As if she's stunned me frozen, I can only watch as her dainty hand reaches out, and slowly, she undoes my pants. She opens her mouth, her tongue curling out, ready to receive me like a hungry siren.

The room, the world, everything blurs...

Chapter 52

Emma

What a great evening that was!

I love that Joar attends those events with me. I know he hates it, so it means a lot.

"Do you like the dress?" asks Mother, snapping me from my thoughts. I only see her at work or for wedding stuff — and only in public places.

I stand in front of the full-length mirror, admiring my reflection in my wedding dress. I run my hands down the smooth satin and ornate beading, a smile tugging at my lips. The fabric is sewn perfectly to the shape of my curves, and at this moment, I am beautiful.

"I love it," I whisper, trying to hold on to my newfound confidence.

As I turn slightly to see the back, my earring suddenly comes loose and falls. I bend down to catch it midair, but a tearing sound causes my heart to sink.

The back of my dress just ripped.

First comes panic, then the weight of insecurity descends. All the doubts and fears about my body that I've tried so hard to suppress come rushing back with brutal force. I look at myself in the mirror, my disbelief draining all color from my face.

"Oh my goodness!" says the sales rep, hurrying over to study the damage I caused.

Tears prick at the corners of my eyes before I can stop them. My hands tremble as I try to breathe past the crushing wave of shame.

Why can't I just feel good about myself for once?

A familiar voice cuts through my spiraling thoughts.

Mother.

She stands beside the saleswoman, arms folded, her gaze assessing the damage with the same cool detachment she used whenever I gained weight before a competition.

"Brings back memories, doesn't it?" she muses.

My stomach drops. Of course she'd say that. I blink hard, swallowing the lump in my throat as old memories rush back. The tight seams of my skating costumes. The silent judgment. The pressure.

Mother's voice is deceptively soft when she asks, "Have you been taking your diet pills?"

I nod stiffly. "Apparently not enough."

She exhales sharply. "Increase it. You only have one week before you marry this man who will cost you everything."

Her scowl deepens, her words laced with disgust.

"A frightening venture without a prenup, if you had anything to lose."

Rage bubbles beneath my humiliation.

"Mom — stop," I snap through gritted teeth. My fingers curl into the fabric of my gown. I may not always believe in myself, but I will defend Joar.

"He doesn't want a prenup. If it costs me my inheritance, so be it."

The saleswoman's brows lift in curiosity. "That's sweet. So, you're marrying a hockey player?" she asks as she pins my dress.

"Yes."

She steps closer, adjusting the fabric around my hips. "Oh. Please stay still. I'm marking where to add fabric and repair the seam."

I tense. "No need to add fabric. I'll lose the weight before the wedding. Just fix the seam."

She cringes, but tries to mask it. "Why don't we replace the zipper with a lace-up back? Then you can adjust as needed."

Mother shakes her head. "No. She'll lose the weight." Her voice is absolute. "For all her faults, she does practice discipline when necessary."

I exhale sharply. I liked the adjustable back idea. But of course, my body has to be the problem.

The saleswoman nods, wisely saying nothing. Then, she changes the subject. "I dated a few hockey players back in Norway, long ago. They're fun."

"You mean controlling? Bossy? Demanding?" I say with a small smirk, trying to distract myself.

She chuckles. "Yes, that was my experience, too. Especially Joar. He was a handful."

My heart stops.

My breath catches as I turn slowly to get a better look at her: Tall. Blonde. Perfect. A golden name tag gleams under the boutique lights: RUNA.

My stomach plummets. *Holy...*

"Joar Sköll?" I ask, my voice careful.

She stiffens. "Oh, um, no," she mutters, but adds, "I bet you're talking about that hockey player in the news? Because that's not the Joar I dated."

Liar.

I push forward. "I know we're talking about the same guy."

She sighs, rubbing the back of her neck. "It was a long time ago. I never thought he'd settle down."

My stomach twists. "Uh huh," I murmur.

Runa forces a smile. "Well, I wish you the best. We'll have your dress ready soon."

I follow her as she turns away. "Joar said you were dead."

She freezes.

"I remember him saying your name. Erik showed me a picture of you."

Runa exhales sharply. "Fucking Erik."

Her eyes dart toward me, lips parting like she wants to ask something. Instead, she flinches. "Please don't tell Joar."

I narrow my eyes. "Why?"

"I just—" She swallows and shakes her head. "How is he? Is he happy?"

"Uh, yeah!" I reply in astonishment.

She only nods, then walks away.

❧ ⊷————•••————⊶ ☙

The game finished an hour ago, but I'm working late to distract myself. Besides, Joar is doing the post-game press conference, so he should come to my office when he's done. The wedding is in two days. I'm not stressing about my weight anymore. I called the dress shop. Thankfully, Runa didn't answer, but I requested a lace up back and they agreed, which put an end to my battle of losing fifteen pounds in less than a week.

My phone vibrates, startling me.

Unknown

> *Picture of Runa in the locker room*

What the...

I race down the hall, my heels clacking against the tile, heart hammering in my chest.

I shove the locker room door open, and there they are.

Runa and Joar.

He stands frozen, his entire body locked, his breathing shallow.

Runa — the woman he mourned. The woman he loved. The woman who destroyed him.

I clutch the doorframe, my stomach twisting as I take in the raw, unfiltered shock on Joar's face. I've never seen him like this—never seen him look at someone like that.

Like she's a ghost.

Like she's something he never dared hope to see again.

"I can't believe it," he breathes, his voice hoarse. "You were alive this whole time?"

I step forward, grabbing his sleeve, desperate to break whatever spell this is. "Joar?" My fingers curl into the fabric, as if holding onto him will anchor him to me. "What's going on?"

He doesn't blink. Doesn't move.

Runa takes a tentative step forward. "Joar..." she whispers, eyes brimming with emotion. "I know this is a shock. But I swear — I'm not the same person I was before. I've changed."

She reaches out, her slender fingers grazing his forearm.

I slap her hand away before I can stop myself. "Don't *touch* him."

He doesn't even notice. He just stares at her like the ground has caved beneath his feet.

And then—

Applause. Slow. Mocking.

The sound sends a cold spike of dread down my spine.

Ophelia.

She strides in, a wicked smirk stretching across her perfect lips, Mei trailing behind her like a shadow.

"Well, well, well," Ophelia purrs, her tone dripping with satisfaction. "Joar, his *fiancée*, and the ghost of his past — what a reunion." She turns to me, eyes gleaming. "Isn't this *interesting*, Emma? Seeing as you met Runa already?"

Joar's body turns rigid beside me, he sneers, "Emma, you knew?"

I nod, feeling ashamed I didn't tell him. But I didn't want him to back out of our wedding! I murmur, "Sorry."

He narrows his eyes, but then, his head snaps toward Ophelia. "You arranged this?"

Ophelia nods. "And Mei." Her smirk widens as she steps closer to him. "I did you a favor, Joar. I *resurrected* your first love." She glances at Runa, her hand skimming her lower back like she owns her. "Erik told me how much you *grieved*. Don't you think you owe me a *thank you?*"

Joar's hands curl into fists. "You *knew* and said nothing?" His voice is low, dangerous.

Ophelia just shrugs. "I wanted to see what you'd do. I know Emma isn't, and if not me, Runa must be the *perfect submissive*, wasn't she? The one who got away."

But Runa speaks first, her voice breaking.

"Joar... I was young and stupid." She wrings her hands, eyes pleading. "I felt you pulling away. You got the NHL deal. You were moving to the U.S. You weren't going to marry me."

Joar's head jerks back, his expression darkening.

"I *wasn't* leaving you!" he snaps. "I just wasn't ready for marriage. So you faked a suicide?"

Tears spill down Runa's cheeks. "I—Joar, I *loved* you! I wanted you to hurt as much as I was hurting. I gave you everything. I did the deal. I was perfect for you! But you still wanted to leave me."

Joar's entire body stiffens. His breath is ragged, his fists clenched so tight his knuckles go white. "I didn't want to leave you! I can't believe you faked your death. Jumped off a boat in the middle of the night... do you know what that did to me?" His voice is ice.

Runa's lower lip trembles. "I didn't think you'd grieve forever—"

"You left a suicide letter blaming me!" Joar seethes, his voice like a blade. "You said I was a sadistic, manipulative dom. That I broke you. That I would've killed you eventually anyway." His chest rises and falls heavily. "They almost arrested me because of your fucking lies, but all they had was a letter."

Runa flinches. "Joar—"

"I thought I was too rough with you, Runa! *Fuck,* I eventually blamed myself."

Ophelia interjects smoothly, stepping between them like she's conducting a show. "Everyone, calm down. Joar, you were never arrested. So why hold a grudge? She feels guilty." Ophelia tilts her head, feigning sympathy. "But isn't this fate? Maybe seeing her again stirs up... old feelings."

I scoff, stepping forward. "Why are you doing this, Ophelia?"

Her sharp gaze flicks to me. And then, for the first time, I see it.

Rage.

"You *always* get the guy," she hisses. "You got Christian. Joar. Even Erik — who wouldn't stop talking about you even though I was sleeping with him! Why? Why do men get hooked on you and not me? I'm better looking! A better skater! And surely, a better fuck."

My stomach drops.

"I didn't know you liked them that much. You like-like Joar?" I whisper.

She laughs coldly. "I tried to get him to sleep with me. But lucky fucking Emma has a loyal man... He said no — a mistake, since I know all his secrets." She leans in. "If I can't have him, neither can you."

She gestures toward Runa. "So here she is. His true love."

I go still, the weight of her words crashing over me. This... this was never about Runa. This was never about justice. This was Ophelia's vendetta.

She smirks, eyes glinting with cruel satisfaction. "You feel pity for him, don't you? You really think you know Joar?" Her voice lowers. "That he's been honest with you?"

Joar stiffens, his grip tightening around my waist. "Don't."

Ophelia shrugs, like she's bored. "Why not? Shouldn't she know that the reason you joined her team was never about her?"

The room tilts.

"The plan was to marry her," Ophelia continues, voice venomous. "To divorce her. And take everything. Erik told me everything."

My heart stops. I look up at Joar. He doesn't deny it.

He doesn't say anything!

For the first time since I met him... he looks nervous.

My lips part, my breath coming in shallow gasps.

Then Mei steps forward, her voice smooth as silk. "Tell me, Emma," she murmurs, eyes glinting. "Now that you know Joar's just another greedy, lying bastard — are you still so foolish as to marry him?"

Joar doesn't speak. And that's when I realize: It's true.

My whole world caves in.

Chapter 53

Emma

I'm in a state of shock. I close my eyes, trying not to pass out.

This man... my everything. He was all a lie. A fantasy? And I fell for it!

I turn to Joar. "Ophelia is lying, right? There was no plan to get my money." My voice cracks as I try to hang on to the last threads of my fairytale with Joar.

But Ophelia answers for him. "Yes! Erik told me everything! Joar always dreamed to own a hockey team. Tell her, Joar. Tell Emma how the deal was just a way to accelerate a relationship and manipulate her toward marriage. How you would retire. Have all the girls he wants. Lots of money. Set for life."

I turn to Joar, my voice trembling. "No, Joar. Say she's lying."

Joar opens his mouth, but Ophelia barrels on, like a woman set on burning everything to the ground. "It's true! He doesn't want to play much longer. His shoulder is shot."

I cover my mouth. "It is? You never told me your shoulder was a problem." I cover my mouth, suddenly remember when he once carried my bag, and had to switch shoulders. How Bri the masseuse found 'the right spot' near his shoulder blade.

Joar exhales sharply, his gaze locking on mine. "Okay. Fine, Emma. That part is true. My shoulder isn't great, and this will probably be my last season. But as for your money and owning the team, it doesn't matter anymore. That's irrelevant now. Yes, the original plan was to marry you for those reasons, but now..." His voice softens, raw with emotion. "I just want you."

I'm speechless.

I feel the world crumbling beneath me. My breath catches as Mother chuckles behind me, her voice dripping with venom. "See, Emma. I was right all along. He couldn't be trusted."

Her words carve into me, and I close my eyes, willing myself not to believe her, but it's hard. The truth is suffocating. I trusted him. I believed in him.

Joar steps closer, his hands gently but firmly clutching my wrists. He bends down so his eyes are level with mine, his voice a low, desperate plea. "Emma, I love you. This isn't about owning a team anymore. It hasn't been for a long time. Please, trust me."

I want to believe him — God, I want to — but doubt is a knife twisting in my chest.

Mother's hand lands on my shoulder, a reminder of every time I've let her dictate my life. "Come, Emma," she says, her tone smug. "His intentions are clear. He only wants to steal our wealth."

I look at Joar, my voice breaking as I search those stormy eyes I love so much. "That's why you didn't want to sign the prenup. You're a liar. I hid the truth about Runa, but this is way bigger!"

His jaw tightens, but his expression doesn't falter. "Your knew about Runa?"

"Don't even try to turn this on me," I warn, determined to ignore every aching bone in my body not to defy this man.

He pauses, then replies, "Emma. These are the moments that define us. This is when I need you to believe me — above your mother, Ophelia, or anyone else. I truly love you. Fuck, Emmy, I'm in love with you. The money doesn't matter anymore. Please, for once in your life, trust someone — Trust me."

Mother's laugh cuts through the tension like a blade. "Yes, Emma. Trust the hockey player who manipulated you. Not me. Though, I don't care what you do, because you won't be getting the team, anyway."

Joar's gaze darkens. "What does that mean?"

Mother smirks at me, satisfied. "Didn't you tell him? We're selling the team at the end of the season."

Joar snaps his attention back to me. "What?"

I nod, my voice shaking. "If you didn't sign the prenup, my parents said I wouldn't inherit the team or anything else.

I chose you." My voice wavers with every word, feeling increasingly stupid. "Looks like I chose wrong."

Joar flinches, his composure cracking. "Another thing you withheld from me. Like the 'vitamins,'" he mutters under his breath.

"They're diet pills. Okay? And my lies served one purpose: to keep you. Your lie was for the opposite. To fool me long enough till you could toss me aside."

His expression hardens, but his voice remains steady. "Emma, listen to me. I don't care about your money or the team. I still want to marry you — whether you inherit a dime or not." His voice lowers, almost soft enough for only me to hear. "I need you to choose me."

"What about me?" Runa whines.

Slowly, Joar turns his attention to Runa, giving her a bewildered look before saying, "No fucking chance."

She frowns, and like a wounded rabbit, she leaves.

Joar clutches my shoulders. "Emmy. Believe I love you."

Before I can respond, Mei scoffs loudly. "Enough of this! I'm tired of him." She opens the locker room door and four officers stride in.

Mei points a commanding finger at Joar. "This is the man who broke into Christian Poole's house and beat him. Arrest him."

Ophelia points at Joar, too. "That's right! He killed his cousin, too! That's him."

"What?" Joar snarls, his confusion giving way to anger as the officers close in. Before he can fight, Joar is tasered. I try to stop the policeman, but there are too many. Joar is handcuffed.

Ophelia's laughter echoes, but it's short-lived. She's handcuffed, too! "What the hell, Mei?"

Mother's expression is chillingly calm. "Runa didn't work. But I always have another plan."

"You bitch!" Ophelia screams, struggling against her captors.

Mother ignores her, her gaze locked on Joar. "Mr. Sköll, I have resources — money, allies, and the will to destroy you. You never stood a chance."

Joar sneers, still catching his breath after being tased. "I figured out your riddles. You've read *The Art of War*, haven't you? 'Victory is reserved for those willing to pay its price.' How far are you willing to go, Mei? Because you'll never break the bond I have with your daughter."

I cut in sharply. "Untrue."

Joar's eyes meet mine, so fierce I have to step back. "Emma. Come to the jail. Wait for me. Don't go home with her. Don't let her get inside your head."

Mother's voice is ice. "Goodbye, Mr. Sköll."

As they lead him out, Joar looks over his shoulder. "Emma. Trust me. Please. I signed the prenup."

My breath catches. "You what?"

"He's lying," Mother snaps. "Don't let him fool you again."

I drop my gaze, my reflex to cling to the obedience she's drilled into me all my life. Her instincts were right, too. He lied. He's the liar. I was fooled. I lied because I love him. He lied to use me.

But my heart pounds in rebellion, screaming to move, to follow him. Yet, I stay frozen, paralyzed by confusion and years of conditioning.

And then, he's gone.

Chapter 54

Emma

I look into the bathroom mirror while the haunting tune of Halsey's *I am not a woman, I'm a God* plays on my phone.

I am not a woman, I'm a God
I am not a martyr, I'm a problem
I am not a legend, I'm a fraud
So keep your heart, 'cause I already got one

I study my reflection in heavy contemplation, feeling the same confusion by the image of a woman staring back at me. From one moment to the next, I change. A girl, an adult, a champion, a loser, a thin woman, a fat woman, and then me, today. I'm none of those, yet all of those.

I'm a woman who has been left wanting... Joar.

As I think about him sitting in jail, I ache for him. Tears roll down my cheeks. My whole life, I've never been alone. My parents were a constant, and always driving my every action.

Except on the ice, I was hardly present in my own body. I lived in my mind.

Being with Joar was the same way. He was a constant who controlled my life. But inversely, he wanted me out of the chaos in my mind, so I could live in my body, and thus, the present — enjoying life with my worries in *his* hands.

We fed off that. It's what drew us together. We both got what we needed. But now he needs me. At least, the guy I thought he was needs me. But someone who wanted to marry me just to divorce — to break my heart — for money... he doesn't deserve my devotion.

With a heavy sigh, I dress for bed. Wishing I could turn off my feelings for Joar. How can I love someone will such ill intent?

But I do. *God*, I love that man, and the feeling only intensifies each second we are apart.

And he loves me... I think. I hope.

Mother walks into my bedroom and gives a small head bow before saying, "Goodnight, Emma. I hope this lesson is lasting, and you remain grounded when selecting future partners."

I stand next to my childhood bed and lift my chin. I wandered home, seeking kindness from the two people who usually support me in my darkest hours.

And then, I'm compelled to do something I once never considered. After drawing in a deep breath, I summon the little energy I have left and say, "Mother, I love you."

She swallows, her face reflecting the same reserved, cold expression she's worn most of my life. The long wait for her to respond grows increasingly unbearable, causing me to grimace in disappointment. I shouldn't be stunned that faced with those words, she still cannot speak them.

Determined not to dwell on that ugly truth, I change the subject. "Why did you pick that dress shop?"

Her eyes close for a moment, as though relieved to escape the awkwardness. "It had a good reputation."

"Mother, it's not like you to lie. Explain why you insisted we go to New York for my dress. There are plenty of other shops in Texas. You knew Joar's ex worked there, didn't you?"

With a slight lift of her shoulders, she answers calmly, "Yes. I hired a private investigator who found Runa."

With a heavy sense of despair and shock, my mouth parts. "Why would—"

"I hoped reuniting them would cause Joar to leave you. Erik told Ophelia her death deeply affected Joar. I assumed it was grounded in affection."

"But *why* would you sabotage my relationship with him?"

"He was using you, Emma! Wake up, you weakling. Christian was a better match."

"Christian and I were not right for each other. We didn't make each other happy."

"Happiness is a Western priority."

I balk. "It's a human priority."

"A human weakness," she corrects.

I shake my head, recognizing our views on the world are so different. Since my happy ending is of no value to her, achieving it myself was never ingrained in me.

With a small voice, I explain, "I wish you had not hunted for reasons to ruin my relationship with Joar. I was happy with him, and that was important to me. Maybe he really does love me."

"Joar was the enemy. I proved that to you tonight. Besides, I would do anything to protect my children."

"No, you would do anything to control your cubs, because you're a tiger mom. The bad kind of tiger mom. The mother who uses that title as justification to abuse her children."

Mother gives a subtle snarl, her round face growing dark. "Clearly, you are ungrateful for all I've done for you. Because of me, you have a legacy, run a prestigious academy, and made it to the Olympics. If you obeyed me more, you would have won gold."

"No. If you controlled me less, I would have won gold."

"Nonsense! If I did less, you would be marrying a liar who would divorce you and take half your wealth."

I sigh and look at my phone. "I called our attorney a few minutes ago. He confirmed Joar signed the prenup the day after I asked him."

Mother's lips purse in a tight line, but she stays silent.

I continue, "When were you planning to tell me Joar signed?"

"It doesn't matter, Emma. His original intentions were to deceive you. A marriage cannot be founded on lies. He's a liar. Therefore, you can never trust him."

"We're all liars, Mother. And Joar didn't trust me, either. He hid the fact he signed the prenup in case I backed out of the wedding last minute. Then he could say he signed it to ease my doubts. I know it is true, because he understands how I think. He's always looking out for me, to catch me if I fall. When you push me down, he's there to help me up. Yes! That's it! And now he needs me to do the same for him!"

"Emma. He's not who you think he is!"

"He's my best friend, my lover, and who I need to undo the damage you've done. I belong to him. I'm going back."

Her hands move to her hips as she shouts, "I won't let you destroy your life for that man!"

I sigh, finally over her threats and mind-control. I turn on my heel, intent on leaving. As I take my first step, I feel a sudden, sharp bump at my ankle. My foot catches, and I stumble forward, losing my balance. Before I can regain my footing, I'm falling, my arms flailing as I hit the ground hard. The shock of the fall steals the breath from my lungs, and for a moment, I'm too stunned to react.

She tripped me!

In that brief instant, my mother, despite her age, moves with surprising speed and agility. She darts past me, her movements quick and precise, reaching the door before I even have time to push myself up. I scramble to my knees, but hear the unmistakable *click* of the lock turning.

As I pound on the door, I hear footsteps hastily retreat from my door. I hurry to my phone to call for help, but realize Mother must have taken it after she tripped me.

Through the window, I hear a car start. I rush to look outside, spotting Mother pealing out of the driveway. She never leaves at night. Where is she going? Regardless, I must get out of this room.

I try to open the window, but it's fruitless. Mother nailed it shut years ago. I side glance, feeling lost for answers. As I stare blankly at the wall, my vision slowly crisps, bringing a medal into view: my Olympic bronze medal.

After I won it, Mother put it in a frame, but never let me take it home. And here it is.

I stand on my old bed and reach high, grabbing the frame off the wall. With all my might, I throw it on the floor, unleashing years of pent up anger from chasing this one achievement.

The sound of glass shattering is euphoric. The medal is freed and comes to a rest beside the bed. I pick it up and wrap the hard circle to the outside of my knuckles, looping the neck ribbon around my fist several times. I study my handiwork, having created makeshift brass knuckles. Then, as hard as I can, I punch the window.

It cracks.

I repeat, causing the first window pane to break. I try again, and again, overriding the pain of my hand hitting the hard bronze medal against my knuckles.

Finally, the window shatters with a deafening crash. I scramble through the jagged opening very carefully.

When my socks meet the slick roof tiles, I'm left skidding on shards of broken glass. I lose my footing, and the world tilts as I tumble, rolling uncontrollably toward the edge.

I drop off the roof, and the ground rushes up to meet me. Pain explodes in my back as the impact knocks the wind from my lungs. As I suck in a ragged breath, I look up just in time to see a flash of something — my bronze medal — spinning through the air, falling straight toward my face.

I have no time to react. The last thing I see is the glint of bronze before everything is black.

Chapter 55

Emma

My eyes flutter open. The night is exceptionally dark, with a sky resembling a pitch-black canvas adorned with tiny, shimmering stars. I rub my forehead, wincing at the tender bump left by the impact of the medal.

My face scrunches in pain as I stagger to my feet. The surrounding houses are dark as I limp inside, grab my purse, and return to my car.

How long was I passed out?

Unable to answer that question, I drive down the road, in disbelief that I knocked myself out with my own medal!

Thirty minutes later, I'm leaving the jail more confused than ever.

Joar was never arrested!

Then where is he?

Since I don't have my phone, I rush to his house. When his home comes into view, I feel better already. He should be there. We'll be together again soon.

I approach the beautiful home through the dark. Just then, I squint, noticing something is off. As I pull my car to a stop in the driveway, a figure steps into the shine of my headlights.

Mother.

"Hello," she says, her voice cold.

"What are you doing here?"

She inhales a deep breath, then replies, "Leave now. You must never speak about this man again."

I smirk at the audacity of her ordering me around when I'm no longer locked in her house. I fold my arms. "So you knew he didn't go to jail?"

She smiles and nods. "The police officers looked real, didn't they? Just some thugs I hired. Joar is inside with Ophelia, but neither is coming out. They are both drugged and unconscious."

"They're what?"

"Yes. It's time for you to move on. Your father and I won't let our only child become a casualty. You're our legacy and always have been."

There is literally nothing she can do to keep me away from Joar, thus I reply confidently, "Sorry, Mother. I'm *not* your legacy, and I don't want your money. I'll build an academy of my own. I'll buy ice time somewhere else. It won't be as big or successful, but it is better than not teaching at all, being under your thumb, and better than living without Joar."

"Emma, it's over. Don't you see? You can never be with Joar. He didn't choose Runa, and I couldn't let Ophelia reveal that our star player murdered his cousin. It would disparage our franchise name. Ophelia will go down in history as a jealous woman who killed a hockey player she couldn't have. Now, it will look like a murder-suicide."

"What are you talking about!"

She shakes her head. From her pocket, she retrieves a lighter. With a gentle flick of the lever, a blue flame glows in the darkness. Just then, the pungent smell of gasoline floats by my nose. I lift my brow as an evil grin curves across her lips.

With a soft toss of her hand, the lighter falls and lands beside the driveway on the grass. Instantly, a blaze of fire ignites and runs in both directions, following the trail of gasoline. The fresh flames are in a race around the house.

My breath catches and I step back. The fire climbs the walls, some areas faster than others. Flames dance violently against the night sky, filling the air with white, blue, and red.

Panic takes over as I sprint toward the front door, but a wall of flames blocks my path, the wood crackling and spitting embers.

"Joar!" I scream, hoping he can hear me through the roar of the fire.

As I circle the house to the back entrance, the doors are unreachable, too. I spot a window which the flames haven't touched, but from my peripheral, Mother pours more gasoline near it. As she flicks the lever, I try to stop her, but it is too late! The gasoline ignites, crawling up the wall surrounding the window.

"Mother!" I scream, horror lacing my voice. "Why are you doing this?"

She turns to me, her expression as cold as ever. "You think I don't love you? Everything I've done is for you. Joar brainwashed you, Emma. Not me. He turned you against your family. If you can't see the damage he's caused, I'll help you see after he's dead, even if it costs me my freedom. A tiger mom loves her cubs. It's not abuse. It's protection."

"No!" I shout, the word tearing from my throat. "You cannot do this!"

"The exits are all blocked," she adds with a chilling finality. "He can't escape. He's sedated anyway."

Desperation surges through me, and I suddenly remember Bergen's dog door, which is partially concealed next to bushes. It's a slim chance, but it's the only one I have. Without another word, I turn and sprint, my mind racing.

"Emma!" Mom calls after me.

The heat is intense, and I race through pockets of smoke that make me cough, but I don't slow down, ignoring the burning in my lungs. I spot the dog door. As I hoped, the stones interrupting the grass did not ignite, the flames leaving the area unlit.

"Emma! Stop!" yells Mother, just as I drop to my knees to crawl through the opening.

I glance back at her and scowl. "I love him. You'll never understand what that means."

I look away, drowning out her words as I crawl forward into the dark house, its walls creaking and hissing.

The smell of burning wood and plastic is overwhelming, but I force myself to move forward into the dying house.

"Joar! Bergen!" I call out, my voice hoarse as I head toward the bedroom.

The smoke is so strong that I bend at the knees, stooping low under the black cloud as I hurry. Once I reach the bedroom, I cover my chest in shock.

The back wall is lit with red flames, but the bed is empty.

"Joar! Bergen!" I call out again, looking at the carpet for either of them. Black smoke billows above my head.

A faint sound reaches my ears, a coughing from some-where nearby, followed by the sharp bark of Bergen. I follow the sounds, navigating through the smoky haze, my eyes stinging and watering.

As I turn a corner, I spot Joar, gripping a chair and struggling to breathe.

"Oh my God!" I cry, rushing to his side. I take his hand as he reaches out.

He looks at me, his gaze is clouded with confusion. "Emma, my eyes are burning. I'm so dizzy. I can't get out." He coughs harshly, having inhaled smoke.

"Well, I'm here, now," I say, my voice trembling. "My mom blocked all the doors and windows. The whole outside is on fire. We need to use the dog door to escape."

I take his hand and lead the way. Bergen follows closely. The fire is closing in, the heat nearly unbearable, but we push forward.

The black smoke thickens, and I have to keep telling Joar to hunch down lower and lower so he can breathe. He seems so confused — so drugged. It could be the carbon monoxide building up in his blood, or whatever Mother gave him. Probably both.

Thankfully, we soon reach the dog door and Bergen jolts through, the flap swinging from the speed of his exit.

"Right here. Your turn," I say, yanking on his muscled forearm toward the opening. I place his hand on the frame as he covers his burning eyes.

"You first," he says, backing away to give me room.

"No! Come on, Joar! Go through!" I plead, not wanting to leave him confused and alone.

He frowns for a second, then says, "Thanks for coming home, sweet girl. I knew you loved me. I love you too, okay?"

"Okay, whatever! Come on!" I yank on him, but he won't move.

"Emma. I can't fit through that."

All the blood drains from my face.

"What?" I look at the dog door's frame and gawk. Through all the chaos, I wasn't thinking. Joar's shoulders are too wide. He's way too big to fit through. I guess my subconscious didn't want to acknowledge that truth. Even though my hips are big to me, they're still smaller than Joar's broad shoulders.

"Go on, Emma. Go through the door," he orders.

"No! We'll be okay!" I reply, clutching his hand tighter. "We'll keep looking for a way out!" I move to lead him in another direction, but again, he doesn't budge. He purses his lips, silently saying what we both know. "But Joar, maybe there is another way!"

He says nothing.

"I don't want you to die!" I cry.

"Emmy. Be happy. You deserve it," he says. And suddenly, I'm being shoved through the dog door.

"Damn it!" I yell and immediately spin around to reenter. As I lean forward, my head thumps against something.

He shut the dog door!

"Joar! No!" I yell in shock, then try to kick the barricade down. The thick plastic shield gives and splits. I retract my leg to give another good kick, but something hot burns my forehead.

Over the roar of the inferno, Bergen barks, prompting me to look over my shoulder. His eyes are sighted above me, so I follow his gaze, spotting the roof glowing red and bowing.

Burning embers flutter as they fall to the ground. Now I realize what burned my forehead.

The house seems to moan as the roof visibly shifts, sending a curtain of embers falling toward me again. As fast as I can, I crab-walk away from the house, flipping over midway and scurrying to my feet just as a large chunk of roof topples to where I once was.

I gasp for air, covering my chest with my hand. I stare at the burning hunk of wood and roof tiles that now block my only path to reach Joar, my life, my everything.

God, no!

Chapter 56

Joar

With Emma safe, I head down the hallway, occasionally feeling the walls as I navigate through the house with blurred vision. Everything is a shadow. Only black, with the faintest of outlines.

I'm groggy, exhausted, and unsure of how I got this way so quickly.

The air surrounding me grows hotter and I know my time is running out.

Soon, I have to crawl on the floor to avoid the smoke. I turn a corner. My shoulder bumps into something. The sound of ceramic against hardwood causes me to squeeze my eyes shut as shards bite at my face. I move forward through the pieces, feeling the rim of a vase under my palm.

I know where I am.

I search the wall until a hot window pane singes my palm. Knowing there is a small chair beside this window, I hold my breath and stand up as high as I can bear the heat. Then I pick up the chair and hammer it against the glass. Again and again, I pummel the window, until finally, the thick panes shatter.

Immediately, the oxygen rich night air is inhaled by the house, feeding the hungry fire. The heat increases, the flames engulfing the window's opening. Maybe I can leap through the window, but how will I survive the wall of fla mes... a wall who knows how thick or if I'll figure out where they end.

Then, my foot brushes against a small rug on the floor, and I snatch it up, wrapping it around my shirtless body. With the fire closing in, I take a deep breath and brace myself, preparing to leap through the flames. All I see is red, like closing my eyes and facing the sun.

"Don't you dare!" says a woman's voice.

Although I can't see well, I spin around toward the voice. "Mei?"

"Tempting you with Aina, having you arrested, bringing Runa back from the dead, setting your world on fire — but nothing will keep you away from my daughter. Why won't you leave us alone?"

I extend my hand toward Mei, searching to grab and pull her close. Although I hate this woman, it's Emma's mother and I can't just leave her to burn alive. Therefore, I'll dive out of the window with the conniving old bitch in my arms.

However, my bicep stings and droplets of a warm liquid roll down my skin. I touch my arm, feeling the wound.

"Did you just cut me?" I say, but soon the burn of a knife slices through my arm's flesh again.

"Die!" her shrill voice cries.

When her blade dives just below my ribs, I pivot from her. "I tried!" I bark, then power forward at full speed, leaping through the window's opening.

I land in what must be fire, as no surface provides relief. I fling off the rug and jolt. I run until I feel grass, then fall down, rolling fast to extinguish the flames charring my body.

Footsteps and heavy breathing soon surround me. Through the blindness, I see shadows. Yells pierce my ears, coming from people whose words I can't discern.

Except for one.

"Joar!" cries Emma. Her small hands pat my head, and I grimace as her palm swipes a particularly painful area of skin.

"You're okay! You're okay, baby!" she says, frantic. However, there is no sincerity in her voice. "Stay still!"

A blanket is thrown over me and what feels like a hundred hands bat down, blotting out the flames that won't quit.

The pressure of their touch is like being lit on fire again. I wail and writhe from their hands. I'm lifted onto what I assume is a gurney. Shortly after, a small pinch nips at the bend of my arm.

My hazy vision grows darker and my suffering fades.

Once my eyes reopen, the blurry room slowly comes into focus.

A hospital room? The sterile smell of bleached sheets fills my nostrils. The beeping of machines and the muffled sounds of the staff create a strange, disorienting song.

I blink against the harsh fluorescent lights, my vision almost in full focus. The pain is present but full, a subtle burning sensation that radiates through my body.

As I turn my head slightly, a figure sits in a chair, facing the television mounted on the wall. A beautiful, curvy woman with black hair slumps in her chair, apparently sleeping.

My little one.

Joy floods through me, and I shuffle to sit up in bed, only to be met with searing pain. I grunt, drawing in a sharp breath.

Emma stirs and quickly rises to her feet, hurrying to my bedside.

"Joar, stay calm," she says softly, taking hold of my hand and delicately cupping my jaw.

She lightly strokes my cheek with her thumb. Her touch is tender and delicate, just as I remember. I stare at her, my mind reeling, awestruck and confused.

"Am I okay?" I ask, my voice hoarse and vision still hazy.

She nods, her eyes filled with sadness and relief. "Yes, you're okay. You were drugged, then got some burns, but mostly on your arm. But you'll be alright."

I can't take my eyes off her, but crack a joke to ease the tension. "I'm homeless now. Can I live with you?"

She chuckles and nods gently, her fingers never stopping their soothing motion on my cheek.

"Is Bergen okay?"

"Yeah, he stayed away from the fire once he got out of the house. He's at my place now."

I smile, glad my faithful friend is safe — my amazing dog who awoke me in that house, helping me survive.

"What about Ophelia?"

"She didn't make it. They only found her charred bones."

"Wow," I murmur, taken aback by the extent of what happened. "Sedation? Is that what those cops injected into me after the arrest?"

Emma nods. "Yeah. The cops were fake. My mother hired them to stage the scene to look like Ophelia set the place on fire in a jealous rage."

"I tried to save Mei, but she stabbed me. Did she live?"

"No." Emma sniffles. "Mother was a controlling woman till the end. Even in her failure to kill you, she safeguarded our legacy. They'll probably never find the men she hired. No evidence of them in the burned house. Mother had the cameras off at the stadium, too. She planned everything to the smallest detail."

"Emma, I'm so sorry."

"Me too. For all my mother's faults, she died protecting me... At least she thought she was." Emma sniffles back more tears before adding, "I think she loved me. She sacrificed herself to keep us apart. I just couldn't get through to her.

I told her I was happy with you, but in the end, we spoke very different languages when it came to love. Thank you for trying to save her, though. God, Joar, I can't believe she did this to you. Your house, your knife wounds... your burns."

I shrug. "I'm just glad you left her. I didn't have to convince you."

"I'll never need convincing again when it comes to trusting you. I wandered too far from you and needed to get back. You told me once I'd miss you too much, and you were right. I did," she explains with a sweet smile.

※ ⊪————•••————⊪ ※

A year later, the stadium is empty, the ice gleaming under the soft glow of overhead lights. The silence is immense, amplifying the sound of my blades slicing through the pristine surface. The chilled air stings my skin.

"I saw you looking at your banner yesterday," Emma says, nodding toward the rafters. My name and number hang immortalized, a reminder of my own legacy. "Will you be okay this year? Without hockey?"

"Oh, yes," I reply simply. "I have something *better* to focus on now."

I couldn't play if I wanted to with my arm, the scar tissue making its mobility poor. But it healed and I can still hold my girl.

She smiles warmly. "Now you'll need another outlet for all that aggression. Maybe I *should* teach you to skate like me."

437

I chuckle, dark and wicked. "I can still lift you, little one, but I won't wear those prissy outfits."

She giggles, those lovely eyes twinkling.

Before she replies, a familiar tapping on the boards interrupts. Her dad leans against the rink's edge, his expression amused.

"Joar!" he booms. "Don't let my daughter turn you into a damn dancer instead of focusing on the championship this year."

I smirk. "No chance. But don't worry, sir. *This* time, we'll win it."

He thumps the boards, grinning. "Good. You're an excellent GM already. Just don't stab another player in the eye, alright?"

I don't flinch. "Only if they *deserve* it."

Emma laughs nervously, squeezing my hand. She doesn't ask about that night, about how *exactly* I handled things with Erik. Some things are better left unspoken — but as far as Sergey is concerned, he leaves us alone now. I made sure of that.

Her dad lingers, his gaze drifting to Emma. "You know, sweety, a father should protect his kids from everyone — including their mother."

The words slice through the air. Emma stiffens, his words more profound than we anticipated. She opens her mouth to respond, but no words come. He can't meet her eyes, then taps the boards once more before leaving. Her dad never *said* he was sorry, but I hope it was enough.

I look down at Emma. "You okay?" I ask, my voice softer now.

"Yes. I feel good. He never spoke ill of my mother, so those words meant a lot."

Good.

Emmy is free. Free of her mom. Free of living in Ophelia's shadow. Free of her dad's complacency.

"I have a surprise for you," I say. "At home."

"You do?"

I give her a dark smile and nod.

She isn't free of me, though.

Chapter 57

Emma

Joar's fingers are slow, deliberate as he undresses me. Every insecurity, every fear, every shameful doubt is exposed beneath the unyielding glow of the overhead lights, yet there is no safer place than this. Than him.

My breath is shaky, my pulse erratic, but I don't flinch. I won't. I know better than to shrink away. I need his touch. Whatever punishment he has planned, I'll take it. I'll take all of it—because I crave it. Because he caught me purging. I go to a counselor now, but I slip. Joar never lets me fall too far. He has his own way of keeping me in line.

And tonight, *this* is my surprise: my lesson.

"Lift your arms."

I obey instantly.

The corset he secures around my waist feels huge in his hands, his grip firm as he wraps it around, making me feel small, delicate — helpless. I hold my breath as he tugs at the laces, tightening, pulling, tying me in lace, yet it feels as binding as steel. My body bends to his will, my waist shrinking beneath his strength, and for a moment, I feel like something precious being cared for.

"Women have such big mouths, yet are so tiny," he murmurs, his voice thick with approval.

"*Some* are tiny," I mumble, refusing to let him fit me into his massive generalization.

His response is swift.

The room spins as he shoves me to the floor. The force of it steals my breath, and I crumble, instinctively cowering as I stare up at him from the carpet.

He grins wickedly. "See. Tiny. Weak."

I should have known better.

He gestures for me to stand, and hesitantly I do as he asks. He trails his fingertip along my neck. "I crave to treat you well. Why do you misbehave?" He resumes tightening my corset, then dresses me in a garter. A shiver runs down my spine as his gaze floats down, checking, adjusting, ensuring I'm how he desires. My breath stutters, half from the unforgiving squeeze of the corset, half from the sheer dominance of his touch.

He closes in, his breath on my ear. "Do I scare you now?"

He's towering, so magnificent. Everything about him screams he can break me. I'm completely at his mercy. And God, I love it, making heat pool between my thighs. I take in a short breath and nod.

"Good. You should be." Stepping back, he studies me, taking his time, his stormy gaze roaming over every inch of my bound, trembling form. I feel the weight of his approval, the way his eyes darken with something raw, something hungry.

That's all I care about.

"Now, lay down and give me your foot."

I move quickly, eager to obey. He stands at the edge of the bed, his large hands warm as he rolls a black thigh-high up my leg, hooking it in place. His fingers linger, smoothing over the sheer fabric, tracing every curve, every sensitive inch of flesh, teasing me without a word.

I swallow hard, biting my lip to keep from *whimpering* — to keep from reaching for him, from begging.

His gaze gleams darkly as he repeats the process with my other leg, taking his time, drawing it out, making me burn.

Finally, he moves behind me. A clasp *clicks* into place.

I freeze.

My fingers brush the thick, heavy leather around my throat.

"Joar," I whisper, pulse thrashing beneath the strap. "Is this a... collar-collar?"

"Yes."

My mouth drops open, followed by a reel of visuals from when I researched BDSM: cages, whips, chains.

"Bend over the bed."

I swallow hard and obey.

The first smack lands hard, followed by another, and another—rapid, unrelenting, his palm leaving a hot, stinging mark on my flesh. My body jolts with every strike, the pain sharp, deliciously punishing. I squirm, but I don't resist.

He spits, and then—

Something cold presses between my cheeks.

Oh.

My fingers clutch the comforter, my breath hitching as I feel the firm, unyielding pressure advance.

"Joar—"

"This is going to hurt."

The metal plug pushes in.

I gasp, my muscles clenching, my face burning as the sensation sends an involuntary shudder through me.

He chuckles. "There."

I strain to look back, realizing he's inserted a plug with a pink gemstone.

"Pretty." His smirk is sinister. "You'll be begging me to fuck that little ass in an hour. But I won't."

I don't know if that is true, but he's usually right.

"Now kneel." The sternness in his voice, the authority, the complete lack of patience for disobedience — I clench with need just imagining him dismissing me. So I lower to my knees without question.

"Good girl."

The praise burns through me like fire, making me ache. He steps closer, his gaze demanding. "Open your mouth."

I obey, my lips parting slowly, my pulse pounding as he slots a ball gag between my teeth. The rubber presses against my tongue, the strap digging into my cheeks.

He tightens it with a smirk. "Much better." His fingers stroke my hair, his touch gentle, deceptive. He loves this. Loves me like this — obedient, degraded, completely his.

Suddenly, he hooks on a leash and pulls me forward.

"Crawl."

The single command destroys me.

The distance to the chair feels insurmountable, but I move, my knees aching, my pride shattered, my skin burning from the friction of the rug.

I crawl, my breath shallow, my mind reeling. It's *more* degrading... humiliating. Yet, I love it.

But, by the time we reach the living room, my knees ache, my pride in shambles, and my arousal dripping down my thighs. Oh? And that *thing* he stuck in me? It's not helping calm the growing *need*.

Joar gestures toward a chair in the corner. "Go. Naughty girls don't get to sit with daddy." He points to a chair across the room!

My heart drops. I shake my head, whimpering through the gag.

His jaw ticks. "Crawl."

I hate it. I just want to be near him. I need him to touch me. To claim me. To show me he isn't going anywhere. To fucking use me like the toy he always wanted.

And by the time I reach the chair, *I'm wrecked.*

The silence stretches as he ignores me, his attention on the television.

I shift. I squirm. I throw a silent fit.

His voice slices through the quiet. "What's the matter — is the sad girl can't get comfortable?"

I shake my head.

"Face me. Feet on the floor. Toes pointed. Sit straight."

Of course, I obey, my posture perfect, eager to please.

"Good." His gaze darkens. "Now spread your legs."

I hesitate. Not out of defiance — out of desire. I already know this is going to turn me on more, and staying seated, apart from him, will drive me into an abyss of sexual frustration. But I want to please him — make him proud. So reluctantly, I part my thighs, exposing everything to him.

His jaw tightens, and I catch his breath hitch. But he does *nothing.* Just looks away!

The ache inside me is unbearable. I *need* him.

I fidget again, my hips pressing forward, my body clenching with desire. Joar lets out a soft chuckle, making me pout.

Finally, *finally*, he turns back to me. "You're hard to put in time-out. So cute over there."

My spirits lift and I pose as sexy as I can, baiting him without words.

He pats his thigh. "You can sit with me — on the floor."

I nod obediently, but inside, he's lost his mind if he thinks I won't find a way to get more from him than a pat on the head!

I slip from the chair and stalk toward Joar on all fours, my knees sinking into the rug as I inch closer. When I reach his knee, I wait for a signal, for a scrap of permission to rise. But instead, he holds up his palm.

"I told you. Bad girls stay on the floor."

I remain sitting quietly. After some time, though, my restlessness . The ball gag in my mouth muffles my soft whimper.

The longer I sit, bare and obedient beneath the flickering television light, the more desire swells inside me. I ache for him — to touch him, to be touched by him, to be claimed in any way he sees fit. *God, just ruin me already.* Just don't ignore me.

I inch closer. I slowly — carefully — place my chin on his knee, once again giving him a desperate, sad expression.

Still, *nothing.*

A lump rises in my throat as I glance up at him again, my chin barely resting against his thigh. I tilt my head, pressing my cheek against the warmth of his inner thigh, nuzzling him.

This time, his lips twitch, the faintest hint of a smirk.

"No," he scolds, his voice laced with amusement.

But I'm too far gone to listen. I shift forward, my face inches from his groin. My pulse pounds as I nudge him gently with my nose, my silent plea clear.

Joar tilts his head, his eyes dark and gleaming. "What's wrong, you obnoxious, *tempting* creature? Do you need Daddy's cock to keep that lying mouth occupied?"

A thrill shoots through me, my heart fluttering with excitement at his dark words. If I didn't have the ball gag in my mouth, I'd smile. Instead, I nod frantically, my need so raw it makes me clench.

He chuckles. "Do you really think that after spreading your legs and teasing me with your pretty pussy, that I'm not starving for a taste?"

"Wha—"

His gaze never wavers as he sinks lower on the couch, then says, "Come up here." He taps his lips. "Put your little cunt on my mouth."

I beam! He doesn't move, though. Doesn't guide me, just watches.

I think I understand, so I step onto the couch and straddle his mouth. My fingers tangle into his hair, gripping tight. His tongue slips out, thick, warm, and wet. Gently, I ride my clit on its slick surface, loving every second. His palms rise up my legs, holding my hips as I grind. Soon my thighs quiver as the euphoria builds.

"Emmy," he grunts, his voice thick with restraint. "Fuck, you're perfect."

His approval is like a drug, flooding me with warmth, soothing every insecurity I've ever had. He inhales sharply through his nostrils, my grip tightening as my fingers dig into his scalp. He murmurs, "Mmm," the vibration sending me over the edge. I tremble more, my knees nearly buckling. He holds me though, his incredible strength keeping me upright as I climax, my teeth sinking into the rubber ball hard.

When I come to, I gaze down as I back off his mouth. His chin glistens with my arousal.

"Look at you, you filthy girl," he praises.

I hinge onto his lap and he undoes the ball gag.

"Um, baby," I say shyly, biting my bottom lip. "Can you please fuck me now?"

"Do you deserve it?"

I freeze, but then realize, he can't take his eyes off me. I've hypnotized him with desire, too, and I love it. Suddenly, *I feel empowered.*

In fact, I've never felt so commanding as I say, "Joar, I'm in control now. And that's all there is to it."

He *almost* seems surprised as he watches me from under his brow.

Confidently, I undo his pants. My breath is shallow, my pulse frantic. Straddling his lap, I take hold of his cock and guide him to my entrance. Just as I am about to feed his shaft into my aching warmth, he clutches my hips.

"Emmy, I'll let you pretend you're a big girl in charge, but first, tell me right now — will you purge again?"

His grip tightens on my hips, waiting, demanding my answer.

"No!" I yip, breathless, desperate to make him believe me.

His stormy gaze bores into me. He searches and when he finds nothing but the raw, trembling truth — he gives a slow, approving nod.

"Good girl," he murmurs. "Now go ahead. Boss me around. Show me how tough you are, my anxious girl."

Relief crashes through me, sweet and overwhelming, and I clutch onto it, onto him, like a lifeline. My lips part, my voice a mere whisper. "Um, you know what I want, Joar. So give it to me."

His smirk is dark, so cruel. He chuckles softly. "I knew that wouldn't last."

And then, in a move so swift it makes me gasp, he thrusts into me, stretching me, consuming me, breaking me. He fucks me from underneath, a slow, torturous rhythm, his body moving like a predator toying with its prey. He knows *exactly* what I need, exactly how to pull me apart piece by piece until there's nothing left of me but want, until I am trembling, unraveling. His fingers travel down and find the gem between my cheeks, teasing, pressing, his touch driving me to madness as his cock simultaneously strokes my g-spot. A sharp gasp enters my throat, my body surrendering to him.

He lifts me, and I'm suddenly helpless under his godlike frame.

Joar takes. He owns. He *devours*. He is my savage. My lover. My protector. My husband.

And I am his toy. His plaything. His *everything*.

I am *his* — and he is *mine*.

Then, the pleasure builds, rising, a tidal wave that swallows me whole. As euphoria shatters through me once more, I moan, "I love you, Joar."

His breath turns ragged, his hands gripping me tighter, pulling me closer, dragging my face to his neck as he thrusts one final time. His body tenses, a deep, primal groan vibrating through his chest as he releases into me.

His voice is a low murmur, rough with possession. "I love you too, my little one."

Then his lips find my temple — soft, reverent — sealing the vow in a kiss that blankets me in everything I've ever craved: safety, devotion, and the kind of love that claims every shattered part of me.

Closing Thoughts

Dear Reader,

Thank you for reading Joar and Emma's love story!

Let me be blunt — many tiger parents are not abusive. This story is not about them. It was inspired by a moment I witnessed firsthand. A tiger *dad* brought his child to work.

Most kids would be restless after spending ten hours in a cubicle, but not this one. She was calm, quiet, obedient. I was impressed and told her father so.

He shook his head. "No, she's not," he said. Then he glanced at her desk, saw she was drawing, and muttered in Mandarin that she should be doing schoolwork instead.

She quickly handed him a stack of papers, explaining she had already finished everything. He reviewed them, found no mistakes. He took away her drawings and gave her a textbook, ordering her to complete the bonus questions, "for fun."

Good wasn't good enough. For some tiger parents, their children will never be enough.

Later, a friend of mine — a therapist in Southern California — told me about the growing epidemic of eating disorders among Asian children of tiger parents. These patients aren't necessarily overweight, but they are starving for something else: a sense of control. Raised under strict expectations, they crave independence. Yet when they finally gain freedom, they don't know how to handle it. They've spent their entire lives being told what to do. Now, suddenly, they must choose.

Balance is absent.

When writing this story, I thought of every little kid who grew up under the weight of an overbearing parent. The anxiety of never having control — and the paradox of struggling with it once they do. That theme became the perfect foundation for dark romance with BDSM, a misunderstood but powerful dynamic that, for some, is deeply healing. It offers a private, controlled way to process trauma, to reclaim power, or to surrender it willingly.

Joar *adored* Emma. He didn't just tolerate her flaws — he craved them. He wasn't the type of dominant who exploits a broken woman like Emma. Instead, he nurtured her, guided her, made her feel safe in ways she never had before.

For someone raised to obey out of fear, love was the ultimate risk. But Joar, for all his aggression and control, was steadfast in his devotion. He was unwavering in his mission to help Emma trust again — to trust him.

That's the heart of their story.

I hope you felt for Emma, understood her struggles, and, most importantly, found solace in her happy ending.

Thank you for being part of their dark, passionate journey.

If their love story touched your heart, I'd love for you to share this book with your friends and followers who enjoy dark romance. Thank you again, from the bottom of my heart.

AND PLEASE DON'T FORGET TO RATE/REVIEW!!! This book had a bumpy launch. It's needs a little love by the readers who enjoyed it!

Endley Tyler

Get sneak peek chapters and news at https://www.endleytyler.com/subscribe

Dedication

To Sophie.

I thought of you many times during this re-write. Your guid-ance — your invaluable advice — was priceless.
You are a very talented story editor, writer, and a cherished friend.

Thank you.

Also by Endley Tyler

Romeo 2.0: A Dark Dystopian Romance

Forbidden Fruit: A Dark Stepbrother Romance

Pretty Ugly Girl: A Dark College Bully Romance

Make Me Feel Series: An Addictive Dark Romance

Punish & Praise: A Dark Hockey Romance (New Edition 2025)

The Whisper that Woke the Stars: A Dark Fantasy Romance

Piggy: A Dark Bully Romance (2025)

Pretty Ugly Boy: A Dark Bully Romance (A Sequel — 2026)

To get latest book releases:

https://www.endleytyler.com/books

Printed in Dunstable, United Kingdom